Happ
Reaa... ♡

WHERE NORTH MEETS SOUTH

By Elle Rhaeser

Content Trigger Warnings

Where North Meets South includes story elements and themes that might not be suitable for all readers. These include graphic violence, strong language, explicit sexual scenes, abuse and death.

Readers who may be sensitive to these elements, please take note, and welcome to the Continent…

For my Fairy Bookmother,

this is all because of you

The Continent

To The Spicelands

ARTICIUM

The Inky Sea

Cailleach Glaciers

Camelleah

Rydan Keep

Eye Bird Ruins

Baffron Isle

Realm Of Sulio

Reashey Isle

Witches Wood

BALCARRAS

Almaid Palace

The Black Lake

Timber Fortress

East ROSHIN

Weapon Forge's

Fighting Pits

The Shallow Sea

City of Linion

Painted Districts

VORRAINE

Rhuus

Atholl

Esiba Estate

Hearts Of Roshin

Sacred Stones

Torrachland

West ROSHIN

Forsyth Manor

BHOLCAN

N

W — E

S

The Southern Pass

To The Drylands

BLOODLINES

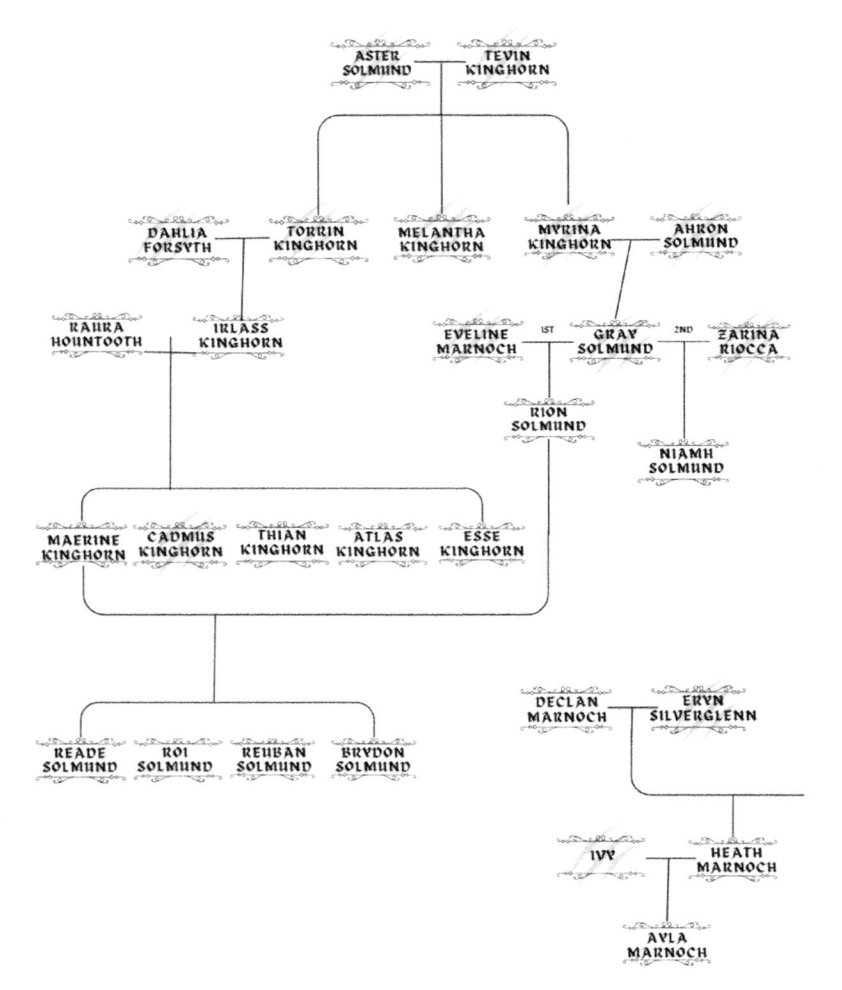

Chapter 1

Ayla's heart surged in her throat as she whipped her head around, one hand shooting to the heavy pocket of her navy skirts. She was sure she'd heard something approach over the wailing gales. Her braided hair lashed rosy cheeks as her panicked eyes trailed the cliffside. But there was nothing to see, she was alone, and thankfully so.

Willing her heart to a steady rhythm, Ayla wandered through the sand-soaked grass, staring out to the silver skirt of shimmering water.

Her fingers itched to pull out the heavy bundle from her pocket.

It was easy to find her favourite spot along the cliffside; where the knee-high blades of seagrass were limp, stems broken and packed onto the sandy earth below. It created somewhat of a nest for her, a shelter from the brutal winds and responsibilities waiting at the castle.

Fishing around her pocket she finally pulled out the stack of letters. Unwinding the fraying leather that bound them, she smiled at the parchment and lifted it to her nose on the off chance it smelled like *him*. It didn't. But if she closed her eyes tight enough, she could remember how he used to smell–sweet, like redberry jam, often smeared on his dress shirt. Evidence of a kitchen raid for his favourite sticky tarts.

She had taken to rubbing perfumed oils on the corner of the pages she sent. The first time had been an accident, the scents on her wrist had not yet dried while scribing. But when his letter arrived the next month noting how lovely it had smelled, she ran as fast as her feet could carry her to the southern market and purchased a fresh bottle to keep on her chamber desk.

Jamming the rest of the stack between her knees, Ayla unfolded the first paper with two hands, pulling it taut as it flapped in the wind. The note was dated from eight years ago.

Dearest Ayla,

It's only been twelve days since you left Balcarras, though I already feel your absence in every moment.

I hope Articium is to your liking. Have they given you a room with a view of the Crescent Bay? I hope it gives you some comfort, but remember it's not forever…

> *I miss you more than words can say. May the days until I can lay my eyes on you again pass swiftly.*
> *All my Love,*
> *Thian*

Though he never *had* upheld his promise to visit her, the pair maintained a written correspondence after her forced departure. His letters dwindled as the years went on, but they would always arrive.

She re-read every word with a smile, the snippets of Thian's life in the central kingdom kept the picture of him fresh in her head. Like when he finally moved out of his mother and father's apartments and into his own. Or when his grandmother made the crossing from Vorraine and scared the ever-loving shit out of him with barbaric stories of the island across the Shallow Sea. Her favourite ones contained charcoal doodles of the silliest things; the cook baked into an enormous pie, a woman entering court in her undergarments, and a set of hounds facing off with rapiers on hind legs.

It had become a ritual of sorts. A way for Ayla to silence the piercing homesickness when it became unbearable. She knew every word by heart, and they filled her soul with warm memories of her childhood.

Re-binding the letters, she tucked them back in the pocket of her skirts. Clutching her knees to her chest she looked out over the bay. The sky was unusually blue for the misty kingdom. But little white capped waves danced in the water, and she knew the weather was turning for the worse. Most days the sun would soak up the sea from the east and pall the land in a foggy mist.

A horn pulled her attention south, to the docks of the trade post.

"Stars," she clipped, rolling onto all fours and tucked her toes under her. The impending storm would rush the departure of the trade ship. The next wouldn't arrive for a full turn of the moon.

As quickly as she got up, Ayla dropped back onto her knees sucking in trembling breaths.

She heard the dull thud of hooves on the sand, loud huffs drawing closer. With all the courage she could muster, Ayla lifted her head over the dancing weeds.

A creature of sharp feathers and powerful hooves, muscled limbs and a distracting grace stood between her and the palace.

A pegasus.

Ayla's hand lifted without her consent and ran along the nasty scar adorning her mouth. Her shaking breath warmed the tips of her fingers. Her blood had been warm too the night of the accident, dripping from her split flesh.

The snap of a twig brought her back to the present with a gasp and Ayla cursed herself for it.

The pegasus' pinna twitched, and the beast turned to face her hiding spot. It's eyes, emotionless.

Shit.

Twisting her head over her shoulder, Ayla eyed the stables to the north, but they were so much farther than the palace. She could bolt, but spooking the beast would make things worse. Besides, a detour would cost her time she didn't have if she wanted to get her letter on that vessel.

The ship's horn blasted again, taunting her.

For the love of Lugh.

Adrenaline pumped through her veins with such aggression she nearly saw stars.

A sharp whistle cut through the air and the pegasus lifted its head on cue, locating its origin. Ayla could barely make out the clicks of the princess' tongue as her pegasus trotted eagerly towards her, deadly feathers ruffling in the wind.

Fear deflated in her chest, and Ayla let her head fell to the grass to pull ensconced breaths.

A different kind of tempest thundered in the air as she rolled onto her back. Staring wide eyed at the sky as the pegasus beat its powerful wings, climbing higher and higher with the princess on its back.

Ayla lay paralysed for one second longer, before she leapt to her feet and sprinted back to the palace.

Although Articium was primarily an archipelago of smaller islands, Almaid Palace sat on the slim territory of mainland the kingdom possessed.

Heaving open the iron-enforced door to the atrium, Ayla slid in, shutting it quickly before the powerful gale sent it swinging. A shimmer of sand fell to the floor as she shook out her dress.

Lungs burning from her charge, she braced a hand on her chest and rubbed soothing circles. Her limbs ached from the cold, but Ayla knew that until she got in front of a fire, there would be no warming her bones in the ancient Almaid.

Marching up the stairs to the nursery, Ayla poked her head inside to confirm the little prince was asleep in his crib.

That explained his mother's sudden departure.

Closing the door softly, she continued along to her own room.

Once inside, she flopped back on her bed and covered her eyes with frozen hands.

Her fear hadn't shown its ugly head like that in many years. She'd never had to encounter the beast on her own, without the princess and others by her side. Sure, she still flinched every time silver wings darted past a window, and her heart beat like a drum when there were no walls to hide behind, but that was nothing like today.

Once the lick of salty sweat cooled on her skin, she shivered.

The horn blasted again. *Right, the letter.*

She moved to her shell-adorned desk and stored Thian's stack of letters back in the top drawer. Reaching for her leatherbound journal she flicked past dozens of pages, each covered in hundreds of scores marking a day since she'd been forced to leave her home. She was nearing the end of her second volume, and though they had made no official date… she had a giddy feeling that by the end of this book, Thian would fulfill his promise.

She flipped through the parchment until she found her place, bookmarked with a sealed envelope of her own making. Grabbing it out the volume, she made haste for the trade post.

"Ayla, wait!"

"Hold on, we're coming!" a set of voices tripped over one another and Ayla watched a pair of golden, curly heads bouncing towards her.

Dandy and Ethel, two young ladies from Torrachland, had been sent to Almaid Palace two years ago. Though their primary aim was to ward the Princess Maerine, Ayla knew they had also been sent there to get acquainted with the triplets, in hopes to one day secure alliance through marriage.

"My, you are fast." Dandy puffed out; cheeks stained a constant shade of pink from the battering winds.

"Mind if we join you?" Ethel asked, lifting a wax sealed letter into the breeze.

"Not at all," Ayla accepted, lifting a twin parchment.

Clasping their woollen shawls close to their throats to keep out the chill, the trio walked side by side beyond the southern castle walls, where the keeper of trade managed the import and exports of goods for the palace. This close to the water's edge, the smell of salt and seaweed was overwhelming.

A shrieking breached the winds and Ayla's heart missed a beat. Her gaze darted around and found three blonde fools pushing one another into the shallow surf.

Her body sagged with relief.

Two of the boys–Ayla couldn't tell who from such a distance–cornered the third on the shoreline, driving him into the water as he flung out frenzied fists while his brothers laughed and waded in.

Dandy and Ethel giggled as they caught sight of the triplets.

Ayla rolled her eyes.

Wrenching open the door against the thrashing wind was no easy task, but Ayla held it wide until they were all in the warm embrace of the keep's musky air.

"Good morning Irwyn," Ayla chirped, "chilly out, this morning!"

"This morning, yesterday morning, and every morning to come I'm afraid." The older gentleman stood from his creaking chair and the pop and crack of weathered joints made the girls wince.

"Not to worry, maybe this will warm you up." Ayla pulled a tightly wrapped linen parcel from her pockets. She unwrapped its fabric, revealing a steaming, golden-brown cheese scone she had pinched from the kitchens. Ayla knew a little warm treat often sped up the exports of her letters she desperately wished to send to the capital.

"Oh yes, yes I'm sure it will." the man said with a smile.

"We haven't missed it have we?" Ayla asked

"By the skin of your teeth." Irwyn replied.

Ayla's shoulders relaxed.

"Got anything for us today, Irwyn?" Dandy asked, placing her and Ethel's letters into the wooden crate aimed for Torrachland.

"Ah yes, as always my ladies." The hunched man shuffled in his worn shearling slippers through to the holding bay.

Since the week of their arrival, some twenty-four moons ago, every week the girls received gifts from their parents in Torrachland, and this week was no different.

Irwyn returned with a pair of boxes and the girls squealed with satisfaction. Ethel grabbed the iron crow and with practiced ease, the lids immediately gave way with a crack.

"They're beautiful, Ethel." Ayla cooed over the girl's shoulder.

"Oh, aren't they just!" Ethel nearly teared up at the box of cut stems. In the dimly lit room, they appeared almost black, though they were in fact the deepest shade of crimson.

"Dahlias. I wonder if they reaped them from the Audlin estate. You remember the Audlin's don't you, Dandy?" she asked her sister, flapping a hand in the air.

But Dandy was caught up in her own excitement. Her box had a bunch of pale pink peonies that were just starting to flower after sailing the Southern Pass for many days.

"My favourite," Dandy whispered.

Dandy and Ethel each thanked Irwyn for his assistance, then grabbed the boxes and raced up the sandy pathway back to the keep. After so many days past cutting, the flowers never lasted very long on the sills of the girls' bedroom. Yet every week, without fail they would arrive. And every week without fail, the girls would cherish them.

Ayla empathised with their homesickness. Though she envied the monthly correspondence they shared with their parents.

"Irwyn–" Ayla began, interrupting the old man as he was about to dive into the still warm scone.

"It's on my desk, my lady," he said with a knowing smile before settling in his rocking chair to enjoy the treat.

"Thank you Irwyn, I'll leave my letter in the box."

She grabbed the letter addressed to her from the desk, turning it over to inspect the wax seal. A white dove, Niamh Solmund's emblem. There was a pinch of disappointment that it wasn't a seal of bloodred, but she was still happy to hear from her friend.

She hadn't spoken as much to the girl in the ten years they lived together than the eight years they didn't.

Plodding back up the sandy path, Ayla tore the envelope open and began to read.

Just as quickly as the wooden door to Irwyn's post fell shut, she nearly tore it off its hinges, charging in to retrieve the letter she had deposited.

Half-choking on his baked goods, Irwyn asked, "You don't want me to send it?"

"No, I'll deliver it myself!" she called back as she fled up the hill towards the palace.

Thian was coming to Articium.

Chapter 2

Today was the day. After twelve sleepless nights and more afternoons than she cared to admit staring at the western horizon. He was to arrive today.

The Kinghorn family along with a company of courtiers were touring the kingdoms to check-in for the sake of diplomacy. Their first stop was Articium, where they would stay at the palace for a week. Ayla thanked her lucky stars. A *whole week* to spend with Thian. Not to mention their tour crossed over her birthday. She was to be eight and ten. Thian was a few years older than her, and she couldn't imagine how he would look after so many years apart.

Upon entering the kitchens with fidgety hands, Ayla found Princess Maerine barefoot at the stove with baby Brydon strapped to her hip. The sight made Ayla smile as much as it made her shudder, imagining how cold those ancient stones must be.

"Hello, sweetling." Maerine cooed with a warm smile, stirring a pot of bubbling porridge with her spare hand. A sorrowful wave rolled through Ayla's empty stomach at the term of endearment–one her mother used to use.

Eight years Ayla had lived with Maerine, and she still didn't have the heart to tell her hostess how much it hurt to hear it from the mouth of another.

As she neared the pot that smelled suspiciously charred, Brydon started to thrash his legs against his mother in excitement. She relieved the princess of her son so she could focus her efforts on breakfast–not that it would help the lost cause.

Ayla swiped an ivory rag from the countertop and wiped the excess dribble from the sides of Brydon's mouth as he gnawed on a spare wooden spoon.

It had taken a long time for Ayla to find comfort in these barren stone walls. The source of her blossoming happiness now sat perched in her arms, pulling her sleeve and babbling with glee.

An unexpected stone hit a pit deep in her stomach. Leaving Articium would mean leaving Brydon behind too. Looking down at his wispy sprouts of bloodred hair, her stomach curdled. When his shining eyes lifted to hers, she turned her guilty attention elsewhere.

"Can I take him for some fresh air?"

"Sure sweetling. He's already eaten. And lunch might be a touch delayed." The princess' sentence was punctuated with an aggressive spit from the pot of oats that was smelling worse by the minute.

Maerine liked to cook for her children from time to time, no matter how often they begged her to stop.

Ayla gave the princess a quick nod before she scuttled to find some warmer layers for Brydon. He kicked and squealed with delight in her grasp.

Ayla had loved to help care for the babe this past year. She felt a closeness to her mother when she tended to him, dancing with fantasies of bearing her own child someday.

Her and Thian's baby. The thought made her heart giddy.

That was a great many years ahead of them though, and she had to remind herself to be patient.

Her stomach refused to untwist its viscous knot. The fresh air helped, so did her little distraction as she held his hands and let him explore the palace walls, feeling bursts of pride as he found new words. Brydon had become the most curious creature in recent months–exploring and climbing and putting just about anything he could reach into his teething little mouth.

She wondered who would take over his primary care after she was gone. Maerine had handmaidens who watched him on occasion when

Ayla needed a break, or when the princess was gone with her husband in the archipelago. And eventually a governess would step in for tutoring. But those women were practically strangers to the boy.

Ayla pushed aside the stab of guilt at the thought.

The western castle walls overlooked the flat expanse of territory that Articium possessed on the mainland. Ayla stood where sandy dunes bled into grassy knolls–not too close to the crumbling edge while in the company of Brydon. Crawling circles around her feet, he ripped up stray stems of blooming machair.

Ayla smiled. Tipping her head back, she breathed in salty air and let it settle in her lungs.

A smidgen of light in the far horizon caught her scrutinous stare.

It multiplied, blurs winding around one another until it became hard to discern. It was so far away it might well be a flock of gulls, but her heart thundered anyway.

Dropping to her knees she places a soft hand on Brydon's head, needing something to anchor her while she stared.

"Ouch!" she squealed, pulling her hand to her chest. The tot had pulled her hand into his feral little mouth and gnawed on her skin with his two blunt teeth. "You cheeky…" She tickled him under his chin and the pain dulled as he giggled.

Pointing a finger to the sky, Brydon strung together an incoherent sentence. Following his eyeline, she found snow-white beasts much bigger than gulls charging through the sky. Three of them. Each mounted by a rider.

Holding her breath, they watched as a silver pegasus circle the coastline before landing into a canter on the sandy banks, tucking its wings in neatly.

Ayla's stomach clenched.

Undeniably beautiful, they were also of great size and power–enough to shake the nerve of any man or woman. Though a genetic relative to horses, the pegasi were almost double the size and their wingspan was thrice their body length. The strength in their wings alone was enough to send a soldier flying, and the weight of their trample would crush every bone in a man's body.

Brydon let out an excited squeal as he watched Niamh landing on Yvie, who wore soft brown barrels of hide around her neck and flank. They were followed shortly by Thian on the back of Racjan, whose grey muzzle gave him away.

Ayla's fingers pulled at the threads of her cuff.

Atlas seemed to lead Ivelle further around the cove, out of sight, letting her scout the area perhaps.

They were early. Half a day ahead of schedule.

The travelling company that carried the King and Queen, who had to stick to roads due to Her

Majesty's fear of heights, wouldn't arrive until sundown.

King Irlass' stud would accompany them nonetheless as a symbol of status to be beheld by all those below. The perfect balance of grace and power, strength and beauty–everything a ruler should possess.

Ayla watched Thian dismount gracefully and walk with haste toward her. Each plant of his boot matched the beat of her thundering heart.

Eight years since she'd last seen his face. Though she could have sworn on a couple of occasions she saw him with Racjan in the distant dunes of the coast to the south. Too far to recognise, so highly possible it was just a hooded gentleman and an extremely large steed. *Or* entirely her imagination summoning him–but that was a darker possibility she didn't want to consider.

At last, he crested the hill, and she met his gaze.

Thian Kinghorn, Prince of the Continent.

Chapter 3

When he finally reached her, Thian picked Ayla up in his arms and spun her around, squeezing with eight years' worth of longing. Once set down on her own two feet he cupped her face and looked down in disbelief. She was standing before him, in the flesh.

"You're here." she said, staring into his onyx eyes.

"I am," was all he could muster, pulling her head into his chest so he could feel her heart beating with life.

She smelt like every letter he had received from her these past few years. Lavender and juniper berries.

"You didn't think I'd miss the chance to visit, my love, did you?" he nuzzled the whisper into her neck, making her break out into an unmistakable blush.

She broke the embrace sooner than he would have preferred.

"Thain," she scooped up the tot clutching her skirts to balance, "this is Brydon."

Thian lifted his nephew's finger in means of a shake, but Brydon–suddenly shy–tucked his smile into the crook of Ayla's neck.

He had so much to tell her, so much to ask. But the thoughts let alone words would not form in his head. All he could do was stare.

Thian had feared she may not recognise him for it had been so long. But he would recognise her face even in a starless night. She danced in his dreams and her laugh rang in his ears whenever he felt blue. She had grown taller and sharper, but so had he, and he remained a solid head above her. He hoped she noticed how his frame had improved over their years apart. Gone were his gangly limbs and chubby cheeks– though boyish dimples still graced his face.

As intensely as his heart bled happiness at the sight of her, a green jealousy churned in his gut at the prospect of others enjoying her too. He didn't like the feeling. It was ugly and sour and if he could rid it from his body at will, he would. But for as long as he could remember it had gripped him fiercely when it came to her.

Before he could break the silence, Ayla's eyes focused beyond his shoulder into the distance. Turning his head to see what he already knew was coming, his heart began to panic.

Ayla moved to meet Niamh on her ascent when Thian grabbed her shoulders in both hands

"Ayla, listen to me," Her smile fell at his sudden switch in tone, but she listened, pulled in by his words. "I—"

An exasperated puffing of breath caught her attention from behind him. Pushing aside whatever trouble Thian was blubbering about Ayla took her friend in a shallow hug.

"I'm so happy you're here," she told Niamh. "You look wonderful."

Niamh blushed and tucked herself into Thian's side, using him as a wind barrier. Her warm blonde hair was gathered into a limp plait and stuffed into the collar of her riding cloak, but the coastal winds soon had their way with it and she tucked the flyway strands behind her ear.

"Oh my Stars! Niamh, you're wed?" Ayla leaped forward and grabbed the girl's hand, watching her ring sparkle even under dull skies. "This is marvelous! How could you not mention it in your letters?"

Ayla's face beamed with delight though Niamh seemed uneasy. The girl's mouth opened. And closed. And opened again, before she turned to Thian who showed no joy for the conversation.

With a tug still pulling her cheeks up, Ayla looked between the pair in the moment of silence.

Something began to sink deep in Ayla's heart. A hollow and dark feeling that quickly filled with bile. As if her body was preparing her for what was coming.

Her eyes took a painful trail down the side of Thian's body, down to the hand that was flexing in anger. And the white gold band that dug into his clenching flesh.

A sharp pain spread throughout her chest. When her eyes met his, they were full of bitter tears. Her lips trembled between sorrow and rage.

"Who's this?" Niamh reached out to pinch Brydon's leather bootie. Ayla jerked him backwards and Niamh winced before stepping behind Thian and began to chew at her cheek.

Ayla held Brydon tighter than before, scared she might drop him given the numb feeling in her limbs. Without another word, she began to march back to the palace with Brydon clutching the neck of her dress.

"Ayla wait," Thian called out, already stalking behind her. Paced by panicked strides he reached for her elbow.

"Don't rutting touch me!" She spat back, not sparing him a glance.

"We didn't discuss it in our letters so I thought you understood?"

"How exactly was I to know if you didn't *tell* me?!"

"*I* didn't tell you because… because I didn't want to accept it as true, alright? I assumed you would have heard it through the wind along with the rest of the continent. I mean, Gods Ayla, it's been two seasons, how have you not heard?"

Fresh pain blossomed in her chest followed by a feeling of fire. "Two seasons?!" she yelled with enough ferocity he leaned back a smidgen. She glared at him in disbelief. Her breathing was so heavy her head was starting to spin. *How on Mother's green earth could he have kept this from her?*

"Since Litha, yes." He spoke softer now.

Her mouth hung open for a second before she ground her teeth.

"You have to know it wasn't my choice, nor hers." He inched closer with caution. "It's for the sake of appearances, you understand. No more."

She tried to listen. But the ringing in her ears muffled reason.

"You promised, Thian." The words broke in her throat.

She could tell from the panic on his face that it pained him to hurt her. Just as she could tell from the spite behind his eyes that he was telling the truth.

"You know that I love you, don't you?" he asked, a pleading look on his face.

Habit kicked in, and she was tempted to sooth his pain. Push aside her own feelings to assure him everything would be alright. But the swelling of her throat prevented the words she did not mean from spilling over. And the sight of the beautiful blonde trekking up behind them only poured salt in her fresh wound.

"I need time to think." She professed. "Go get your wife, Thian."

Chapter 4

B rydon squirmed in her arms the entire way back to the palace. As soon as Ayla burst through the southern doors, she shoved the babe into Roi Solmund's arms and stomped towards the closest staircase.

"Woah! What are you doing?" he asked, holding his brother at arm's length. "Do I look like a wetnurse?"

"Do I look like I care?!" she hissed back over her shoulder.

She could hear his brothers sniggering as the triplets passed their brother between themselves like a ball of nettles.

The minutes it took to ascend the stairs to the living quarters were counted as shallow breaths and restrained tears. Ayla's arms swung strong with each stride, propelling her forward alongside her simmering rage and stinging eyes.

"Maerine?" she called out.

She checked the duke's cabinet, and the wing's solar with no trace. She so desperately needed to talk to someone. When she got to Maerine's bedchambers she swung the door open without hesitation.

"Mae–" The name was cut off with a sharp gasp, slapping her hand over her eyes while her mouth hung wide.

"Oh gods." Maerine whispered, followed by a thud as her husband, Rion, rolled off the bed. With her eyes still covered, Ayla retreated and pulled the door almost shut.

"I–I'm sorry, Mae. I'm *so* sorry. T–that was foolish–I wasn't thinking." Ayla was spluttering all over the place. "I–I can't think." A sob escaped her.

"It's alright, sweetling." Maerine soothed, slipping through the cracked door in her pearl-white bedrobe. Maerine hugged her tightly and the reason why she'd sought the princess out dawned on her again.

Ayla jerked back; her eyes boring into Maerine's desperately. "Did you know?"

"Did I know what?" The princess asked, face etched with concern as she brushed Ayla's hair off her tear-stained cheeks.

"That Thian and Niamh Solmund are wed?"

For a moment, Maerine looked taken aback, and Ayla latched onto the possibility that she *hadn't* known. That this was all a cruel conspiracy locked up in the highest chambers of Balcarras Castle.

And then that possibility shattered.

"Of course I did. He's my brother, Ayla. Not to mention I was there–"

Ayla yanked her head out of the princess' grasp with enough force to hurt her neck. "How couldn't you tell me?" She spat, anger overshadowing the sorrow on her face.

"Ayla," Maerine said in warning. "We did."

Ayla laughed. Then she dropped to the floor and laughter slipped back into tears. "I don't understand."

Maerine tightened the belt of her robe and joined the Ayla on the floor. "I *swear* to you, we told you. But that week, you fell ill with the red fever."

Ayla's sobs reduced to a jumble of hiccups and clogged sniffles. She watched the princess shake her head and tuck her chin.

"It never even occurred to me you wouldn't remember. You cried when I told you, but I thought that was because you didn't want us to leave you here in such a state of health–which I would never dream of. We didn't make the trip until the fever broke and I was sure you were safe from death's clutches."

The pressure in her head spread over her face, throbbing from the inside out. Ayla tried to remember that week. But couldn't recall much other than sweaty skin, naps bleeding together and being submerged in icy baths to draw the heat from her blood turning her skin cherry red.

Pressing the heel of her palms into her swollen sockets, Ayla shook her head and tried to make sense of it all. "I'm sorry I accused you of keeping it from me," She croaked out, throat rough. "I trust you more than anyone, Mae. I just panicked."

The princess smiled but her eyes were full of worry.

"I presume this means my brother has arrived ahead of schedule?" Maerine asked.

Ayla nodded. "Along with Atlas and Niamh. You didn't see them fly in?"

There was nothing shy or sheepish about the smile on the princess' face. "I was otherwise engaged."

"I am so sorry, Mae." Ayla repeated once more, humiliated hands finding their way to cover her tear swollen face.

"Enough of that," Maerine pulled the girl's hands away and used her own silk sleeve to wipe the remaining dampness. "It was a mistake. We all make mistakes, Ayla. The important thing is to forgive when they happen."

Ayla's nod was lethargic. It was early in the day, but the army of emotions raging war on her body left her feeling drowsy.

"Now go and take a breath. I will prepare myself to receive the company in something a little more pertinent." The princess declared as she rose to her feet, pulling Ayla up with her.

Chapter 5

Ayla's room wasn't far from Maerine's but she padded right past it in a stupor state. She walked aimlessly through halls that she'd always thought of as temporary. A transient displacement before she returned home. And now her means to return was slipping through her fingers.

At the top of a set of stairs, she considered throwing herself down them. Only because she was so convinced this was a horrid nightmare that she needed to jolt herself out of. Alas, she descended a spiral staircase plod after sombre plod.

Passing a window-like hole in the stone near the bottom she spotted the last rider approaching.

Her limbs froze as soon as she saw him.

There had been rumours of his accident, but she was yet to see the extent of his wounds. Some said he had lost control of Ivelle when mounting her, others claimed it was Thian atop Racjan that had caused the damage.

Whatever the case, Atlas Kinghorn had been scarred by feathers that slashed like steel.

Just like she had been.

Sucking in a breath, she pulled herself together and stood inside the grand doors to greet him. Catching a glimpse of her barmy appearance in the reflection of a polished sconce, she blushed before smoothing down her windswept, walnut hair.

The castle exhaled as the doors were opened, and a gust of wind danced through her dress.

"Prince Atlas," she said, with a friendly smile and gracious curtsy.

She never addressed Niamh or Thian with their formal titles, for it had always been more natural to address them like siblings–they all grew up together after all. But Atlas made her nervous, inciting the feeling she had to be more formal with him. A primary reason being not to drum up jealousy from Thian. Silly, she understood, but it wasn't worth the trouble.

"Ayla," he replied. A rare, tender smile on his face and Ayla had to remind herself not to stare. "It's good to see you."

Three gashes lacerated his neck at an angle, spreading from his ear to beneath the collar of his leathers on the other side. It was a miracle he had survived the blood loss alone. Whispers said he'd been lucky he had not come into his voice yet, for the marring of his deeper chords would've meant the loss of it altogether.

Atlas kept a respectable distance from her side, taking in the interiors of the palace for the first time. The atrium was bare with the exceptions of intricate etchings made into the stone, their shape rounded and soft from time. His eyes latched onto a shell sitting proudly on a lip of stone. He plucked the thing gently from its perch, turning it in inspection.

"It's beautiful, isn't it?" Ayla noted.

It was one of the smaller shells in the palace. The biggest she had spotted over the years was in Maerine's bathing chamber, an enormous clam basin used as a tub. It was the most magnificent thing Ayla had ever seen, until she'd realised a creature just as big had to have once inhabited it.

Rolling the husk in his hand, his face pinched. "It's sad."

"Sad?"

"Hm." He ran the pad of his thumb over the scalloped lip. "It's pretty. But it's hollow. It used to be full of life, and now…" placing it back on the rough ledge he turned his attention back to her. "It could find purpose again someday, but not trapped within castle walls."

Unsure how to respond to such a statement, Ayla cleared her throat. "I seem to have misplaced your brother and Niamh, but I'd be pleased to take you to the kitchens for refreshment. You must be famished after your journey." She stepped aside, leading the way for him to follow.

An awkward tension billowed in the air as the two walked through the keep. All Ayla could think about was Thian's predictable upset if he found them alone. *Not that she owed him an explanation after today's developments,* she reminded herself.

Even though she'd spent six out of seven days with the younger prince since she was born, Ayla could count the number of conversations shared with Atlas in private on one hand. He wasn't shy, but he used his words carefully. Unlike his brother who would ramble to his own reflection if no one was there to listen.

"I always knew you were jealous of my scar, Atlas, but so much so that you felt the need to earn your own?" Ayla regretted her words immediately. Atlas slowed his pace, and she could feel his eyes boring into her. Cheeks hot, she tried not to cower.

"Well," Atlas dragged each letter, his deep voice making it sound half admonishment, half purr. "You wear yours so well I thought I might give it a try." Ayla tilted her head to meet his eyes and was met with an amused grin instead.

"Hmm." She smirked at the ground, praying he wouldn't catch it.

When they reached the kitchens, she stepped to the side of the door, recognising the voices already inside and not wishing to join them. "Here we are." She said quietly.

A beat. "Aren't you going to join us?" Atlas asked, lowering his volume to match hers.

She shook her head and clamped her lips shut in a tight smile to keep from crying.

His eyes flicked to the doors she was hiding from. "You didn't know."

She shook her head once more, slower, more resigned.

He dropped his head, and she could see his jaw working with tension. He didn't look at her as he wrenched open the door and joined his brother and Niamh.

"Oh good, you found us," Niamh said as the door fluttered shut.

"Took you long enough." Thian offered.

If Atlas gave a reply to either of them, she couldn't hear it as she scurried away on the balls of her feet.

Chapter 6

T he welcoming of the King and Queen left Ayla fighting back yawns so big they threatened to unhinge her jaw. She sat in the stalls next to Dandy, Ethel and the few handmaidens Maerine kept, just to the side of the duke's dais.

Training her eyes on the floor was the only way of ignoring any temptation to look at *him*.

Thanks to the formality of the affair, Thian had to remain at his father's side, though he looked as miserable as she felt whenever she succumbed to peeking.

King Irlass looked much older than she remembered. Still handsome but weathered. *Tired*. Queen Raura on the other hand looked like she hadn't aged a day. She could be mistaken for Maerine's elder *sister*, not her mother.

When court disbanded, Ayla scurried from the room to ensure Thian would not catch her. She slammed the door to her chamber and latched it with the flimsy hinge. Then she pressed her face against the frozen wood panels.

Listening for signs of movement outside proved challenging while her own panting skewed her senses.

When she was sure no one had followed her, she marched to her desk and grabbed the two journals, clutching them so fiercely her nails nearly pierced their leather jackets.

Striking a match on the stone beside the hearth, it hissed to life as she threw it atop the waking coals.

Opening the first book, she ripped a few pages and threw them into the flames. With shaking hands, she went back for more and more, pulling and ripping pages covered in scores. Thousands of them.

Her heart felt as if it was falling apart, burning alongside those pages of hope that kept her going all these years.

Gripping too many pages at once, she pulled and pulled but they would not rip, so she chucked the whole thing, leather and all, into the fire. She watched as the flames devoured the paper. The leather binding shrunk and cracked but refused to burn.

A sob escaped her. A sudden mourning for that *stupid* girl that really believed she was enough to marry the heir to the continent. She had *nothing* to offer the crown or its people.

Slipping into her bed, she didn't bother removing her dress. Pulling the comforter tight up her neck, she used the rough cotton to swipe at her sniffling nose.

Without his ring on her finger, how was she to get back home? she pondered. *They'd already cast her out as a useless waste of space. What made her worthy now?*

Ayla listened to the wind singing through the walls as she stared upon the cold stone. Beyond that billowing song, Almaid palace was quiet, and so, she slipped into sleep.

A relentless knock pounding on the door woke her. Cracking her eyes open, Ayla realised the room had melted into darkness. Only a deep lavender colour filtered through the window from outside. Her body shivered as she slipped from her bed, brows crunched in drowsy confusion.

Habit drove her steps, guided her way to the door she opened softly, "Ayla–"

She tried to slam the door back shut but his booted foot wedged it open a sliver. She pressed her full body weight into the door. "Please go away,"

"No, I need you to listen to me,"

"I don't want to hear it."

"Well, that's too bad," Thian said as he pried the door farther to let himself inside. "Because I cannot *live* knowing you are in pain. And I need you to understand."

He shut it behind him, guarding her only escape.

With a resigned sigh, she reached for a bottle of matches on her desk and began to light up the room with candles. "Who told you where my room was?"

"No one," he replied. She could hear his smirk as she watched wax drip while a wick caught alight. "I tried every door in the damned palace. Would you believe me if I told you this was the very last one?" His tone was laced with playfulness.

"I don't care, Thian. Say what you have to say and be done with it."

His smile melted off his face. "How can you speak so coldly to me? Do I mean nothing to you?"

"You mean everything to me! That is why this hurts so much. You told me you loved me; you promised me–"

"I do love you–and I know what I promised you. Believe me I want nothing more."

"It doesn't look that way to me."

"Don't be a child Ayla. How dare you think I would plot callously behind your back. Why would I want to marry Niamh? Hm? For *love*? Don't be ridiculous–"

"Alright! You've made your point."

"You seem to have forgotten the fact that my title means nothing to those above me. I am simply a more expensive piece to move around the board." His laugh was cold and spiteful. "Why else do you think my dear sister ran as far away from our crown as she could?"

Crossing her arms tightly across her chest was the only defence she could wield. "That's not what–"

"When they told me they had picked out a bride, I nearly drove a stake through my own heart. I thought we had more time…" His voice grew small. "They wouldn't let me see her. Wouldn't tell me her name. Claimed it was for her own protection until the day arrived. But it was just another layer to the cruel joke. They knew exactly what I would have to say– what I would do if I found out the truth." His jaw was so tense Ayla thought it might break. "I had my escape all planned out. Armed with a pouch of crushed foxglove, I intended to feed it to the girl at the great feast after the union."

Ayla's heart sank at the pitilessness of the plot.

"Once she fell cold, I would flee under the guise of heartbroken madness. I would fly straight here and wed you without a moment's wait.

"But when they pulled back her veil, and those familiar green eyes stared back at me, I knew… I could never… I just couldn't–"

"Of course you couldn't. Niamh is our friend. You would never forgive yourself. And neither would I. Even if it means that we can never be together."

Ayla took a beat to consider what they'd told Niamh. If she knew who and what she was walking down the aisle towards, or if they pawned her as cruelly as him.

Tucking her chin, she shook her head, eyes squeezed shut. "I'm sorry they did that to you. But *you* kept it from me. Made me look like an ignorant fool for months."

"I thought you would have heard–"

"For the love of the Gods Thian, why would I *want* to hear it from anyone else? Why would *you*?! So I would assume the worst without hearing your side of the story? To leave me believing you have forgotten me here on the edge of the world, and had no intention of bringing me home with you?"

"You're right. I wasn't thinking of you. I was stewing in my own self-pity and hatred." His voice was quiet now. Honest. "But you listen to me, Ayla. I told you I would marry you. And I intend to do so." Her heart swooped, while her rational brain cursed its lunacy. "When I am King, no man on the continent will have the power to object to an annulment of my marriage to Niamh. Hells, I could take a second bride, if I so wished. But no court of law or man of Gods will allow me to do so as long as my father walks this earth with that crown on his brow."

Ayla latched onto the statement as a spark of hope. If there was a sliver of chance that his words held weight, then she wanted it. It would take longer than she had hoped, but one day…just possibly…

"In three years, my father is going to pass the throne."

"He is?"

A nod. "His heart… it's not as strong as it once was. He's reigned well and reigned long, but the council agree it is time for a new ruler to bear the weight of the continent."

Her mind wandered to the king downstairs. The grey hairs that now decorated his bloodred hair and peppered his beard. All the years of service behind each of those strands. Impossible decisions, endless duty and a constant target painted on his brow. That pressure would take its toll on any man's heart.

"*Three years*, Ayla. That's all I ask. Wait three years and then I can make good on my promise."

Her mouth was dry.

Three years. *She'd already survived eight, what was three more?*

Drunk on an elixir of emotions, Ayla looked into his deep eyes and nodded. The smile he returned made her heart glow warm.

His eyes latched onto the puckered flesh above and below her mouth in an angry slash. She dipped her head, and thinned her lips, as if she could swallow the scar that adorned them.

His hand cupped her cheeks softly. Forcing her to look him in the eye. "Forgive me?"

Her rage now settled to a simmer, she gave the faintest of nods and he pressed in closer. His lips dusted hers and he smirked at the way she pressed up on her toes to get closer. In the end, he planted a firm peck to the corner of her mouth.

Smirking down at her pouty lips, he nudged her nose with his. "Can I stay?"

She jerked her head back. "I…but Niamh?"

"Will not mind, I assure you." He was already kicking off his boots. Ayla remained glued to her spot as he rounded her bed and climbed atop the covers. Slinging one arm behind his head, the other was stretched out beside him–summoning her. "Just lie with me, Ayla."

Pulling the long sleeves of her dress over her fidgeting fingers she feigned a chill. "I'll raise the flames."

Turning to the small hearth next to the door she dropped to her knees.

"I'll keep you warm." She could hear the smile in his voice.

Throwing a grin over her shoulder she poked the embers and fed it lumber. "And who will have to feed you soup at your bedside when your summer-bones catch a chill?"

"If I recall, you loved to play bed nurse."

She scoffed, dusting her knees as she rose to her feet.

"In fact, I could have sworn you brewed me malefic teas from your mother's collection just so you could nurse me back to health."

Ivy Marnoch had kept every herb under the sun in her personal collection. Her knowledge of medicinal remedies rivaled even the royal healer.

"Don't be ridiculous," Ayla chuckled as she climbed above the frame and nestled in beside him. "Alright, perhaps *once.*"

"I *knew* it!" Thian began to tickle her in punishment, leaving her limbs thrashing as she begged him to stop. "You threaten the future of the continent by poisoning its heir for your amusement?" He straddled her hips, trapping her beneath him.

"But you were such a good patient!" Her laughs were on the edge of hysterical. "Please! Please, Thian stop!" she managed between wheezes. "I'll do anything you want!"

That piqued his interest.

"Anything?"

Blowing a wisp of hair from her face she nodded, "Anything."

His face morphed into mischief. Dipping his head closer, she could feel his breath fan her scar. "Kiss me."

Her cheeks felt hot. Her palms were sweaty. He left his where they were, planted either side of her head but didn't move an inch closer. Forcing *her* to make the claim.

Her head hurt with the fresh wounds of the day's revelations. Too many to untease and think clearly. So, she didn't think. She listened to her heart, instead. And her heart wanted what it had for eight long years, to kiss the boy of her dreams.

Tongue darting out over her dry lips, she didn't miss the way his eyes followed. Her hands found their way to the sides of his face, a slight tremor caught in them. Her breathing felt shallow. Her nerves were seething and before she knew what she was doing she closed her eyes and surged up, mashing her face to his.

She must've missed, because she felt more of his skin than lips against her own. Moving her head side to side she tried to shimmy over.

The tension in his body made her anxious. And when he started to chuckle against her mouth she wanted to die. Dropping back down to the bed she covered her face with her hands in a groan. "OUT! Get out!"

He was still chuckling, tugging at her hands that concealed her pretty face. "Ayla, please,"

"I can't believe you made me do that! As if today wasn't embarrassing enough."

"Don't be embarrassed. It was sweet."

"No, it wasn't. It was horrible and I hate you." Though there was no malice in her voice.

The feel of cool air as he rolled off her was both a relief and a disappointment. Peeking through her fingers she watched him readjust the throw pillows and sit himself lazily upright beside her. "No, you don't." He said with a grunt as he dragged her on top of him. "It was just the first one."

She was transfixed by his smile. On the dimples that were too innocent for someone like Thian.

"The first of many," his voice was liquid. He grabbed the back of her neck and yanked it forward. She braced her hands on his chest. As she stiffened, he squeezed the roots of her hair between his fingers. "Slowly."

She attempted a nod in his tight grip.

This time she listened. Her mouth moved unhurried, enjoying the budding anticipation before the reward. With fluttering eyes, her lips skated over his in a part, tasting his breath as he stole hers. When she was ready, she pressed more surely.

Spurred on by the languid roaming of his hands and the pleased sounds he was making, she continued in her exploration. Kissing him at her own pace. Until his fingers pinched her skin and she broke away.

"That's enough." His voice was strained.

She licked her lips as she nodded hesitantly.

Rolling off him she lay on her side, back to him. She ran the pads of her fingers over her mouth. For once, not focusing on the puckered flesh that marred them. But the beautiful, tingling feeling that made her smile.

The mattress dipped and bounced as he pressed in behind her. "Ahh," he exhaled in contentment, throwing his arm around her and pulling her close.

They lay in silence. Chest to back. Having just napped for half the day, Ayla wasn't desperate for sleep. But laying here with him felt so good, her eyes soon felt heavy.

"Ayla?"

"Hm?"

"I missed you."

"I missed you too."

His whisper fluttered against her neck. "Three more years, Ayla. I promise."

Chapter 7

T hian could feel it. A coldness, thawing between his ribs. It felt like hope.

Laying with her, as he closed his eyes and feigned sleep, the steady rise and fall of Ayla's breath soothed his soul.

Running fingers through her hair he tried to keep his tears at bay.

He wanted wine to numb the pain. Numb everything.

Thian Kinghorn was a cauldron of emotion, brewing into something dark and unforgiving.

He hated how strongly he felt all the time. It was exhausting. His emotions did not pass easily as he saw in others, like Niamh and Atlas. Instead, they festered and bubbled and coiled round his heart until they were simply too much. The moments spent with Ayla were soothing–a dose of happiness that balanced the sourness that infected his soul.

His limbs ached, a souvenir of his hasty journey to get to her. They needed to be stretched, bathed and oiled, or else they may tense up and tear. But nothing so trivial as *pain* would move him from this bed next to the only thing that brought him joy in this world.

Tears pooled at his ears as he stared at the ceiling.

And then Ayla released a delicate snore, and the simple sound pierced through the darkness mottling his mind.

He smiled. Resisting the chuckle that sat high in his throat. Once dusk fell to darkness a feast would be held to entertain all the palace guests. But she could sleep for a short while longer.

Warmth bloomed in the cold cavern of his heart.

Chapter 8

The king's laugh was infectious. Every head turned longingly towards it.

Atlas could feel the vibration from each chuckle his father discharged. Comforted by the calloused hand coming to rest proudly on his shoulder.

"An honest offer, but Atlas has many a year before we will consider it." the king replied to one of the many faces gazing adoringly.

"Very well, Your Majesty, we will revisit the proposal in due course." a nobleman said, dipping his head in gracious respect.

The twisting knot in the prince's stomach loosened slightly at his father's dismissal.

"By then he may well be as handsome as myself," the king pronounced to the amusement of the crowd who cocked their head in mirth at the reddening tint to the boy in his father's step.

"The prince is already of great beauty–"

"He has his mother's divine eyes–"

"Any maiden would be blessed to share the company of his grace–"

Fawning onlookers tripped over each other in appraisal. Irlass thanked them for their kind words and good judgement until someone uttered the words, "He looks just like Cadmus did at his age…"

The mumbled flattery startled to a collective halt. Wide eyes darting between the king and the stone balcony in uneasy discomfort.

The king's strong smile fell slowly, softly.

The woman who had made the innocent remark turned a ghostly shade of white at her lapse in tongue. But Irlass did not shout. He did not berate. He simply looked at the boy standing in tow and regarded her words as they were–honest.

Irlass led his son away from the crowd to a balcony overlooking the Crescent Bay. "What do you recall of him?" the king asked his son, gaze firmly set on the waters before them, shimmering under Arianrhod's light.

The water from which Cadmus never returned.

Atlas sifted through the hazy memory of his brother. "Little. I remember how Thian idolised him.

How they would tussle and laugh and wear matching smiles."

His father chuckled. "That they did,"

Cadmus Kinghorn had been heir to the crown. Though two years younger than Maerine, a heated meeting in the closed counsel had concluded that Cadmus would take the throne–not Maerine. The princess departed shortly after to Articium. But now he was gone, and Thian was next in line.

"He wasn't made to be a king." Irlass confessed to the sea before them. "He was born an explorer. To discover this world and all its offerings." He wore a smile knotted with grief. "He made maps– hundreds of cartographic parchments from his views in the sky."

Atlas listened to his father intently, grateful for memories of a brother he had known only briefly.

"They were magnificent, detailed beyond my comprehension, better than any I had seen before. Your mother burned them after we lost him." A crinkle interrupted the space between his brows. "She said they smelled of him. I saved only one–"

"Your Majesty–" a footman interrupted with a back breaking bow. "The Queen requests your presence for the toast."

A curt nod in thanks, and then Irlass' attention swayed back to his son. A hand on his chin he inspected the boy's face with great interest. "Hmm," he mused, "no, you won't be as handsome as me. I suspect you will be more." A tug of his lips and he was gone.

Atlas stayed outdoors a few moments longer, sweat dripping down his spine. The crowds, the candlelight and the steaming food smothering every table inside had created a heat most unbearable. It didn't help that he'd worn his smartest black leather vest and boots.

The result was dizzying.

That was the reason for the blush of his cheeks, of course. Not the sight of the girl inside that kept swaying in and out of his field of vision.

Making his way back into the feast, his eyes snagged on tapestries of the coast and depictions of local legends covered the walls, divided by white gold sconces holding flaming candlesticks.

The Solmunds preferred the natural materials of their kingdom; sea glass that regifted itself upon their shores was refined into buttons and accents for silverware and weaponry.

The higher-class tonight were dripping in saltwater pearls of beautiful organic shapes, each one unique. Maerine was no different, she donned a seafoam-coloured gown with a pearl belt slung low on her hips. Pearls also lined up her forearm, trickled from her ears, and dozens were laced through her up-tied hair.

The more working-class residents of Articium, most of them fishermen and whalers living on the larger islands of the archipelago, were jewelled in shells. Men and women alike wore them roped into their hair, around their limbs, and sewn into their garments.

Atlas watched his father take his seat next to Maerine and Rion at the head of the table, while his mother sauntered down to the other, his baby sister falling in step. After Raura took her seat, Esse climbed into the chair adjacent, sandwiched between their mother and one of the Solmund triplets.

With Their Majesties sat, everyone else dropped back into their chairs.

Chatter erupted in the hall. Glasses were filled generously, and fruits and breads were picked at from the central spread before the first course was served.

Through the racket of the feast, Atlas tuned in to the words between his father, sister and Rion Solmund.

"Surely you could spare three," the king said to his son-in-law on his left.

"We could, but we won't, Irlass." the duke replied. "It's not just iron and wood aboard those ships that you send out there, there are men and women too. Lives that you seem to throw away without care."

"Do not mistake my desperation for lack of care, Rion. I will provide my own men for the voyage if that is what causes you to question."

Atlas kept his eyes trained on his plate, pushing food around while he listened keenly.

"The sailors of The Mouth have no idea what it's like beyond the bays of Roshin. The only people prepared for the eastern seas are my men." Rion continued

"Do you know many ships you have sent out in the past decade, father?" Maerine asked. Their father hesitated in his answer.

"Twenty-three." he bit out finally.

"And how many have returned?"

"Seventeen." he replied

"With all their men alive, and the ship intact?" Rion clarified.

The king chewed his meat, sipped at his wine, and clenched his jaw. "None."

Atlas stomach clenched.

"There is nothing out east, father. Nothing to gain, only to lose. If you need resources then look west to the Spicelands, or south to the Drylands. At least the destination is certain."

"The Drylands have less food than we do, and the Spicelands are hostile savages. They would sooner wage war and invade if they sniffed out a weakness like ours." the king replied.

"Irlass you cannot deny that is only half the reasoning of your pursuit. Your fascination with the unknown, it is an itch you can't scratch. And it would be selfish to put more lives at risk to tame this obsession with the uncharted east. Whatever it was, wiped out Bholcan. Don't tempt it to draw west." Rion spoke plainly.

Atlas sifted through his memory on what he knew of Bholcan. Its cities had collapsed long before he was born.

Flicking his gaze up, he noticed Maerine's eyes drifting to the other end of the table. Specifically, the head of the table, where their mother sat, doting on Esse the entire time–wiping her mouth with a napkin, or reminding her softly not to slouch in front of company. Every word spoken with softness. Every time Maerine's eyes returned to her plate, she chewed her food with just a hint of aggression.

"Send us men and coin for new ships and we will train them up to catch. Half of whatever they pull in can be carted to the capital, without charge. We will regulate their domain, so they do not compete with Articium's catch." Rion offered.

"That is very generous of you," Irlass replied. Clearly not what he wanted, but not an offer they could refuse. "The Crown would be very grateful for such a proposal. In return we can dispel taxes by ten percent, as a measure of goodwill."

"A fair offer, Father, thank you." Maerine said, placing a hand over his own.

As the conversation moved on to much lighter topics, Atlas' interest bounced around the room until the three identical idiots stole it.

They helped themselves to their food before the King and Queen, snapped their fingers at servants for attention, and cut over each other–as well as everyone else–to interject their most unbidden opinions. There was no charm to their behaviour. It wasn't ignorance, it was arrogance, plain and simple.

Atlas couldn't comprehend how three brats could behave in such a brazen way. They had received the best tutors and governess' coin could buy since they were fresh off the breast, in order fill in for the gaps that their parents could not. One of them would take their fathers post as Duke of Articium, and yet they acted feral among court.

"You are *not* a better sailor than us, Reade," Reuben called over Etheline Forsyth's head to where his brother was boasting about his marine skills of late.

"*Yes,* I am," Reade replied bluntly.

"Fine, then let's all agree I'm the fastest flyer," Reuben said.

Beside Atlas, Niamh's fingers began to shake, cutlery rattling her porcelain plates.

"Come off it Reuban, Reade and I could fly circles around you any day!" Roi countered from opposite Ayla.

"The only place you fly *is* in circles, you never have any bloody idea where you're going, even if the world is laid out below you like it's a goddamned map!" Reuban accused.

"That's rich coming from someone who couldn't even mount on their own until two years ago" Roi sniggered.

"Shut your mouth." Reuben snarled

"Come over here and *make* me," Roi challenged.

Niamh rose so fast her chair toppled behind her.

Atlas righted the furniture before it clattered to the ground, but not before he could catch the princess.

Chapter 9

"Let me." Ayla said to Atlas as she jumped out her chair to follow the blonde hair cutting through the crowd.

Weaving through merriment, Ayla followed Niamh to the balcony that clung to the feast hall.

The princess clawed at the stone balustrade, and Ayla's eyes landed on the stunning ring that decorated her left hand. And tied her to the prince. A stab of jealousy wrung through her heart, but she recalled Thian's words from this evening.

Three years. She just needed a little more patience.

"Are you alright?" Ayla asked, stopping hip to hip with the girl.

Niamh was schooling her breathing with long exhales. "Just a bit loud in there." Her teary eyes avoided Ayla's.

Wringing her hands, Ayla speared ahead to spare either of them any further discomfort. "Niamh, I wanted to apologise for this morning. My conduct was cold and unfair."

"It's alright. You were upset. I understand."

"I was." She nodded, rolling her lips. "And still am, if you want the god's-honest truth. I don't understand why you wouldn't tell me. You wrote to me every turn of the moon, but failed to mention something as momentous as this?"

Soft green eyes looked deep into her own. "I knew it would make you unhappy. And I thought if I were the one to tell you, you would be angry with me."

She opened her mouth to protest, but her earlier attitude only affirmed Niamh's stance. "I've known you a long time Niamh, I know you don't want to hurt *anyone*. But in the future, I'd rather you just be honest with me."

The princess bobbed her head. "Of course."

"Good." Ayla sighed, releasing the remaining tension bunching her shoulders. "I like your dress" she said with a smile.

Niamh looked down at her dress, muddled. "Thank you."

The piece was nothing special. A simple frock of saffron with petal sleeves and a fabric belt was an uncommon choice for a formal feast such as tonight's.

Her long blonde hair was woven back into a loose plait to keep it out of her face. She wore no gems or jewels except the sparkling rock on her finger.

"Have you spoken with Rion?" Ayla asked.

"Mhmm." Niamh offered back, finding the moonlit waves more interesting. "He said he'd tour me around the palace personally."

"That's nice of him."

"He got distracted by the others." Niamh added, her jumpy gaze flickering around the bay.

It was hard to read Niamh's feelings towards her half-brother. Resentment and sadness would be perfectly valid given her circumstance, but she displayed neither.

"It's chaos at the moment, but I'm sure he'll honour his word once everything calms down."

Niamh had been handed over to the royal palace by her half-brother after her parents' demise. He was a grieving young man when it happened, yes, but he wasn't anymore. He had settled into his position and built a family of his own in these many walls, not once offering to have her back in her rightful home. At least as far as Ayla was aware.

Articium held a natural beauty somewhat lost in the densely developed cities that sprawled out of Balcarras, one that Ayla felt would suit Niamh well.

Ayla offered, "Is there anywhere in particular you would like to see?"

That piqued the princess' interest. "My nursery. I'd like to see if there are any trinkets or toys that I can return home with."

Being only weeks old when her parents' vessel wrecked on the voyage back up the eastern coast, it was impossible that she would remember anything that had belonged to her. But Ayla understood wanting a piece of her youth with her. Something her mother would have purchased and displayed proudly, longing for the day her daughter was old enough to play.

"It's Brydon's nursery at the moment, but Rion put all the precious belongings you left behind in a trunk for safekeeping." Ayla assured her.

Niamh nodded but kept her head down. Her nimble fingers spun her ring. "And perhaps the gallery? I would love to see fine works of the islands. I hear some are textured by crushed shells, and others adorned with scales that shimmer like diamonds."

Ayla had no idea Niamh was so taken by art. She had Roshin blood, so perhaps it was innate. Despite knowing her for eighteen years, she was still learning new things about the princess. Niamh wasn't a secretive person, but she didn't think to share things with others unless they were brought up in conversation. She guessed Niamh was like one of those works of art she loved, complex and layered. With each viewing you discovered something new

The princess lowered her voice. "And I'd like to see my parents. I've probably walked past their portraits already, but I have no idea what they looked like." She tacked on an airy laugh.

"Trust me, when you see them, you'll know. You're your mother's double."

"Really?" Niamh asked, suddenly sounding small and unsure.

"Without a doubt. Rion takes on more of your father's design, but you could be mistaken as Zarina's sister."

Zarina Riocca was a striking figure in the royal gallery. Standing out against pale skin and crimson hair, her sallow glow, golden hair and remarkable green eyes were staple traits of the Royals of Roshin, her place of birth.

She smiled softly, "Mhmm. Are you ready to head back in?"

Niamh nodded and the pair waded back through the busy feast to their chairs opposite one another.

"Now this is more like it! I was beginning to think my dear sister was allergic to fun." Thian dropped into the chair next to Ayla, and his smile warmed her from the inside out.

"Some people like the peace and quiet of a private palace." Niamh mumbled.

Thian dropped his head to his chest with a feigned snore.

Ayla smacked him on the shoulder with the back of the hand. "Stop it. Not everyone needs entertainment every hour of the day." She said pointedly.

"And be left alone with my thoughts? Pass." Thian reached through many plates to pluck something that took his fancy.

His other hand found its way to Ayla's thigh.

His grasp was firm enough that she felt it under the many slips and petticoats. Slowly it sank further up and further over from her knee, gripping tighter.

A teasing ache began to build between her legs, and she squeezed his hand between her thighs, purely out of reflex. To that Thian lightly choked on his Roshin red.

Atlas rose unexpectedly, whispered something in Niamh's ear and left the table. He did the same to his mother, gave Maerine a polite bow as thanks for her hospitality and then retired.

Merry music and dancing soon erupted. Thian and Ayla danced and laughed until her feet ached and brow sweat. Every missed step or stomped foot was accompanied with breathless laugher. The two of them sniggered at the outrageous steps established in times long past. When Reade had surprisingly asked for her hand Thian bestowed such a deathly stare that said all he needed to say. So, Reade asked Niamh instead, to which Thian grimaced, but did not mind as much.

Ayla made her way to the far wall covered in trays of decadent desserts. She'd been eyeing it up since her plates were cleared from the main course, but only found the courage to go and grab some when

Thian asked her to grab her a slice of whatever looked the sweetest.

Suddenly flanked by Dandy and Ethel, she made a point of cutting a daintier slice of malted pecan pie for herself.

"Do you know where Atlas ran off to?" Dandy asked, craning her neck over her shoulder.

Ayla paused. "Bed?"

"Shame. I wanted a dance." Ethel added, Popping a candied date into her mouth.

Her sister snorted "Or *three*. Why didn't you tell us he was so good looking?"

"I–I guess… I thought you were interested in Reade, Dandy?" Ayla didn't like being interrogated in this way about him. Didn't like how it made her stomach twist.

"That doesn't mean I can't appreciate pretty things. Plus, what kind of sister would I be if I didn't help dear Ethel gain the favour of a *prince.*" She gave a shit eating grin, before looking over and waving at Reade who pretended he hadn't been watching her the entire time.

Ethel twirled the end of the ribbon that tied up half her hair, surveying the prospective pool of eligible gentlemen. "Not to worry, plenty of fetching faces here tonight. But if Atlas returns, Ayla wave me over, will you?"

Ayla scurried away without saying another word, two plates of cakes and fruit, one of which she placed before Thian.

When the candles were burning out and the pitchers running dry, Thian offered to walk her to her chambers. She scouted the room for Niamh first, though the princess had already retired to her rooms. Only then did she agree and took polite hold of his arm.

Leaning against the cold wood of her door, she swung her arms around his neck, smiling up at him,

"Thank you for the escort, my prince."

"Don't you mean, *my husband*?" he countered to which she very loudly shushed him with a hand, laughing in her tipsy state.

"Will you be quiet! I do not think your family would think highly of such a plot, Thian," she chided. Her chamber was located far from the guest suites that were housing visiting members of court, but one could never be certain who was listening to the stone.

He grabbed her wrist from his face and began smothering her palm and wrist with kisses, making her giggle. He trailed up her arm, to her shoulder, then her neck, and then her face.

He paused, staring at her cerise painted lips and the damned scar that crossed them. Out of breath from laughter, her gaze was just as hungry as his own.

Then he pushed her against the wall and planted a deep kiss on her mouth. Reaching up she grabbed the back of his neck, pulling him closer before she pushed him off.

"Was that my name day gift?" she grinned.

"I'm afraid not. That was entirely for me." he jested, earning him a slap on the chest. "No, your gift will be ready tomorrow." he promised.

Looking up at him with wanton eyes, her teeth pulled at her bottom lip. She wanted more, but she would continue in her practice of patience. She slipped into her room before her desire would betray her virtue and she would ask him to join her.

Instead, she readied herself for bed. Thinking only of how his lips tasted upon hers.

Chapter 10

S auntering through the narrow halls away from Ayla's door, Thian rubbed his fingers over his lips in a lame attempt to wipe away a giddy smile. The hum pouring from his lips fell as he rounded a corner to face his mother.

"Lost?" she asked.

He cleared his throat. "Not at all,"

"Interesting. I distinctly remember your chambers being but two doors along from mine in the northern tower?"

An exhausted sigh. "No need to fret, mother. I'm just exploring."

She didn't seem to blink as she stared straight past his eyes and into his lying soul. Handing her tea light off to a flanking handmaid, Raura looped arms in his, "You are dismissed. My son will escort me to my rooms."

As they began a leisurely pace, the queen's sugar-plum skirts audibly dusted the stone beneath her velvet pumps. "Thian."

"Yes?" he asked with a raised brow. His mother only bothered to speak to him when she required something of him.

Raura slipped a half smirk at his intuition.

"You seemed to be enjoying yourself this evening"

"Was I not supposed to be?"

"In the company of your goodwife, of course my dear. But latched to the side of the Marnoch girl is another matter."

He realised it would've been hard not to notice the pair glued to one another the eternity of the evening.

"Might I remind you that you are no longer a *spare*. Your heir will carry this continent into the future one day and you whoring around so blatantly is only going to cause destruction."

"Mother–"

"I'm not done talking." she snapped, turning to face him head on. A sharpness to her voice but a respectable volume to the slumbering members of the household.

"Tomorrow you will announce to the court that Niamh is expecting."

The world stopped turning.

He stared at his mother's face, white-gold circlet glinting in candlelight. Nothing of her expression was joking. Or more likely, *lying*.

"She…she's–"

"Expecting. Correct. We are far along enough to be sure it will take. With the gathered houses here it is an ample opportunity to make a grand spectacle of it.

"Does father know of this plot?" he asked. Tears welling behind dark eyes.

"It was his proposal. Announcing it amongst her kin is an excellent play."

That's all it was to her. *Play*. A game. And he was no more than a pawn to move around at will. He couldn't talk through the thick swelling in his throat.

Raura's jaw worked as she mustered up her best attempt at empathy. "He only wants what's best for you, Thian. He recalls your fondness of one another in your youth."

Poppycock. Everyone knew that Atlas and Niamh were far closer and better suited to wed. The quartet had always been split as such.

She reached out to touch his face and he flinched back with a disbelieving scowl.

"I do not care what you do with your *desires,* Thian. But you will not flaunt your adultery to the gods-damned continent without consequence. Do I make myself clear?"

Her icy eyes pierced him with her glare.

Forgoing him the opportunity to respond, Raura turned on her heels and paced on without escort, nor candlelight to make it back to her rooms. He had no doubt she had every route in this place mapped out in her head after trailing it only once.

He however, suddenly felt very lost.

Wandering around the keep in dim sconce-light, only half his thoughts were on his steps ahead. The other churned with battling emotions.

Thian saw marriage as sacred, *not that anyone had cared to ask.* There was a reason that the romantic tales were always his favourite. The hero and the maiden always married and went on to have a happily ever after. He wanted that. All he had ever wanted was that. To marry for true love.

And they took that from him.

Niamh.

The moment Thian had laid eyes on the girl when she was placed in the nursery with him, he had been in love. As much as a child nearing two *could* be. She had been so precious with her soft skin, fair hair and curious eyes. He would sing rhymes to her as she slept, and bring over his wooden horses to share, and pass her flowers cut from their stem. But Niamh had been a fussy baby. Extremely sensitive and he never comprehended why she wouldn't love him back, when he wanted to give her everything.

After two years of trying to make Niamh smile, Thian had given up. Then he met another girl. Ayla had given him a smile so bright and gummy he thought she was made from sunlight.

He hadn't done *anything*; had made no effort for her affection, yet she had given it to him freely. Even if in the smallest of ways.

Reaching down into the bassinet to touch her, she'd grabbed onto his finger with a tiny chubby hand. Squeezing it so tightly Thian had found himself chuckling in astonishment, as if he couldn't believe she was real.

"*Can I keep her?*" he'd asked his governess–the girl's mother–Ivy.

She'd laughed at his innocence. "*She's not a pet, Thian. But she's not going anywhere, don't worry.*" That had soothed a faint panic already budding in his heart–that this was temporary, a fleeting moment in a happy dream.

Every day he'd played with Ayla. Being four years her senior, she hadn't really known *how* to play in the beginning, but he tried, nonetheless. He would share the horses he once brought to Niamh and tell her stories of brave knights and scary beasts. When he grew rather excited and roared in her face she didn't cry as Niamh did–instead she would burst into fits of laughter. The sound of which had made his little heart grow warmer.

All his aimless wandering had somehow led him back to the door at which he started. There, the tears began to fall silently. He reached out and touched the wooden panels, resting his head against the splintering cold.

Chapter 11

Ayla was watching over Brydon run around the grassy yard, birthday dress feeling tight over her heaving ribs when Thian finally emerged from his slumber. Her heart did not flutter as it usually did, instead it thrummed with inexplicable ire.

Taking the hand he offered, Thian pulled her up off the sandy grasses. But she leaned away as he tried to pull her close, hands pressed at the small of her back. He looked positively puzzled.

"Where were you last night?" she questioned sharply.

Niamh had been all too forthcoming about her predictions of his whereabouts at breakfast.

Suddenly his face shifted, realising he'd been caught, though he defended his actions. "I took Ser

Maitland to explore the livelier docks of the archipelago…he deserves a bit of fun now and again, what with the poor hand he's been dealt, in charge of me…" He was teasing, but she was in no mood.

"And did *you* have a bit of fun?"

Niamh stated over crumbed pears that he'd stumbled in after sunrise, smelling like debauchery.

His face fell "Ayla…Niamh is pregnant. I was informed late last night."

Her stomach did a little flip. Though nothing as painful as yesterday's news. Heirs were an inevitability in any noble marriage. "And you are not pleased?"

He released a pained breath, as if this conversation was very inconvenient for him. "What do you think?"

Instinct urged her to say sorry, but offering sympathies for the blessing of a child felt wrong.

He looked around them taking a deep breath. "She is not my wife by choice, Ayla."

A bitter part of her calmed as she tried to understand. Tried to put herself in their shoes–trapped in a loveless marriage. "Does Niamh know?" she asked, "about your–*our* plans for the future?"

"I haven't told her. Have you?"

"No," Ayla shook her head softly. "But don't you think she ought to know?"

A short-tempered exhale. "Believe me, Ayla, she doesn't care. She doesn't love me. She does not value our vows, nor wishes to be queen when my time comes." He said the words so matter of fact, but Ayla detected a hint of sadness behind them. "I suspect when she *is* told, it will be a relief–the weight of the crown off her shoulders. But until then, I do not wish her to know. She knows I love you, and that is enough. The less people know of our plans, the safer the secret. Until I bear that gold on my brow, I do not have the power to keep them from parting us. And if they…" he ground his teeth to dust, "If you were hurt, or *worse*…I wouldn't survive."

He once again tried his luck and pulled her flush against his sternum with a devious smirk, "Now will you please drop this, so we can go and see your long-awaited gift?"

Anger slipped through her grasp with every second he looked at her like *that*. Flashing his dimpled cheeks until her traitorous heart fluttered despite itself.

Resigned to silence, her frown unfurled into a defeated smile. Ayla gave a nod to one of Maerine's handmaidens hovering nearby to take over watching Brydon and Thian covered her eyes as he led her out the castle walls.

"I do hope you're not peeking." he said, breath fanning her cheek.

"How am I supposed to peek between your enormous fingers?" she replied, her own hands finding purchase on his wrists that framed her face.

"Believe me," he rumbled, "one day you will be grateful for my enormous fingers." Emphasizing his promise with a wet kiss on her throat. She squealed at the sudden touch in her vulnerable state of cecity.

She had barely caught her breath when it was stolen from her once more, as his hands fell to reveal her gift.

It was a horse.

A beautiful stud with a chestnut coat that glimmered in the rare sun of Articium.

Ayla's hands began to shake by her sides. She'd never taken to the animal, not since the accident. They were smaller, and tamer, sure, but resembled the pegasi far too much for her to feel comfortable in their presence.

Thian picked up one of her hands in his own to stroke the short-haired coat and down the head to a soft fleshy nose. With his confidence behind her, her nerves settled.

"Girl or boy?" she asked.

"Boy." Removing his hand from hers, Thian scratched under the horse's jaw. "He may not be a pegasus, but a fine ride, nonetheless. He is in need of a name though…"

"Hmm…" Ayla considered it. *Beast, monstrosity, abomination all came to mind.* "Olive." she pulled out of thin air.

"Olive?" Thian questioned with a disappointed face "Why?"

"Why not?" She instantly regretted the impulsive choice but stood her ground. "I rather like olives. I've never tasted anything like them until Roshin, and I've craved their saltiness ever since." A chuckle. "Don't laugh at me!" She hit his chest.

"Olive it is then." Thian lifted her up by the waist without warning to sit on the unsaddled mount. Swallowing a squeal, every muscle in her body locked up.

She dug her claws into Thian's hand to keep him close.

"He was a draft, so he won't give you any bother." Thian assured, looking slightly concerned. *Presumably at the terror he saw in her eyes.*

They lapped around the palace walls and with each plod, Ayla relaxed a smidgen. Olive wasn't in any rush, and he had a steady rhythm she soon found soothing.

"Know any private coves around here?" he enquired, "I feel like swimming tomorrow."

"We can't, it's not safe to swim here." she replied.

She had assumed that moving to the seaside would allow her to learn how to swim, but she was sternly warned upon arrival not to venture into the waters. Creatures of old, tales of which trickled down through generations, occupied the seas between the islands. Any skeptical child or visitor who had taken their chance never returned home for supper.

"Why ever not?" he asked, a puzzled look on his sharp features.

Stammering for a moment, Ayla considered if telling him the truth was wise. So, she landed on "The wildlife of the waters is… hostile."

He scoffed and wrapped a gentle hand around her ankle. "I'm sure I can protect you from a few angry fish." he taunted with a grin.

She smiled but shook her head. "Not just *fish*. Seals, white-spot whales, both carnivorous and territorial. Stinging jellyfish for heaven's sake! You can see some as tall as me floating in the shallows of the Crescent Bay. I'm not pissing on your foot if you get stung."

He scrunched his nose "Why on Mothers earth would you do that?"

She nearly threw her arms up but tightened her grip on the leather reins instead. "It's just what you do– calms the sting, better than any seaweed poultice a healer can conjure."

He looked like he was about to argue again so she reached down to grab his arm, knowing it would attain his full attention. "Promise me that you won't swim here? Please?" She spoke with doe eyes and a saccharine tone.

He exhaled dramatically. You'd think she just asked him to trek across the continent barefoot by the charged disappointment on his face. "Alright. Just for you." he replied.

By the time they looped back to where they started, Thian lifted her down, and she found herself voluntarily giving Olive a thank you scratch behind his ears.

Meanwhile, Atlas stood in Niamh's chambers, watching out a slitted window as his brother gave Ayla her birthday gift. A gift that he had only picked up this morning on the way back from his exploits the night prior.

"It looks like she's enjoying his gift," Niamh said, peering out from behind his shoulder, "have you given her yours yet?"

"Not yet," he mumbled.

Chapter 12

Later that day Ayla took Thian for a walk along the cliffs. Niamh and Atlas joined them. The winds were a soft caress on their flesh instead of the weathering brutality they normally lashed with.

Duke Solmund was escorting the King into the archipelago to a shipyard that Irlass was considering investing in. Maerine was entertaining her mother with Brydon which left them free to traverse the coast.

Thian and Ayla walked a small distance ahead of the others, where Niamh was politely wrapped under Atlas' arm. Looking back every so often her gaze snagged on Niamh's stomach. No swelling was detectable.

Niamh had never expressed interest in motherhood, though it was presumably an unquestionable expectation given the station of her marriage.

As they walked closer to the rocky face, Thian kissed her cheek several times, fully aware of who was watching behind them. Ayla giggled at the cheeky advances, but felt it was disrespectful in front of his wife, loveless marriage or not, so she always pulled away.

Thian teased Ayla further, pretending to push her off the cliff only to have her scream, followed by a hysterical laugh.

Ayla introduced the three to her 'nest', the trodden patch of grass for them to sit for a while and enjoy the rare rays of sun and sea views. Sitting beside Thian she leaned back onto her palms.

Ayla took a moment to realise how happy she was. The four of them together, just like the days of their youth. The only thing that was missing was her mother.

A deafening shriek followed by a gust of wind snapped her out of a daze. Racjan and Yvie–Thian and Niamh's pegasi–were chasing each other in playful loops.

Ayla jolted up, grabbing onto Thian's leg in a fit of fear.

Thian laughed and pulled her into him. He proceeded to tickle and roll on top of her.

"Get off me!" she screamed in between laughs.

"No!" he bellowed back, "for I am a pegasus and I will feast upon you." while pretending to eat her neck and shoulder, which only caused her to howl more. She knew fine well that a pegasus was an herbivorous animal and he was just mocking her fear.

When Ayla's eyes ended up on Atlas, he looked as though he was ready to snap.

"Prince Thian, the Queen requests your presence." Ser Maitland interrupted their games.

Thian huffed before pulling himself off the ground, leaving a disarrayed Ayla to burn under the gaze of Maitland, hands over her eyes in utter embarrassment.

Ayla's heart was still racing when she opened her eyes to stare at the winged beasts roaming the skies.

"Where do they come from?" she asked aloud. Her mother had once schooled her that *fear was simply a lack of understanding*. And she was fucking *terrified*, so it was worth a shot.

"Our history suggests there was a darkness consuming our land, north–far beyond the Inky Sea" Atlas started. "The people were dying, the land was being destroyed by…" he shook his head as he tried to comprehend, "*something*. One day the Gods parted the heavens, and light cascaded upon the lands as they sent through ten silver pegasi. Enough only for the family of my ancestors to mount with nothing but the clothes on their backs to flee south to the unknown. Once settled on the continent, they established themselves in a new, uninhabited kingdom as rulers.

"The Gods chose us. They gave my family a chance of survival." Finally, his gaze returned to Ayla–who had been staring at him the entire story, entranced by his words. His words and… his eyes, that looked so unfamiliar, even though she'd known them her whole life.

While his brother and Maerine had their father's obsidian irises, he and Esse bore his mother's blue ones. The palest shade that reminded her of the Articium sea on a cloudy day. She wondered why she had never noticed their beauty before as she toyed with the new locket at her chest.

When snapped out of her trance, she remembered his words and pressed further, "Why would they do that?"

"That is a question for the Gods, I'm afraid. One that puzzles me also. Our records depict my ancestors as farmers, they worked and lived off the land. They were of no importance to their kingdom nor had they anything special to offer the world. Alas, someone above deemed them worthy of life. There has never been a species like the pegasus before or since. They don't reproduce, but they don't die either."

"What do you mean?"

"They have been wounded in battle before, but never fatally. And the wounds always heal beyond recognition. They never seem to age or wither."

"Are you… are you saying that these ten are the same ten that made the journey to the continent thousands of years ago?"

"The very same."

A wave of bewilderment washed over her. "But that's not possible. Every living thing dies. No animal can live forever."

"But they were not *born*. They were God-made. Evidently, the constricts of time don't apply to them. If they can be slain, is yet to be determined, but no man nor steel has come close to finding out."

Ayla's face stiffened as she tried to wrap her rational mind around such concepts as God-made creatures that lived forever. "I knew they were old–older than us, anyway–but immortal…"

"It didn't seem fair to discuss them with you. Not after… I know you fear them. But they were our saviours. And we owe them our respect".

Ayla swallowed a lump in her throat. She wasn't planning on riding one anytime soon–or getting within ten paces as a matter of fact–but an ounce of fear seemed to melt away as she understood just a little bit more about them.

Atlas stood and walked over to the leather satchel that had left Ayla curious. Out he pulled a small jar wrapped in brown paper.

"I believe I owe you a name day gift…"

She looked at him, trying to read past his unreadable mask of emotions.

"Thank you," she said politely.

The jar was heavy and… sloshing? As she peeled back the paper, she knew exactly what it was.

A clipping from a lavender bush in Balcarras Castle gardens.

Ayla used to enjoy exploring the flora of the garden. It was something she had bonded over with her mother. But her favourite was the lavender. Ivy had shown her how to rub the petals gently so you wouldn't pluck it from the stem, but the oil transferred its glorious scent onto the skin.

One day Ayla had eagerly shown the princes the trick, and while Thian had found it dreadfully boring, she didn't realise Atlas had remembered after all these years.

"The grounds keeper tells me in the mist of Articium, it might thrive here even more so than Balcarras."

She lifted the clear jar close to her face, inspecting the end stems that were already sprouting little white root hairs to soak up the water.

"They've always reminded me of you," he said.

Her mouth was dry.

"These are nice." he brushed the backs of his fingers against the glittering jewels that fell from her ear.

"A gift from Maerine," blinking away her stare,

Ayla reached up with one hand to finger the silver casings. They were worth more than all her possessions combined. but they didn't mean merely as much to her as the jar of stems she held against her stomach.

"They suit you." Atlas replied.

"Thank you–for these."

Time seemed to disappear as the pair stared at one another, for even Niamh took notice. She simply looked up at them with a coy smile, thinking how well they fit together.

Chapter 13

The soothing winds of Articium were singing through the stone of Almaid Palace. The sound was eerie upon Ayla's arrival many years ago, but it had become pacifying over time. A constant whisper that lulled her to sleep.

Tonight, that sweet sound of breathless chorus was overpowered by giggles in the darkness. She had once considered if the draughty whine *was* in fact the spirits of old whispering to one another in the dead of night. Though childish laughter…

"Ayla…" the giggles dissipated into a calling.

"Ayla, wake up…" they persisted.

She scrunched her eyes as the burning light of a candle invaded her sleep. She had never seen an apparition in the palace walls despite the tales of footmen, but she had no reason to disbelieve them.

Sleep pulled her thread of consciousness deeper into its grasp, even as a chill slithered over her flesh. She didn't remember pulling down her sage quilt, but she raked it back up immediately after feeling its absence.

It was only when something cold and clammy touched her shoulder that she bolted upright with a horrified yelp.

"It's alright!" someone said in a whisper. Her eyes were adjusting to the blinding light, but she could practically hear the smile on the lips of whoever spoke. A second voice accompanied the first in only a symphony of sniggering.

"What's going on?" Ayla asked through her drowsy confusion.

"Get dressed and come with us." Ethel said. She could see them clearer now. Ethel and Dandy. Ayla slunk out of bed and reached for her dressing gown and slippers.

"Not those," Dandy instructed, "you'll want something warmer where we're going."

"Where *are* we going?" Ayla snapped. *She wasn't exactly a morning person*. The golden-haired sisters ignored her tone and gave each other a knowing look.

After changing into her only pair of breeches and boots, Ayla slipped into a short leather jacket with a fur trimmed hood. The Torrachland sisters mirrored her garments save for a thick knitted scarf looped around each of their throats. Ayla was fantasising strangling them with said scarves if they did not justify their interruption of her beauty sleep promptly.

The three walked through the empty halls of the castle by candlelight. Unlike the royal castle in Balcarras, Articium did not post guards in every hall and chamber. Only a select few were on duty overnight, mostly around the outskirts of the castle and at any entry point to the keep. Scouts monitored from the tallest spire and would ring a large iron bell if they caught sight of an attack. The bells had not been rung in many years, but the guardsmen still slumbered in their rooms deep in the belly of the palace with blades by their bedside–should they need them in the dead of night.

"*Where* are we going?" Ayla asked again, frustration mounting.

Nothing.

"Alright." Ayla announced, stopping in her tracks and not bothering to whisper, "This is ridiculous, I'm going back to my roo–" she was cut off by the loud creak of a wooden door.

"Told you they were here." Roi said smugly, still clinging to the inner iron handle and gesturing to the girls in the hall.

"Congratulations, you have working ears." Reade quipped.

Ethel and Dandy skipped inside giddily and left Ayla to gawk in the hall. Her suspicion peaked when two figures approached her from behind. One of which slung an arm around her neck.

"Good, you're here," Thian mused as he led the rest of them inside.

Atlas closed the door of the records room behind but looked just as impatient and skeptical as Ayla. They were on the second lowest floor of the keep, between the dungeons and the treasury. A large windowless cavern with floor to ceiling shelves stacked with scrolls and tomes from all over the continent. Most were untouched for decades, though it wasn't a dusty tomb as one might think. If the draught of the castle was good for one thing, constant airflow left little to no settling grime. Ayla frequented the room to visit a certain section in the back left corner she was interested in. The library of the palace–erected two floors up–was much grander and extensive, but only contained works of fiction, which she was less inclined to pick up.

The octet stood around a stone slab table in the middle of the room. But there was only one person missing.

"Is Niamh joining us?" Ayla asked hesitantly.

"No, she wouldn't be of any use in her *condition*." Thian replied, cringing on the last word as if it wasn't the miracle of pregnancy his wife was undertaking. Turning his attention to Ruben, he asked, "Did you find it?"

Ruben answered by smacking down a huge scribe of paper on the stone table, weighting its curling edges with decorative metal ornaments. The girls placed their tea lights down to help illuminate the parchment.

It was so old and weathered Ayla was surprised it hadn't crumbled to dust under the supervision of someone as clumsily aggressive as Ruben. The markings were faint, even more so given the yellow ageing of the paper but it *could* be deciphered if you looked close enough.

"A map." Atlas voiced, unimpressed.

"Very astute observation, brother." Thian feigned a smile and gave a less than loving clap on his back.

Ayla kept her mouth shut. Waiting for a long overdue explanation to whatever business this was about.

"Not just any map," Roi said lowly, "a treasure map, *oooo*"

"Shut up," Reade hit him over the back of the head.

"What do *you* want treasure for?" Ayla asked "You have dungeons full of gold downstairs. Even split between the three of you, you will rival the wealth of the other lords of the kingdom." They were sitting on a mountain of wealth thanks to Articium's fishing and whaling exports.

"Ah, but it's not gold that we seek." Thian said, "The lads and I have located a map to something far more precious…magic."

"Magic?" Ayla echoed with suspicion and doubt. She could feel Atlas rolling his eyes from beside them and matched his urge to leave the lot of them to their nonsense.

Reade explained further, "There's rumour of an object housed in one of the islands on the outer rim. It's a tale told in every bait shop and tavern throughout the kingdom. A '*Wishmaker*'. Most chalk it up to myth and legend, some are too scared of the cost to try and find it. Any that *want* to find it have no bloody idea where to start."

"Then how do you know *this* is the map to your *Wishmaker*?" Atlas asked, bored.

"Because this is from the oldest collection of cartography in the castle. It's dated five years after our ancestors' arrival. And the title has been written in *Alpische*, not the common tongue. So, most would never understand its importance." Roi flipped the parchment face down to reveal the alleged date and title. "Giver of Starlight," he translated for the girls who were uneducated in Alpische–a near dead language of his displaced kin. "That's the literal translation, but it's the closest word to magic we can find. Probably a correlation to wishes placed on shooting stars"

"Wishes!" Dandy practically squealed, "Can you believe it?" The triplets grinned proudly at the girls' excitement.

After some convincing, Ayla agreed to accompany the group on their mission. If it turned out to be a steaming pile of lies, then all she would have lost is one night's sleep. Better that than missing the chance of adventure with the rabble.

Atlas seemed hesitant, but his decision was secured once Ayla agreed.

The group of eight split into two boats down at the docks.

The triplets had each received a small sailboat from their father on their fourteenth name day and spent more time on the sea every year. They were all similar in design except the shades of blue on the main sail which distinguished them. They'd been gifted without names, so their captains may choose accordingly. Reade had received days of ceaseless teasing after naming his 'The Dandelion' but had weathered it proudly as it granted him Dandy's favour.

After five awfully boring minutes of squabbling between the triplets over which boat would be left behind, the group split in half, boarding the two vessels with darker sails. Ayla, Thian and Atlas in Reade's boat with the deepest blue sail, Ruben, Dandy and Ethel in Roi's slightly paler one.

Ayla was silently glad that Ethel was separated from Atlas. She could just picture the girl using the

cold night air as an excuse to rub up against the prince–
and the chaos that would follow when the triplets
noticed how her head turned from their own affection.

"The object that we're looking for," Ayla
started, "what is it exactly?"

"Not sure," Reade replied casually, "The cook
claimed it was a chalice you drink from, my milkmaid
said it was a pen with which you write your wish. Most
accounts suggest it's a ring you wear while you profess
your desire to the nights sky. That the stone set in silver
was a fragment of a fallen star and that's what gives it
power."

Great. Ayla thought to herself.

Was it too late to jump ship and abandon this
wild goose chase for an ambiguous, *hypothetical*
object?

The royal tour and all its soldiers were camped
on the west side of the castle, which put them out of
view for their departure. The boys took midnight sails
around the isles often, so it wouldn't be unusual to the
watchmen in the palace towers.

Roi and Reuban's boat took the lead, one of
them looking off the rear to follow the guiding flashes
of light, relaying that information to his brother who
manned the rudder and navigated the narrow entrance
to the Crescent Bay.

If anyone tried to siege the palace by boat, they
would be a wreck of floating debris before they
reached the shore. The palace however, communicated

with their own boats with enormous mirrors, one posted at either side of the keep and reflect them in the light to signal the incoming vessel. Whichever mirror would flash, informed the captain to veer either left or right to avoid the lethal reefs. During the day, sunlight was the source manipulated to bounce off the polished mirrors. In the hours of darkness however, bowls of flame were ignited as a substitute.

Reade tucked his boat behind his brother's, following close. Even in shallow sailboats such as these, the lethal coral of the bay would wreck it thoroughly if they strayed from the guiding directions of the men in the towers.

Ayla clutched Thian's hand, holding her breath until they breached the bay unscathed.

The moonlight shone over the misty waters, glittering its reflection like a sea of starlight.

Atlas was studying the map thoroughly, perhaps doing his best to memorise it. The trail led the navigator from the palace to the outer rim which would take about two hours at the hasty speed they were going at. It marked the location of the 'treasure' with a classic X-marks the spot, on a tiny almond shaped island. No instructions as to what they were to do once there. *If the boys expected her to get on her knees and upturn the soil of the whole island, they had another thing coming,* Ayla decided.

"You're off-course." Atlas said dryly.

"We can't take these to the outer rim," Read announced, slapping his hand on the lip of the little sailboat. "We will dock in Bannen Port and charter one of the whaling boats."

From the day they could walk, the Duke of Articium acclimated his boys to the tides on which they ruled. He'd quickly realised they fared better on smaller vessels, especially when they were put to work. Having command of the sails and rudder gave them a sense of physical control which did not turn them as green. Not to mention it was hard and busy work that distracted their stomachs from the sway of the tide.

After tying up their quaint vessels in favour of one large ship, the boys paid a bearded captain handsomely for his service. Tipping even more with assurance their destination be quickly forgotten upon departure. All the Duke and Princess would know is that the youth of the palace escaped for a night of fun in the town's port. For they *would* know.

Ayla had no idea how early it was. The dawn was already paling the midnight sky and before they knew it the palace would be raving mad about eight missing souls. Several of which were of high importance to the aristocracy.

Roi had made some joke about *leaving a note,* but it wasn't looking like a bad idea now that it was assured the palace would wake up without them.

As they sailed further away from the mainland, the islands became smaller and more fragmented. Ayla stood at the starboard side against the railing overlooking the waters. Thian stood behind her, arms braced on either side of hers on the railing and she enjoyed the warmth he had to offer.

Something made a splash in the water. She scanned the area for the school of busy fish or–

"A girl! Stop! There's a girl in the water!" She pointed to the head that bobbed out of the water, but the captain and the triplets just laughed.

"That's no *girl*, love." the captain shouted as Ethel and Dandy, also curious, ran to the starboard side to see.

Ayla did a double take. It *was* a girl. Wet orange hair stuck to her face, only her nose and eyes remained above the water. Those eyes pierced through their beholder in a glowing frosted silver. Unlike any Ayla had encountered before.

"It's a selkie." Reade professed. As if on cue, the face of the girl pushed into the water and a tail splashed up in its stead. Not that of a fish, scaled and slimy, but the thick mottled hide of a seal.

"Terrible beasts," Roi muttered with distaste. "They eat fish mostly–but so do we. Our fishing interrupts their food chain and they get hungry enough to feast on flesh if a boat gets too close."

"Won't they attack us then?" Thian asked.

"No, they don't touch the whaling boats." Reade answered plainly.

The foreigners were quiet, expecting an impending explanation. The triplets looked to the captain, as if for permission to share trade secrets. He gave them a once over, deciding if they were a threat to the secrets of his livelihood, before scoffing. "We've come to a mutual understanding. They are predators, but they are also prey. The white-spot whales in these parts see their tales and mistake them for their seal cousins. We whalers reduce that threat with each catch. So, they let us pass unharmed to go about our business."

Articium was the largest export of saltwater produce. But they also hunted whales that reaped a much prettier penny. The blubber and oil harvested made the territory one of the most valuable. Everyone craved that precious oil that burned in their lamps, maintained their torches and polished their leathers. The whales lived in no other kingdom that bordered the ocean, which was a financial blessing to Articium. No part of the animal was left unused; its meat was sold off to eat, even the bones were sewn into corsets and carved into children's toys by tinkers in Roshin.

"How do they know which boats are for whaling?" Atlas asked.

The captain scoffed and shook his head, "Don't underestimate their intelligence, boy. They're half human after all."

Even though the creature had disappeared into the depths, Ayla could still feel silver eyes covering her skin, luring her closer.

As expected, the island marked on the map had no dock to reach. The captain remained aboard the vessel offshore and set the party down on a tiny rickety rowboat. It was so small they had to sail three trips to get everyone from the boat to the island.

The light of the morning was cresting, but the fog was much denser there.

After they ascended the rocky cliffside to the grassy plain atop, everyone stopped.

Chapter 14

Large stone pillars encircled the outskirts of the island. The haze was densest inside the ring, nothing could be seen within despite it being only a few dozen feet away.

"What now?" Ethel asked faintly.

"Well, if this isn't a good sign, I don't know what is." Thian replied.

Atlas didn't know what gave his brother such fearlessness. Everyone could feel the bad energy surrounding this place and yet he swaggered on in, disappearing in the fog almost as soon as he crossed the threshold.

Dandy clung to Reade's arm as they too crossed over, followed by his brothers and her sister.

Atlas and Ayla gave each other a quick glance before they joined them in the unknown.

The mist seemed to swallow all sound. The resulting silence was thick and unnerving.

Atlas could see Ayla, for he was shoulder to shoulder with her. But there wasn't so much as a whisper nor shadow from the others. They left no tracks in the soggy grass and made no reply as he called out to them. He resisted the urge to take Ayla's hand. The last time he did, there were sickening consequences.

Instead, he looked to the sky for a clue as to where they were. The sun was still rising so its direction would indicate east, but he couldn't find it through the pall of fog. The light simply dissipated through the droplets, blending into a hazy grey for as far as the eye could see.

Time was inconsequential in the fog. Atlas tried to keep count of how long they were walking, and to maintain a straight course–gods-forbid they veer and walk right off the cliff–but he kept getting distracted. Defensiveness coursed through him as he clutched the humble dagger strapped to his side and cursed his stupidity for not bringing more weaponry.

And then he stopped so suddenly that he made Ayla jump.

"Atlas!" Ethel was shouting, jumping on her toes through the thinning fog.

The clearing before them was a wet green landscape. No trees or bushes to be seen, just sodden

100

grass. A creek cut through it like a fracture, running from one side down the slope to the other. Right past a cottage that sat dead-smack in the middle.

The tiny white stone building wore a thatched roof, two little windows on its outer face and a bright bloodred door.

The group took a collective swallow as they made tentative steps toward the promise of treasure.

An odour emanated from inside the dwelling. A reek that pledged death. Whoever lived here was so remote that no one would find them when they died. Atlas braced himself for the fact they may be about to walk into a room of maggots festering over flesh.

The triplets pushed Dandy and Ethel behind them. Thian drew his dirk and walked to the stained red wood. Only hesitating when he reached the handle.

A distinct humming resonated.

Not from inside the house, but behind it. An eerily merry tune, mixed with the trickling of water that ran through the land.

After an exchange of glances, Thian led the group around the dwelling, white knuckling his blade.

Beside the creek, a woman was on her knees.

Her grey hair was plaited over her head and her clothes were modest and weathered. But she seemed unsurprised to have strangers on her secluded island.

"Hello children," she cooed, not looking up from the clothes she was scrubbing on a washboard.

Atlas could feel Roi gathering the strength to correct her that they were *not* in fact *children*, and if he did, so help him Gods, he would slap him silly.

"What is your name?" Atlas asked first.

"You can call me Beanie." She replied.

"We've come for the treasure," Thian stated, pointing his blade in her direction in a casual threat.

"Treasure?" she asked, though her tone was mocking.

"The Wishmaker." He responded.

"I'm sorry pet, I've no idea what you speak of." She returned to her chores with a hum.

"Then you won't mind if we take a look inside that rotting hole of yours." Thian pushed.

"Mind your tone boy." Her voice became painfully calm. "But I've nothing to hide, you're free to look as it pleases you."

Atlas waited a beat for the other shoe to drop but it never did.

The crone looked up and found Ethel's eyes. "Your shirt is awf'y dirty pet, want me to give it a wash?"

Ethel blanched at the attention; a fawn caught in a wolf's stare.

"Invalid." Thian muttered as he backed away and stormed into the cottage. Two of the triplets followed while the third hesitated at the doorframe with the girls.

When Ayla entered through the short frame, she expected to see the boys ransacking the place, but there wasn't much to turn over. It was very, *very* bare. A tiny one-room cottage, with a loft-bed overhanging a table and single chair. A shelf of dried goods stood beside several skinned rabbits hanging on a line, their furs drying over the fire.

Ayla peered out one of the slitted windows on the southern wall to the little old lady on her knees washing clothes that would never have a chance of being truly clean in a life like this.

No one with access to magic would live like this. She had no wealth to be seen, nor comfort in life. No signs of family, friends or even passing company. Nothing in her life spoke of wishes granted.

Exiting the cottage, Dandy took her place, rummaging carefully through the dried herbs and spices in her food store.

Walking over to where the old woman worked, she knelt, noticing the single tiny piece of clothing. It was so old and threadbare; her harsh scrubbing only worsened the holes in desperate need of darning.

Clasping her trembling hands in her lap, Ayla peered over her shoulder to confirm they were alone this side of the stone.

"It's you, isn't it?" She said softly.

"Is *what* me, pet?" Beanie asked, still scrubbing harshly.

"The magic. The *Wishmaker*. It's not an object, it's you."

The old woman stilled and lifted her head. The grin she gave was not one of evil or malice, but one of pride and a touch of surprise. Just as soon as she lifted her head, it dipped to resume her work.

"What do you wish for Ayla, daughter of Camelleah?" she asked.

A thrum of fear chased through Ayla's lungs. No one had named her since their arrival to the island.

What did she wish for? A million possibilities coursed through Ayla's mind. But she found it hard to settle on one. She mulled her answer with great care before answering.

"Nothing from you." she said mousily, with no intention to offend.

"No?" Warm eyes flicked up to Ayla's chest like they could peer into her very soul. "I can see what it is you wish for. The secret you hold in your heart. You need only speak it," the old woman offered, still focused on her work but her movements had slowed.

Ayla paled. She felt utterly naked before this being that could see past any lies she told, to herself or others. She knew—somehow, *she knew*. "No. Magic has a cost. I must sacrifice something to receive something. Am I wrong?"

"You are not."

"Then it would be foolish for me to bargain. The thing I want most in this world has already been set into place, I just need to be patient a little while longer."

"Curious." the old woman muttered, returning to her full pace. "Leave me. I don't take well to liars on my isle." And she hummed her tune once more.

Ayla rose to her feet and brushed the grass off her sodden knees. When she returned to Atlas and Ethel, they were watching the boys from outside the door.

"What did she say?" Atlas asked.

"Nothing of importance" Ayla replied.

Magic was tricky business. Even the books she'd once considered fiction preached so. Oaths and bargains struck without understanding the repercussions...the devastation unknown until it was too late. She didn't want to condemn any of her friends to such a fate. And she didn't trust the three idiots pulling apart an old woman's bedspread to make a sensible wish in the first place.

"There's nothing here!" Reade yelled in frustration.

"Your map was utter rubbish!" Thian yelled back. "This was all for nothing!" his face was growing red, anger bubbling under his skin.

"It was not for nothing." Ayla chimed in, "It was an adventure. It was fun– we got to see more of the islands,"

"And a Selkie," Dandy added.

"Yes, and a Selkie!" Ayla echoed with a smile. "Let's put her place back together and head for Bannen Port. We can have breakfast there before we face the wrath of your parents."

It was convincing enough for the boys to comply. Thian walked ahead of the group in a moody sulk on their return to the boat.

Ayla and Atlas found themselves behind the rest once more as they passed through the haze, this time guided by Beanie. Ayla tried to keep one eye on the Wishmaker, but she could hardly make the old crone out in such thick smog. The energy of the grey scape was charged, and it upturned her stomach. She tried to keep her focus on the person next to her, instead of letting her fear fester irrationally.

"If it were true," Ayla started, "what would you have wished for?" she asked Atlas.

He seemed to consider his answer. He wore a small smile, though his eyes were downcast, and Ayla realised that was likely all the answer she was going to get.

They passed by one of the stone pillars and the smog cleared again. The vessel–thank the Gods–was still waiting for them beyond the rocky shallows. One by one they descended the lopsided path onto the stone beach where the rowboat was waiting for them. The boys went first to test the footing, while the girls trailed in the back.

Ayla hit a patch of moss and lost her step, clinging to the grass banks as she hauled herself up. She looked behind her to warn Ethel but was halted. Her breath hitched as she beheld Ethel still at the top of the cliff, hand in the calloused grasp of Beanie, who pressed a thin kiss on the back of it.

"Ethel!" Ayla called out, trying to mask the concern in her voice. When the girl turned, she gave her a wave to hurry up and join the others.

Gods. She really hoped that hadn't been what she thought it was.

Chapter 15

T he sun was moving the wrong way. Instead of lunging up out of the horizon as they had left it, now it seemed to plunge back into distant waters. Their time on the almond shaped island had felt like a handful of hours at most, but as they docked back in Bannen Port, the sun bid the day farewell on the surface of the choppy tide.

The hunger in her stomach was only further proof to Ayla that an entire day had passed. The feeling seemed mutual among the group. Famished, the temptation of popping into the closest tavern for a hot meal was inviting. But a full day of absence by the heirs and spares of not just the Kingdom of Articium, but The Continent would wreak absolute havoc on the palace of Almaid. Ayla was surprised Bannen port wasn't swarming with pale swords of the Royal Guard already.

Of course, they could hardly expect to be rewarded for their childish exploits with a bowl of spiced fish stew. So, sleepy eyes climbed into the two blue-sail boats anticipating crawling into their feather-down beds with empty tummies.

"Race back?" Reade called out to his brothers on the boat next to his own.

"Losers take the brunt of mother's fury?"

"You're on."

With two against one, Reade must have felt extremely confident in his abilities. Without warning he pulled a rig and the sail went taut, jolting the boat into a new speed.

The boys next to them were scrambling to follow. In an attempt to catch up, Ayla could hear Roi screaming at Reuben to veer right and weave between the islands instead of taking the route they had that morning.

"Fools," Reade muttered, looking ever secure in his impending victory.

The walk through that endless veil of fog had left misted beads of water clinging to their clothes, leaving each of them a jittery heap of dampness in the breeze of the open water.

Wringing her pale, chilled hands, trying to rub some warmth back into her skin, Ayla noticed the stain of green moss on the back of her right. She brushed over it with the pads of her thumb, but the mark wouldn't budge.

Cursing under her breath, she leaned over the edge of the boat. The icy water would sting for a moment, but she didn't want the natural dye to set completely. Better to scrub it off now and be done with it.

The moss was stubborn. Her fingers appeared ghostly white as they lingered under the surface of the saltwater, but she had no doubt they would swell an angry red once out.

Hissing at the cold lapping up her wrists, Ayla could finally feel the green smudge loosen under the rigorous wash of her fingers.

Her movements slowed as she looked upon her reflection on the water. Her dark brown eyes of her father's house looked... silver. She swayed her head, but the reflected eyes did not follow her movements.

Because they did not belong to her.

Frozen hands surged out the water and grabbed her wrists in a vice. Her scream was cut short as she was dragged over the edge of the boat into the water of Articium.

"Ayla!" Thian screamed as his heart surged into his throat. He leaned over the lip and scanned the choppy waters. But they were still sailing, the winds of the night pulled the mainsail taut, and the speed of the vessel was greater than feeble legs could swim.

Reade jumped into action, loosed the knot of the halyard, which dropped the mainsail. The boat decelerated, but not quick enough.

Thian was shedding his clothes with shaking, desperate hands. He knew from many summers swimming in the Mouth of Roshin how clothes weighed a man down. Tired limbs can only tread so long before lulled into the arms of the God of Death.

Atlas and Reade were shouting at one another. But Thian couldn't hear them over the panic ringing in his ears.

He shucked one heavy boot off and reached for the other when a splash breached the water. His eyes had never left the surface, trying to track the spot she was sent under so he could swim back and grab her.

A head broke the waves, mouth gasping hungrily for air. Thian called out her name again, offering a beacon to swim toward. But as he saw her arms thrashing around, her head dipping under the water, he realised she couldn't swim. *She had all but told her as much the day prior,* he recalled.

Thian dove in headfirst. Refraining screaming into the freezing water was nearly impossible, but he would need all the air his lungs could hold. He counted twenty strokes before he lifted his head to check his progress. She had disappeared again.

"No, no, no!" he chanted over and over in a hurried pursuit. The saltwater was only clear for a few feet before the depths skewed the vision of mortal eyes. And as dusk bled into night, the water appeared black as tar.

There were no bubbles of breath to pinpoint her location. The choppy tide slapped against him, masking any trace of movement.

"Ayla swim!" Ayla heard Atlas call out from somewhere over the tide.

She looked towards the cry, just fast enough to catch sight of the mainsail boom pole swing, clubbing Atlas in the head. The thud of the wooden beam against his skull carried over the water. Without the mainsail drawn, there was no tension to keep the boom from swinging as the wind willed it.

Ayla gasped in horror as he collapsed. The draw of breath just in time before that familiar sharp grip locked around her ankles and pulled her under once more.

She had managed to kick the selkie and escape her grip, but now the half-breed was back for vengeance.

After being tossed, turned and dragged for so long, Ayla had no sense of direction. No clue which way was up. Should her captor release her, she may well swim straight down towards the endless ocean floor. Not that that was very likely given the selkie's steadfast grasp.

Ayla willed her eyes to open–feeling even more vulnerable without the ability to see around her– but her lids refused to comply.

She continued kicking–and missing–the head of the creature, only skimming through the hair surrounding her head. As she did, pincer sharp nails of the half-girl punctured around Ayla's ankle just above her boots.

Her lungs were on fire. As much as she understood the rules in place forbidding her to enter the kingdom's waters, she cursed them now for they left her without the ability to swim.

Seals lived in colonies. Chances were this monster did not live and hunt alone either. Which meant more of them would soon be tearing her apart. Roi had mentioned that they only threatened human life when they were hungry, while the waters were depleted of fish. As much as she empathised for any starving, living thing, she had no desire to become something's dinner.

She had no weapons to defend herself, and no strength compared to the whipping blubber tail pulling her along. Blindly shucking her heavy leather jacket gained her some mobility of her upper body. As she tried to pull at whipping strands of orange hair something cold was knocking against her nose. She reached to her neck, clawing for a silver chain.

The locket Dandy and Ethel had gifted her for her name day. She clutched the thin, long chain in both her hands as she took it off. Using whatever strength she had left to scrunch her body until her legs were bent and her torso overhung her knees.

Praying it would be enough, she reached out, hoping the long silk hair would guide her to her target. Hooking the loop over what she hoped was a head she pulled, but it didn't catch against anything.

Missed.

Even behind closed eyes she was beginning to see spots and her chest screamed for her to open her mouth and draw breath.

She lunged again, *further* this time and pulled down and back towards her chest.

Possessive hands released her ankles and scrambled to the chain at its throat. She could sense the half breed's panic as it clawed for the hands behind her, pulling at its frozen neck.

That gave Ayla a last push of adrenaline, of *hope*, that she would make it out of this. But to do so would require pulling with unrelenting strength long enough to send her to sleep. And Ayla didn't have much strength left.

Suddenly her shoulder breached the water into the night air. The selkie, in her panic, had pushed the pair to the top. They flailed around in the water, tumbling over each other. Ayla drew desperate breath when her face popped above the waves, but the lapping water poured into her open mouth, and she spluttered.

Ayla pulled and pulled, hoping the small silver links were strong enough to withstand the pressure. Her grip was feigning, slacking against fatigue. She didn't know if she was making noise but, in her head, she was screaming bloody murder.

A wet hand grabbed her shoulder, and she was ready to concede to her sealed fate, when instead of being dragged down, she was hoisted up into the cool air of the night, spluttering out saltwater.

Only the frigid locking of her knees kept her standing upright. Cold thumbs wiped her eyes of the trickling water, pushing back her sopping hair and pulling her impossibly close.

Her teeth chattered violently. She was whimpering sounds of fright and relief all at once as Thian beamed down at her.

A rough splash jolted her out of her feeling of safety. They all peeked over the edge to see the creature's tail spasming, slowly coming back to consciousness.

Ayla's eyes caught on the flaming red line marring the neck of her slate-white skin, and the silver locket still looped around her neck, its pendant floating in the water.

There was a feeling of relief–knowing she hadn't killed a living thing. A thing that was at least *half* human.

Thian all but growled as he lunged for his blade slashing it at the water's edge. Ayla jumped forward and grabbed the bicep of his raised arm.

"Thian no, don't," she pleaded through rattling teeth. Her tongue tasted of salt, and it was an effort not to gag. He didn't even look at her, taken by his rage.

"It tried to kill you." he gritted back.

"She's just hungry," Ayla whispered. "It was my fault for reaching into the water. I was tempting them."

He reluctantly dropped his weapon, and Ayla rewarded him with a kiss on the cheek and pressed her frozen forehead against his.

When her eyes fluttered open, a limp form behind him caught her eye.

"Oh gods!" she sucked in a breath. Tears finally flooded her lashes as she dropped to the younger prince's side.

"He's breathing," Reade assured, "just out cold."

She cradled Atlas' head and winced when she felt the enormous bump swelling on the side, right where she'd watched him get hit.

Chapter 16

Thian squirmed under the covers, cursing the chill that he couldn't rid himself of. After a thorough berating from his father and a stare that promised death from his mother, guards had been posted outside the rooms of each of the teens with strict instruction not to let them out until sunrise.

He hadn't seen his mother so incensed since he'd dyed his hair pink with wine when he was ten. His father though… he'd never heard his father scream like that. Nor had he seen tears in his eyes as he reminded his foolish sons that he'd already lost a child to the eastern seas.

Cursing with colour, Thian wanted more than anything to go to Ayla–to ensure she was alright and soothe her through the onset shock. Instead, he was a prisoner within his own dreary room.

The door ground against its hinges as Ser Maitland let in Niamh, carrying a tray of something steaming and spicily scented. She had left their rooms as he stripped out of his sopping clothes–announcing she was hungry for supper.

Unlike their apartments in Balcarras, where they occupied multiple rooms, on this tour they would share a bed every night.

Clenching his jaw around its chatter, he watched his wife pad over to the dresser and place down the tray. Picking up the husk bowl and spoon she made her way to his bedside and perched on the soft edge.

He barely blinked as she dipped the spoon in the hot broth and lifted it to his mouth in silent offering. He barely had time to identify any flavour in the dish as he swallowed instantaneously, revelling in the burn that trickled down his throat and coated his insides.

"I thought you were hungry?" he said.

"I've already eaten." she replied, not taking her eyes off the spoon she scraped on the lip of the bowl to catch a drip. "I didn't want you to sleep on an empty stomach."

"They let you take seconds?"

She smirked. "I'm pregnant, Thian, if I asked for the moon, they would do their best to lay it at my feet."

His stomach twisted.

It was rare for the two of them to spend time solely in each other's company. She favoured spending time with Atlas, and he preferred the company of…well, anyone but Atlas.

She continued to spoon feed him, wasting not one droplet.

"Thank you." he croaked. The words foreign on his tongue.

When the soup was finished, she moved over to the hearth where she had a small cauldron set over a humble fire. She dipped her hand in the cast iron and pulled out a soft cheesecloth rag. After ringing it free of water, she returned to his side and laid the hot fabric over his forehead. He refrained from groaning at the warmth that seeped into his skin.

Shedding her chamber coat of soft knitted cream, she moved to the foot of the bed. Thian hissed as she pulled back the covers, exposing his flesh to the night chill.

She wrapped his frozen feet softly in the fabric, offering what little else was available to warm him.

Moving over to her side of the large bed frame she hefted a pelt from her pillows and draped it across his still shivering chest.

Thick layering of mattresses made it a bit of a climb, so she groaned as she clutched the spread. Thian flinched, considering offering aid, but stopped short when she made it independently. Slipping her feet under the covers, she nestled into her pillows.

A large, embroidered cushion laid between them–positioned so by Thian to allow her space. She placed her ringed hand on the soft fabric and pressed until it bowed, allowing them to gaze at each other.

"What would you have wished for?" she asked quietly.

He looked inward, searching for the true answer he had not fully considered.

The scales of his heart were already toppled, weighed down with bitter rage, disappointment, longing and jealousy. With each beat of the organ, he could feel their threads weaving thicker, trapping him in an endless web of darkness from which he could not escape.

He said nothing–only stared into her eyes. His wife's eyes, that were such a beautiful pale shade of green that he had never taken the time to appreciate.

"I'm sorry." Niamh whispered.

So was he.

Chapter 17

Eighteen Moons Later

A yla stared at the unsealed parchment, re-reading its contents at least half a dozen times, refusing to let her heart celebrate until she was certain her eyes were not misunderstanding.

She held an invitation. An offer to move back to Balcarras Castle and serve as Governess to Niamh's baby girl, Twyla.

Suddenly the excited tremor in her hands spread through every bone in her body and she launched up out of her chair, jumping up and down like a child, clutching the papers to her chest.

After nine long years she was finally going home.

Ayla skipped down the worn stairs of the palace, their stone rounded from time. She burst into every room looking for Maerine until she finally found the princess in a cosy drawing room on the second floor.

Out of breath, Ayla didn't bother apologizing for barging in. She stared at the princess of the palace, perched in front of a window, the pale light of Articium casting a cool glow on the divine figure who had shown her so much affection from the day she had met her.

Still clutching the paper between her fingers, Ayla's smile started to wobble beneath her cheeks. And then she burst into tears.

Maerine leapt to her feet and pulled her into a soothing embrace, shushing her softly and rubbing her back in circles. "What's wrong sweetling?"

"It's not wrong, I swear–It's *good*. I don't know why I am crying," Ayla said with a chuckle that slowly dissipated into more sobs.

"That's alright," Maerine assured "I'm here."

Once reduced to a sniffling mess, Maerine guided the Marnoch girl over to an upholstered chaise and pulled out a handkerchief from the sleeve of her dress. Ayla wiped her eyes that were so puffy she could hardly see, but refrained from blowing snot all over the princess' pretty ivory rag.

"Tell me?" Maerine asked softly.

But Ayla couldn't form the words without her throat closing up. So, she instead handed over the now-crushed letter that contained the news she could not articulate.

Maerine tensed for a moment, then smiled softly as she read Niamh's pretty cursive. "This is wonderful news."

"I know. It's what I've always wanted." Ayla grimaced at herself, at words that made her sound ungrateful for everything Maerine had given her. "Though I didn't think it would be so hard to leave," she said, voice cracking. "I'm going to miss you so much."

And with that Maerine's own eyes glazed over, until all that was left to do was pull each other into another hug. "I just hope for your sake the girl is more like her mother and less like her father and myself."

Ayla's puzzled face was enough for Maerine to continue, "Oh yes, I was a dreadful child. A truly rebellious rascal, easily bored by the lectures my governess had for me. Sometimes I would protest by not saying a word to her for days on end. Others, I would reply in Alpische, knowing fine well she didn't understand a word. I scared away quite a few in my youth. Eventually one resorted to bribery; one uninterrupted lesson in exchange for one visit to the arena."

"I had no idea," Ayla confessed, "you're nothing like that here."

She tucked a lock of white hair behind her ear and shrugged. "I found happiness. It took me a long time to realise why I behaved the way I did. It didn't seem to matter what I learned or how I behaved because I was perpetually a disappointment in my mother's eyes. Then I started making friends–your mother being the first–and began feeling companionship and care that went beyond the duty my teachers and overseers held. And then came my husband, and now my boys. I can only aspire to be the best version of myself for them."

"I can't speak for the boys," Ayla said "but these past nine years, you have been the best mother I could ask for. You made it more than a place; you made it a *home*."

Both erupted into another fit of tears, occasionally taking a break to laugh at the ridiculous appearance of one another.

Though spiteful about her circumstances at the time, Ayla was grateful for Maerine's kindness in bringing her back with them to Articium.

She was not her mother, no, but sometimes it felt as though she were.

There was something Ayla needed to do before she left for the capital. Down on the sand of the Crescent Bay, Ayla cradled the shell close to her chest as she watched the calm waters ripple with the wind. No one would notice the thing was missing from the palace. Not with the thousands of others littered around. But for some reason, she needed *this one* to be set free.

Reaching down, she softly placed the shell on the ground, where the surf lapped at the sand. Standing back, she watched as the rising tide gobbled it up.

There was a chance it would tumble for a while, beaten by sand and sea, only to be washed up again. But there was also a chance it could find a new life, see new things and visit new places. And that was worth letting go for.

"Bye sea," she whispered to the Crescent Bay.

Turning on her heels a gust of sand smacked her in the face. "Good riddance, you salty nuisance."

Walking back up the slope she eyed her old bedroom window. "Thanks for keeping me cosy."

A voice carried over the wind and Ayla turned over her shoulder to catch Irwyn waving on his deck. She waved back on her toes with a smile. "Thanks for keeping me sane." She whispered.

By the time she made it back to the palace gates the carriage was packed with two trunks, filled with every item Ayla owned in this world.

She stood outside its wooden doors to make her final farewell.

Crouching to the ground, she took Brydon's hands in hers. "Promise me you will keep working on your letters, so you can read when I write to you?"

"I promise," he said with a cheeky grin that told her he didn't mean a word.

"Good boy," she smiled, nonetheless. With just shy of four years to his name, he didn't understand the full nature of what was going on. That he wouldn't see her every day as he had since the day he was born. Ayla dreaded the day he did.

Ayla waved to the western facing window of Dandy and Ethel's room. They promised to visit if she ever felt homesick. A sweet sentiment, but home *was* Balcarras Castle. Ayla had been homesick for nearly nine years. And finally, *finally*, she was going back where she belonged.

Rion planted a chaste kiss atop Ayla's head. "Good luck, little one." was all he managed as he moved back to stand beside his wife. Bloodred hair whipped around his proud eyes.

Ayla didn't dare look at Maerine as she entered the carriage, they had said their goodbyes, and looking at her face would only make it harder to leave.

A whip cracked, and Ayla let go a shuddering breath.

Outside she could hear Brydon start to whine and then cry out. She closed her eyes and refused to picture his arms stretching out, pleading for her to come back and hold him.

The line–up beyond the gates dissipated the farther the girl's carriage tumbled down the path. A bittersweet sadness was felt at the departure of the long-term resident.

Rion took a strained step forward–

"Don't." Maerine warned, grabbing his hand within her own. "Let her go."

He said nothing. Grinding his jaw, he set his brow painfully low.

Chapter 18

I t didn't take long for the smell of the capital to hit as the carriage wheeled through the cobblestoned streets of Linton. Ayla's nose cringed.

Her skin itched with desperation for a wash. She didn't need a tub, just a basin and some soap would do. *Gods, the first impression she was to give to the castle was that she had been dragged through a hedge backwards.*

Peeking out the little window to her left, she watched the streets and the people on them. Inspecting the hanging bracket signs, she carded through her memory if any establishments rang a bell or were new additions in the past nine years.

The long days of travel had given Ayla plenty time to think. And worry. And then dread.

Blinded by excitement, she hadn't stopped to consider what her life would look like under employ of the castle. She wasn't a child anymore, none of them were. So, they wouldn't spend every minute of every day together as they once had. She was there to do a job. Perform a highly coveted duty that many would argue she was unfit for.

What business did a girl with no bairns of her own have nurturing the most important infant in the continent?

It didn't matter what anyone else thought, she had to remind herself. *In a little more than a year, the King will step down and once coronated, Thian would uphold his promise and tether them together for eternity.*

Any anxiety fluttered away when the castle came into view. The familiarity of the dark stone perched upon the dormant volcano made her smile.

Niamh wouldn't even let Ayla visit her new room before introducing her to Twyla, who was occupying the same nursery Ayla, Thian, Atlas and Niamh had grown up in.

The nursery was exactly as she'd left it all those years ago. The rugs were a little more worn and the curtains had been swapped from a pale blue to a vivid purple, but she was flooded with happy memories of her youth.

Though with the happy memories, also came a touch of grief and longing. Never again would she create a beautiful memory with her mother in this room.

Blinking away the sorrow, Ayla turned to Niamh who saw through the smile she tried to plaster.

"I know," Niamh croaked out.

Sitting on a tufted rug was the little princess. Playing with wooden Pegasi, very similar to the wooden horses Thian used to own–though hers possessed tiny, intricately carved wings.

Niamh dismissed her handmaiden and dropped to her knees, placing a delicate hand on the girl's head, "Ayla... this is Twyla." Picking her up, the girl snuggled into her mother's side, shielding her pale green eyes from the stranger.

Ayla joined them on the floor.

After giving her a cautious once-over, Twyla crawled over to her new governess and raised her arms in a silent plea. Ayla, happy to comply, placed the girl in her lap.

She couldn't believe how small and precious she was. It hadn't been that long since Brydon was this age and yet she found it hard to believe he was ever this tiny.

Twyla had a beautiful chubby look to her, radiating health and happiness. Blonde shocks of hair were tufting in patches of her head that Ayla smoothed over absentmindedly.

"Niamh?" Ayla asked softly.

"Hm?" she replied, not looking up from the figurines she was setting up into a neat little row.

Ayla took a minute to consider how she wanted to address it, "Are you… happy?"

Niamh suddenly looked pensive. "Perhaps I could do with a glass of water, but yes, I think so."

Ayla smiled at the innocence of her response, but pressed, "I meant happy here, in this life, with Thian." A pause. "Do you love him?"

She dreaded the response, but it needed to be asked. Never had she explicitly asked Niamh about her feelings for the prince. It was an arranged marriage, not one of purest love. But perhaps, she recognised, she was seeing what she *wanted* to see and believing what she wanted to be true. She wasn't sure what she would do if Niamh declared she *did*, in fact, love him.

Realisation dawned on Niamh's face, and it softened into understanding. "I have never felt love the way you have, no."

Relief washed over her. But another question crawled up her throat.

"Does he hurt you?" The words felt acidic on her tongue. She had seen no bruises or signs of harm on the princess, but bruises can be hidden, as can the internal destruction it does to one's soul. Thian promised to marry Ayla after his coronation, *after* the dissolvement to his marriage to Niamh. But patience was never Thian's virtue.

"He has never laid a hand on me." she replied.

Ayla's chest felt mountains lighter with that kernel of assurance.

She watched mother and daughter before her. Mirror images of one another. Being two years younger, Ayla had never known Niamh at this age and could hardly recall what she looked like until she was at least seven or eight, but imagined she'd looked an awful lot like the little princess in her lap.

"Did you want to be a mother?"

It took Niamh less time to answer this one "No. But I didn't have much of a choice."

Ayla's heart fell for the girl.

Niamh went on, "I was very happy when she was born, though. She was so tiny and perfect and *mine*. She used to be such a simple thing. When she cried, I knew it was because she was hungry, or tired, or needed to be fed. But now that she's growing… she has all these complex feelings I can't understand." Her eyes went glassy and her voice small. "I don't know why she cries or gets angry or scared. And she's too little to tell me how to make it better. I ask her to stop crying and she just wails harder." She met Ayla's eyes with desperation shining in her own. "It hurts my heart when she's upset."

Ayla offered a sympathetic smile "I think that's normal, Niamh. It makes you human–makes you a mother." She reached out to touch Niamh's trembling hand. The princess released a shuddering breath and squeezed a thank you back.

Sitting in the nursery with Niamh and Twyla, Ayla found the peaceful contentment she had been longing for, and she knew she would be happy here.

She almost forgot that someone was missing.

"His majesty has important work to attend to. He doesn't have the pleasure of entertaining staff."

Ayla winced at the queen's remark. She hadn't meant any offence when she'd enquired how his majesty was fairing. Nor did she expect him to be there. The fact that she was dining with Raura herself was a surprise.

Instead of stumbling through some kind of apology, Ayla dropped her head with a submissive nod. Her eyes flicked up across the table to where Niamh sat stiffly.

A hoard of servants flooded the space with an egregious amount of food for the four of them to eat, cutting the tension brewing in the air.

A slight boy served the queen a plate with a little bit of everything that Raura nodded to. Once she was satisfied, he removed the plate to a sideboard along the far wall where a handmaid took a modest bite of each dish.

"How is the archipelago, Ayla?" Raura brought her attention back to the table. "Thriving I hope?"

Ayla's fingers twitched beside her fork. Niamh was helping herself to roast goose, but it felt like a trap to begin eating before the queen herself.

She cleared her throat. "Very well, I believe. Trade is strong. The weather is, well, dreich."

Raura smiled politely, but it didn't quite reach her eyes. "And my daughter?" She picked up a crystal goblet and brought the water to her lips. "How is the princess?"

Ah. That was why she had been brought to dinner.

Raura wanted insight into Maerine's life without reaching out directly.

"Her Highness is very happy in Articium." *Shit, did that sound like an attack?* "But she misses her family here greatly." she tacked on for good measure.

One of Raura's perfectly manicured brows pulled with suspicion. She turned her head to her royal taster who dipped her head with a curtsey. The servant brought the silver plate back to the table and placed it before his queen.

Raura then personally moved half its contents onto a scalloped plate in front of her daughter.

Ayla had barely caught a glimpse of Esse when they came to Articium around her eighteenth name day. The beautiful girl was growing into her ears, that poked through a curtain of bloodred hair. She wore a simple navy dress with a white lace trim and a headband smothered in pearls behind her ears. Ayla had to wonder if they were Articium pearls, perhaps a gift from her elder sister.

After Esse began to eat, Raura couldn't seem to peel her gaze from her daughter, watching every bite, chew and swallow. She wore her icy white hair down, with a silver netted headpiece from which tiny rubies fell like droplets of blood.

"We don't normally take on a governess with so little experience for a child of the Crown, but Niamh here was quite insistent."

Ayla looked to Niamh who seemed content being left out of the conversation.

Queen Raura continued, "You are however a second generation, and grew up under the instruction of the finest."

Ayla smiled at the compliment in her late mother's honour.

"For the first ten years anyway."

Ouch.

"Niamh suggested you have an affinity for languages?"

"Yes, Your Majesty, I speak four fluently and can read with some confidence in one more."

"Good. Learn three more by the time the child is five." The Queen watched her daughter eat every mouthful with sharp eyes. "Attempts at education for the moment would be futile, but we expect you to further your own education regardless to prepare for instruction."

"Of course, Your Majesty."

They were surrounded by empty chairs. The head of the table, for His Majesty. One for the youngest prince, who was somewhere in the borderlands, training with the royal army. And one she'd hoped would be filled tonight.

Chapter 19

There wasn't much to unpack, but Ayla enjoyed finding new homes for all her things. There was plenty of room in the ornate wardrobe for new gowns over the years, and she was already eyeing the deep windowsill prime for planters.

She wouldn't be staying in the apartments her parents had lived in with her as a child–which was somewhat of a relief. No need to be haunted by the grief of her past every day.

Glad to see a steaming basin already drawn for her, alongside a neat pile of washcloths, she peeled off her heavy dress skirts and made way for the bathing chamber.

Closing her eyes, she exhaled into the steaming fabric, savouring the tingling feeling of heat as it seeped into her pores.

After settling in and readying herself for bed, Ayla heard a knock, so light she thought herself going mad.

She treaded lightly to the door. "Who is it?"

No reply.

Gathering her nerve, she opened the door.

Thian swaggered in, eyes shadowed with exhaustion. He looked her up and down, surprise and something darker rolling over his face.

"My love... you're here." He strode over and lifted her.

Ayla gave out a giggle, "Yes! And where in the hells have you been?!"

He gave her a pout as he sat on the edge of the bed, trapping her between his legs.

"My apologies, I simply got my days mixed up..."

Ayla tried to suppress a grin, but who was she kidding. Here he was. She ran her fingers through his snow-white locks–or lack thereof.

"You've cut your hair..." she stated. It was shorn right to the root, and in the dim candlelight its silver colouring shone iridescent like an Articium saltwater pearl.

"Do you not like it?" he questioned. "Say the word my love and I will grow it out for you here and now!" Throwing her atop the bed, he straddled her, tickling his short stubbled head of hair over her face, which was now bright red.

She squealed. Laughing harder than she had in years.

Finally, she caught enough of a breath to grab his head with both her arms and pin it to her chest. His body conceded as it slumped atop her.

"You're home." he murmured.

"I'm home." she echoed, a smile tilting her cheeks.

"I'll never let them take you again, I vow it."

She kissed the top of his head.

Continuing to languidly stroke his stubbly hair seemed to lull him to sleep, and she lay there positively smitten.

"I had dinner with your mother."

"My condolences."

Her scoff bounced his head. "I had hoped you'd be there."

Soft, sleepy breaths tickled her skin.

"I know you're faking it, you little terror." She shook his shoulders.

He peeked up at her with a guilty smile. "I'll make it up to you."

Continuing her languid strokes she said, "Twyla is beautiful, Thian. You're very lucky."

He returned his cheek to her chest and murmured "The luckiest."

Ayla's thoughts drifted to the baby girl with big green eyes and soft blonde hair.

"Thian?"

"Hmm?"

"What will happen to them…after?"

"What do you mean?" his words were smooshed against her sternum.

"After the coronation, what will happen to Niamh and the baby?"

He was silent for a moment.

"Whatever they desire I suppose. Niamh will have the freedom she was never given, and I will support wherever she wishes to reside. She wants to live in Articium with her brother? I'll cart her off with the finest footmen. She wants a new palace opposite mine? I'll order the sandstone. If she wants to wed my brother and live under my nose just to spite me? So be it."

Ayla swallowed

"What about others though? Our support aside, how will the rest of the world see her? *Treat* her? Damaged goods? Unworthy of a king's love?"

"Ayla, since when did Niamh prefer the company of others?"

"That doesn't mean she's immune to their judgement. It's a cruel world, that's all. I worry for her."

"It will be no crueler for her then than it is now."

Ayla chewed on the sad sentiment.

"And Twyla?"

A beat. "She will stay with her mother."

"With the marriage annulled, will she still be your heir?"

A sigh. "Ayla the hour is too late to tease out details of a far-off future."

But it wasn't far off. Not anymore. It was a little over a year away. Wars have been fought longer.

"Sorry. I just… she still doesn't know?"

"Not yet."

Ayla rubbed her hand down the prince's spine, thumb tracing the divot between muscle

He kissed her sternum. "Everything will be perfect. I promise."

Chapter 20

T hings weren't quite as Ayla remembered.

She was learning, day to day, what lived up to the memory she'd held on to over the years. As well as what was a little more disappointing.

Turns out, the throne room ceiling was not, in fact, a thousand hands high. And you couldn't *actually* smell cooks' lemon shortbread wafting all the way from the gardens. The kennel hounds weren't quite big enough to ride. And you couldn't see *all* the way to the Mouth from the tallest tower in the keep.

There were other things too. More disappointing things. But she tried not to dwell on those so much.

It had its upsides too, this biased memory; realising some things weren't quite so bad as she recalled. It was blessedly a lot less than a million steps down to breakfast from her rooms, and the sentinels didn't snarl like dogs whenever you walked in their path.

As Ayla waked through the streets of Linton, she smiled as vendors sang praises of their own produce and children ran in fits of giggles from their mothers' wooden spoons.

There was a slim section of the day when Linton could be considered lovely, wholesome. The hours after the hooligans and thieves of darkness scurried back into their holes, before the ladies of the night got hungry and began to prowl the streets for their next meal.

And so, Ayla had chosen this time of day when the sun cast brightest to wander into town by herself, scouting for a suitable tailor to make some alterations.

In the month since her return to Balcarras she had indulged in all that she had missed; time with Thian, basking in the gardens, and gobbling up the wondrous desserts the kitchens whipped up each morning. Though she had no regrets, exploits of the latter had affected her more than she cared to admit, and several dresses needed to be let out a little.

Carrying said dresses in a deep wicker basket on her arm, she pottered through the cobbled streets, ignoring the temptation to buy whatever baked goods were flooding the block with such glorious smells.

She had considered buying a few new dresses that fitted properly, but her payment as governess was primarily room and board. The gold feather coins she saw were few and far between. The heavy basket contained five simply spun dresses, but she needed to get a quote from the tailor to make sure her coin could cover alterations for all of them.

If Thian knew she needed coin for this–for *anything*, really–he would have her room filled to the brim with gold. Ayla knew this. But she was admittedly a little embarrassed to admit the reason she needed the coin in the first place.

Hopping over what she hoped was a puddle of well-water, she turned down the ally of silk spinners.

Stepping back out into the fresh air, Ayla muttered a string of unladylike curses, avoiding the appalled eyes of judgmental townsfolk passing by.

After trying each and every tailor on the block, she had returned with a face of shame to the cheapest one. Even then, her coin only covered two out of the five dresses she intended to be altered.

Shoving a near empty purse back into her heavy pockets she brushed off the frustration and readied herself for the walk back to the castle.

"You there!" a voice called out behind her.

She didn't recognise the man addressing her, so Ayla hurried her pace, breathing through her racing heart.

"Ayla!"

Her eyes blew wide, and she ceased her steps. The man's clothes were finely made but well worn, the pommel of his sword was tarnished, so obviously not just for show. He had young skin, but the short stamp of hair around his mouth aged him considerably.

Ayla waded through every corner of her mind, but she could not place him.

Feeling the security of the bustling street around her, she did not retreat when he sauntered towards her. She did however, clutch the basket of dresses a fraction tighter, testing its weight, deciding the strength required to haul it at his tanned head if he got too close.

"Forgive me, I didn't mean to startle you." the stranger said with an amused smile. "You *are* Ayla Marnoch, are you not?"

"And *you* are?" she would not confirm her identity until he forfeited his own.

"Knox, my lady." he said with a courteous dip of his head, long arms reaching for her free hand to place a chaste kiss upon her knuckles. She tried not to recoil.

"Knox," she echoed. "Thian's friend?"

"Ah, so he's spoken of me."

"No actually, he hasn't." she replied honestly. It was Niamh who had mentioned the name on a couple of occasions.

A chuckle, "Well, he's certainly spoken of *you*." It was fair to assume that went beyond her role as his daughter's governess. That warmed her heart a little. It scared her, just a fraction more. "He's just down the road, if you'd like me to take you to him?"

She studied Knox' face for any sign of ill intent. But she *was* curious, so she gave a brief nod and Knox turned on his heel, sweeping his arm as he led the way.

Down the road clearly meant something different by the stranger's standard.

Nearly an hour later the two reached a string of taverns and inns on the west side of town, her guide descended some cobbled steps to a cellar door. The sounds of laughter, clinking glassware and a smooth pianoforte drifted through.

Wearily, Ayla descended the steps into the vault.

She let her eyes adjust to the sudden darkness, only candlelight emitted a faint glow into the space. It was disorienting–this deception of nightfall. Making it impossible to tell what time of day it was, nor how many hours had passed in this den of sin.

The space was loud, every seat full and even more players spilling out onto the bar. Most tables were covered in coin and cards. Others were drenched in ale from tipped tankards.

"Can I buy you something to drink?" Knox asked.

"Water, please."

Knox let out a dangerously low laugh. "You'll find no water here, I'm afraid."

Ignoring his tone and resuming her search for Thian, she soon picked out his pearlescent head of hair.

Beyond the glimmer of surprise, there was a gladness in the prince's eyes at the sight of her. He stood, folding his cards and abandoning his coin without second thought. He flung his gaze to Knox and the man cleared off to the bar.

Shielding her from the view of the cellar, he planted a kiss on her cheek.

"What brings you down here?" he asked once he pulled away.

"Your friend spotted me heading home and offered to take me to you. I was curious where you spend the ungodly hours of the day when you're not with me." She batted her lashes at him in that way that made him grip her tighter.

He stroked his hand down her arm to the heavy basket that left an angry red welt on her skin. "What's this?"

She looked down at the three dresses she couldn't afford to be altered. "New dresses." she replied, more mousily than she'd intended.

His onyx eyes flicked between her own. "No, they're not. You wore that one three days ago." he proclaimed, fisting the gown of heather grey. She swallowed. "Don't you know you dance around my head in all your pretty dresses? I have the way you look in each one committed to memory."

The musty heat of the cellar was getting to her. She felt a flush spread across the breadth of her chest under her light cloak. "A few needed darning, that's all."

"Are you lying to me, Ayla?" he asked with a sinner's grin.

Behind them, a growl of frustration exploded into violence as a patron, unhappy with the way the dice fell, flipped a table. Silver and copper feather coins scattered everywhere and before she could blink, people were on their hands and knees, scurrying around for any they could pinch in the panic. A large man leaped over the bar and grabbed the disruptor by the scruff of his hairy neck, driving him right to where Ayla remained by the door.

Thian pulled her aside with fluid grace and started towards his old table with her in hand.

Flicking her head around to inspect more, Ayla noted one definitive difference from any tavern she'd ever set foot in. There were no women. Normally, girls sat in the laps of their lovers while they drank and played, women of the night flashed unspeakable amounts of flesh at potential customers and occasionally a noble lady or two would sneak into one to witness the lust filled debauchery that took place in establishments such as these.

Just as fast as she made the observation, it was shattered as she peaked a slender neck and exposed shoulder that most certainly did not belong to a man. The unfaced woman sat at the farthest table from the door, her back to Ayla as they weaved through the main floor. She had sickly-sweet honey coloured hair– cropped shorter than most women at court, just below her jaw that flared out at the ends.

Ayla wanted to enquire as to what made her special, why *she* was permitted in the company of these men above all other women, but Thian stopped beside the chair he had been occupying.

Without needing to be asked, the player next to her vacated his seat for the prince to sit with his lady. But Thian had other plans. He offered a hand to Ayla, patting his thigh in a silent request. She lowered herself onto his lap and he wound his arm around her waist.

If the prince had noticed the extra inches Ayla had recently acquired, he had never mentioned them. In Fact, he seemed more pleased than ever in the nights he spent clutching her. Her heart did a little flutter just thinking about it.

"The game is King's Army, gentleman." A man shuffling a deck announced to the table of about seven players including Ayla and Thian.

Thian tucked a piece of hair behind her ear so his whisper would tickle her skin "Want to play?"

Smiling, she slunk her hand into her pockets to pull out her nearly empty coin purse.

"Buy-in is ten silver feathers." the dealer stated, not taking his eyes off the flying deck he shuffled.

Ayla stilled her retrieval, her smile wobbling slightly. "Maybe the next round. I'll watch and learn the play this time." she whispered to Thian.

He looked into her eyes so deeply she knew, *she just knew,* he saw through her lies. "Very well," he conceded. "A kiss for good luck?" he chanced. And she obeyed happily. A maidenly touch to the corner of his lips before their company whose attention was surely on the Prince of the continent and a girl who was surely *not* his wife.

Feeling his disappointment when she pulled away too soon, she whipped her red stained cheeks back to the table who was waiting for him to pick up his hand.

She watched him play four rounds. They were relatively short lived–despite six players partaking in each. Thian lost each round. But to her surprise, he lost with a gracious smile each and every time. Even offering congratulations to the winners on their lucky hand. Though, despite her being new to the game, she could have sworn she saw him hold winning spreads in the last two games.

"You're killing me, Slater." Thian exclaimed to the game master who gathered the discarded cards to reshuffle for the next round.

"Apologies, my prince. Perhaps the Goddess of Luck favours myself today." the dealer replied.

"Don't listen to him, love." Thian murmured to Ayla. "He has that Goddess of his wrapped around his prick every day." There was no malice in his words. Slater chuckled at the crude remark, muttering in a foreign tongue that Ayla picked up on. The pair were obviously far from strangers.

"Is your family originally from Vorraine?" Ayla enquired as Slater scrambled the deck. Besides the dialect, his fiery hair was a staple of the kingdom, and his name was not a popular one in Balcarras.

"Yes, my lady. A little town just outside of Rhuus."

"And the bastard was going to leave me and go back, can you believe it?" Thian stated, taking a swig from his freshly refilled tankard.

"Business was slow–too slow. The locals here didn't trust my family to run a house of cards." Slater wore a smile, but his ticking jaw spoke of something other than amusement. "They called us cheats and tricksters before they even played a hand within our walls. We win because we are *skilled*, not because we cheat. They saw my hair of the gambling land and assumed I wanted to strip them of all their coin." Ayla tried not to look pitifully upon the dealer, assuming he wouldn't appreciate that. "I want their coin–to pay my keep and feed my family, not for *greed*. We offer fair terms and a chance of wealth. It's not my fault this kingdom is full of shit players." He cast a final grin at the prince across the table.

Thian didn't look the least bit moved.

"It doesn't seem as though business is slow now?" Ayla noted the sounds of laughter tumbling over the tables towards them.

"No, my lady. Not for many years." he split the deck and used his thumbs to bend them until they bowed, eventually fluttering into one stack once more. "Prince Thian was–*is* a loyal patron. He bought the property from the previous landlord and gifted it back to us."

Ayla turned to Thian, who cast his eyes down– as if embarrassed by his own charity.

"Ah but see," Thian finally said, "it was rather selfish of me. For in return, I ask them to open their doors to me and my friends during the day–to avoid the rabble of the night."

She wanted to kiss him. Hard. Harder than the polite peck of luck from before. Thian liked to hide this side of himself–the softer side, the side that cared–but it was there. And she wanted to see more of it.

"Care for a hand, my lady?" Slater asked. Ayla turned her attention back to the dealer who was yet to hand out cards. King's Army had a buy-in she couldn't afford. But there were other games.

"Could we... Do you know Twenty-One?" she asked, hand clutching the velvet pouch in her pocket. A nod of the head and two cards were placed before her. Several players of the table left the private hand to refill their cups or join a new game elsewhere. Ayla placed a single silver feather on the table. Slater matched her quaint bet on the weathered oak between them.

She could feel Thian's stare, so she nuzzled his cheek with her nose as she whispered, "Best practice a little before I risk more."

Peeking under her cards she smirked. Twenty-one was a crowd favourite between the Solmund boys and the Forsyth girls back in Articium. Many late, candle-lit nights were spent throwing around Reuban's decorative deck, betting for future deserts and morning buns as opposed to money. But it gave her enough practice to feel confident here, even with a Vorrainish Master of Games.

She won the round. And the three after that. Each time her winnings doubled, so did her next bet. By the end of the day, she walked away with her velvet purse bursting with silver.

Perhaps she would treat herself to a new dress after all.

Two days later, when Ayla retired to her chambers after nightfall, she was startled to see a second wardrobe had been added to her room, brimming with a dozen beautiful new dresses of every colour of the royal garden.

She didn't know how Thian knew her measurements so precisely, but every dress fit her flawlessly.

Chapter 21

"How did you learn to draw so well?" Ayla asked, not lifting her eyes from the parchment she was scoring on.

"Cadmus."

Thian watched her wince.

"I hated it at first, but he assured me that I had the right eye, just had to refine my technique. The more I drew the better the sketches became, I suppose." he shrugged. "I'm sure I've sent you some gods-awful drawings in the past."

The pair had made a studio of sorts in Ayla's room. Night had long fallen, and so dozens of candles lit up the space. Thian had insisted on them, knowing that their warm glow casted the harshest of shadows on a sitter's face.

Both sat upon Roshin rugs and plump down pillows, Ayla's back pressed against a bed post while Thian sat opposite leaning against the old stone of the wall.

"They aren't *awful*, I love them. There's no doubt you've improved, but I adore every one of them. They tell me a story of where you were in life at that time." she insisted, shifting her legs and the wooden board that supported the paper on her knees.

"You kept them?"

Ayla nodded, eyes still downcast on her sketch, a healthy blush setting into her cheeks.

Humbled by her words, Thian watched how concentrated she was on her work. His eyes roamed over the tension in her brow, and how she absentmindedly bit her lower lip ever so slightly.

"Can I see them?" he asked, brows raised. He couldn't even remember what he had scribbled on his letters over the years. Mostly he added them just to fill the empty space he didn't have words for.

"No, you may not. I don't trust you to not berate yourself and take them away."

He scoffed, "Very well. But I'll need to draw up a big stack to leave with you, a reminder of just how talented I've become."

"Oh, how I missed your humility." she jested, lifting her eyes through her lashes to remind herself of the details of the subject of her design.

"Are you finished?" he asked impatiently.

"No, not yet! You're much faster than me–you said yourself you've had the practice. I want it to be as good as it can be." she chuckled out.

Long finished with his own drawing, Thian leaned back against the wall, a pillow wedged between himself and the rough sandstone. He lazily sharpened one of the blunted charcoals with a knife.

"Do you want a bigger apartment?" he enquired.

She shook her downcast head. "No, I have everything I need here."

Thian shook his head in silent disapproval. Looking around Ayla's bedchambers was painful. A simply carved poster bed, a few white gold candle sconces to brighten the place up, but even the rugs and pillows were a mundane shade of beige.

Any flavour of personality in Ayla's room was clearly implemented herself. Dusty coloured blue and green dresses poked out of a doorless wardrobe next to the ones he had commissioned. Some small, hardy potted plants sat neatly on the inner windowsill, and he spotted a familiar babydoll tucked away on a chair in the corner.

She deserved more. She deserved *everything*.

***

"Alright, I'm ready... *Don't* laugh at me." Ayla warned Thian sternly, clutching the paper close to her chest despite being ready to hand it over.

"I would never. One," Thian began counting.

She didn't understand why, but her heart was beating very fast. It was just a silly little sketch. There was nothing rational to be nervous about.

But here she was, *nervous*.

"Two," he went on, "three."

There was an exchange and then a moment of silence.

Ayla didn't even look at the drawing he had passed over, feeling too much anticipation over his reaction to her own work. She scanned his face, his posture, for any telling signs. He was biting his lips together but the crinkle around his onyx eyes gave him away.

"What?' Ayla insisted "Oh, it's dreadful isn't it! Give it back!" Lunging forward she ripped the page away, crumpled it up, but before she could throw it into the hearth, Thian snatched the mess.

"Hey! No, this is mine, now."

When she finally conceded, he deftly opened up the scrunched paper, smoothing out some of the newly acquired folds. A week or two under a stack of tomes would probably re-flatten it.

"I will cherish it forever." There was amusement in his features, but a softness in his eyes that was pure.

It was not the work of masters, but he didn't seem to care. There was a childlike quality to her design. She hoped he wasn't offended by the presumed enormity of his ears poking out beside his head.

Ayla then took the time to finally appreciate his own sketch. 'Sketch' seemed like such an inappropriate word for what she was looking at. It was gorgeous. He had fearlessly shaded and smudged and amended, where necessary.

She had never thought herself an ugly girl, but her confidence *had* wavered upon Dandy and Ethel's arrival to Articium. The way the triplets had fawned over the golden-haired sisters made her aware that they had never shown her the same interest.

Seeing herself through Thian's eyes like this though, made her feel beautiful.

Having never been the subject of his artwork in the past, this one instantly became her new favourite. Ayla looked up at him and cocked her head with a smile. "Thank you." Then she leaned over and gave his rosy, flame-lit cheek an audible peck. "Sign and date it for me?"

He did so, though didn't seem to understand the importance of it.

Shifting to her feet Ayla waddled over to her desk–legs on the verge of pins and needles for sitting in one position for too long. Placing the paper on the corner of her black pine chamber desk, she positioned a brass paperweight over one corner to hold it down.

After petting the paper a couple of times, she turned around to see the prince on his feet too, stifling a yawn and stretching his gangly arms over his head. A line of flesh peaked from his belt to his naval which made her blush.

He toed off his boots and collapsed on the plush bedding.

Ayla scratched behind her ears. "Niamh informed me Atlas is returning tomorrow."

"Hm." Thian crossed one long leg over the other. "You should stay away from him"

"Thian," she started with an amused laugh. "We are not children anymore. And I am not a toy that you don't wish to share."

His sleepy eyes held hers with a smile. "If you are not a toy then why are you so fun to play with?"

She scoffed. Climbing atop the covers, still in her day-dress, she tucked herself into his side.

Chapter 21

The excursion to the Temple of Three Sisters was annual. A time where the royals offered clothes, food, and toys to the orphans living with them, as well as stock the stores that were handed out to the needy as the Sisters saw fit. Usually in exchange for prayer to their three-faced Goddess, or citizens committing themselves to their temple. In truth the king made such donations on every moon, but once a year the royals attended in person, to pay respects and appease the egos of the priestesses.

Twyla was perhaps too young to understand the full meaning behind the trip, but it was important for her to get used to royal duties. And presenting the prince and princess with their child was a stronger, united image that the crown liked to project.

After the princess was up and dressed, Ayla left the little girl's suite room through the main hall, not the adjoining door to her mother's room. As Ayla petted down the curling strands of Twyla's hair, she heard sniffled crying.

Hiking the princess higher on her hip, she quickened her pace as her heart bottomed out. Just before she burst into Niamh's room, she heard a voice from inside, causing her to hesitate at the door. She stood with her back pressed against the cold stone while she listened in, praying Twyla wouldn't make enough noise to give away their eavesdropping.

"All you have to do is sit there, shut up, and look pretty." someone spat, a woman's voice. "This is an important day, and it will not be soured by your hysterics, do you hear me?"

Niamh's only replies were smothered sobs.

"I chose you because you were agreeable, Niamh. Not to mention your blood was prime. All you have been is a stubborn thorn in our side. Clean yourself up."

The sound of flat pumps knocked against stone as the woman made for the door. Ayla froze up, and with nowhere to hide, pressed herself into the wall, a mere stride away from the entrance. Luckily the visitor was so consumed by her own spiteful frustration, she didn't notice Ayla on the other side as she stormed off in a huff. Ayla watched the icy hair bounce down the corridor.

Turning inside the room, after placing Twyla on her own feet she beheld Niamh crumpled on the floor, wiping her reddened eyes with a handkerchief, as if she had literally been on her knees before the queen, begging for excusal.

"Niamh, what's wrong?" Ayla asked softly, coming to her side and helping her to her feet.

"Nothing. Nothing at all," the princess replied in a far too cheery tone for someone who still had remnants of tears drying on her cheeks.

"Niamh." Ayla persisted, but the princess simply looped her hand through her daughter's and tugged her out of her rooms.

"I'm alright, honestly."

"No, you're not. Niamh, talk to me. What did Raura want?"

Niamh shuddered a breath. Her composure slipped through her fingers. "She wants me to try again." she whispered, keeping her eyes trained in front of her. "She wants another heir."

Lost for words, Ayla said nothing. She looked at her friend who was so broken by the mere request of having another child.

"Niamh, you're a great mother to Twyla. I Know it's scary but–"

"I can't!" Niamh snapped for the first time in her life. "He hasn't touched me since you returned. I cannot provide her with anything!"

Ayla reared back. A guilt as strong as steel wrapped itself round her throat.

She couldn't find words as they walked to the courtyard and climbed into the carriage. When Thian finally joined them, Ayla's worried stare never left Niamh.

The crack of a whip and the carriage jolted forward. Twyla, climbed up Ayla's chest, grasping at the iron lattice windows to peak at the streets as they tumbled by.

Thian's hand found Ayla's knee beside him. She stiffened and shook him off. She could feel the scowl he burned into her side.

Have you ever been inside?" Niamh asked, voice a little nasally in the aftermath of her tears.

Ayla shook her head dumbly in response. She knew her mother had been raised there, but the temple did not hold happy memories for Ivy, and she hadn't cared to recount them.

"It's as boring on the inside as it is outside." Thian drawled next to her.

"That's not true," Niamh insisted. "There are beautiful pieces of artwork, sculptures, paintings, tapestries, all depicting accounts of the Gods. Each one a story you must depict for yourself. Every onlooker may interpret something different."

"And all it will cost you are bruised knees and welted palms." Thian muttered.

"It's not on us to judge how they repent." Niamh countered.

"It *is* on us to protect our people they abuse."

"Well, some people *deserve* to be punished!"

The carriage rolled to a stop as Niamh's outburst rung out in the enclosed space.

Ayla stared with wide eyes. And she was pretty sure Thian's mouth hung next to her. Twyla dropped her bloomers back into Ayla's lap, a dribbly finger in her mouth as she stared at her mother uneasily.

"Just…Just *stop,* Thian." Niamh's voice broke on the plea.

She raised her palm to enclose her throat, squeezed her eyes shut and inhaled a steadying breath. Then, in but a second, she rapped on the carriage door and a footman helped her descend.

Ayla blinked through her shock, and tears, before she followed.

Her eyes instantly found Niamh on her haunches, scratching a scrawny cat under the chin while several High Sisters glared down at her in distaste.

Ayla caught Thian rolling his eyes. It was well known that while Niamh had an affinity for animals, Thian did not.

When the princess was ten, she'd been gifted a kitten by Atlas. Ayla could recall its smoky-grey fur and black stripes over its body. Just like some of the exotic animals from the Spicelands to the west. One day Thian stole the kitten from her basket in Niamh's rooms, and threw it in the kennels with the hounds. He didn't bother sharing his knowledge of its whereabouts, even in the day Niamh spent in floods of desperate tears. It wasn't until the kennel master went to check on the pups the next morning that it was found.

"Your Highnesses," a High Sister announced as several curtsied in front the ornate temple door. "It is an honour to have your presence grace us. Please, follow me."

They wore dresses of muted, modest colours, but Ayla could tell even from a distance they were constructed of fine fabric. Fine, *expensive* fabric. She couldn't help wondering how many meals could've been bought for a starving family by the cost of those pretty dresses. It was understandable that they had to appear presentable–as heads of an institution and dealing with people of court often. But why go to the trouble of disguising an expensive gown under the colour of commoners?

Ayla let Thian and Niamh take the lead, trailing with the toddler and a wicker basket behind them. She and Twyla had spent the morning baking lemon loaves for the orphans. A personal offering.

As they passed through the temple they were bestowed with lengthy tales of the religion's history. The Goddesses had been known by many names over the years; Mother, Maiden, Crone. Birth, Life, Death. But their domain was constant: Creation, Growth and Transformation.

Thian's boredom was palpable, and before long he slipped out of sight.

Niamh assured their host's they could continue without him, so they ascended the stairs to the living quarters of the priestesses and the orphans they took in.

Ayla held Twyla's hands as they walked up, determined to let the little girl learn how to do it for herself even if they fell behind.

Whispering giggles chittered above them. Little boys and girls hid behind curtains, peeked out behind furniture, and dashed between pillars. She looked at their faces, full of youthful mischief. Her mother had spoken of how her guardians tried to beat her into conformation with canes.

She was expecting solemn faces and sadness perfuming the air. But these children appeared... happy.

Ayla put the basket crooked on her arm atop a small trestle on the first floor. Pulling off the linen cloth, a delicious scent exploded into the air. Children emerged slowly, creeping toward the smell of lemon and sugar. Ayla passed a slice of loaf to Twyla and nodded to the boy who was closest. The girl waddled over to him and handed over the goods. He bowed his head in thanks and scurried off. Piece after piece the little princess handed them out to all the children with the help of her governess.

Ayla spotted one of the Sisters in the corner watching them. Rising off her haunches she wiped the cakey crumbs off her skirts. "There are toys, also–they should be unloading them as we speak."

"You are the Marnoch girl, yes?"

Ayla hesitated. The woman's tone was sharp, and she felt she would be berated for simply saying *yes*. She nodded, and as she did the woman's face softened slightly.

"Hm. Your mother was under my charge as a girl." she professed. "It was I who named her." A faint smile hinted at the women's lips. "No matter how many times I cut it back, the incessant weed continued to stretch toward that babe in her crib."

Ayla had no idea that's where her mother's name stemmed from. Hadn't even considered that it hadn't been her parents' choosing.

"I'm sorry, she didn't speak of you. Or much of this place, either." Ayla confessed.

"No, I suppose she wouldn't. She was practically running out of here when she came of age. Did she tell you she wanted to study at the Siam?" The woman laughed. "Really, that girl was something else."

Ivy *had* told her daughter about the Siam Institute. She had explained how desperately she had wished to be placed under the mentorship of a healer so she could develop her love and knowledge of herbal remedies, and more importantly, put them into practice. She had swiftly been shut down by her overseers. Eventually she'd soothed her soul by telling herself, if *she* was not permitted to use her knowledge, she might as well pass it onto someone who had the power to. Shortly after she took the position of governess to Thian.

Ayla gave a polite but pretend smile. "Shall we rejoin the Princess?" she asked, already making her way there. She found Niamh sitting at the desk of one of the Sisters, and Twyla clambered onto her lap and nestled in.

Niamh petted her daughter's hair and bloodshot eyes peered over her shoulder. "Has Thian made a reappearance?"

"Not yet. Should I go and look for him?" Ayla asked.

"If you wish." Niamh replied, turning her attention back to the table.

Ayla needed some air anyway.

She descended the strange structure and exited through the back, into lush gardens. Deeper and deeper she waded until she arrived at the cemetery. A garden of headstones as far as the eye could see. Some were intricately carved, others raw stone just to mark the placement of a loved one. Wilted flowers rested against the heads of some, small candles were lit before others.

She walked through the sea of stone, reading the names etched into some. Far too many read dates of too few years. Children. So many children.

Eventually she spotted the pearly shimmering head of hair sitting in the grass. Hunkering down next to him, she crossed her legs in the thick layers of her skirts.

Her heart seized in her chest when she gazed at the stone in front of them.

Ivy Marnoch.

Tears threatened to spill. She had never been to her mother's grave. There had been plans to move her body to Camelleah to be buried with the Marnoch family remains, but her father had abandoned everything after she died, so The Sisters had swooped in and claimed her body as theirs.

The pair sat in silence. Staring at all that was left of the first person each of them had loved.

Ayla watched the sharp blades of grass dance before the stone. The earth that concealed her mother's rotten corpse.

She felt nothing.

Her mother was gone.

But Ivy was more than a body of flesh and bone. She was warm morning cuddles on a winter's day. She was soft thumbs that dried tears and promised to banish pain. She was extra helpings of desert kept secret from father. She was a never-ending love. Even here, nearly a decade later, Ayla felt the love her mother bestowed upon her.

Silent tears slipped down her cheeks.

"I thought it would lessen over time–how much I miss her." Thian said. "It would seem I was wrong." He stared at the stone. "It was like a pillar of my being had been ripped away before I was strong enough to stand on my own. But I had you, and I thought we could find strength in each other. Then they took you away, too. And I crumbled."

"I… Thian, I didn't know."

"Well, I didn't tell you. She was your blood, Ayla. But she was a mother to me too. Not to make it a competition, but she was mine for four years more than you," He nudged her with a teasing smile that quickly faded. "I come here quite often, actually. I hate the temple and the bloody Sisters, but when I sit here it's just me and her. And call me a damned fool, but sometimes I feel like she's listening."

Ayla tried to swallow but her throat was tight with tears. "When I left, it took nine days by road to get to Almaid in Articium. *Nine days*. But by the time we got there… I had forgotten how she used to smell. I assumed it was the grief muddying my mind and it would clear when the last of the tears fell.

"By the first turn of the moon, I still couldn't remember. I knew what oils and perfumes she liked, but I couldn't remember *her* smell, and I panicked. I spent a sleepless night writing down every little detail I could recall so I would never forget. Her hair, its silky feel and mystic, inky shade. Her thinly manicured brows that were always so expressive. The softness of her skin, the shape of her hands and the tone of her voice. I filled three pages with colourful descriptions that I could read every night, so I wouldn't lose her in my head forever. I still read it from time to time, and *factually* it's her, but she's still fading in my mind. A little more blurred every day. And the harder I try to picture her the less I can."

Thian took her hand in his and interlaced their fingers.

"Thian…why didn't you come and see me in Articium?"

"Because I didn't think you were coming back. And I didn't want to feel that pain, seeing you settled and happy without me."

She swallowed. "Thian, they were the hardest years of my life. Yes, I found moments of happiness– It was nine damned years. But I was never *settled*. It wasn't my home because it wasn't with all of you. I didn't run away in the night and charter passage back to Balcarras because we both know that would've been futile. I wasn't welcome yet. I had patience and hoped that fate would lead me back to you. And it *did*, prematurely thanks to Niamh's invitation. But I cannot tell you how much it would've meant to me if you'd come to see me. To break up the years of sorrow with bursts of joy." She gave him a watery smile.

He smiled back.

"Well, you're back now. And I'll never let you go."

It was the second time he'd shared the sentiment since her return.

"Don't you trust me to stay?" she asked with a grin.

The sparkle in his eyes dulled a little. "I trust you to stay. I don't trust that others won't take you away."

"Well unless you know something I don't, you're stuck with me."

He pulled her into a long, languid kiss. She lost herself in his soft lips and sweet taste.

She looked back to her mother's stone, wondering what Ivy would say about her budding relationship with the prince.

The flutter in her stomach quickly soured.

"I'm worried about Niamh." Ayla whispered.

Thian's eyes drifted to their joined hands, where his thumb brushed over her skin. "Me too."

Three was a divine number. A cruel one too.

"Your mother is making demands of her."

"I would talk to her, but it wouldn't do any good."

"But you could talk to Niamh."

"And say what?"

"What you've told me, that you support her. That you'll protect her from the pressure of others. Now, and *after*."

"I'm not telling her about the annulment, Ayla."

"Why not?"

"Because I don't trust her. I don't trust *anyone* but you. What if she decides she *wants* to be Queen, rats my plans out to my father and insurances are put in place to prevent the annulment?"

Ayla's voice was mousy. "She wouldn't do that."

"How can you be sure? What if she tells my mother, *in earnest*, seeking excusal from duties and Raura quietly calls for your head?"

"You really think your mother—"

"Would kill you? With her own two hands if she had to. Raura has already had two failed heirs, she would rather raze this city to the ground than be dishonored by a third."

"Alright. If you think it's better to leave Niamh in the dark, then I trust you. But you should still talk to her."

Leaning in, Thian brushed a kiss against the tip of her nose. "I will."

Letting out a cathartic sigh she said, "Come on, let's go to the kitchens. I'm in the mood to make something." Pulling him up to his feet, she asked "Do you still love redberry tarts, or have you grown out of your sweet tooth?"

"Grown ou–never! Simply impossible!" He fell back to his knees and clutched his heart in jest. "Ayla, you must learn to love me as I am! Faults and all!"

"You're ridiculous." She pushed his shoulder as she rolled her eyes.

He rose to his feet. "Ah yes. But you love me for it anyway." Pecking her cheek again, he slung an arm over her shoulder. They made for the exit.

Ayla stole one last glance at Ivy's grave, silently saying goodbye.

"Wait, wait, wait!" she said, pulling him back from the front door.

"What's wrong?" he asked.

She chuckled. "I've got to get Twyla. Wait here and we can go back together."

Joy slipped off his face.

"Oh. Well, you go back with her and Niamh. I'll take one of the empty carriages."

"Are you sure?"

"Positive." He plastered on a smile she wasn't sure was entirely pure. "Seems like Niamh isn't in the mood for my company anyway."

"Alright. Well, we will meet you in the kitchens after supper?"

"No, you two just have fun."

"You're not going to join us?"

"I'll just see you tonight." And before she could ask him why such a sudden change of heart, he fled.

Chapter 22

After the morning excursion, Niamh seemed particularly sensitive. Regressing into herself she detached from those around her. And so, Ayla took Twyla away so her mother could rest.

She was still learning how to address and comfort Niamh when she would have such spells. She wasn't sure leaving Niamh by herself was the best option, but Twyla's screeching and tugging at her skirts were making her mother visibly upset and so Ayla decided it was best to remove her altogether.

Instead, Ayla requested to one of Niamh's handmaidens to fetch Atlas. He was far more adept to care for her.

The younger prince had returned around daybreak.

So, Ayla found herself in a quiet corner of the kitchens with Twyla. The toddler sat atop the oak counter in the centre of the room, battered and stained from years of service. Her legs dangled off the side and Ayla kept one hand on her knees, in case she slipped off.

Twyla gripped a large wooden spoon in her tiny hand and mixed a sweet tart filling in a ceramic bowl, occasionally dribbling into the mixture. They would have to write these off as a lesson expense of sorts.

Ayla had many fond memories with her mother in this side of the castle. On Ivy's one day off a week from her own governess duties, she'd spent time solely with Ayla.

She'd shown Ayla how to bake sour breads and sweet cakes. While she was always in the company of her mother the other six days a week, Ayla loved the one-on-one time she got with Ivy on those precious days. It was there that the kitchen staff got to know Ayla too, and they had adored the young girl.

Those that that had remained under employment of the crown had been delighted at Ayla's return to Balcarras Castle. The other staff around the castle, had not been so warm in their welcome of her.

They treated her coldly, whispering about her when within ear shot. And her time spent with Thian did not go unnoticed, either. If the prince took a mistress–or several–there would be no retribution for him. In fact, history suggested it was almost *expected.* It was Ayla's reputation that would be shattered if she engaged in unvirtuous acts before marriage.

Not that they'd crossed that line. Ayla refused to cross that line, and Thian was gratefully understanding. Content with simple kisses and lounging in each other's company until the coronation. Even then, she would wait until they made their own vows to one another.

"Last step, Twyla, can you pour the sugar in?" Ayla handed a small wooden bowl of measured sugar to the princess, keeping one hand out just in case she felt the urge to throw the lot into the air. Alas, she tipped it in neatly, just as instructed.

"Well done, now give it a big mix." Ayla passed her the spoon once more.

When the filling was put to rest, they got to work on the dough.

Twyla was now kneeling on the flat surface, sitting between bent legs. Squishing a mound of crust-dough between her chubby hands, she occasionally lifted a raw chunk to her mouth, which Ayla swiftly removed and redirected her attention to kneading.

To her surprise, another visitor entered the kitchens through a stone archway.

"Atlas." She addressed him with a tight smile.

There was a hint of surprise mixed with fear in her eyes. Fear of what brought him here.

"Ayla." he returned her smile with a small nod.

There was a moment of silence between them as he took in the sight of the pair covered in flour and jams. She tried not to redden in embarrassment.

Ayla waited for an instruction or request to be made from the prince but when neither came, she opened her mouth to speak. He beat her to it, "I have come to collect the princess."

"Is everything ok?" Ayla asked with a small lump in her throat, and her grip on Twyla tightening ever so slightly.

"Quite." Atlas stepped further into the kitchen.

Twyla crawled over the surface through sprinkles of flour and flaky pastry to meet him. He lifted her up with a smile so wide it was foreign to Ayla. "The queen thinks a visit from her granddaughter would brighten the king's spirits."

"I see. Is His Majesty well?"

King Irlass had suffered a few bad spells with his heart of late. It wasn't something made public, but Thain had mentioned it was a prime reason behind his upcoming abdication.

"He will be."

The sureness in Atlas' voice soothed any worry for the king's health. Nosiness got the better of her as she pressed, "And why couldn't a page deliver this message to me?"

"I've been away too long. I missed the princess' chubby smile." he said as his gaze fell to Twyla on his side and he pinched her cheek, making her giggle as dribbles poured out unbridled. Ayla rounded the table and pulled a handkerchief from her sleeve, wiping up the girl's face. There was now flour dusted all over Atlas' coat, but she didn't dare clean him up too.

"Do you need help bringing her to His Majesty's chambers?" she asked innocently, looking up at him.

"I'm sure I will manage," he replied. Twyla was clinging to him with such eagerness she wasn't sure she'd be able to peel her from him if she tried.

"Have you enjoyed your time back in the capital?" he asked, not blinking an eye at the floury hands Twyla was printing on his fine jacket.

She chewed on her cheek. "Not everything is quite as I remember."

"You're disappointed?"

She opened her mouth to deny but closed it to consider her words. "Nine years, and all I've ever wanted was to come back home. Now I'm here... I don't know what I want anymore."

"You're not happy?"

"No, I am, I just... you know what, forget I said anything. It's silly." She waved him off with a smile.

Ayla took a step back but didn't leave. She looked up at the pair, gaze wandering over Atlas in particular. He had changed since she last saw him, just shy of two years ago in Articium on her name day. If he had been the same height as Thian then, he obviously hadn't finished sprouting. He must be at least a head over him now.

While Thian had shaved off his hair, Atlas had grown his bloodred strands out. As a boy he kept it cropped and neat, but now it was long enough to reach his temples at the front and the nape of his neck at the back.

Still well-kept and regal, but the length allowed the kink from his maternal line to poke through. *Yes, he suited it greatly,* Ayla thought.

Her eyes dropped to his throat and the vicious scars that poked above his collar.

Atlas stiffened and his gaze hardened.

It wasn't the first time she had seen it, but he clearly held a great deal more shame about it now. Ayla wondered if it was the doing of his military experience. He had left a broken boy, and they had built him back up cold and heartless.

"Didn't your mother teach you it's rude to stare?"

Ayla's heart sank at the coldness in his words but didn't break his stare, "I guess she didn't have time for that one." With tears threatening her waterline, she made a swift exit.

Wringing her wet hair into a small bath cloth Ayla walked past all the trinkets gathering dust in her rooms. Almost every day for a full moon after returning to Balcarras, Thian had brought her little presents to fill her new rooms. She didn't spare them a glance as she walked over to the window.

There was no pane of glass to separate her from the world outside. The huge bay that started at her waist was covered only by thin gauzy curtains when she wanted, and tied back when she didn't. There was no need for glass when the climate of the capital was so agreeable–warm winds and sunlight were all that penetrated her room. It was a far cry from the tiny window in her Articium room latticed with iron to reinforce its strength against the gale.

She reached down to pet her freshly potted lavender she had uprooted from the garden.

Lost in a haze of her own thoughts she wondered how the lavender Atlas had brought her in Articium was faring. She had planted it in her 'nest' along the coast, a light barrier from the harsh winds. It needed no tending to on her part, the morning mists and daily showers provided it plenty of water. She hoped one day she would return to visit and find the entire cliffside sprawling with its enchanting colour.

Bringing her fingertips to her nose she inhaled the soothing scent of the herb.

A couple of hours passed before a servant knocked on Ayla's chambers, informing her that Twyla was ready to receive her in the nursery. After cleaning herself up from the mess in the kitchen, she continued to the west wing.

At the doors, she hesitated–hearing a familiar male voice. Peeking around one of the doors, she spied Twyla at the window, in the arms of her uncle. He was pointing out the archway to the sky, no doubt to whatever pegasus was swarming above. Twyla listened intently.

The way Atlas interacted with Twyla was such a contradiction to the stone-cold soldier she had come to hear whispers of. In the months of living back in Balcarras she had never seen Thian spend much time with his daughter. And when he did, she suspected it was only to be in the company of Ayla herself. He found it hard to connect with Twyla, she'd noticed.

Though Ayla tried to move soundlessly as she entered the room, Atlas' head snapped to her almost instantaneously. There was an awkward silence as she tried to maintain professional composure despite the hurt lying under her skin.

He walked over to the large hand-woven rug and placed the toddler down to play with some stacking blocks.

"Ayla, I owe you an apology. I spoke without thought." Though his voice was as emotionless as ever, there was sincerity in his eyes, even if he kept them cast downward.

"I didn't mean to stare," Ayla confessed "I know from experience how it can make you feel. But…" Suddenly her heart was beating fast, and she felt the words swelling in her throat. "I wasn't staring for the reason you think…" *She should shut her mouth. Shut her mouth and say nothing more and forget any of this because it is ridiculous and pathetic and–* "I was just thinking that the Gods were balanced in maiming you. For otherwise you would be perfect. And that just wouldn't be fair to the rest of us."

Attempting a smile, she waited for a reply.

She had meant her words to be polite, give him comfort and perhaps even confidence regarding the insecurity. One that she was all too familiar with.

Sometimes Ayla would pity Atlas for covering his scars with obscenely high collars when he wanted. For hiding his true form. But more often than not, she envied him for the option he had to do so. It wasn't as if she could walk around the castle in a muzzle.

An innocent complement had been her intention, but she suddenly felt a flush of red infect her face as the reality of embarrassment set in.

Still he said nothing and she wanted the rug to swallow her whole.

The two stared at one another, neither one with the confidence to speak until–

"Brother," Thian stood at the door, brows pressed slightly but he kept his wits as he questioned calmly, "What are you doing here?"

Ayla dropped to her knees to play with Twyla. Her first instinct was to back away from Atlas, but that would have looked suspicious–made her look *guilty*. But she had done nothing wrong. So, she continued to stack the blocks until they fell, offering sweet smiles at Thian that went unnoticed as his gaze was locked on Atlas.

"I escorted the princess back to the nursery after a visit with her grandfather." Atlas said flatly, but did not move an inch away from Ayla, who realised she was practically kneeling at his feet. It would seem it wasn't just Atlas' *body* that had changed over these past few years. The boy that would once cower before his brother's cruelty had grown a confidence she hadn't seen before. Long gone were the days that Thian could physically overpower Atlas.

"Ayla," Atlas offered her a polite bow of the head as he made his departure.

As Thian made his way into the room Ayla prayed the flush from her cheeks had dissipated. He didn't come over to join her and the princess on the floor, instead he sat in an armchair a good ten paces away.

Ayla tried to wrap her head around it. He hadn't had the gift of present and adoring parents in his own childhood, but Ivy had raised him with as much love as she held for her own. She showed him kindness, silliness, and compassion–all traits he proved he possessed as he conveyed them to Ayla every day–and yet he offered none of that to his own kin.

Ayla had once dreamed of having Thian's babies. Lots of them. But now the thought of him as their father, as *this* kind of father, to her children made her feel a little sick.

Chapter 23

As always, the sun was gleaming over Balcarras Castle and its gardens. This day, however, was filled with celebration for more than just sunshine–Princess Twyla was turning two years old, and a celebration was being held in the gardens.

The stone pavilion was wrapped and wound in thorns and roses, housing every kind of cake known to the continent–a fine gift from the Duchess Vora Riocca to her great niece.

Each guest greeted the shy child with congratulations and grand presents. There was a mountain of painted paper wrapped gifts and lush boxes towering next to the stone pavilion.

Ayla had gifted the young girl a baby doll, one she had adored in her own youth. It had hollow porcelain limbs and head, but a cotton body that was stuffed with wool and rice. Its face was carved into a sleeping pout, the lips and cheeks held a faded rosy tint.

Maggie was her name. Or at least what Ayla had named her when she was five. She'd introduced the baby doll to Twyla with such a name, but understood the princess may decide to rename her.

Maggie was one of the few cherished possessions Ayla had brought to Articium all those years ago. It was a gift from her mother, but seeing as she didn't play with her anymore, Ayla decided that Twyla would make a much better owner. The only updates Maggie had received was a new lemon coloured dress Ayla had stitched up herself, made from a similar fabric to the one Twyla wore today.

The princess' dress with little puffed sleeves and a thick white bow tied at the back was short enough that her frilly cream bloomers would peek out as she crouched to pick up her presents.

The King, Queen and Princess Esse sat at a private table on a dais, shaded by soft gauze. Twyla toddled up to her aunt of six years with her treasured wooden pegasus in one hand and the babydoll in another and offered to share. Esse looked up to her mother, but Raura did not meet her stare, nor release her grip on her hand. The answer was clear, and the child's hopeful face dropped with disappointment.

Ayla bit her tongue.

Scooping the tot off the ground, she propped Twyla on her hip and curtseyed to Their Majesties.

"Come on Bumblebee," she whispered to Twyla as they headed for the glorious smell of sweets. "Which one would you like?"

Twyla pointed to a pink sponge with buttery ivory icing and strawberries on top. "This one? Alright, let's get a piece for you," she cut a small slice and plated it "and a piece for Maggie." She cut an even smaller piece for the doll, who she now realised would be inseparable from the young girl for the foreseeable future.

The duo sat on the grass on a woven quilt and ate the cake, taking breaks to 'feed' Maggie too.

Onlookers cooed and awed at the little princess. Her blonde hair almost reached her shoulders now in wispy white strands that curled up at the bottom. She had Niamh's green Riocca eyes and was lightly speckled in pale freckles over her nose from endless days playing in the sun.

Ayla leaned back on her hands as she watched Twyla in her own world, mumbling to the baby doll and hugging her intermittently. Her gaze however, soon turned to the castle walls on their right. She squinted her eyes and lifted a hand to her brow in attempts to shield them from the sun.

A curious feeling washed over her that someone was watching her. It was entirely possible— there were three dozen small slitted embrasures on the face of the castle, over many floors. Her eyes dotted around a few, but the sun streaming in her eyes skewed her gaze and she blinked away the watery result.

The outburst of whispering ladies captured Ayla's attention and she turned to see Niamh being escorted to the party by Thian. The girls of many ages blushed at his handsome presence, but he seemed entirely focused on his wife.

The pair were rarely seen solely in each other's company, and when they did, it felt very plutonic. Today however, they were holding hands. A chaste act, but one of tenderness–something Thian rarely offered Niamh. At least in Ayla's company.

Ayla stood and led Twyla by the hand to greet her parents. She curtsied politely–in proper fashion with an audience present. Niamh broke their grasp and knelt to greet her daughter. "You look just delightful, my darling," she praised, "And who is this?"

"Maggie." the princess replied, smiling through the dribbly finger in her mouth.

Thian strolled over to the pile of presents, rattling some for clues, straight out opening others. When he flipped the addressed tag of the largest ribboned box, he scoffed with an eye roll and walked away to a table of grapes and bottles of… more *refined* grapes.

"Are you feeling better?" Ayla asked Niamh.

"Yes, much. Just needed a rest," she assured. After gifting the adorable new dress to her daughter Niamh had become overwhelmed with the excitement of the morning and took her leave. "Is Atlas here yet?" she asked.

Ayla looked around, but she already knew his presence was missing. "Not that I have seen, no."

"Ah, well not to worry. I know which present is his. Shall we go and open it, darling?" She asked her daughter, taking her hand.

Twyla pulled on the silky white bow of one of the bigger boxes and let it fall to the ground. Ayla picked it up and read the card tied to it *'For my little princess, love Atlas'*. She smiled a little at the flawless handwriting that she recalled from their studies together.

The princess' squeals of excitement were enough to get the attention of all the guests who broke out in awed applause at what they saw.

A beautiful rocking horse with carved wings. *A rocking pegasus, if you will.* The appraise was worthy of the craftsmanship. While Roshin were artists of almost every medium, this woodwork was the specialty of Atholl. The timber kingdom on the west of the continent was a landscape of forestry. The lumber extracted was exported to the rest of the kingdom for use. It was said, that whatever magic was left on the continent was densest in those woods. So, they were not felled with haste by those unfamiliar with the land and its inhabitants–whatever they may be.

Twyla tried desperately to mount the new toy with one arm, the baby doll still under the other. Ayla relieved her of the latter and assured her it would be safe with her, while Niamh helped her mount by stepping on the crook of the wing. This inanimate wing could not lift the rider up to the saddle like the ones of flesh, but this one was also only four hands tall.

Ayla grasped the doll in her arms, tucking her chin to her chest, she inhaled the familiar scent of its body.

Once when she was seven, following a growth spurt, her mother took her down to Linton to buy new slippers, and she asked Thian to look after Maggie in her absence. The trip was only a few hours, but upon her return from the cobbler she'd found the doll discarded on the floor with a slit in the fabric of the torso, wool spooling out of its centre. When Ayla showed the doll's condition to her mother in tears, Ivy stitched it back up neatly. However she'd added some dried lavender to the stuffing beforehand, the smells of which were still lingering even today. Ayla never asked Thian what happened to Maggie that day. But needless to say, she never asked him to watch the doll again.

Instead, she secretly delegated such a task to Atlas. He always returned the baby doll in perfect condition. In fact, Ayla suspected on an occasion or too he had washed the porcelain limbs, as they always came back sparking.

"Are you well?" Ayla asked Thian after leaving Twyla with her mother momentarily. He squinted in the sun, grinning at her familiar voice.

"All the better for seeing you." his gaze roamed over her body, noticing the doll in her arms. He reached out for it, and Ayla subconsciously tightened her grasp. She intercepted his hand with her own and maintained polite distance in a sea of guests.

"Gods, it's embarrassing. She's a *princess* and she acts like an invalid." Ayla overheard someone say, from the cohort of ladies congregated nearby. She traced the eye line of the amused women to Niamh who was mindlessly crawling on the grass with her daughter, to pet some of the stray castle cats.

The social leader of the group was Lady Elowen Henson, a girl of Atholl origin. "They should lock her away. She's an embarrassment to the crown." Elowen added with a cruel giggle.

Ayla's heart soured.

As if on cue, Niamh looked over to Ayla with a smile that suggested she take over Twyla again. Leaving Thian's side to rejoin Twyla on their quilt, Ayla could still hear snickering coming from the flock of ladies nearby.

"Twyla, could you bring this over to Lady Elowen?" she instructed the toddler, handing her a silver goblet of wine. The young princess bobbed over with both hands barely wrapping around the cup which was filled to the brim and splashing over the sides with each step. As grass turned into pave she stumbled and the cup tipped over, gushing Roshin red all over Elowen's chalky cotton dress.

Ayla beamed at the execution of the plot and rushed over to the group who were brushing off phantom splatters from their own dresses.

"Well, I never!" Elowen stood mouth gaping like a fish, unable to chastise the princess of the continent.

"Oh dear!" Ayla chirped in as she arrived at the scene. "Twyla and I thought you looked rather parched Lady Henson. And Twyla is learning it's polite to keep your guests refreshed. It's important for young children to learn their manners, wouldn't you say Elowen? Without them, who knows what kind of monsters they may grow up to be?" she said with a civil smile.

"Who do you think you–"

Each word was matched with a step in Ayla's direction until a tall figure stared down at her with both an icy presence and flaming eyes.

"My prince," Elowen curtsied and blanched under his punishing stare. Atlas offered no reply, and she scurried away. The rest of the ladies followed like chicks tailing a mother duckling.

"Are you alright?" he asked quietly.

"Mmhmm" she murmured back, fighting the urge to check over her shoulder to see if Thian was watching. Instead, she picked up Twyla, placing her between them, removing the fingers from her mouth now and again.

"I shall have to send her lilies to apologise." Ayla said, heart still racing from the exchange.

"I do believe she is allergic to such flora."

"Exactly."

Grins reflected back at one another, though nerves prickled at Ayla's skin.

He pulled out a flower from his pocket, a small blooming tulip with a rosy colour. "For the princess," he declared as he handed it to Twyla who clutched it to her chest. "And for the lady," he pulled out a second stem, one of lavender.

"Thank you," she managed.

Realising after a moment that she had been staring, she hitched a breath and put several steps between them.

"Enjoy the party, Atlas." she said with a dip of the head and a slight curtsy.

Willing her feet to move at a normal pace, she headed back to their lunch spread on the grass. Picking the blades that poked free around the border of the quilt, keeping her red cheeks downcast, praying Twyla wouldn't toddle over to her favourite person in the kingdom and force another interaction between herself and Atlas.

Chapter 24

T he hour was late. Fire reduced to embers and ashes; candles burnt to the wick. The night's sky was so thick with fog that no moon nor starlight could penetrate it, leaving Ayla's chambers submerged in complete darkness. Not that she minded–she was lost in a world of dreams.

The creaking of a heavy wooden door caused her to stir, barely lifting her head from the pillow. "Thian?" she called out, still half asleep.

It was not uncommon for the prince to sneak into her chambers at ungodly hours of the night. More often than not drunk off his face after a night of fun down in Linton with his new friends. He would stumble in, too wasted to hear her whispers of kindness, give her a kiss on the forehead and promptly pass out draped over the edge of the bed. It wasn't very romantic, Ayla recognised, but she was content any time she got with him alone.

Tonight however, there was no answer.

The room was chillingly still.

Lifting her head Ayla gasped. A tall figure shrouded in shadow stood against the door.

With a speed she didn't know she possessed, Ayla reached around her headboard for the hidden dagger strapped to its back. When she whirled round with her heart in her throat, she stared into empty darkness.

Blinking her eyes to decipher between furniture and predator, she leapt out of bed. The shock of cold stone on her feet only heightened her rousing senses.

It wasn't the biggest of apartments, far from it, but there were plenty of places to hide. Especially in the pitch black of night. With trembling legs, she moved to the hearth. One hand spilled the bottle of matches all over the mantle while the other kept a terrorised grip on the blade.

With practiced precision, she struck the match, and the head burst into flames. After tossing it into the pit, she didn't wait for the lumber to catch, instead she threw in a handful more after the first, that hissed and lit up in symphony.

She shucked a breath as the burst of light illuminated the room in an amber glow. In the temporary brightness, her eyes searched manically to every crook and corner. Though the light was a comfort, the way the shadows danced as the flames flickered made Ayla flinch.

When her eyes failed to locate anyone obvious, she darted to the door. Holding the blade out in front of her, she blindly reached for the brass loop and pulled.

The door rattled but it did not open. Her eyes flickered to the closure and with both hands she pulled. It wouldn't budge.

The door was locked.

Gooseflesh erupted on her skin. Bracing two hands on the pommel of her dagger, she tiptoed towards the only other entry into her room. The white gauze drapes lay still over the windowless frame. With the fire beginning to gobble kindling, the starless sky beyond the fabric was a dark abyss in contrast. Ripping the curtain to the side, Ayla peeked over the lip of her windowsill, side to side, and even up, for good measure. There was no sign of any intruder.

The next window down was much farther than the span of a human, and the embrasures that dotted the stone face were far too narrow to step in for purchase, if someone wanted to scale the wall.

Clutching a hand to her throat she felt her own pulse thunder under her thumb.

She turned back into her room.

She had *seen something. Right?*

A glint in the flame-light pulled her attention to the floor. By her door, the ornate key to her room lay peacefully. Ayla always locked her door before washing for the evening and checked it a second time before slipping into bed. Never, in the months of living in these rooms, had the key fallen from its chamber.

Which meant that it had been pushed.

From a key on the other side.

The door knocked and Ayla yelped, spinning on her heel.

"Ayla?"

She closed her eyes in relief at the sound of Thian's voice. With shaking hands, she picked up the ornate key and worked it into the lock.

As soon as Thian crossed the threshold, his face of languid pleasure soured into concern. "What's wrong?" his eyes flicked down the trembling blade in her palm.

"Nothing." She said, dropping the weapon on a sideboard next to the door. "Just the dark playing tricks on me."

"Are you sure?" his voice was slurred as his eyes darted around the shadowed room.

"Mhmm." She hummed unconvincingly.

After poking around a few corners of the room, Thian deposited himself on the sofa in front of the hearth.

Suddenly sick of the darkness, Ayla tended to the fire. She poked the coals with an iron prod, ushering flames to spread.

Once happy it wouldn't burn out, she prepared the prince to rest. One by one she unlaced his boots and shucked them from his feet. When she grabbed both his hands and pulled, he made no effort to lift himself from where he sat.

He was perfectly lucid, just lazy.

Conceding with a smile, Ayla dropped into the cushions next to him. Almost instantaneously he shifted his position, so his head rested on her chest like a child being coddled by their mother.

With a resigned sigh she scratched his bristly head of hair.

"Your heart is beating fast." He noted.

She chose not to accredit that to the figure she was sure she'd just witnessed on the wrong side of the door.

"Well, you make me worry when you're like this."

"Like what?"

"*Like* you don't even have the strength to stand on your own."

"I have the strength, just not the will."

Jest or not, she did not laugh.

"I was just having some fun, Ayla. There really is no need to fuss."

She considered his words. But this wasn't just an isolated incident of too much indulgence. It was a nasty habit. One he turned to, far too frequently.

"Sometimes I think you do it to punish yourself."

"Why would I punish myself?"

"I have no idea, Thian. But abusing your body like this isn't kind to yourself."

"Ayla–"

"Don't deny it, Thian. You wake up with cuts and bruises you don't remember receiving. You surrender control to sheer luck that somebody doesn't take advantage of your state of mind. As heir, you are not only in a powerful position, but a vulnerable one. The amount of people who want you dead simply for *what* you are, not who you are, could fill a kingdom in itself. You consciously lower your defences and make it easier for an attack of any kind. Yes, you have guards, but you make it harder for them by turning yourself into a useless ragdoll every night. You roll the dice every time you sleep on your back and pray to the gods you don't drown on your own upchuck."

As she spoke, she compensated harsh words with soft touches. One hand caressing his scalp while the other rubbed lightly over his shoulder blades. "Now, tell me what upset you tonight. And don't *lie*."

He waited a long time. So long in fact, Ayla dropped her head to check if he had fallen asleep in her arms.

"I promise it will be soon." He vowed.

"What will?"

"Our happy ending."

Too many emotions swirled through her that she was left useless in forming a response.

"Sometimes I wonder if I shouldn't just take it for myself."

The murky landscape of emotions cleared into a valley of dread. "How?" It was only one word, but she stammered through the whisper.

"I don't know. I'm not sure I have the patience to wait until the coronation." He continued.

He leaned in for a kiss, but she grimaced and turned her head at the last moment, resulting in his lips landing on her cheek. Filled with instant regret she refrained from opening her eyes, afraid of what she might find.

Eventually she did. But what she found was a face not full of anger, but of concern.

"That *is* still what you want, is it not?"

Every second of hesitation was an answer in itself. So she scrambled for a coherent answer.

"I… I don't think I'm ready yet." She whispered. "For what comes after, what would be expected of me."

"I wouldn't expect anything from you."

"But everyone else will. The kingdoms deserve more than what I have to offer. At least right now."

The thought of sitting on a dais, with thousands begging for help she had no idea how to give, demanding decisions she was ill-equipped to make, blessings she was unworthy of bestowing…made her feel sick.

Thian's dark eyes glinted in the firelight. "You will be perfect, because you *are* perfect. They have had to put up with my mother's ice-cold heart for thirty-six years, having you next will be a blessing."

She smiled down at him. "It takes more than kindness to rule."

"Which is why you won't be doing it alone." He rested his cheek back on her sternum as she tried to picture herself atop a throne. "If it wasn't what you wanted…I would run away. From the crown, from my family, from it all. I would run for you."

Ayla closed her eyes as her heart clenched. "I'm not asking you to do that. I just need a little more time."

Chapter 25

Balcarras Castle was buzzing. A hive of worker bees busy to please their queen. A tournament was a couple days away, and knights and lords alike were arriving in the capital by the hundreds. It was a tradition conducted annually by Queen Raura to honour the Goddess of War.

A celebration Ayla found barbaric and wholly nonsensical. The continent hadn't seen a war in centuries. Not since the unification of the kingdoms under the Kinghorn crown. Sure, there were squabbles over borders and clashing clans, but war? Definitely not. And *that* was something that should be celebrated, surely? The *lack* of war. Instead, the queen found it appropriate to celebrate the brutal maiming of men and women for sport.

Most of the visitors stayed in Linton, but noble families were invited to reside inside the castle walls. The staff of the crown were working tirelessly to both accommodate the guests and prepare for the grand event, which would be followed by many smaller feasts and celebrations.

Ayla found the only place of peace during the chaos was in the gardens, so that is where she and Twyla spent most of their days.

She used the time to recall her own childhood days running around the flowerbeds with Thian. There wasn't an inch of the garth they hadn't explored together. Except one little corner hugging the eastern wall of the castle.

Unlike the rest of the gardens, a little wrought iron fence parted its contents and onlookers. It was no more than a foot tall. More of a psychological barrier than anything. For inside its iron rungs, delicate flora with deadly capabilities grew. Foxglove, hemlock, gympie and lilies of the valley, to name a few. Deceptive pretty petals, given their poisonous quality when ingested.

No one had permission to pluck the flowers from their stems without the King or Queen's consent, and the area was safeguarded by castle soldiers from dusk till dawn in inconspicuous corners of the garden so as to not draw attention to the powerful toxins.

Ayla tried to play her favoured game of peek-a-boo with Twyla, recalling the endless laughs she shared with Thain in their youth, though the princess didn't find the joke nearly as funny as she had.

Twyla was precious, but she didn't remind Ayla of Thian in any way. Where he was loud and boisterous she was quiet and gentle. Obviously, Ayla concluded, the princess took after her mother more than her father.

Ayla followed the princess around, a few steps behind, letting her explore at her own pace. Often following a trail of ants or staring at how the bees floated from flower to flower feeding on pollen.

After a while of toddling around and discovering all the buds of the flower beds, Twyla grew tired and nestled into Ayla's arms. Sleep briskly followed. So, Ayla carried the princess around, enjoying the peace of the grounds and the views of the city below.

Eventually Niamh came out to join them, escorted by her brother-in-law. Ayla felt her chest tighten slightly.

Twyla stirred as the pair approached, she wriggled out of Ayla's arms and stumbled over, not to her mother, but her uncle, arms outstretched to be lifted while squealing, "Atee!"

That tightness in Ayla's chest turned into a flutter as she smiled and questioned the name, "Atee?"

"Hmm." was Atlas's only reply as he looked upon his cherished niece, now resting in his own arms.

"Ayla, you may have the afternoon to yourself, I wish to spend time with my daughter." Niamh politely offered, stroking the thickening blonde curls sprouting from the princess' head.

"Thank you, Niamh, in that case I think I will visit the stables."

The stables were a refuge. About half a mile out of Linton, down one central road south, lined with pink blossom trees that cut through the entire city out into the wooded landscape. Far enough from the castle that it was quiet enough to think. From there Ayla would take Olive out of the city where she was free to ride the woods and rolling hills.

"How lovely," Niamh cooed, "Atlas will escort you." Earning a wary look from the prince.

He simply nodded with an agreeable "Hm".

Ayla wished to argue but the castle was exceptionally busy, the streets were full of bustling new strangers, and the guards were indisposed containing the chaos in the town.

Gods she knew she would regret this.

The two made the walk in silence. Every so often Ayla thought she saw a shadow of wings cast on the ground around her, but when she looked to the sun above, she spotted no pegasus. Nevertheless, she remained tucked near Atlas just in case. Atlas too, kept close but half a step ahead of her, anticipating trouble.

She could feel his tension. A full body stiffness practically warped the way he walked. Something was troubling him. But it wasn't her place to ask what, or offer counsel, so she kept her mouth shut.

The southern road was a glorious sight at this time of year, cherry petals falling like snow–at least how Ayla imagined snow would look. Balcarras, being central in the continent, was blessed with a pleasantly neutral weather regime. It did not suffer from the deadly colds of Camelleah in winter, nor the scorching suns of Roshin in the summer. It was far inland enough to avoid the smog that carried over Articium and the violent winds and storms that breached Vorraine on the west.

When Atlas and Ayla arrived at the stables, a few grooms bowed to the prince before making leave. The scent of straw and wood was not enough to mask the everlasting smell of horse shit. Restless hooves and impatient snorts echoes through the seemingly endless row of stalls, each stud and mare desperate for some time out in the paddock.

It had taken time to become comfortable, let alone confident with Olive back in Articium. But he was a gentle soul just as Thian promised. The rush of riding him along the coast had become addictive. Her heart would race, not with fear but exhilaration. And though he wouldn't stand a chance outrunning a pegasus, just being mounted on a strong saddle that could run much faster than her feeble feet eased a bit of fear when beyond the castle walls.

They hadn't quite made it to Olive's stall when Atlas turned to Ayla. She stopped to look at him, his tension had spread to his brows, which were now pinched together.

"You should not have come back." he stated flatly. A darkness behind his eyes of light.

Her heart tumbled, unexpecting *that* of all things to leave his mouth. Hers, in turn gaped with a complete loss for words.

"Excuse me?" is all she could manage.

His teeth clamped down, as if resisting whatever he wished to say. He turned to make an exit, but Ayla grabbed him by the arm. *He would explain himself right now or she would absolutely lose it.*

"Atlas!" she called as she tugged him back to finish their conversation. The flickering flame behind his eyes burst into a devastating inferno as he grabbed her wrist and in answer pushed her flush against the wooded wall of the stable.

Seething, he immediately pulled back.

"You should not have come back here. You should have stayed away from him–from… from all of it." he repeated in a low warning.

"Why?!" Ayla's eyes were wide in shock and confusion, but she would pull the answer from Atas no matter how much he resisted.

"Because he is a monster," he spat. After regaining composure once more he continued, "Stay away or you will get hurt."

"Thian would never hurt me," she insisted with confidence.

"Wouldn't he?" Atlas began to close the gap between them once more, "He's done it before…" he brushed over the scar over her lips with his thumb, and she jerked her head out of reach and backed away.

"That was an accident." she argued, her voice less sure of itself.

He scoffed, turning to leave, "Some scars maim much deeper than flesh, Ayla. If you knew… if you knew what…" he could not finish the thought. Whatever sentiment he feared, he had it so tightly leashed, his tongue refused to share.

Ayla didn't like the way her name sounded coming out of his mouth. She didn't like the way it made her feel, either. Didn't like the feeling of being unwanted here in her own home–by the very people she came back for.

Staring at him as he left, the words rose out of her throat on their own accord, "Why did you come into my room that night?" she asked, voice shaking.

Her mind had tumbled for days after the intrusion, warring with the possibility of her own delusion. It had been dark; she had been half asleep. But the more her head argued it was just a silly mistake, her heart knew it was something more. And it seemed to know exactly who it had been, too.

Holding her breath for the answer to the accusation, she waited.

Atlas paused in his tracks but said nothing to confirm or deny. Didn't even look at her, simply stalked off into the distance. And once he was out of her eyeline she stared some more, paralysed by her own spiraling thoughts, trying to rationalise the doubt he'd planted in her head. That seedling of uncertainty that threatened everything.

She didn't have the strength to ride Olive that afternoon. So, she aimlessly brushed his hide, while her mind waded through everything she ever thought she knew about Thian.

Chapter 26

A tlas Kinghorn did not know why he had been cursed.

It couldn't have been retribution for his own actions, for the affliction had resided inside him as long as he could remember–before he could stand on his own two feet or form words on his tongue.

His heart was bewitched. Decidedly hexed to another.

It was nothing so meagre as love, it was *obsession*. A carnal enchantment he could not control if he tried. And he *tried*. Every day of his life he leashed the beast that threatened to ruin everything.

It *had to be* the work of witches. This was not natural–it felt so otherworldly that it consumed him entirely. Perhaps his mother or father had upset a coven in passing through the Witches' Wood of Atholl. And perhaps this lure was a plot they had scribed in the stars. A haunting he could not rid himself of, until it destroyed him. And perhaps, everything and everyone else in the process.

The enchantment on his heart was only half of the curse. The other wound the threads of fate so that he could not have her. Evil circumstances that would have his brother fall for her first, have her love *him* wholeheartedly and then rip her away from their life in shared walls.

Every day he had been blessed with her presence, dared to steal glances and wished with his whole being that she would look back. It had been torturous–to have her so close and yet allowed to move no closer.

But then she was gone, *really* gone, and she'd taken a part of his heart with her. Incomplete without her, he hadn't felt like himself since. He couldn't stand the wrongness that plagued the place he called home in her absence during that first year.

Risking the wrath of consequence, he'd take the three day flight–that took him *five* in his inexperience of being a new rider–to the coast. Just to check on how the other half of his cleaved heart was faring. He'd spend the day hiding in the dunes, just trying to catch a fleeting sight of her.

And then he'd be spellbound all over again.

There was an aching in Atlas' chest as he blinked into the new day. Unlike strained muscles–proof of a good training session or long ride in the skies–this did not seem to stem from flesh. Pushing the heel of his palm over the plain of his sternum he tried to find the root, the trapped nerve or tight tissue that needed to be worked out. The pain had been sharp last night as he tried to find rest. As his head spun in useless circles of guilt and shame and regret and hate.

He'd said too much. Too much and yet he feared not enough. Not enough to make her listen, to heed his warning and move far away. But how could he? What could he say to convince her to leave without explaining the truth that he clutched to his chest closer than any secret.

A secret that was not wholly his.

Rising off his featherbed only seemed to make it worse. Breathing seemed exhausting.

Drifting into his bathing chamber the tub's morning water was already cool. Obviously, he had slept in longer than usual, but perhaps a brisk dump in the cold was just what he needed to shake this off.

The Gods were laughing at him this morning.

Whatever cruel enjoyment they gained from his torment was far from amusing. He'd slipped on the cold stone as he'd stepped out of the tub, landing on his arse. His glass of pressed juice shattered when he'd knocked it against the mahogany table, shards of it cutting up his trousers. The buttons on the first *three* shirts he put on popped off as he was doing them up.

Atlas Kinghorn knew how to control his temper. But that did not mean he was immune to irritation. Unlike his brother who wore his emotions on his sleeve, Atlas preferred to contain them within–showing only what he wished others to see.

But this morning was already thoroughly pissing him off.

Heading for the armoury, the prince's mood did not improve. Slow steps of meandering ladies that refused to part arms and let him overtake them had him grinding his teeth. A sea of overlapping ladders lined the halls so men could string merry bunting ahead of his mother's blessed tournament made him reroute his path to the armoury. *Twice.*

And then he saw that head of wondrous dark hair swaying with each step, almost dusting over the curve of her backside. A cruel temptation of what he could not have. Ayla walked with a solemness that seemed to mirror his own.

Suddenly flooded with guilt he hated that he was most likely the cause of it.

She walked through the intersection of halls adjacent to him, turned around by decorators that redirected her so as not to interrupt their work. She huffed out a frustrated breath and planted her hands on her hips. As her head turned in his direction his heart seized in his chest at what he saw.

Starting toward her in an aggressive march, he wore a face like thunder. So startling that she turned behind her to check who had silently offended him enough to elicit such a reaction. But there was no one else in his eyeline.

By the time she whipped her head back around, he was on her. She sucked a gasp of fright as he cupped her face softly and continued to stare like vengeance incarnate.

"Did *he* do this? How did he do this?" he demanded, a mere breadth from her face.

She stared back wide eyed, pushing at the arm that held her in too intimate a fashion for the gossiping halls of Balcarras. "Do what?"

He brushed his thumb a touch harder, and she winced, reminded of the violet welt blossoming on her cheek. She huffed a laugh, pushing hard enough to release his hold.

"I fell," she snorted, "My new slippers have no traction, and I hit my dresser."

"*Don't* lie to me." he growled.

"I'm not," she snipped back, obviously as vexed as him. "The only one to leave bruises on me is *you.*" she spat, pulling up her long shirt sleeve that hid another deepening mark of purple.

He stumbled back a step.

Whether or not she was protecting Thian, if he did or did not in fact mar her face, *he had* hurt her. There was no denying that–the proof was written in her skin. His hands began to shake at his sides. As time stretched without a response, she pulled down her sleeve and marched past him to wherever she was needed for the morning.

Forsaking training for the day, Atlas wandered down to the arena. Numb inside his own head. He didn't trust himself around weaponry today. It didn't matter how blunt the practice instrument was, his heart called for blood.

Chapter 27

T he castle released a collective exhale as guests enjoyed the great feast on the eve of the tournament.

Atop a dais at the back of the hall, was a throne, gilded in white gold, with forged metallic wings unfurling behind it.

The cavernous room, normally barren save for the throne itself, was packed. Men and women of many titles and ranks sat side by side drinking and laughing and provoking each other before they would fight and potentially kill each other the next day.

The King and Queen sat at a table atop the dais, he on the grand winged throne, she on a more modest one beside him. Irlass looked dashing in his white coat, and his wife never tore her eyes from him the entire evening. The ballads written about Their Majesties love simply didn't do them justice, Ayla decided as she stole glances at them.

Amongst a sea of distraction, Thian was brave enough to be a little too handsy with Ayla. The young royals sat at a table on the main floor with the rest of the rabble, though theirs was surrounded by about twenty of the royal guardsmen, ready to pounce on any threat.

Ayla was wearing a midnight blue gown of thick fabric that clung to her shape and draped effortlessly off her hips. She had wanted to wear the new lavender two-piece she had purchased in Linton after her winnings, but it had short fluttering sleeves that would've exposed the bruise blossoming on her left arm.

Her skin was dreadfully sensitive, and she would mark easily from any scratch or bump. It held no pain when she grazed her fingers over it.

No physical pain anyway.

She'd packed on as much powder as she could followed by rouge dust to mask the matching mark on her cheek, but it still peaked through.

Her hair–which she wore most often free to fall as it pleased–had been braided back by Niamh, into a crown over the top of her head while the rest tumbled down her back.

While Ayla may have inherited the colour of her father's hair, the texture was all her mothers. Heath

Marnoch, like his northern kin, had a curl to his locks, while Ivy's fell as straight as a cleave.

Sometimes Niamh would get carried away when braiding Ayla's hair and she would end up with an intricate style as depicted in the history books of Vorraine. Thian liked the way she wore those braids, claiming she looked like royalty while he teased her, bowing at her feet.

Thian leaned in to whisper into Ayla's ear. She cast a cautious look around the hall in case eyes lingered on them. While it was entirely possible, the hall was so full and loud, all manner of things going on simultaneously that no one paid much attention. There was dancing in the little space that remained between tables, servants and ale boys flitting around to provide nourishment to guests, slamming of hands on tables by men as they chanted old war songs, even a fight had turned into a murder as one not-so-gentleman drew steel.

"You look good enough to eat," Thian whispered in her ear, before nibbling on the lobe. To which Ayla closed her eyes and tried to steady her breath.

"I'm glad to see you still have an appetite," she jested, nudging the three empty plates in front of him, which once held seasoned chicken, pork and breads ladled in sauces before Thian most ungracefully devoured them. It hadn't been an attractive sight, but Ayla couldn't help but smirk at how he ate without care of how others perceived him.

When she opened her eyes they found their way to the other end of the table, to the one person who *had* noticed the intimate exchange.

Atlas stared at her with a stone-cold face and eyes that roared a silent warning. The same warning he demanded she heed in the stables; *stay away.*

She shielded from his gaze, turning her attention back to Thian, but he too had noticed the onlooker.

"Still missing the balls to compete, brother?"

Neither of the princes had volunteered to fight in the tournament–it had been years since Atlas had faced a worthy opponent, and Thian just couldn't be bothered. But Ayla had a sickening feeling Thian's question was not in regard to the tournament.

"Is that a challenge, Thian?" Atlas answered coolly.

It was Ayla's turn to flash Atlas a warning glare. Reprimand poured from her eyes, threatening him silently not to take the bait. She knew of the warrior he had become, and how Thian–whilst once competent and showed great promise–scarcely visited the training wing anymore. Atlas would destroy him. Ayla knew this–hells even Thian probably knew this.

Luckily Niamh broke the tension, asking Ayla to join her on the dance floor. More than happy to escape whatever primal performance was going on before her, Ayla accepted. She couldn't help but return her gaze to the table every couple of steps just to check that the princes were not tearing each other to shreds.

Not yet anyway, that will come tomorrow.

Niamh danced with a natural grace that seemed displaced in someone so seemingly uncaring. It reminded Ayla of their lessons of etiquette, how envious she used to be of Niamh's deep curtsy, strong spine and elegant strides.

Every so often, after a spin or a partner swap, Niamh would become disoriented. Her movements would cease as her eyes flicked through the crowd. A face so full of emotion yet void of any at all.

"Are you alright?" Ayla asked as she grabbed both of Niamh's hands softly, her feet still shifting weight with the music.

Giving Ayla's hands a squeeze Niamh nodded with a deep inhale.

Ayla watched the life return to her friend's eyes after a moment. "Do you need a glass of water?" Niamh shook her head but already looked distant again. "Niamh I think you should–"

"I'm going to bed."

A pause. "Are you sure? If we sit down for a while you might feel be–"

"I'm going to bed. I've stayed long enough. I've done enough." She was speaking to herself now. Muttering the sentiment quietly as her hands slipped from Ayla's.

Watching the sugary-pink gown wade through the crowd carelessly, Ayla stood unsettled. Niamh made her leave past their former table. Atlas rose as soon as she was near, concern marked his brow. They exchanged a few words before she left, and he retook his seat.

Shoved off the dance floor by a spinning shoulder, Ayla paced back before standing on her toes in search of Thian. His seat was vacant from their table, so she scanned the rest of the room for his distinctive head of hair.

Her gaze snagged on a pair of honey-coloured eyes that were watching her intently. Those unblinking eyes were paired with a soft mouth in the slightest smirk.

Ayla began to walk away, but the woman's eyes tracked her every step.

Dropping herself back at her seat, she avoided Atlas' glare.

The Master of Ceremonies banged his staff against the basalt, and the commotion of the throng stilled. Ayla craned her neck from her seat to see who was joining the feast so late in the evening.

A voice boomed. "All rise, for her highness Princess Maerine Kinghorn and Prince Reade Solmund!"

Ayla's mouth dropped open while she rose with the sea of guests, a wave of whispers rolling through the throne room.

The crowd parted with dipped heads as the princess and prince made a for the table atop the dais.

Ayla managed to close her gaping mouth before Maerine veered of her path towards her.

Bracing her in a shallow hug, the princess whispered in the girl's ear, "I missed you, sweetling. We'll talk tomorrow." Pulling back, she leveled her eyes with Ayla and offered a smile. Then she made her way to another table, speaking too quietly for Ayla to discern in the chittering throne room. The couple stood and followed Mae to the royal table where she curtsied before her mother and father. Three new chairs were brought to the table by footman, and the newcomers took their seats.

Ayla blinked.

She hardly recognised the princess.

Back in Articium, though Ayla thought all the princess' gowns to be delightful, they were not very stately. They never featured boned corsets or layers of endless tulle underskirts or impractical sleeves, trains or hoods. Neither did she accessorise with unnecessary finishes like veils, circlets or beaded nets like her mother did.

Tonight however, bore all of it.

Maerine preferred to embrace the natural offerings of the sea; pearls of all shapes and sizes, refined sea glass and wonderful shells strung into belts and necklaces and brooches alike.

But here she was, smothered in rubies.

Her waste long strands of salty curls Ayla loved so dearly were sleek and lifeless. Clearly the work of hot irons.

And then there was the bump that protruded from the from the front of her silky gown.

"She didn't want to make leaving any harder for you." Ayla turned to where Reade had snuck up beside her. "That's why she didn't tell you."

"Hi." She said densely.

"It's good to see you, Ayla." Reade said with a smile.

She gave him a shallow hug. "You as well. Are your brothers here?"

"Just me and mother I'm afraid."

Another strange concept. As long as she'd known them, the triplets were sown at the hip. To see Reade as an individual was... strange.

"Cousin." Reade nodded across the table to Atlas who dipped his head in acknowledgement.

"Please, sit." Ayla gestured to Thian's vacant seat beside hers. "What brings you to Balcarras?" She hoped she masked her worry. The only time Maerine visited the central kingdom during Ayla's tenancy in Almaid was for her brother's wedding. Other than that, she sneered at the mere mention of the capital.

Reade reached his hand in the air and a server was there a moment later, filling a fresh goblet with wine. "Just some business to run past the King and Queen."

Ayla's eyes flitted back to the royal table, where Queen Raura was glaring at the female guest Maerine had ushered to the table with her.

"How's *The Dandelion*?" she asked with a smile.

Reade looked at her with a lack of understanding.

"Your boat?" she clarified.

"Oh," he exclaimed, dropping his eyes to his lap.

"It's called 'The Etheline' now."

When she left Articium, Dandy and Reade were a smitten pair, it would seem that Reade had moved his affection to her sister.

Ayla's head spun with the bizarreness of the evening.

"Reade, who is your mother speaking with?"

The prince swallowed another mouthful of bitter white and said, "Angus Forsyth and Lorenna Fairheart." He wiped a dribble from his chin.

Ayla's head whipped back to the table in question. "Dandy and Ethel's parents? Are they alright?"

Before Reade had a chance to answer, the King rose to his feet and tapped his cup with a golden fork. The feast hushed at the behest of their beloved monarch.

"My friends, it is an eve most special, for I have just blessed the marriage of my eldest grandson, Reade Solmund and his new bride-to-be Etheline Forsyth!"

The crowd burst into cheers and applause.

Ayla's eyes were dry with how hard she stared at Reade, who got up and joined his mother at the head table, shaking hands with his grandsire and Ethel's parents.

It was always expected for one of the girls to marry a Solmund heir and tie their families back into the royal bloodline. Ethel and Dandy's father was Duke Forsyth of Torrachland, a fertile farming kingdom, and therefore the largest export of food on the entire continent. An alliance like that would take some of the strain off the crown's current issue. Too many mouths and not enough food. The royal coffers were plenty full, but no amount of money in the world could speed up the harvest or increase the land mass of fertile soil.

No great wars had been fought in many centuries, and while such peace was a blessing, it was also a logistical problem. The population was rising at an exponential rate. Hungry bellies fled to the capital seeking out work or charity. The King was generous to provide both where he could, but it didn't stop the overarching problem.

But Reade and Ethel were so young. Less than a year ago he was lovesick for her sister, his immature lust flitting from one flower to another. It seemed too soon, in Ayla's eyes. But if Maerine had come all this way to a place she despised wholeheartedly, there must be a good reason.

When it was clear that Reade wasn't coming back to her table and Thian hadn't shown his face for some time, Ayla decided to take her leave for the night.

WHERE NORTH MEETS SOUTH

Chapter 28

Even back in her chambers, the rowdy sounds of the feast filtered through the stone to meet Ayla's ears.

Just as she began to unlace the front of her dress, the door slammed open. An unannounced Atlas Kinghorn burst into her room, not bothering to close the door behind him.

"Atlas!" Ayla jumped at the intrusion but fear soon overshadowed her shock. "Get out!" she demanded, lacing her dress back up with shaky fingers.

Not even looking at her, he made his way over to her wardrobe. His eyes snagged on a cube of straw that sat in the corner of her modest room, its frayed fibers scattered the surrounding stone and it's out of place nature was enough to give him pause before he continued to his mark.

Rummaging through until he found a thick hooded cloak, Atlas pulled it from its hanger and threw it harshly at Ayla before grabbing her elbow and pulling her out of the room.

"What do you think you are doing?" she protested his grip, squirming and leaning all her weight back in resistance.

"Put it on and be quiet." he ordered. "You want to know where Thian is this evening? Hmm?" he asked rhetorically, "Then I shall be the one to show you."

He led her out of the castle and down into the city under the cloak of darkness. They each had nearly twenty years to their names now, so no guardsmen protested the prince's departure, nor were they required to find a secluded exit as they had when they were children.

At some point the grip on her elbow had slipped into her hand and they walked with fingers interlaced. She had noticed but did nothing to correct it.

The streets indeed were packed, the hour late and chaos spilled out of taverns and keeps into the muddy cobbled roads. He remained half a step ahead of her, just as he did on their way to the stables, pushing the occasional drunkard out of the way before they stumbled across their path.

Ayla's chest was tight with anxiety about being in such a place at night. Danger lurched on every street, every corner, every building–especially for a young woman. It reminded her of how fortunate she was to grow up under the protection of the crown. Her free hand gripped Atlas' bicep, cowering behind him just like she'd done in the arena all those years ago.

The path they took got noticeably more vulgar as they went on, whores draped out of windows, pouring out of doors, exposing their breasts, and intimates. Atlas wore his hood up so as to not draw attention to his distinctive royal hair, but it was as if they could smell it on him–his status, his wealth, his power–and they were hungry for it. They called to him, walked up to him, some even dared to touch him–to which he pushed them away just as aggressively as he had the drunk males. Holding Ayla's hand tight, he offered silent reassurance she was safe with him.

Suddenly, without warning Atlas dragged her behind a cart of various flora, holding onto her as she stumbled over her own feet. She looked to his face for an explanation but found him staring intensely down the street at one of the brothels called 'The Red Cockerel'. His brows pressed and something akin to anger threatened his icy composure. Ayla followed his gaze, though it was not the establishment itself that drew his eye, but the person standing outside it.

Arm slung over an obvious Lady of the Night, teetering in the street was Thian. The pair were surrounded by half a dozen other women who would on occasion stroke his hair, or down his tunic. Ayla couldn't hear the words spoken amoungst the crowd but between every sentence Thian seemed to roar with laughter, head flung back, threatening his balance. Eventually he seemed to bore of whatever they were discussing and landed a sloppy kiss to the brunette under his arm.

Ayla's heart cracked though her face remained neutral.

When Thian dragged himself and the female inside the establishment, their onlookers–Knox and several others she recognised–swiftly followed.

The compulsion to follow them was strong and she took off in a march from behind the wooden cart, stopped only by Atlas' words

"You do not want to go in there…".

She halted in her tracks and turned on him with a sharp, cruel scowl. "Do you think I'm so naive that I do not know what goes on inside a brothel?"

"I do not think you are naive, Ayla. But that doesn't mean you should have to witness what he is doing."

She looked at the crumbling stone building and winced. Then she turned her glare back towards Atlas and took off back towards the castle. She did not take his hand for the ascent though, nor did she walk beside him. It wasn't a newfound confidence so much as being temporarily blinded by emotion. Atlas must have felt it radiating off her as he let her take the lead without negotiation.

A million thoughts raced through Ayla's head. As quick as she tried to sort through them and rationalise each one, the next swarmed her mind.

"Did you take me there to hurt me?" she blurted. A cold sharp tone. But inquisitive not accusatory.

"No," he replied "I took you there to enlighten you. To show you with your own eyes where Thian spends his nights. And occasional days." he muttered with distaste. "Does that look like love to you?"

She stopped in her tracks and poked a pointed shaking finger into his broad chest. "Don't speak of what you do not understand. Thian does love me. Even going to such places is a testament of his love, of his respect for me." she strode off again, he followed.

"*How* is that respect?" he gritted through his teeth.

She turned on him once more, "Because I am a maiden! And I will not give myself to him until we are wed! He knows this and so he takes his… *needs* elsewhere."

Atlas' face paled with each word, and it dawned on Ayla that the logical passage of thought would lead to the question of what would happen to Niamh.

"*After* their annulment.*"* she tacked on to assure the princess' safety in the situation.

That was the plan, as it had been for two years in a secret pact. But the words felt silly in her mouth.

They seemed ridiculous and impossible, and suddenly her eyes were filled with uncertain tears she had no good reason to shed.

"Atlas," she started again, measuring her words carefully, "we are not children anymore. I have declared myself to Thian and I intend to uphold that promise. Please, drop this... I just want us all to be friends."

She looked at him with pleading eyes, desperate for the hostility between them, between the princes, to be over so they could all move forward together.

"I have no intention of being your *friend*, Ayla. Stay away from Thian." he repeated for the third time. He stalked in front of her and her heart sank once more.

Chapter 29

A yla had spent the morning pacing around her rooms debating whether to find Atlas before the tournament and beg him not to go through with the fight, or at the very least to spare Thian from injury.

She considered stopping by Thian's rooms before breakfast and drugging his morning meal–with nothing fatal of course, just a small concoction that would deem him wakeless for the next handful of hours. Long enough for the tournament to end and the window for fighting to close. The idea was colourful, but not very feasible seeing as though she had no access to toxins of any kind.

Feeling very vexed with the both of them, a teeny, tiny unladylike part of herself wanted to see each of them in pain. *Just a little bit.* Besides, there was no way Thian possessed the skill to seriously hurt Atlas and the guards would intervene if Atlas *were* truly about to murder Thian, being heir to the throne and all.

Holding the young princess' hand, Ayla ascended the steps of the roofless amphitheatre that was constructed just on the outskirts of Linton. Twyla protested every step.

Raura had specifically requested to leave Maggie behind in favour of the smaller carved pegasus–stating that such a show of affection of the former was a display of weakness. The decision was much to the princess' disgruntlement and Ayla refrained reminding Her Majesty that the girl was *two*.

The whining of the tot was already grating on Ayla's fragile nerves as they made their way higher and deeper into the stadium.

Built in Her Majesty's name, every year new intricate carvings were etched into the wooden structure. It was a modern take on the ancient sacred hippodromes from her homeland.

Reaching the royal box, the pair were ushered down to the front seats before the railing, overlooking the stadium. As Ayla's first time at the amphitheatre, it took her a moment to take in its sheer size. The boys had attended the tournaments as spectators since their first year on this earth, but Ayla had been spared the gore by Ivy's demand she stay with her father on the castle grounds during such events.

Settling into the newly upholstered bench that offered some comfort for what was sure to be a long and unbearable afternoon, Ayla tried not to let her mouth hang.

It was hard to believe that this space was modest, a mere tenth of the colossal size of the ancients on Vorraine.

The floor of the arena was designed in a triskele. One ring of grass, one of sand and one of mud all butted up against a giant monument of The Morrigan. The Goddess of war, faithfully carved from a yew trunk, held a spear in one hand, and a raven in the other.

In each sizable ring, different forms of combat were already under way.

Twyla perched in between her mother and governess, petting the carved trinket on her knees as her feet swung carelessly off the bench. Thank the Stars, her short stature meant she couldn't see much past the railing before them, unless sat upon the lap of another. Ayla's stomach coiled tight at the likely possibility in which Raura called upon her granddaughter to sit with her and bond over the blood of the fallen and the roars of the victors.

In Ayla's opinion it was quite villainous to bring children to an event such as this. Although the Queen had insisted on Twyla's presence to observe her father's duel.

Ayla grimaced, noticing a table of refreshments erected in the back corner of the tiered box, which ruled out the option of excusing herself for refueling after some time.

By the time the King and Queen arrived at their seats every stand was filled with spectators of every class, from every corner of the kingdom. They cheered and waved handkerchiefs gleefully at their sovereign.

Spectators from Vorraine threw dark calla lilies into the triskele as a humble offering to their Goddess in her arena.

Members of the court may don fancy attire and speak in sophisticated tongue, but they still enjoyed the carnal thrill of watching men beat each other to death for sport. All while complaining about the prospect of war.

The hypocrisy was rancid.

The fights were varied in nature. Some men fought with longswords in full chainmail, others fist to fist in little more than light leathers, and a few chose the newer custom of a joust upon steed.

Three Vorrainish females had fought in a triad, for which the Queen sat a little straighter and smiled a little wider. The women of Raura's homeland proved their worth as warriors, which was seen as unfathomable on the mainland of the continent. Any men who had doubted their capability in the fighting pits, who had sniggered and heckled as they took to the sands, were well and truly shut-up by the time it was over.

Though declared as a tournament, the victors never again showed their faces to be crowned the champion. No one seemed to care, either. The whole affair was about pacifying a carnal and brutal demon that laid dormant deep within the hearts of bloodthirsty men and women.

When it came time for the princes' duel, many more onlookers flocked to the stands for the show.

"Niamh, do you want a drink?" Ayla asked, leaning over Twyla's head. Niamh shook her downcast head lightly, fixing her eyes on the small ball of yarn she was finger-knitting with. The princess kept her elbow tucked into her sides and the crafts close to her stomach so the Queen could not catch sight from behind her and demand she pay attention to the gore before them.

As Ayla ascended the shallow steps to the back of the box, her eyes drifted over the King and Queen sat proudly in their finest garb. Irlass' attention was firmly set on his Queen. From the look on his face, you would not know he had been married to Raura for the better part of four decades. Pure awe was cast over every feature as he beheld her in a flaming dress of scarlet.

In the period after their union, there had been whispering gossip speculating that Raura was a witch, when a bright young man like Irlass was so strongly lovestruck by his new bride from the west. His entire world suddenly revolved around her in his eyes, and others speculated she had somehow charmed him through magical means to achieve such a feat. Though at the time of his marriage, he was not yet king, merely prince, he still had duties to perform. Those duties became secondary once she was in his eye.

Poppycock, Ayla thought. *A ridiculous notion.*

Raura was beautiful, and just as intelligent as her husband. *That* is what he fell in love with. He was only human, after all. The whispering gossip mongers were most likely men of the royal council dumbfounded that he suddenly found his wife more interesting than them.

Just as Ayla reached the table of pickings and beverages, the crowds went wild.

The clash of steel commenced.

Despite herself, her fingers trembled as she attempted to fill a glass with water.

A sudden tear ripped through her soul as she fought the contrasting urges to run to witness the outcome, and to run from this place completely.

"*Tosse.*" Raura hissed in her mother tongue, leaping from her chair and ignoring the aghast looks of the waiting staff around them. That idiot girl had tripped on her descent back to her seat, spilling the entirety of her glass on the queen's crushed velvet skirts.

Hissing, she wiped off what droplets resisted sinking into the thick of the fabric and perched back on her throne, not sparing the fool another glance as she professed her apologies and scurried back to her seat next to the princesses.

Raura had never felt a swell of pride so strong. Her sons before her, fighting for glory with the entire city watching. She used to oversee their instruction from a modest corner of the training wing when they were younger. The glances of approval offered to Thian when he showed no mercy to his opponent were reflected back with a face of honour. Those glances soon cast toward Atlas as his refusal to concede and determination to exceed perfection moulded him into something stronger and sharper than his brother.

It was the only time she saw herself in her sons. She shared some physical resemblance to them; Atlas' icy eyes, Thian's prominent dimples and thinner nose, but nothing beyond that exterior.

During the fight, however, her blood, her heritage, her *pride* lit up in their eyes as they struck and parried and raged on through the pain.

If someone was talking to her, she could not hear it. If her husband was soothing her clenching fists with his calloused hands, she could not feel it. Her body may have sat upon a dais, but her soul was down there, with her sons.

Vorraine was the only kingdom that did not strictly adhere to the custom of ascension by blood to rule. At the passing of each duke, a championship would be held, the victor seizing control of the kingdom.

The Vorrainish valued strength and power over all else, they expected their ruler to be the supreme in both aspects. This order of law meant that Raura was not of royal blood, like all the other dukes and duchess' of the continent. She hailed from a strong and noble house that bred fine warriors though, whose name often took up the mantle of ruler over the centuries. There was no promise her younger brother would follow their fathers footsteps as duke, and if Vik dared to enter those fighting rings he would either win or die. There was no mercy for the losers of the pits.

Her sons had opted for grounded combat. Thian bore a heavy, decorated longsword while Atlas wielded a lighter short sword. Raura had to control her temper as they'd entered the grassy ring. *The easiest ring*.

All other battles had ceased as the princes held the city's attention in the palm of their hands.

Raura's eyes narrowed in on Thian's movements, clearly fueled by unspoken rage. But it was clear almost immediately that Atlas was in control. He was holding back, not needing to display his full capability for a measly out of shape opponent such as Thian. However, he didn't show-off nor exhibit insufferable cockiness. He remained poised with a deadly focus, always on guard.

She had half the mind do go down there and join them. Shed this ridiculous dress and swaddle her skin in the familiar feeling of leather and steel. Ever since that bitch, Fairheart, had invaded her table last night, her skin itched for a fight. Lorenna had the audacity to sit there with mirth at the welding of their houses. At least the foal will breed the Solmund name, not her own.

Atlas let Thian tire himself out swinging creatively as the crowd lapped up his showmanship. He waited patiently, parrying and blocking each blow.

After he seemed to grow tired of the dance they were engaging in, he took Thian down. A brutal blow to the leg had Thian roaring in pain, but he did not fall. So, Atlas flipped his short sword and slammed the hilt into Thian's face. Which subsequently had him dropping like a ragdoll.

Raura felt her silent husband stiffen beside her.
Though no stranger to violence, Irlass detested it among kin.

The crowd cried out in applause, but Atlas did not gloat in the glory of it all. He bowed to his parents, and once she flashed him a proud smile, he left.

Chapter 30

For the days that followed, Thian was bedridden. His leg was swollen and bruised with a large gash that needed redressing every day. His face looked positively dreadful–a black eye practically swallowed his ability to see. Other than that, just a few scratches and sore ribs.

Ayla fed him soup and read to him every day while he lounged on his canopy bed. Without a particularly sophisticated palate when it came to literature, Thian requested only the stories that Ivy once had–tales of knights saving princesses, slaying monsters, adventures across the seas in the Spicelands, that *always* ended with happily ever afters.

Other than that, the two just dozed in each other's company. Ayla tried to kiss him, but his pained wincing was remarkably off putting. She always made her leave before the queen's daily visit around supper time, but her visits had not gone unnoticed by others.

After yet another night of broken, unsatisfactory sleep, Ayla awoke. Groaning and cursing into her pillow that morning was already upon her, despite her desire for a restful slumber.

She regretfully pulled back the linens and drew her legs over the side of her feather bed. Hissing as her feet touched the cold slabs of stone, she made her way to the window, peeking behind the gauzy cream curtains that blew in the breeze.

The sun shone dutifully upon the dozens of plants peppering her windowsill. She had collected quite a few in her time back in Balcarras, mostly clippings from the gardens that she propagated and eventually rooted.

She soothed over the leaves of some with a smile, as if to say good morning. When she got to the potted lavender, she bent over to inhale its wondrous scent.

A curling vine of ivy crept over the sill toward the moisture and nutrients of the potted soil. She cocked her head and heaved a sigh. Its thin and delicate tendrils were deceptive. If left to spread, it would suck the life from her potted flora. She leaned her waist over the sill to reach down as far as she could and gripped the vines before ripping them away from the wall to which they clung. They seemed to sprout from the stone itself, since there was no root in the gardens below. She had checked.

"It seems you don't know how to do what you're told."

Ayla's shock almost had her falling out the window. "Sisters save me!" she grasped at her chest as if to reach in and calm the racing muscle beneath. When she opened her eyes, she found Atlas lounging in an upholstered chair in the corner. He was so cat-like, still and silent she hadn't even registered that he was there.

"Gods above, Atlas? Get out!" she said, covering one arm over her chest and pointing the other at the exit suddenly all too aware of what she was wearing. A short summer sapphire chemise that rested halfway up her thigh, the edges trimmed in black lace.

She tried to scurry behind a wooden modesty screen, but he stalked after her.

"You've been visiting him every day. I told you to stay away." His tone was low and controlled but frustration lurked beneath.

"And I'm telling *you* to get out!" She suddenly felt trapped, prey, cornered by a predator. She needed to change her tactic. "I appreciate your concern Atlas, and I believe it is earnest, but I am happy with Thian. Truly."

"No, you are not."

"Excuse me? How can you presume to know my feelings?" Her polite smile soured into disgust.

"You're not happy. You have just been dealt such a cruel hand in life that you have convinced yourself that this contentment is happiness."

He was impossible.

"Please leave."

"I will not leave you condemned to a brutish future with him."

"He treats me well, whatever fiction you have deluded yourself with will not change my mind!"

"It is the truth, and you damn well know it. You are just too scared to admit that there might be something better for you out there. Too scared to try and reach for it because you risk the comfort you have come to know."

"Atlas! I am growing impatient! I don't know how many more times I can tell you I am where I *want* to be! So please either stop this incessant pestering, or…"

Shit. She hadn't meant to say that out loud.

"*Or* what?" he questioned with a sudden curious face, moving towards her, herding her into the stone corner. "What would you rather have me do, Ayla?" His voice was too quiet and intimate.

She shook her head softly, incapable of forming words. She wanted to crumble into herself, disappear through the walls.

"Say it." he whispered, inching closer and closer with confidence until he towered over her, with her back pressed firmly against the stone wall. His gaze traced her face, her lips, down her pale neck, to the swell of her breasts that rose up with every heavy breath. Each step he grew closer she felt her nipples harden beneath the silky nightdress.

She watched him, as he looked at her. She watched his eyes dance around her body, his mouth pulled back with a smirk as he saw some features, his jaw clenched with restraint as he glanced at others. His hands by his side fisting until his knuckles paled, further demonstrating the strength it took him to touch her only with his gaze.

"Tell me what you want. *The truth*. Let me give it to you."

Ayla's veins were burning. A pool of fire began to flood her stomach. Her breath was so short it was almost audible as he moved his head lowered to hers. She did not retreat; she urged her neck forward.

Closer, closer, closer.

The door swung open, and Ayla nearly jumped out of her skin a second time.

"Ayla?"

Thian.

Fuck.

Fuck, fuck, fuck. If he knew who joined her in her room, Gods knew what he would do.

Unsure if she did it to protect herself or Atlas from his unquestionable wrath, she jumped out from behind the modesty screen before he would come looking for her.

"Thian, my love," she ran out from behind the divide and gave him a kiss on the cheek.

Atlas peered through a crack in the divider and watched with a scrutinising stare. Hand on his blade, ready to draw should the situation turn for the worst. He did not wish to kill his brother, but if Thian were to find him with Ayla like this, he would need to be put down.

"Why are you so out of breath?" Thian questioned, hobbling around the room with a cane to support his healing leg.

Ayla's overcompensating smile wavered momentarily. "Just happy to see you…" she planted a long and loving kiss on his lips to distract him from his line of questioning. The sight made Atlas' heart blacken with jealousy.

"I came to take you to the gardens… but perhaps we could stay here…" a devilish smile consumed his face and Atlas' grip on the dagger tightened at the thought.

Luckily Ayla cut him off before he could follow through. "I would love a walk in the gardens. Just give me a moment and I'll change." She gave him no time to argue as she ran to the closest, pulled out a suitable day dress and then retreated once more behind the wooden screen.

With a desperate but threatening glare, she mouthed silently to Atlas, "Turn around."

He did not move a muscle. He stood, eyes locked on her with a pleased smile drawn on his face, all too happy with the circumstance he now found himself in.

Ayla closed her eyes in clear fury, being trapped with no choice but to change in front of the prince. So, she instead turned herself around.

She slipped the nightdress off her shoulders, and it fell to the ground, leaving her only in her underwear, before she pulled the dress over her head in haste. She was only without cover for a moment, but Gods it was enough to enchant Atlas.

Her milky skin was perfect. Even the stretches of growth that patterned around her hips were exquisite. The curve of her waist between her hips and breasts was... criminal.

Atlas thanked the Mother that she had turned around so she did not see how desperate he was for her.

His jaw slacked and his mouth gaped ever so slightly.

If that's what she looked like from the back, then Sisters save him what awaited him in the front?

His trousers tightened cruelly at the thought, and his hands damn near reached out to touch the vision in front of him. *Not yet,* he had to remind himself. But soon, Gods, Atlas needed it to be soon.

He did not want to spend another night in his bed without Ayla by him. Or under him. Or on top of him…

His thoughts ran away, and Ayla ran out the room as quickly as she could, linking arms with Thian and practically dragging him with her.

Chapter 31

Are you sure you're feeling alright? You look flushed."

It was the third time Thian inquired into Ayla's current appearance. This time, like the two prior, her cautious heart missed a beat and she was sure that only encouraged the stain on her guilty face.

His eyes were not full of suspicion or disbelief though, only genuine concern. It warmed her soul. He always looked out for her, took care of her, loved her in his own way.

"I'm quite well, I promise." she replied with a shy smile and a hold on his arm. They walked–or limped in Thian's case, given the state of his leg– through the gardens arm in arm. *At least his black eye was almost back to normal.*

"I have news," Thian started. "I have been ordered to remain here in the capital whilst my... *injuries* heal." he said through gritted teeth. "I cannot mount Racjan, and even if I made the voyage by road with you, it has been decided the cold would only prolong my mending."

The tour. Of course. Ayla had forgotten amidst the stupid tournament that there was a royal tour planned to venture to the northern kingdom and check in with the Duke of Camelleah and other nobles of the area.

"Oh, not to worry. I can stay here with you then." Ayla professed.

She had been invited not only to accompany Twyla, but as a daughter of Camelleah, the royal family was eager to show the Marnoch's just how well they were treating one of their own.

The task had been delegated to the next generation of royals. To form bonds and alliances with their subjects so that come Thian's ascension to the throne–with Niamh as his queen–they would be in a steady political position to rule.

Thian slipped his arm from Ayla's, winding it around her waist and tugged her in close, sheltered by the spindly rose bushes. She beamed up at him, basking in his touch. Until the memory of a phantom touch from just moments before soured her stomach.

"As much as I would love to chain you to my bed and keep you here, all to myself," he murmured in her ear,

"I'm afraid the Queen insists upon your presence in Camelleah. Just promise me one thing, hmm?"

"Yes, my prince?" she jested, lifting her hands to his chest and running fingers over the fabrics of leather and linen.

"Promise me you won't fall in love with Camelleah so deeply you wish to never return."

She broke out in a laugh at the thought. Ayla had never been to her ancestral home. Never met its inhabitants, her kin. In Balcarras Thian was her family. Thian, Niamh, Twyla, and–much to Thian's distaste–Atlas.

She met his fear with comfort, lifting his hands and placing a chaste kiss upon his knuckles. Perfectly proper, just in case any eyes were upon them.

The journey had taken about one week. One week by *road* that is. Atlas and Niamh brought Ivelle and Yvie. A reminder to the realm of their heritage and power they possessed. The pegasi were much, *much* faster than the rest of the travelling company, so while they would ride them throughout the day, they would always circle back to the rest of the group and travel most of the time by carriage.

There were seventeen massive wagons in total. Ten held provisions. One held a small armoury should any trouble arise along the way. Three stuffed full of tents and sleeping rolls for the nights too far from a hospitable lord's keep. One kept a number of handmaidens and pages for Atlas and Niamh. The last two were solely dedicated to the royals; one for the prince and princess, one for Twyla and her governess', Ayla, Hensella and Phena.

To *that* Ayla heard the grumbling discontent from the handmaidens and squires, complaining among themselves that they were almost twelve in one carriage while she got one to share with only three. As it they were too dim to realise the carriage was not *hers,* it was Twyla's, but her occupation demanded her staying with the princess.

About a hundred royal guardsmen on foot and horseback travelled with them. Olive was among the stallions, and when Twyla was asleep or with her mother and uncle, Ayla was able to stretch her legs and get some fresh air riding. That is, until she inevitably heard the beating of powerful wings, then she always felt a sudden compulsion to return the wagon.

Though she would hear them outside, Ayla dared not peek out the window. She thanked the Gods that she had another eight years before Twyla would mount one of her own. If Ayla remained her governess, it would be *her* job to escort the princess down to the arena. And she never wanted to set foot in that place of nightmares ever again.

After a large lunch, Twyla dozed off in Ayla's arms. Though she could have placed the babe in the bassinet on the floor, she couldn't bring herself to. The little princess wouldn't be this size for much longer, so Ayla was savouring every moment she could with her cradled in her arms.

Niamh was working on an embroidery hoop. A peculiar task inside a bumpy, tumbling carriage, but the princess wore a small white gold thimble and didn't prick her skin once, nor did she make a single mistake. The canvas design was a heather-faced mountain sitting in a blue loch, the sigil of the Marnoch clan.

The sun was setting, and with it the warmth of the day. The sky was painted an array of golden tones, but the air felt icy and thin as they crossed the border into Camelleah. It was rather early for the light to fade, but the days in the northern kingdom were shorter. More cruel and unforgiving. Despite being in a plush carriage, Ayla pulled up the hood of her cloak and held Twyla a little closer.

Ayla caught Niamh staring at her with a faint smile.

"What is it?" Ayla asked curiously.

"You look like her," Niamh answered, already back to her stitching.

"Like whom?" Ayla questioned further

"Ivy."

Ayla's throat bobbed and her eyes stung with the threat of tears. Niamh never spoke of her late governess. And Ayla was thankful. It was a subject that she pushed down inside herself, lacking the strength to discuss. She wasn't sure what would become of her if she did. But spontaneous combustion into a puddle of tears wasn't off the table.

"Nearly there," Ayla mumbled into Twyla's scalp.

Despite herself, she was feeling quite anxious about their arrival to Rydon. It was a part of her history, her family, and yet she had never laid eyes on either.

They arrived by nightfall the following eve.

As she descended the carriage steps Ayla gazed upon the historic stone keep. It was modest in size, but it had a proud feeling to it.

The ground was frozen solid beneath her feet, a silver frost crawled over everything but to her disappointment, there was no snow blanketing the landscape. A sprinkling of grass encased in the frost that crunched under her boots with every step. Even patterns of mud were frozen solid as whatever form they had been mushed into during the warmer months.

The little princess bundled in layers upon layers of fur lined garments, and a yellow knitted bonnet, shivered as she exited the plush wagon. Her little chin wobbled as her teeth chattered within.

Ayla tucked her under her own cloak in effort to share heat, but feared she didn't have much to offer. "We'll get toasty soon, Bumblebee." she promised.

The girl didn't look put off by the cold, though. Her eyes scanned their new surroundings. New buildings, new people, new landscape. She seemed fascinated   by   it   all.

During the formal welcome procession in the grand hall, a young herald did his best to announce the names and titles of the visiting royals, his voice breaking every few words. Ayla did her best not to cringe. To her surprise, one final name had been added to the roster.

"Ella Marnoch," he boomed as assertively as he could.

"*Ayla.*" Atlas quickly corrected the boy, and the court.

The herald flushed, looking momentarily frightened at Atlas' gaze before repeating her name with the correct pronunciation. Ayla's head sank and the embarrassment was abysmal.

She turned to make her way to the back of the court where she belonged, where she'd always belonged, but to her surprise, Atlas softly grasped her elbow and led her to stand next to himself and Niamh.

She looked up at him, confused, but flattered that they presented her like family. Then her smile dropped as she realised the truth. It was exactly that–a presentation. A facade, an attempt coordinated by Raura to stay in the good graces of the Kingdom of Camelleah.

A good number of bodies pressed into the hall helped heat the frozen keep.

A dull, aching fear beat behind Ayla's breast. Her eyes flitted around from face to face, expecting to see her father's amongst them. She had been told in her youth it was suspected he went beyond Rydon to the mines, but how could she be sure?

She didn't want to spot his rugged face among these people and yet her eyes kept searching for it.

Court droned on and Ayla could hear Twyla grow fussy with Phena near the back of the hall, so snuck out with her for fresh air. They stayed inside the estate walls but wandered around the once grassy plains.

There were no gardens or vegetation in Camelleah, only evergreen trees hardy enough to survive the bitter colds of winter.

The trees in Balcarras Castle gardens were mere saplings compared to these giants. She couldn't help but don a giddy, childlike smile at their strange appearance. Their lack of leaves substituted with bristly tendrils which looked like they would prickle, but were surprisingly soft.

The pair stood under a fir tree so large, the bottom branches were several feet higher than Ayla's head.

"Atee," Twyla muttered and did her best to waddle over to her uncle without slipping on the frosty ground. He scooped her up and tucked her up under the warmth of his coat.

"Your kin are eager to meet you, I'm sure."

"I'm not here for them, I'm here for her." Ayla replied, rubbing some warmth into her gloved hands.

"Aren't you curious to see where you come from?"

"I don't come from here," she insisted.

A sickening thought wormed its way into her head. "You're not going to leave me here, are you?" she asked, eyes full of furious accusation.

He didn't skip a beat before the hurt was visible on his face. "I would never leave you. *Ever.*"

His words should've been comforting, but they were said with such ire it made her skin itch. "Why not?" she challenged. "You told me to stay away from him, why should I believe you wouldn't conjure a plot like this just to get rid of me?"

His face was made of stone. But his body radiated darkness. "Don't you trust me?"

She swallowed. Twice. Looking within she expected the answer to be clear, but it wasn't. Atlas Kinghorn was shrouded in a storm of uncertainty.

When it was clear she didn't have an answer to give him, Atlas turned on his heel and marched away with Twyla in his arms, her heavy head resting on his shoulder.

Chapter 32

With Twyla asleep in her mother's room, Ayla bathed and changed out of her frozen clothes.

There was a loud knock on the door and the announcement of Declan Marnoch's presence. Declan–her paternal grandfather–had been missing in court when they arrived. His eldest son Harris had overseen things in his stead.

It would seem that the Kinghorn's were not the only ones preparing a new generation for duty.

Ayla fell completely still. Her heart pounded and she suddenly felt very nervous, though not entirely sure why.

"Come in," she croaked. The door opened, soundless despite its ancient appearance, and a large man entered. His once dark hair was completely grey, save for a few strands clinging to youth. He was weathered and pale but wore a warm smile. Ayla's heart eased when she discovered he held no apparent resemblance to her father. She really didn't want their first encounter to be one with tears.

"Ayla," he greeted, walking over and bracing his hands on her shoulders, taking her in. She didn't expect such a familial welcome from the Duke of Camelleah. "It's good to have you here with us," he went on.

"I'm happy to be here." She lied politely.

In truth, she hadn't felt very merry since her arrival. Though no one had done anything to make her feel as such, she felt like an outsider. An imposter. She hadn't expected Rydon to feel like home, but a small part of her had wondered if it would. The only time she felt comforted here was when in the presence of Twyla, Niamh or Atlas.

Ayla offered the duke a seat in front of the humble fire, and he questioned her graciously about her life in Balcarras. Not in a political sense–to learn more about the royals or conflict with the crown. But with genuine care and curiosity of her welfare there.

This place may not have held any familiarity or sense of belonging, but this man made her feel welcome.

With so many sons, daughters and subsequent grandchildren, Ayla was surprised he even remembered her existence. He left no gaps for awkward silences, instead filled them with anecdotes of his house and kin that gave Ayla some insight into the thick branch of heritage she knew nothing of.

The question she had been chewing on all day sat on her tongue. "Is my... erm, is–do you know if–"

"He's not here." Declan spared her further floundering.

Ayla let out a breath she didn't realise was bunching her shoulders high. After a moment of relieved silence, she said "I'd heard he was in the mines."

Declan nodded. "I've heard that too. I don't know where he is. No one has seen nor heard from him since the week your mother passed. The week I suspect a big part of him died too."

Ayla didn't know if that was supposed to be a comfort.

"Your mother wrote to me often, you know." *No, she didn't.* "I only knew her for a short while, but she sent me countless letters over the years."

"About what?" Ayla asked, puzzled.

"You, my dear," he chuckled to himself before going on, "she wrote to us about *you*. About how you grew and learned and blossomed into a lovely young lady."

Ayla's eyes stung but she fought back the tears.

Declan seemed to sense the pain and moved on, gazing at her hand. "You don't wear a ring. Are you married yet?"

Breaking out of her spiraling thoughts, she rubbed her undecorated finger and cast him a shy shake of her head. "No, not yet."

"With your beauty my dear, I'm surprised you don't have half of Balcarras begging for your hand." She blushed but he went on. "Your mother always thought you would marry the prince someday."

Ayla's heart skipped a beat, but she kept composure with a soft smile. The thought that her mother knew, that she understood Ayla's love for Thian and had imagined a happy future for them together made her chest warm.

"Prince Thian and Princess Niamh make a fine pairing," she said.

"Oh no, not Thian. Prince Atlas."

All the blood seemed to drop from her. Her heart was running rampant, and she found it hard to breathe as he continued. "In her letters, Ivy would tell us how she had never seen a young boy so in love. She was sure one day he would ask for your hand."

She was going to be sick. She felt fucking nauseous, and she was going to throw up.

Luckily the door opened, and a footman summoned the presence of Declan to oversee the preparations of the feast tonight to welcome the royals.

Ayla thanked the Gods for the interruption, and Declan's leave before stumbling over to the chamber pot.

Her whole body was practically shaking but no vomit arose.

Ayla sat with Niamh and Atlas at the head table with the Marnoch family.

Twyla was tucked in and asleep for the night, watched over by Hensella and Phena, as well as two trusted members of the royal guard. Which meant Ayla was attending the feast as a guest, not as a governess.

Somehow that made her feel uneasy, without purpose or reason, and she couldn't stop fidgeting.

Several of her Marnoch kin gave her welcoming smiles, though no one conversed with her. They spoke and laughed among themselves, and Ayla found herself deciphering their words underneath thick accents.

Their dialect was so different from her own, having grown up in Balcarras castle. She began to tune them out after realising how similar they sounded to her father.

Niamh wasn't interested in making conversation that night either. She was very quiet and lost in her own head. Dark circles haunted under her eyes and Ayla worried they weren't just due to the taxing journey north.

Ayla reached out to touch the princess' hand, but Niamh winced and pulled away.

Despite being sat opposite one another, Ayla tried her damned hardest to avoid Atlas' gaze. When he lifted out of his chair and moved to the wine table behind him, she relaxed her stiff posture. Only when his back was turned did she have the courage to look at him.

She missed Thian. He always knew how to distract her from her own head. How to make her laugh even when she felt like crying.

And she did feel like crying.

She mulled over the words Declan had spoken. What had her mother seen when they were mere children.

A slim, gorgeous young lady with dirty brown hair and eyes as blue as the Roshin Sea approached the prince as he filled another cup of wine. She was standing a little too close for Ayla's liking and an ugly green jealousy seeped into her veins. Whatever the girl was saying to Atlas had him grinning and Ayla chewed her charred vegetables a tad more aggressively.

The prince looked over his shoulder, eyes meeting Ayla's. She flinched and averted her gaze, suddenly finding the contents of her plate very interesting as she pushed around honeyed carrots and potatoes.

What was wrong with her? She thought. *What business did she have being jealous of young maids?*

Perhaps she was just being protective, a familial urge. He deserved to be as happy as she and Thian were. And perhaps when he found that happiness, he would stop this nonsense about her staying away from Thian.

Air. Ayla needed some air.

Excusing herself, she wandered outside to see Olive in the temporary stable, erected for the travelling company. It was colder than freezing, and the stable held very little insulation, but the horses were tightly packed, sharing body heat and each wore wool coats under their saddles.

Pulling out an apple from her cloak pocket, she halved it–intending to share. But when the horse next to him gave her a *look*, she stroked the silver stallion's nose and offered it to him instead. "You're very beautiful." she murmured to the white horse who devoured his share of the apple in about two chomps. Olive huffed and pushed his head between them, begging for her attention. She laughed at the silly stud. "Yes, you're very handsome too. I'll come and see you tomorrow." she vowed with a kiss on his forehead.

"They like you."

Ayla whirled around to find the voice that spoke. A man in his later years smiled from a respectable distance.

"They like *apples*." Ayla countered, dusting the fruit juice from her gloves. "This one's mine." She said, giving Olive a scratch.

"You're both a long way from home."

Even in the darkness, the man's angelic eyes pierced her through, yet she couldn't look away.

"Olive here is, bred on Vorraine before he found me on Articium."

"Yes, I used to have one like it in my youth."

"Oh, are you fro—"

"You have to make a choice, Ayla." He cut over her enquiry and she stilled. "You have to let go."

Unease swarmed her chest. Little bells ringing in her head.

"I'm sorry, do I know you?"

The stranger smiled again, lighting up his whole face. "Not yet." Taking a step backwards he said, "My name is Aithris." He kept walking backwards with a kind smile until he turned on his heel and spoke. "It's nice to finally meet you, Ayla."

A shiver that had nothing to do with the cold raced down her spine. She kept her eyes on the stranger as he ascended the slope back into the frozen keep, the strong warm huffs of Olives breath steadying her.

Now that her fingers had turned numb and her nose red, the cold was too much to bear. Heading back to the archaic keep, she took in its design. Dark stones of all shapes and sizes piled atop one another in a random fashion. presumably hauled here over decades by the original Marnoch family. The lack of uniformity was mirrored in the many buildings that made up the keep. like a small village, they stood at many heights and lengths, butting close together, but never touching.

Opening the door to the guest wing was a blessed warmth. Stretching out her stiff fingers she recalled the words of the stranger outside.

When she was almost at her room Ayla stopped abruptly and tucked into an alcove around the corner. She picked out two familiar voices. Atlas talking to Niamh.

Gods it was late, and she didn't have the strength to argue with him, nor explain herself for lingering eyes at the dinner table. She peeked around the corner, frustrated that she was too far away to hear what they were saying.

Niamh looked visibly distressed and clutched Atlas' jacket.

Gods please leave. And please go the other way when you do.

He didn't though. Atlas pushed into Niamh's chambers and closed the door behind them. Ayla waited a few moments longer, expecting him to re-emerge, but he never did. So, she tip-toed past Niamh's door down the hall to her own as quietly as she could.

Chapter 33

U p at the crack of dawn, Ayla needed some space. She missed the walks along the cliffs of Articium. The peaceful breeze and tickle of long blades of grass brushing her fingertips.

Dressed in riding leathers instead of a dress, she shrugged on a thick winter coat of forest green, and gloves lined with rabbit fur. After retrieving Olive from the stable, she subconsciously headed south, towards home.

Several hours of walking, trotting and cantering around the plains of Camelleah later, Ayla overlooked a great valley before her.

The crumbling drop was several hundred feet, and the valley walls were smothered in a wild heather, resulting in a purple hue as far as the eye could see.

Olive roamed free along a verge, snacking on some sprouting along the edge.

It was so quiet. Ayla loved the quiet, the nature. There wasn't much of either in Balcarras.

When suddenly something plummeted into the earth and a thrash of wind made Ayla stumble to the ground.

Ivelle.

And with her, Atlas.

For fucks sake.

Even in a land as vast and desolate as Camelleah she couldn't get one moment's peace.

The great beast glared at her momentarily and she swallowed hard, questioning if it was wise to regain her footing with haste. If she startled Ivelle, she would suffer the consequences.

Instead, Ivelle turned to Olive, displeased by his skittish display and began rearing and beating her wings fiercely. One knock to the steed had him lose his own footing. The stallion gave out a heartbreaking cry as he slipped on the fragmented edge, tumbling down the valley's edge and landing on a wide lip twenty feet down.

Ayla's eyes widened and her mouth agape. Suddenly anger overshadowed her fear, and she bounded to her feet and marched closer, screaming at Atlas.

"That was my horse!!" She bellowed.

"For a girl who is afraid of pegasi, you're rather brave to be shouting at one." he said in a voice loud enough to be heard from a distance but in an infuriatingly casual tone.

"I am not shouting at Ivelle, I am shouting at you!" she screamed back, storming ever closer.

"Why? *I* didn't push your horse." he replied dripping in sarcasm.

She was seething. That horse meant something to her. Olive may not be as valuable or grand as a pegasus, but he was *hers*. One of the few things she owned in this world. One of the few things that granted her freedom. She had worked hard to overcome her fear of him in years past, and he cared so little, he felt the need to joke?

What. A. Cunt.

Atlas dismounted and positioned himself between Ayla and the cliffside, so she couldn't see the result Olive's fall.

She continued with venom on her tongue, "Oh I'm sorry, I thought that pegasi obeyed the commands of their riders? Or am I mistaken, and Ivelle does as she pleases and you're just along for the ride?"

It was his turn to step forward and he peered down his nose at her. She wondered if it was wise to come this close, provoking him and his beast. Nevertheless, she held her ground.

"I assure you… I am in control." His tone was wicked enough for Ayla's stomach to drop out. He brushed past her casually, leaving her speechless.

"Your horse will be fine. This way, we flew over a tavern nearby." She didn't move an inch–out of protest, naturally. "Or if you'd rather spend your afternoon with Ivelle…"

She had forgotten how close to the creature she was and nearly jumped out of her skin when she turned behind her to see sharp feathers mere inches away.

Suddenly she started in a pathetic run towards Atlas, looking back every so often to check they were being followed by the winged monstrosity.

He was right. They were close to a tavern. Despite its name, *The Rat and Mouse*, it was actually rather charming. Unlike the establishments in Balcarras which were built from dark stone, this place felt warm. Everything was made from timber and the candles dotted around gave it an inviting atmosphere. The smell was not of filthy drunkards and stale ale, but of the most delicious northern food.

Ayla hadn't been to many taverns, but a few nights when Thian had pulled her away, he had shown her a couple of his favourites in Linton. With the exception of Slater's Den of Games, she didn't like them. They induced the feeling of vulnerability.

However, walking into this place, she had no unsettled nerves. The only thing that risked ruining her mood was her company.

Walking through, the pair gathered a few gawks from the pub's patrons. The bloodred hair of the Kinghorn and Solmund families were legendary to the people of Camelleah. A shade of dark and brooding crimson. Ayla could not blame them for their stares. Atlas possessed the most beautiful head of hair she had seen in her life. Not just the shade of it, but how thick and heavy it was. The way that it moved as he walked. The way it bounced when he fought. The way it danced as he flew.

Gods she could stare at that hair all day.

Walking up to the bar, Atlas didn't need to call on service as several tankard girls elbowed their way past one another to assist him. "There's a horse in the heather valley north of here in need of a groomsman." he declared evenly. "I suspect he may need a stent and help navigating out of the slope, as well as shelter until he is healed enough to travel." It was hardly the work normally delegated to barmaids, but no questions were asked as he set down a pouch of gold feathers.

Atlas found them a table in a corner and didn't need to wave for service before two cups were dropped before them.

They sat in silence as he stared at her so surely, and Ayla avoided his gaze. She found drinking to be the best distraction, so it wasn't long until she polished off her first tankard of ale.

"What are you thinking?" Atlas inquired, breaking the silence.

She looked at him momentarily, concocting a lie, "Well my beloved steed was just pushed off a cliff, so naturally I'm mourning my days in a saddle."

"I'm sure you will find a new ride soon enough" he replied, causing Ayla to choke slightly on a gulp of ale. He smiled at that, which let Ayla know his choice of words were quite intentional.

Well, if he wanted to get a rise out of her, then she could do the same.

"Last night" she said, mulling her words over carefully. "You spent the night in Niamh's chambers…" She watched him intensely, looking for any non-verbal telling's, but he gave nothing away. "Why?" she added, when he didn't jump to correct her statement.

He took his time to answer. "She was upset. She can find people overwhelming. Last night was especially difficult for her. She was growing hysterical, afraid of being left alone in her own head, so I stayed with her."

"Why not have one of her handmaidens keep her company?"

"You know Niamh, Ayla. They do not understand her as we do. Nor can they comfort her as we can. I can hold her–soothe her."

Ayla didn't know what to think of it.

"Is she feeling better now?" she asked.

"Yes. Whatever goes on in her head… I don't know how to rid her of such a burden. It can grow to be intense… too intense for her to handle alone."

Ayla knew all this of course. She hadn't just spent her time at court with Twyla, she was rarely parted from Niamh. And unlike her husband and stuck-up members of court, Ayla paid attention to her. Though it would seem, so too had Atlas.

"The more pressing question, however… is why were you spying on me last night?" he changed the subject and drew a cruel smirk over his face.

"I'll have you know I was avoiding you, actually. I have to pass Niamh's chambers to get to my own. When I saw you outside, I thought it better to wait it out than face you."

Atlas narrowed his eyes.

Ayla asked a barmaid for a plate of whatever was causing such a mouthwatering smell. The girl brought out a skillet of baked batter with sausages and vegetables nestled throughout, the whole thing drowning in a steaming onion gravy.

"Why did you have to fight in the stupid tournament?" Ayla asked around a mouthful.

"I was challenged. It's the noble thing to do."

"Horseshit. You've been challenged every year since you were four and ten, and you've never entered the triskele."

"I have nothing to prove to attention-hungry lordlings."

"And you have something to prove to Thian?"

"Not prove, no. Thian needs reminding once in a while that there's someone bigger than him. Stronger than him. That he's not all-powerful and there will be consequences should he cross certain lines."

Ayla snorted. "You really believe he thinks of himself as all-powerful?"

Atlas held her stare. "I believe he thinks he will be, in several moons time."

Her stomach flipped.

Ayla stared at her plate like it held answers to questions she couldn't comprehend.

Once her stomach was full, skin toasty, and no thoughts of duty or responsibility on her mind, Ayla settled into the prince's presence. Content to be tucked away from the world in this little candle-lit pub just the two of them.

Even in those moments of quiet, Atlas watched her though she held the world in her palm. Something akin to fluttering bloomed in her chest, which she hastily smothered out.

"Atlas."

"Ayla."

"Don't look at me like that." she said, her tone stern.

"Like what?" he asked with a shit eating grin.

Her voice was little more than a whisper, "Like you don't care about the consequences."

He clenched his jaw. When he opened it to speak, he was interrupted by the splash of sweet ale set down before them.

"Uhm. no," Ayla said, "I can't stomach anymore today." A slur in her voice that wasn't apparent moments prior. She stood to put her cloak on once more, and the headrush she got reminded her of just how much she had drunk.

She wobbled a bit, but Atlas offered her his arm which she reluctantly took. She only hesitated out of habit–if they were in Balcarras, in the same vicinity as Thian, she simply couldn't risk it.

Just as she reached for the door to leave, Atlas pulled her back. He tossed a bag of coin to the girl who had served them generously this evening, "One room."

Ayla aggressively pulled her arm from his grip. "Excuse me?" she demanded.

"Ayla," her name on his tongue was a soft purr, drawing her in against her will. "In case you haven't noticed, the sun has gone down, and I hear the cold nights of Camelleah are not particularly forgiving." he said.

Looking through the tiny window set between timber she saw only impending darkness.

Shit. He was right.

Maybe it was one too many cups of ale, or the atmosphere of the tavern putting her in such a relaxed mood, or maybe it was simply because she was starting to enjoy the prince's company, but she nodded her head.

Not before rolling her eyes, of course.

Atlas put his hand on the small of her back as he led her up the stairs despite her slurred protest that she was perfectly capable without.

"Wait a minute," she paused on the narrow staircase and pointed a finger into his chest, "only one room? No, no get your own".

He smirked down at her. "Two rooms?" He led her further up the stairs to the room with the number matching the one on their keys. "What do you think I am? Made of money?"

"Atlas Kinghorn, was that a joke?" She almost snorted a laugh as her back pressed into the door, and she faced him.

He smiled down at her. A smile so pure that her heart melted. Even in her drunken state she recognised he didn't pass those often.

He reached to her side for the door handle only to have her slide her body over, covering it.

"Ah, ah, ah… not so fast," her smile dropped, and she braved as serious a face as she could. "Give me a legitimate reason for sharing a room…"

He looked down at her through long lashes and sleepy eyes. "You might not be royalty in Balcarras, Ayla. But here you are a Marnoch. You are of status and power whether you see it or not. Others may try to… take advantage of that. I will not allow it."

His words were proper and polite, but she could tell by the way his face contorted in disgust what he meant. She could be taken for ransom. Or much worse…

"Okay…" she announced as she grabbed the handle and stumbled into the room, "but you can sleep on the floor"

"I will do no such thing."

Ayla was too tired to argue.

She took in the room. Charming, just like its counterpart downstairs. Small and humble, but the wooden furniture made her smile. They were intricately carved, and she ran as she ran her fingers along the grooves of the canopy bed, she noticed they weren't patterns. It was a story. The beam that wrapped around the overhead told a *story*.

Screwing her eyes to steady her vision, she beheld the tale written in wood. A girl and a boy, falling in love. The girl becomes with child. She tells the boy. Has to run away, but he doesn't go with her. She boards a boat and... Ayla rounded the corner of the beam too fast, and her head spun violently.

Collapsing on the bed, she slipped off her fur lined boots and threw her coat on the ground as Atlas poked at the fire.

Ayla slipped under the furs, snuggling into their natural warmth. She watched Atlas as her eyes fluttered and threatened sleep. She watched him take off his boots. Then doublet. Then her heart began to quicken as she wondered how many more layers he would peel off. How much she would have to see. How much she would *get* to see. He took off his linen undershirt, which momentarily stopped her frail heart, but that was as much as he took off.

Thank the Mother.

Her eyes traced him as he rounded the bed. As he climbed in, Ayla shifted her position to face him on her side, so her back was lined up with the edge of the bed–*practically falling out*–and crooked her knee up, creating as much of a barrier between herself and the prince.

Atlas hadn't even fully laid down before he corrected this distance. He hooked the leg she volunteered to drag her towards him, causing Ayla to let out a yelp.

"Hey!" she whined, trying to peel herself away, but Atlas gave no release on his grip. Her leg now rested atop his own, and his arm wrapped around her back pulling her closer.

"The Duke of Camelleah would have my head if one of his own froze to death on my watch." he argued, eyes closed with a smug smile on his lips.

"If it's so rutting cold then why did you take your shirt off?" she questioned, feeling rather smart, chin tilted up to gaze at him, but his eyes remained sealed.

"I run hot." he said flatly.

And with that she backed down and bit her smile. She had to admit, it *was* cold. The fur pelts would've done the trick but feeling his scorching skin flush against hers was a luxury.

She felt as if she was melting into him, his hold, his warmth, his smell. Gods if she wasn't already wasted, she would find herself drunk on his scent. Being pressed against his bare skin was intoxicating.

"Goodnight Ayla." Atlas professed, as if commanding a child to go to sleep.

"Goodnight, *Atee*." she teased, smirking once again into his flesh. The nickname admittedly sounded just as adorable on her tongue as it did Twyla's.

Sleep found her at an embarrassing speed. Not for Atlas though. He too had indulged in the fine ale of Camelleah, but he intended on savouring this moment. Something so mundane as sleep wasn't going to rob him of it.

Looking down at her, a faint smile rested on his face. He spent some time rubbing his thumb in circles pressed into her back. Then he moved to her hair, brushing it off her face after it fell over her eyes. Then finally to her face. He cupped her cheek and his thumb, unsure of itself, traced its way down to her scar. The scar from that damned night that haunted his dreams. Dreams of her screaming and crying and bleeding. The night that Thian's stupidity and jealousy had marked her. The night when he couldn't protect her. The night when she sobbed into his hands, blood pouring out her mouth and down his arms.

Memories of that night pulled the smile from his face and replaced it with a remorseful frown. However, the more he stared at it, the more he felt she rather suited it… she looked fearsome and glorious.

Perhaps one day, he thought*, she too could come to think so highly of his own scar.*

Chapter 34

The brightness of the rising sun almost blinded Ayla as they emerged from the inn. She had awoken with what felt like a blacksmith working within the compounds of her skull, hammering true. Wincing as she hid her eyes behind ivory hands, she followed Atlas out the heavy wooden door he held wide for her.

In this moment she couldn't understand how Thian could drink so much so often. Running off with his newfound rabble almost every night for fun always ended in inebriation.

She couldn't for the life of her fathom how he felt the effect was worth the consequence–feeling like *this*. But then she suspected that her reasons for drinking were very different from Thian's. Ayla drank to relax, unwind and indulge every now and again. Thian drank to escape.

Walking across the frosty plain, Atlas took note of her discomfort. "Don't worry… it's noting some fresh air through the sky won't clear up."

Ayla stopped in her tracks.

The pounding in her head seemed to travel down to her heart as she digested the words, dissected their meaning.

Through the sky. Fly. Olive was not there to bring her back to Rydon. Fuck. No.

"No," Ayla whimpered. Too afraid to even voice her understanding of his intention. Pure animal instinct overcame her and one minute she was standing as still as a doe and then she was running.

Or at least she *tried* to run.

Atlas lunged toward her, grabbed her wrist, and pulled her back to him before he hauled her over his shoulder and marched up the hill toward where she could now hear the beating of Ivelle's wings.

"Atlas Kinghorn, you have no fucking right! Put me down now!!" she screamed at him, pounding her fist into his back, legs thrashing, but he held her firm.

As Ivelle landed, the thundering hooves matched the erratic pounding of Ayla's heart. Her smashing on his back melted into clawing instead, grasping his leathers and pleading to be set free.

"Atlas, please don't do this! I will walk back, it's not that far, please!"

Atlas finally put her down, grabbing her wrists before she had time to bolt again. She held panic in her eyes, so much raw terror that she was practically shaking beneath his grasp. He tugged her in closer, forcing her to look him in the eyes.

"Do you trust me?" he asked flatly.

Her shaking seemed to still.

Part of her wanted to spit in his face and run for the hills. But—and she couldn't comprehend why–deep down she felt the answer. Yes. In the shadowed depths of her heart, she knew she trusted him. Even with her life.

She stared at him while all of this ran through her head before she gave the tiniest of nods. Atlas' grip loosened. He nodded to the beast on his left but held her gaze.

"Climb." he instructed flatly.

She just about reached the pommel on the saddle if she stood on her tiptoes. Atlas gave his pegasus a brush and the gentle giant folded her wing enough for Ayla to stand in the crook. All the while Atlas' hand rested in the low arch of her back, anchoring her. The wing stretched taught backward, subsequently lifting a squealing Ayla to a height at which she could mount the saddle.

Once sat, the absence of Atlas' touch was chilling and black spots dotted her vision as her heart raced in record time. Only when she felt Atlas join her on the enormous saddle did she open her eyes. Open them to find… Atlas facing her. He hooked her knees over his thighs to give him more room to sit flush on the saddle.

"Very forward of you, Ayla." he said with a distracting grin.

Ayla looked around her. With the fear of the ascent, she had mistakenly mounted backwards, currently facing Ivelle's rear.

After a quick assessment of her mistake, she scoffed, unamused, before very slowly, and *very* carefully turning herself around the correct way.

Atlas looped his arms through hers, one hand spread over her torso, pulling her close. The other reached for the reins.

He left the pommel free for Ayla to hold onto. She gripped it with one hand. The other rested upon Atlas'.

He leaned his head in to whisper into her ear, "You trust me?" And once more she gave him a quaint nod, her breathing already short with anxiety over what he was about to put her through.

Atlas knocked his heels into Ivelle, the faintest of pressure was all the creature needed to start into a fierce canter. A pegasus could not flap its wings and shoot to the sky with a jump like that of a bird. Their size and weight required a running start before they had the momentum to take off.

Ayla refrained from shrieking mostly since she was breathless, chest heaving.

Survival instincts screamed at her to run away from this. But there was nowhere to run.

After a few minutes to comprehend what was going on, Ayla noted how different flying was from riding. Where Olive's canter was fast and hard and rugged, to fly was smooth and fluid. Powerful, but in a different way...

Something flickered in her chest, and she couldn't believe what she was considering–that she was enjoying this.

A seedling of a smile sprouted on her lips.

She felt herself getting braver and loosened her hand off Atlas', and then off the pommel... trusting that he held her there.

She had seen Atlas and Thian fly. And she knew this leisurely speed was a mere fraction to what Ivelle was capable of.

Her hands lifted, arms straight to either side of her. Feeling the wind beat against them as she kept them stretched. As if she were the one with wings, soaring through the sky. She let out a laugh as the wind whipped against her hands, her arms, her face and she leaned back into Atlas.

Overcome by the experience, adrenaline shot through her veins, fueling her with a feeling of fearlessness. She slowly lifted her outstretched arms above her head, elbows bending to reach back for his head. Arching her back, her head dropping to his left shoulder. Her eyes fluttered shut as she felt his warmth seeping through their clothes.

The heartbeat she felt through his leathers mirrored the erratic state of her own. Hard desire pressed against her arse. When the feeling finally registered through her elation, her mouth fell open and a light whimper escaped her.

Fighting the strength of the wind, she pried her long lashes open wide enough to look at him, her head still resting on his shoulder, though now cocked so they were eye to eye. So close were they, that her breath dusted his lips.

"Look down," he whispered.

After a beat of hesitation, she bid his command and peeked past the wings of Ivelle to behold the landscape of this beautiful land where north met south.

The winter sun shone over the frost dusted land making it shimmer like stardust. Ayla was suddenly overcome with the desire to see everywhere from this angle. This height. With this rider.

She knew they had flown south because streams of ice were trickling through the land toward the capital. Cutting through the land like veins; feeding the life of this wondrous land.

Once they circled back to Rydon Keep, they landed a safe distance from the stone, behind a wall of evergreens dusted in frost.

Atlas descended without the aid of Ivelle's wing, jumping the impressive height without a second thought. While Ayla could have descended the way she ascended, she didn't protest as Atlas lifted her by the hips and gently placed her on the ground.

Her breath hitched at the touch, but he didn't relieve his grip even when she was safely on the frozen earth.

Ayla held his stare with such conflict and confusion brewing inside of her. A raging war between her head and her heart. But she was still riding the high of the thrill of flight, and before she could even comprehend what she was doing she grabbed his face in both hands and pulled him into a crushing kiss.

From the moment their lips met, a fire was lit within her. It was all consuming, and yet she wanted more. She wanted to burn in this inferno that was Atlas Kinghorn.

She melted into his punishing hold and when she came up for air he slipped in his tongue to taste her deeper.

His kiss was a brand. An everlasting mark that she would never forget.

This was wrong.

The compass inside of her that promised to lead her to a happy future was spinning off axis.

He wasn't Thian, and he wasn't hers.

But something about it felt too right to deny.

Chapter 35

T hey heard her before they saw her. Niamh was running with skirts in hand around the wall of trees, calling after Ayla.

The tangled pair broke the kiss, but Ayla found it hard to pull her face from his completely. The thrum of her heart was an ancient song calling her to connect with him once more, fuse their bodies and souls.

"Ayla!" Niamh called again. Though her tone was more joyous than concerned. "You're back just in time to get ready for the festivities!"

The princess didn't ask where the governess had been the past day. Nor why she had just arrived to the keep on a pegasus–knowing fine well Ayla was petrified of them. *Or at least used to be?* She wasn't exactly thinking straight enough to comprehend her position on the matter.

When Ayla's eyes regretfully left Atlas', they met Niamh's, and she rushed alongside the princess to the stony compound. She didn't have the strength to turn and look at him, but every step felt like she was going in the wrong direction.

Ayla shuddered, hoping to physically shake off whatever strange chemical compulsion was wreaking havoc over her feelings toward the prince.

The *wrong* prince. *Gods, maybe she* was *still drunk.*

As they marched arm in arm through the cold, draughty keep, reality started to rush back to Ayla's head.

"How is Twyla?" she asked, tone laced with guilt.

"Oh, she's just fine, Phena and Hensella watched her while you were away."

A sliver of guilt lifted from Ayla's conscience. Phena and Hensella were the official governesses for Twyla during this leg of the tour to give Ayla freedom of acting like a guest, with her kin.

"Would you like me to braid your hair up? Or should we leave some down?" Niamh questioned when they arrived at Ayla's chamber. She only realised how ridiculously thirsty she was when she saw the silver pitcher of water next to her box-bed.

Ayla poured herself a glass as she replied to the princess. "Some down I think." She swallowed until the cup emptied and she was out of breath but already pouring herself another. "I like how it dances when I do." she said, only half listening to her own words.

"Lovely, I'll leave you to wash up and I'll be back before sundown to fix it up before the ceremony."

"Thank you, Niamh. You know you don't have too though. *You're* the princess, I should be fawning over *your* hair."

"Nonsense, I quite enjoy it. Perhaps one day if Twyla's hair is as long and lovely as yours, you'll be spared the torment." she jested. Ayla just smiled as Niamh made to leave before adding "Oh! And wear the sapphire earrings." and with that, she was gone.

Ayla polished off a third glass of water before bathing–this one however, hit a pit in her stomach causing her to question if she underestimated her hangover.

She felt disgusting in her day-old riding leathers.

The lingering smell of pegasus fueled the urge to scrub her skin raw. Her hair felt dry and matted after her trip through the skies. And to her dismay, Ayla knew her underclothes were ruined by the heat that had emanated from the apex of her thighs.

Peeling off her clothing she threw them in a pile on the floor in the corner. A shameful heap of sin and betrayal.

She fetched a vile of lavender oil and dried eucalyptus leaves from her leather trunk, adding a few drops to the steaming water, along with various salts native to Camelleah.

The warm, glorious smells hit her nose and with each exaggerated inhale her head seemed to clear. Blurry memories became explicit images, hitting her hard one after another. Her stomach soured and her heart raced, though it had nothing to do with whatever alcohol remained in her system.

The water eventually cooled around her, but she did not leave the bronze tub, paralyzed by thoughts and feelings. Parsing through the events of the day, that felt so good in the moment but made her feel sick with guilt and shame now.

She suppressed the compulsion to look over her shoulder at the door, feeling that Thian was about to burst through her door and chastise her for such reckless betrayal. *When she returned to Balcarras, would he see it in her eyes?* She chewed on the likelihood.

Emerging from the tub with shivering and pruned skin, she wrapped herself in a bathing robe and hunkered down before the fire.

Wiping soggy hands on the thick linen of her robe, Ayla reached into her trunk and pulled the parcel of letters from their pouch.

Sitting back on her heels, she unfurled the leather that kept them neatly bound. Guided by habit, she lifted the stack to her nose and inhaled. It still didn't smell of him, it never had. But now her heart pinched as she realised he usually smelt of wine, not sticky tarts anymore.

Opening the top letter, her eyes scanned the page, reading familiar words. Ayla waited for the flutter that always made her chest feel warm, the involuntary lift to her lips.

Dropping the parchment, she opened the next, gaze flittering through scribbled nonsense and thoughtless prose.

Brow pinching, she reached for the next. Then the next. And the next. Looking for that feeling that had kept her afloat for nine years.

Ayla read each cherished letter numbly. A tear fell from her cheek, droplet smudging ink.

The door knocked and Ayla's shoulders jumped.

"Ayla?" It was Niamh.

"Come in." Ayla scooped the strewn letters in a heap before dumping them in the trunk. Raising off her knees, she wiped the salty streak off her cheek before she turned to greet the princesses.

Twyla giggled as she ran toward her governess who fell back to her knees to embrace her. Ayla squeezed her tightly in her arms before peppering her in kisses. "I've missed you Bumblebee, have you been good for your mother?"

Twyla became far more interested in the trinkets of Ayla's room to answer.

"Your hair!" Niamh gawked, running her pale fingers through still-wet-locks.

"I'm sorry, my mind ran away with me…"

"It's alright, I can still pull something together" she soothed with a smile. Ayla was happy to see Niamh in such high spirits.

Settled in a comfortable chair, Twyla climbed into her lap as Niamh attempted to braid a section of hair out of Ayla's face.

It was easier to focus on Niamh than herself. "You seem in a good mood today?"

"It is a happy day, full of happy people…" Niamh replied absentmindedly as she concentrated on the hair being held back in strands between various fingers. "Do you think they will like my gift? It is not very regal, but I heard the bride has a fine collection from all over the continent." Niamh continued, referring to the now finished hoop she had been working on during their journey north.

"I think it's lovely. And I bet this will be the first in her collection made by a *princess*."

Ayla was beginning to forget her knotted stomach when she saw a flash of bloodred hair cross past her window. The fright was so sudden she squeezed Twyla's arm, and the sharp pinch made the toddler burst into tears.

"Oh no, I'm sorry bumblebee," she tried to soothe Twyla through her tears, meanwhile that pressure of guilt was building tenfold. "It's alright, I'm sorry, I didn't mean it." Ayla kissed the red patch of skin and rubbed it softly until the crying subsided into weak sniffles.

Meanwhile Niamh stepped farther and farther from her daughter. Eyes glazed over as if she was only there physically. She made no attempt to comfort the child but was displeased by her upset state.

Still shushing and bouncing the princess on her knee, Ayla refocused her gaze out the window to the mop of hair responsible for all the fuss. The sight of Atlas brought on contradictory waves of relief and unease.

Ayla stood, tot strapped to her hip and turned her back to the window, determined to keep her focus on those with her in the room.

The ceremony of the northern couple was beautiful. Man and wife coming together under the stars, ordained by the Duke of Camelleah himself.

Camelleah's roots gave worship to Arianrhod, Goddess of the Moon and her children of Stars. Constellations depicted heroes, reminders of ethics and morals to abide by. So naturally weddings were performed in the cover of darkness lit by starlight. It is said that if a wedding night is clouded and the stars are not visible, the Gods deem the pair unsuited and deny them their blessing of union. Some couples choose to go ahead with the marriage, though most fell victim to the superstition and part ways.

The freezing temperature gave the bride a rosy glow to her cheeks and the tip of her nose. Her husband was all too smitten by the sight of her.

Guests flooded the ruins of Ryn Kirk, spilling out of its many fissures.

Ayla gazed up inside the roofless kirk as the stars sparkled in approval. She and Twyla took up a nook at the back, where the princess could toddle around and touch the ruins. Niamh had offered she stand by the altar with herself and Atlas, but Ayla had politely refused. It may have been the coldest place she'd ever been in her life, but she could feel her cheeks heat at the mere thought of it. She couldn't even look at him when Niamh had posed the question with her arm in his.

Ayla missed the start of the feast that followed in favor of putting Twyla to bed, fueled by the guilt that she had left her yesterday. When she returned to the great hall it was alive with merry song and laughter. She hesitated before she took her seat. Niamh had left her a space between herself and Atlas.

Great.

Swallowing her pride she took the seat.

Several guests at their table looked drunk and Ayla felt the sudden urge to catch up. Anything to quiet her unrelenting swirl of thoughts. She emptied her glass of sweet red wine and waved over a page for a second.

She could feel Atlas' judgement burning into her side.

The hall was so loud and bustling, so many distractions, and yet try as she might, Ayla could not for the life of her think of anything other than the man sitting on her left. Or the way her breathing was noticeably short, and the wine wasn't doing its job to amend it. Or that she could practically feel the energy radiating off him, making her shiver. Or the fact that he made no effort to talk to her, to touch her which–*regrettably*–made her a little sad.

Niamh, who was often overwhelmed by rowdy crowds such as these, seemed to be in a world of her own, humming and singing quietly as she ate her dinner and pulled threads of her napkin.

Gods, the three of them must have looked pathetic and miserable in each other's silent company.

The bride and groom announced their departure to the honeymoon suite and the hall erupted in thunderous applause and cries. Some of which were well-wishers, some were less savoury. Luckily there was no bedding ceremony–nor had there been in Camelleah in many years.

Massive bonfires were erected in the courtyard and a band of strings and drums was set up next to them, encouraging members of the court to enjoy the space. Ayla was admittedly hesitant to agree when

Niamh had asked her to explore but was glad she did. The heat from the bonfires flooded the courtyard beautifully and she suddenly didn't care that she wasn't wearing a cloak. Just her midnight-black gown, with some tiny sapphire gems sewn into the wrists. The fourth–*or perhaps fifth*–*glass* of wine was doing wonders for her internal temperature also.

Feeling giddy, Ayla pulled on Niamh's wrist, ushering her to where the musicians were stationed and several young lords and ladies danced. The music toed the line between classical folk rhymes and something darker.

Atlas had sulked after the pair when they left the great hall and took up residence in one of the lounge chairs scattered over the yard.

When she opened her eyes as one song ended and another took its place, she locked eyes with him instantly and froze. After a beat she snapped her entire body to face the other direction.

As Ayla closed her eyes and let the music guide her movements, her rolling hips and snaking arms caught the eyes of a few. One set of those wandering eyes stalked through the crowd to the pair.

"I'm sorry to interrupt, but your jewels are quite amazing…" he purred, and Ayla couldn't help but laugh at such a strange attempt at flattery. The young man was barely taller than her but traditionally handsome for a man of Camelleah. Light reddish-brown hair hung in curls around his face, which donned thick, well-kept stubble.

"Thank you," she said, clearing her throat and regaining composure. "They were a gift."

"Well, someone must love you very much to gift sapphires of such quality. Though I don't find that hard to believe, given your own beauty." he drawled, stepping closer as if she would hear him better. She tried to move away, continuing to sway foot-to-foot as if it was all part of her dance, and not an urge to remove the man from her personal space.

She looked for Niamh, but she had found another dance partner and was twirling a young boy—with no more than ten years—who was absolutely beside himself to be dancing with a real-life princess. Instead, Ayla found the eyes of Atlas, which still clung to her, as if they had never stopped. Something in her soothed that he was there, watching.

"Forgive me, I haven't introduced myself. Fergus Goldsworth." He picked up her hand without warning or permission and placed a lousy kiss on the back of it. To which Ayla leaned back, trying to hide her cringe.

"My family owns the largest emerald mine on the continent. The irony of our name is not lost on me." he poured out these words as he circled her, and she suddenly felt a lot like prey.

Her heart drummed very fast, but not for the right reasons. Not in the way it had this morning, with

Atlas. No, this was a different feeling. One she did not recognise at first. Fear.

He too moved as if he were dancing, casually swaying towards her, around her, before he grabbed the side of her neck and leaned into her ear, lips ghosting over the lobe. Ayla's shoulders shot up in discomfort and she tried to push him away, but he would not relent.

"I could cover you in emeralds from crown to cunt." he whispered in her ear.

Before Ayla could even muster a response, someone yanked him back and landed a devastating punch to his face, sending him plummeting to the floor. Fergus' eyes rolled as he stirred, groaning in pain.

Ayla steadied herself as she watched Atlas Kinghorn beat the man's face bloody. Again, and again. A rabble began to form around them, some cheering in encouragement, others calling guards for help. A sudden panic returned to Ayla at the thought of Atlas being dragged away and punished for protecting her.

He was unrelenting. She did not dare step between his fist and what remained of Fergus' face so all she could do was speak.

"Atlas," she croaked out. Barely a whisper. But it was all he needed. It was a beacon that snapped him out of whatever frenzy possessed him. He looked at her with wild eyes and noted the fear in her own. He stood back up, bloody hands dripping by his sides.

Ayla didn't know what came over her as she grabbed said bloody hand and pulled him away from the scene, running into the keep until they reached her room, where she flung him inside before slamming the door shut.

Chapter 36

S he was out of breath, chest heaving. But the run seemingly did not faze Atlas' lungs as he just stared at her.

"Ayla... I'm–" his apologetic tone was unnecessary.

"Thank you." she breathed, pulling him into an eager, breathless kiss. Her hands roamed the back of his head, fisting that gorgeous hair and pulling him deeper.

He stiffened at first but took no time in reciprocating her impatience. Both his arms wound round her so tightly she wasn't entirely sure her feet were touching the floor. His blood-soaked hands smeared over her dress, but frankly, she didn't give a damn.

Atlas walked them toward a stone wall, pressing her flush against it. He pulled away but their mouths remained parted, panting, drawing in each other's breath.

"Are you alright?" he asked, brows twitching with anger, referring to the unwanted touches she had just received.

"I am now." she promised, tugging his hair in a desperate plea to which he obliged, scorching her lips with his own. Slanting his head so he could explore her deeper, harder, she moaned into his taste.

Her knees went weak, but his hold was strong. He hooked one of her legs up over his hip and kneaded her arse with bruising force. The feel of which had Ayla grinding into his evident desire.

He broke away from her lips and traced kisses along her jaw, down her neck, and to her exposed chest. These were not chaste pecks; they were hungry ravenous claims that made Ayla whimper with every swirl of his tongue or nip of his teeth.

She let one hand fall from his face only to pull up her dress past the knee lifted by Atlas' side, hiking it up as high as it could go. Atlas replied by tracing his hand up the same path, thumb rubbing teasing circles as it went. It stopped however, when he reached a foreign object.

He looked down to confirm his suspicions.

A dagger, strapped under a garter. It's making was modest, but the blade peeking through its cover was sharp enough to cut air. Ayla chuckled at the confusion engulfing his face and chose to take mercy on his curiosity.

"When I arrived back for my position, it was made very clear that my life was of no importance next to the princess. And that I should lay it down in an attempt for her survival, if need be." Ayla explained with a humourless smile. "They tossed me a dagger and left. Made no attempts to show me how to use it, protect myself *or* Twyla with it. Just left me to wallow in my own lack of worth. I have to admit…" she averted her gaze down, slightly ashamed by the admission, "I wasn't sure I was ready to die for anyone, even Twyla, as much as I love her. But I knew I was willing to kill for her."

Her gaze raised to his mouth which she watched like a woman entranced, a wicked smile drawing over her own. He said nothing to her divulgence, but admiration poured from his eyes.

He gave her a softer kiss as he resumed his trace past the dagger–not bothering to remove it on his ascension. When he reached the apex of her thighs, he tugged the undercloth to one side and grazed across her flesh.

"You're soaked." he groaned with a smile into her lips, and she whimpered with a nod, brow still pressed against his.

In all honesty she hadn't stopped being after that morning. Even after a long bath. Every fleeting thought of Atlas left her body wet and wanting, even if her mind hadn't caught up to the fact.

He started circling his thumb over her tight bud, and Ayla's head threw back against the stone wall–hard enough to hurt, but she was feeling too much pleasure to notice. The speed of his thumb increased, as did the pressure applied to the bundle of nerves which had Ayla's jaw unhinged, eyes screwed.

She bit her lip in an attempt to hold back her moans. Atlas leaned in and replaced her teeth with his own. She couldn't stop saying his name. It was forbidden on her tongue, and she wanted to taste it.

Atlas kept working his thumb but teased a long, strong finger at her entrance. She pushed her hips toward him, practically begging for more, to which he grinned and obeyed. She hitched a breath, and Atlas caught her in another kiss, lapping up every sound she dared to make.

"More…" she pleaded breathlessly, opening her eyes to find his own glazed with a hint of concern.

"Are you sure?" he asked, and she smiled at his assumption of her innocence before nodding in agreement.

He added a second finger, pumping at a leisurely speed.

Fuck, he was ruining her. Her own fingers would never be enough again.

That familiar tension was mounting in Ayla's core and her breathing became erratic as she writhed against his hips. Atlas kissed her chest once more

308

before using his teeth to pull down the off-the-shoulder neckline of the dress to expose her breast.

Fighting her impending eruption, she wanted to know what he was going to do next. He licked across the line of fabric up to the other side and dragged that down too.

Atlas leant back momentarily, and his fingers stilled inside her. His face presented unmistakable hunger.

Ayla whimpered at the sudden lack of friction but cried out his name when he resumed, this time taking one breast in mouth, sucking and tugging the rosy brown bud that was painfully hard.

Ayla wanted to feel this forever. To have him worship her body like this forever. But it felt too fucking good, and her body couldn't hold on any longer as she built and built and built and cried out his name, fisting his hair so tightly he must've lost a few strands.

The sight and sounds were so raw and lewd, paired with the feeling of her clenching around his fingers, she couldn't come down from this high. Atlas didn't stop moving his fingers or tongue until she stopped writhing against him, riding out every wave of euphoria. Until she went limp and slumped against the wall with only Atlas' body pinning her against the wall.

He rose from her breast and brushed a few stray hairs off her sweating face with a tenderness Ayla could hardly register as she saw stars.

As she stood against the wall and slowly began to regain feeling in her limbs and clarity in her mind, Atlas never peeled his body off hers. His hands remained cupping her face, rubbing gentle, adoring strokes along her flushed cheek. He gave himself only a couple inches of room between his face and hers, so she could regain her breath, and he could taste hers.

"You're perfect." he cooed in a low raspy voice.

Ayla registered the words enough to open her eyes. He looked at her as if she were the stars in the sky or a god at an altar. *How could he possibly see such things in her?* she thought. Instinctively she lowered her chin to her chest.

"Don't hide yourself from me," he said flatly, "or anyone else."

Those knees of hers that were finally feeling some strength again found themselves wobbling.

Ayla's tongue felt thick and heavy, but she forced it to form the words, "Then why do you hide from me?" Her voice was laced with fear as she eyed his own scars poking out above leathers. Despite the jest they seemed to share in Articium when she first beheld his scarring, he seemed to have grown far more sensitive to its mention in passing years. That much was evident after her return to Balcarras, where in the kitchens she had merely looked at them and he'd snapped.

But things were different now. Defensive walls between them were beginning to crumble and Ayla wanted to tear his down and reduce it to rubble. To have him lay bare before her.

He lifted his hand to his neck, slowly, chest puffed as he revealed the most fragile, shame-filled part of himself.

Time seemed to slow as he unfastened the hooks between leather, separating the high collar all the way down to his chest.

Ayla understood what this meant. How personal and vulnerable it made him feel.

Maintaining a neutral face, she lifted her shaking finger to caress the lines of scar that ran across his throat, from one ear to his collar bone on the other side. She counted four slashes. Four feathers that had caused such destruction, both physically and mentally. Her own wound was so slight and inconsequential next to his. His scarring was fresher and so much larger that the tender skin was still trying to heal itself.

Ayla pressed her palm flat over the expanse. Smiling up at him softly, converting more than words could possibly say. *Thank you for showing me. I understand your pain. You are no monster in my eyes.*

Her transfixion on his scarring was soon eclipsed by the urge to continue unhooking his leathers, to see more of him. She did so slowly and carefully.

Peeling back the fabric, she found a dagger of his own strapped inside. She gave him a knowing glance before removing it from its confines. Far bigger and prettier than hers, at first glance she assumed it was forged by a blacksmith of Vorraine. Black-soaked-leather bound the pommel. The blade itself was etched with slanted lines, not enough to be serrated, but enough to resemble a feather. Ayla refrained from snorting at the intended irony.

Her fingers trailed down to what *really* caught her eye. A Jewel set into the end of the hilt.

"Why a sapphire?" she asked, transfixed on the shimmering orb. His royal ancestry was covered in clear diamonds all the way back to the first king and queen of the continent. The Princess of Camelleah at the time had belonged to a house of diamonds. Their gems were set into tradition ever since. And his Vorrainish kin had an affinity for rubies–due their close resemblance to blood no doubt–so his choice was not an obvious one in placing allegiances.

He in response said nothing, but lifted his hands to her ears, playing with the gems adorning them. *Her* sapphires. Ayla had to fight a whimper climbing her throat at the sentiment. Her second hand reached for his face and pulled him forward until their brows rested upon one another. Under which he could feel hers bunching.

"I feel like I've missed you..." she whispered. "All these years I have known you, but only from afar. And yet my heart has missed you, *longed* for you. Is that foolish?" she tacked on, suddenly self-conscious about such a blatant admission.

"We both know our distance was not the desire of either of us. But I swear we will not fall back into it. Never again." he reassured, followed by a tender kiss. The moment their lips pressed, the hunger in both of them reignited and it grew more passionate, ravaging. He growled before he forced himself to tear away.

Removing the tagger from her hand, he returned it to its keep.

"Sweet dreams, Ayla," he said with a sombre grin, fingers working the buttons of his shirt.

"Where are you going?" she asked through kiss-swollen lips.

"Unfortunately, I have made a mess that needs cleaning up." he replied, grinding his teeth.

The thought of Atlas facing the consequences of his actions by strangers starving for revenge made Ayla feel nauseous. Goldsworth was not some nobody that had picked a fight in a tavern. He was of a noble family, one with great wealth–which translated to great power.

But Atlas was a Prince of the Continent, she reminded herself. He may have a temper, but he was diplomatic and knew how to handle a situation such as this. It also didn't hurt that they had brought a small army north with them that could aid if things turned ugly. Civil war was unlikely but had been started over lesser things than a man's bruised pride.

Atlas opened her door and just before he slipped out Ayla couldn't help but slip the words "Be careful."

His face softened at her worry for him. "Do you trust me?" he asked knowingly.

"Always." she replied without hesitation, and he left her room.

After Ayla collapsed on her bed, her head spun. Not from the copious amounts of alcohol she had indulged at dinner, but the words and touches that felt burned into skin.

How could two days change so much between them? She pondered.

But it wasn't just two days. It never had been. Those feelings, desires, in both of them had lingered for years. Suppressed by courteous and respectful boundaries. Separated by fear of consequence.

But here, far from the reality of life at home, they had broken. Succumbed to the curiosity that burned inside of them. And now Ayla never wanted to return home. To reality. She didn't want those walls to be rebuilt. Nor the boundaries reset.

She wanted *this*. Freedom to choose him. And they were leaving tomorrow.

What in the Gods' good graces was she going to do now?

Chapter 37

A yla's cheeks were raw after less than half a day into the journey home to Balcarras. It would take just over a week at the tumbling speed of the tour, but the impending reunion was already filling her with dread.

Her teeth nipped and pulled at the flesh as she mulled the words over in her head. Trying to string together adequate explanations for Thian.

Because how could she explain? Explain how she still loved him dearly, but the feelings she held for him were entirely different from the kind she felt for Atlas. That they ran deeper. *Harder*.

How could she explain that the thought of his touch had turned sour in her head, and she'd rather just remain platonic. Friends–*best* friends. As they'd always been.

How could she explain she didn't need him to uphold his promise of marriage to her one day. He could remain faithful to his wife and child. And she would remain in his life regardless, in their home, as governess to his children and maybe one day something more to Atlas.

Wincing as she hit a particularly sensitive spot, blood pooled around her tongue. The coppery taste brought her back to the night of the accident in the arena with Racjan. This time though, she didn't dwell on the image of Thian's anger, or his face seething with betrayal.

But her memory cracked open to recall how Atlas had scrambled over to her–ignoring his pain in favour of her own. How he held her so tenderly at such a young age. How she could see in his eyes the concern for her well-being, then the rage at his brother for causing her such pain. The same rage he had put on display the previous night when Goldsworth had put his ruddy hands on her without consent.

She had to admit the sight… excited something in her. The thought that Atlas would throw his life on the line and destroy anything that threatened to harm her heated Ayla's core even as she sat in a rolling frozen carriage.

Twyla was restless, trapped in such small confinements for hours on end. After futile attempts to settle her, Ayla decided they both needed some fresh air.

She knocked on the wooden wall of the wagon and it reared off to the left–allowing those behind to continue on–and came to a stop.

A footman opened the creaking hinged door and offered a polite hand to Ayla who graciously accepted as she descended the frozen steps. She turned around to pick up Twyla from the open frame and set her on the ground, not before she flew her around in the air as if she were a pegasus, making whooshing and cheering noises.

Twyla giggled profusely and clawed at Ayla's cloak once on the floor for a second flight. And so, like a good and fair governess, she did.

Phena and Hensella barely registered their departure from the bench opposite, in a dozy state after such a late night prior.

Ayla scooped the infant up and strapped her to her hip. She walked slightly off the worn and muddy path–away from risk of Twyla being trampled before letting her toddle as far as her little legs could carry her.

Ayla herded her back towards the group now and again when she strayed too far, but mostly let her explore on her own.

Neither girl had ever seen a landscape like Camelleah before. Everything was new and demanded analysis: the frost covered blades of grass, foreign species of flora that were suited to the freezing temperatures, even the animals. They spotted a couple of dusty-coloured hares hopping around the open plain. They froze as they beheld the toddler running in their direction, before chasing the poor things down into their burrows.

As the winter sun fell from the sky, bleeding into magical swirls of pinks and orange, the company stopped and began to set up camp for the night.

Just as they had learned on their journey northward, there was a long stretch of land over the borderlands between Rydon and the next Lord's keep.

Twyla had run off all her cabin fever but now a hungry tummy had her whinging for another reason. So, Ayla was glad to smell food being prepared as they made their way back through the encampment. With one hand holding the princess' they wound through the crowd busy pitching tents, unloading carts or seeing to the cavalry horses.

Ayla had to admit the sight of the latter made her heart twinge with pain. The fact that Olive wasn't returning to Balcarras with her was just another on the list of reasons she did not wish to go back. She hadn't forgiven Atlas for that yet. She knew it wasn't entirely rational to blame him for Ivelle's actions, but she couldn't help the suspicion that Atlas had influence over the incident.

In a few months she would take a handful of days leave to travel to the border and collect him from the address the barmaid had scribbled on a piece of parchment before their departure from the Rat and Mouse.

When they reached the three tents erected for the royals, Ayla asked a posted guard which was for Twyla.

When he lifted the flap to the canopy to his left, she thanked him and led the princess inside. Phena and Hensella rose from a plush bench as they entered and offered to take over. Ayla thanked them for the offer but dismissed them to eat and relax. The girls left the tent in favour of their own, but not before eating something hot and smokey and shamelessly flirting with several members of the royal guard.

Ayla popped her head out of the tent flap to request the guard find a page to fetch hot water for the princess.

Twyla was filthy after an afternoon of running around the northern plains and she worried she would catch a chill if she stayed in her muddy linens any longer. She had been piled up with layers of furs, but the chill had seeped through to her skin.

Exhausted, Twyla picked at her food, eyes half lidded and chewing slow and sluggish. Hanging a bath sheet by the fire so it was nice and toasty after the princess' bath, Ayla left Maggie nearby to dry off her stuffed torso.

The governess did everything in her power to keep the girl awake until the bath was ready, bursting into song now and again, spontaneous tickle attacks, or tearing up bread between her teeth like a ferocious beast.

Once in the tiny tub–more of a cauldron really–Ayla scrubbed her softly with a porous sponge. She dropped some of her lavender oils in the water, an attempt to replace the earthy smell clutching at her skin. It worked like a dream, but the aromatherapeutic qualities of the substance were making the princess' eyes drooped lower and heavier.

"Twyla," Ayla soothed and distracted from the allure of sleep, "If you had a pegasus, what would you name it?"

That wasn't how it worked, Ayla recognised. The ten mighty beasts had held the same names longer than Balcarras had stood. But for the sake of the game, it was innocent to ask.

The girl looked at Ayla then at the steaming, oily surface of the water as she thought about her answer. Then it came to her all of a sudden and she cried out "Atee!" followed by a string of giggles, which Ayla matched with her own.

"Atee? Well, we need to let him know he holds such an honour."

"Ayla," Twyla said, "can I have a stowy?"

"A *story*?" Ayla whispered back. She tapped her chin dramatically while she pretended to think of one. Though she always settled on Twyla's favourite.

"Once upon a time, there was a little bumblebee, who was sweeter than honey. Her mummy was the *Queen Bee* and one day she might be queen after her. So, her mother taught her to treat everyone with the kindness in her heart. She told her little bumblebee to share her toys with the other bees. To learn how to make honey, even if the others were willing to make it for her. To always tell the truth, and never lie." Ayla shook her head and widened her eyes to emphasise the point.

The warm water was making Twyla's eyes heavy as she listened intently.

"Some nasty bees were unkind to the little bumblebee, even though she was nice to them. But the little bumblebee had made lots and lots of friends with her goodwill, and they stood up for her when she needed them. And together they pushed the nasty bees out of the hive, which made it a happy place to live for everyone."

The earth tremoured and Ayla's face paled at what she'd come to understand was Ivelle and Yvie landing close. Atlas and Niamh had returned to camp.

Swallowing the lump in her throat, Ayla continued to wash away the grime of the day.

Ayla lifted Twyla out the tub and wrapped her in the warm bath sheets, careful not to get her dirty with her own mucky dress. After she tucked the little princess into her bed and kissed her goodnight, she left her sleeping to the clattering sound of the camp. She nodded politely to the who stood guard at the door as she walked away.

Entering Niamh's tent, Ayla found both her and the prince finishing dinner inside. Her heart stumbled as she acknowledged the latter.

"Oh, I'm sorry, I didn't mean to interrupt." she announced, already backing out the way she came.

"Nonsense," Niamh glowed. She always felt better after a ride with Yvie. "Have you eaten? Come, join us." she continued.

Atlas said nothing but his stare did not break from Ayla, even when he took a long sip from his goblet. Eyes twinkling.

Ayla accepted the invitation to sit. Niamh's tent was much like her daughters, only slightly larger. Candles ignited the room in a soft warm glow. The floor was layered in straw then covered in rugs and plush pillows.

The prince and princess sat at a small, round, wooden table, one that Ayla found herself picking at the edges of as soon as she sat down.

"Did you have a nice afternoon?" Ayla said, breaking the silence. She suddenly felt the urge for wine.

As if sensing her thoughts, Atlas emptied what was left of the pitcher into his cup and slid it over. She hesitated but accepted. Bringing the silver chalice to her lips.

Thinking only if the rim would taste of him.

She looked to Niamh for the answer, but the princess seemed to have forgotten the question. "Yes, we did," Atlas answered on behalf of both of them. "You come from a very beautiful place, Ayla."

The word *beautiful* sent a shiver down her spine, recalling how he had used the word to praise her the previous night.

"I don't come from here. Not really…" she said softly "And as beautiful as it is, I'm not sure I could ever call it home."

"Why not?" he pressed.

She weighed her words. "I–" Ayla was cut off by Niamh standing abruptly, a shade paler than she was before.

"I'm not feeling well, I think I'm going to sleep." the princess decreed.

Atlas rose as quickly as she did, rounding the table and taking Niamh's arm in his hand. His other hand rose to her cheek, inspecting her face. "Are you alright? Do you need anything?" he asked.

Niamh shook her head, but her eyes were glazed and Ayla wasn't sure she was actually listening to his words.

He walked her to the side of her bed and pulled back the furs. He helped her remove the outer layer of her dress so she could sleep more comfortably, and Ayla felt the urge to turn away. This display of affection seemed too intimate for prying eyes. He covered Niamh in several warm layers of bedding before smoothing over her face.

"Do you want me to stay with you?" he asked. She only shook her head again, but this time wore a soft smile.

As he walked away from her, Niamh's eyes drifted to Ayla's and her smile grew wider before she gave her a wink.

A wink.

If Ayla wasn't gawking before, Mother knew she was now.

Atlas grabbed Ayla's hand on the way out of the tent and didn't let it go until they were inside his own. Only then did he snake it around her waist and press her up against the central post of the tent.

Ayla was understandably caught off guard by the act, and it must've shown in her eyes. He let out a low chuckle at the sight. Moving slowly towards her face, Atlas gave her the world's most tender kiss. Slow, deep, *loving.*

"I've been waiting all day to do that," he grumbled against her cheek, nipping along her jaw.

"Then what took you so long getting back here?" she jested.

"That... *mess*, required extra attention." he stiffened.

"Are you alright?" Ayla's heart flooded with worry, even knowing he was back here in one piece.

"I am now," he echoed her words from last night to her with a grin.

"Is Niamh going to be alright? She seemed so happy tonight and then suddenly–" Atlas cut her off with a grunt, pulling his head away but not his body, that remained pressed against hers. His heat seeped through their clothes.

"I have a sneaking suspicion that Niamh knows exactly what she was doing, putting on a little show…" he said casually. Ayla's brows pressed, unsure of what he was insinuating. He answered her question before she could pose it. "She wanted to remove herself from our company, so we could be alone."

Ayla's mouth gaped like a fish, before she choked out, "Why would she do that?"

He gave her another smile, softer than before, as he raked fingers through her dark brown locks. "Niamh has always thought that… you and I would end up together. I think she knew how I felt about you even before I did. Despite my protests over the years, she never believed my denial."

The words hit Ayla like a ton of bricks. *First her mother and now Niamh.* Thian's company and affection had occupied her mind so thoroughly, she hadn't stopped to look at anything else in her life. Blinded by a promise she'd made when she was ten. The ignorant bliss she lived in, was being shattered every day away from him.

Atlas' face darkened and his brows pressed. He dropped her gaze and worked his jaw. *Whatever he was about to say he really didn't want to say it.*

"You can't marry Thian," he stated, low and pained. "Anyone else, Ayla. Just not him. I can't stand by and watch him hurt you. I don't want to have to kill my brother…"

Ayla swallowed, the thought of Atlas slaughtering Thian for her was significantly less attractive than the hypothetical stranger she had imagined. She tipped her chin back to meet his gaze.

"Anyone else?" she whispered.

He ground his teeth so hard they must've cracked. He nodded. "I won't behave the way I did yesterday. There are plenty of suitable matches for you besides that piggish northman. You will have the crown's support, and I will control Thian–" she cut him off with a kiss.

She wanted to devour him whole. He thought, *even now,* that she didn't want him. That *he* was the problem.

When she pulled back for air she asked, "And… if I want you? Can I, have you?"

His face was a concoction of shock, disbelief and hope.

"Ayla…" he started, and Ayla's tears gathered along her lashes as she steadied her heart for impending rejection. For him to laugh in her face and reveal the cruel game was over. That he didn't want her and would never be hers. "… you've always had me."

After a flush of relief, sunshine flooded her veins. A feeling of happiness she had never come close to feeling before. Her lungs opened so wide she didn't feel the need to breathe. A single tear fell to her cheek before being snatched up by Atlas' lips.

He ripped apart his doublet, snapping the fasteners without care. Baring his scars to her proudly. The act itself made Ayla weak. It was a declaration; *I give all myself to you.*

Chapter 38

Ayla moved slowly, never breaking his stare as she circled him. Until it was he who was pressed up against the post. She dropped the thick winter cloak off her shoulders and his jaw worked with pleasure as he noted the bruises that dotted her skin. *His* bruises. Made with his tongue and his teeth.

Atlas loathed his brother for his display of possessiveness against Ayla over the years, but in this moment, he found himself a hypocrite. For all he wanted was this girl in front of him to belong to him, forever. To slay any man that dared touch her, protect her from the many evils of this world.

She unhooked the remaining fasteners of his doublet, latch by latch at a wicked pace. When he shrugged it off his arm, she made quick work tugging his linen undershirt over his head.

She moved impossibly close, staring at his eager lips but keeping her own an inch away from satisfaction as she ran a hand down the plain of his torso. Lower and lower until she met with his waistband. She slipped a mere fingertip between flesh and fabric, running it side to side until he understood her request and laced his trousers.

Her gaze slid from his mouth to his eyes as she slid her dainty hand down the opening, watching his pupil swallow the icy blues of his iris'.

Hard as he tried, he couldn't keep the groan that escaped his throat. Ayla's lips parted in wanton desire at how hard and ready his silky flesh was. And *fuck* he was ready.

He hadn't lain with a woman since Ayla's arrival back in Balcarras. Every time he saw her, she drove him crazy. He thought about her divine form as he took himself in hand every now and again just to release the built up want for her. *Only* for her. He had thought about those damned nipples ever since he saw them pebble beneath her silk chemise many weeks ago. And when he'd touched her after the bonfires. *Stars above.*

Ayla removed her hand and peeled away an inch, only to lower herself to her knees while keeping her eyes locked on his. She hooked the banded top of his leathers and pulled down to his mid-thigh. She sat back on her heels momentarily and swallowed, salivating at the sight of his cock jutting out, ready to take her.

Keeping him locked in a sultry stare, she placed her icy hands on his hips and moved her head to one side of his length. She licked up the left side in a painfully slow stroke. His needy cock twitched in response. She moved her head to the right side and showed it the same affection with her tongue.

He hissed a breath and clenched his hands.

Ayla broke her glare to look before her as she took his head in mouth, moaning at the salty beads already forming at the tip. She kept him shallow as she swirled her tongue over the end, sucking like it was the best tasting rock sweetie she had ever tasted.

"*Fuck*, Ayla." he groaned. "Have you done this before?"

She pulled him free and kissed his swollen head before the tiniest of nods.

A bolt of carnal jealousy shot through him. He leashed his emotions.

"Not with him though." Ayla whispered.

As much as Atlas wanted to look at the goddess kneeling before him, overcome with pleasure his head was forced back against the wooden pillar. So, all he could do was watch her through his bottom lashes. "Please don't stop."

Relief washed over her face before she moved him deeper into her mouth. Her long, white-tipped nails dug crescents into his hips. He welcomed her marks.

Ayla pulled all the way back to the tip and the threat of leaving her hot wet mouth caused Atlas to snap. He snatched her hair with his hand and pushed himself deeper down her throat. She moaned in surprise, screwing her eyes as she tried desperately not to gag on his length. She was a vision of beauty and the sounds she made were angelic.

Faster and faster, he pushed and pulled her head. Faster and harder his pants heaved from his lungs. Both sweet and filthy words of encouragement dripped off his tongue, Ayla's name front and centre in most of them.

Atlas watched in awe as she slipped hand down her dress to relieve her own pleasure.

It tipped him towards the edge, and he fisted her hair to the point of pain as the muscles in his legs and torso clenched. He came with a groan, as cum trickled down Ayla's throat. She kept going though, sucking him dry until he had nothing left to give. When his body slumped and his hands released her hair in favour of cupping her face, she released him with a sensual pop.

He guided her back up to standing and pressed his forehead against hers. He beheld her, the crazed hunger glinting in her eyes, a mixture of sweat, saliva and seed glistening her lips. Like a man unhinged he grunted and licked it all up before tasting himself on her tongue.

He repositioned her, so the back of her knees were flush against his bed. Guiding her back so she lay before him, he planned on repaying her threefold for the bliss she had just blessed him with.

Ayla's eyes blazed with desire.

Atlas didn't have the patience to remove the entirety of her dress. Instead, he raked the skirts up from her ankles all the way to her hips in desperation. He got to his knees, tugging her down to the edge of the bed so he would have the best access possible to her.

The smell of her drove him crazy. Yes, she was always coated in lovely lavender and eucalyptus, but something about the scent of her skin… a smell he could not articulate or recreate. It was so perfectly *her,* and he wanted to drown in it until the end of time.

Mumbling sweet nothings against her thigh, Ayla released a breathy giggle. Her giggles morphed into subtle moans as he worked his way higher, and higher and–

Ayla shot upright.

"What's wro–"

"Shh!" she snapped in a whisper.

Atlas removed his head from her skirts with a displeased grunt. But when he beheld her face–full of panic and unease–that displeasure transformed into a murderous fear.

"Crying…" she said. Eyes wide but voice still no louder than a mouse.

Atlas brows' pressed as he tried to hear this phantom crying, but he couldn't. There were bustling sounds of the camp, but no crying.

Then Ayla jumped off the bed, nearly kneeing him in the face on her way down "No, *screaming…* something's wrong with Twyla." She ran out the tent not bothering with her cloak.

Atlas fumbled to piece himself back together, breaking into a run as he watched Ayla charging full speed into the little princess' tent.

His own fear snapped into vengeance at the sight of no guards posted outside her canopy. If anyone or anything threatened to harm that little girl, there wouldn't even be bones left. Just the ash of them and everything they ever loved.

He caught up with Ayla inside the tent. Nothing. No one. No Twyla, or Hensella or Phena. No royal guard. Just Ayla, frantic and hysterical as she tossed up the pillows and rugs on the floor, as the princess was hiding under there.

Atlas marched over to her and grabbed her hand, interlacing their fingers to hold her as tight as he could. He dragged them out of the tent and bellowed orders and accusations to several men of the royal guard who looked aghast at the disappearance of the princess. They gawked at one another like they didn't remember whose turn it was to take watch.

He would deal with their ineptitude later.

For now, they ran to Niamh's tent, Ayla stumbling over her own feet as she tried to keep up. Atlas burst through the double layered flap. His heart bottomed out as he found the second tent also empty. No sleeping princess in sight.

His blood iced over at the massive gash sliced through the back of the canopy blowing in the wind. There was no matching sign of intrusion in Twyla's tent, though it was highly likely the assailants brought the princess and her two governesses into Niamh's make-shift chamber before departing with all four.

Ayla was sobbing and shouting at him, but he heard nothing over the ringing in his ears. He walked over to the slashed fabric and pushed through. Two guardsmen that were posted at the rear lay with slit throats.

He pushed Ayla back inside as she tried to join him, before she saw such horror. They exited the front of the tent once more and he bellowed orders to a now frantic encampment. He commanded several high-ranking men to prepare for a search.

Whoever was behind this, they had just stolen two princesses.

It was an act of war.

Atlas retook Ayla's hand and pulled her toward the outskirts of the camp.

"Where are we going?" she asked, clinging to his arm with her free hand.

"We'll get a better view from above." He didn't even look at her as his face returned to that familiar stone.

Unreadable except for a promise of death.

Chapter 39

T he mounting of Ivelle was no less nerve-wracking the second time than it had been the first. The high anxiety coursing through Ayla's veins mixed with that deep set fear of the creature before her, resulted in full body tremors of unease.

After saddling, some of that fear subsided into something else. Power. To stand before a beast of such might was menacing. To *mount* one was a privilege. A gift.

Atlas sat in front of Ayla this time. He needed better access to control. They shot through the sky with perilous purpose. Unlike their first flight that was purely for pleasure, each thunderous beat of Ivelle's wings was harder, each turn faster.

The sting of the icy wind against their faces was brutal.

Ayla's hands clung around his torso from behind. An anchor of sanity and hopefully a slight comfort to the red spiraling of his mind.

The trail from camp was deep and clear. Multiple assailants, moving in a disorganised hoard. No stealth or attempt to hide their numbers was apparent. Even in the hour of the owl as the night blanketed the land in darkness, the moon shone bright over their crime, guiding the way to justice. *Thank Arianrhod.*

After some time, the line of trees thickened into a dense evergreen forest and there was no sign of tracks from above. They circled back to the mouth of the woods and descended from flight into a rampant gallop. The company was making haste, but their cavalry could not match the speed of Ivelle, so it would take them some time catching up. Atlas clearly had no plan on waiting.

The thick canopy of the woods blocked out most of the light provided by the moon. Soon, at the speed of Ivelle, any tracks were blurred together in the darkness.

"Atlas I can't see their trail!" Ayla shouted with concern, Ivelle's rough pace causing her voice to pitch on every second syllable.

"Atlas," she tried again. Her words were every bit a question as they were a statement.

He let out a frustrated growl and stopped Ivelle's stampede. The beast reared with protest before she turned and made for the path from which they came, tucking her wings neatly. The pair cast their eyes down as they cantered at a much slower pace, seeing nothing but Ivelle's trail of hooves much larger than that of a horse.

Two miles they had ridden in the wrong direction. The kidnappers had made a turn west on horseback in a thick section of brush, confusing tracking.

Not so incompetent then.

Ayla and Atlas made to start west, until a fleeting flicker of light was seen in the distance. They waited until the company arrived to lead them the right way in the dead of night. Every passing second was torment. Any kidnapping was a race against time, and the more time separated was distance between them and the princesses. A greater possibility of harm becoming them.

A diminishing chance of finding them.

The heat radiating off Atlas was carnal. Not the kind Ayla experienced earlier, when she'd knelt before him. That was a pleasure. This was rage. Pure and unbridled, it seeped from his skin so freely Ayla was surprised he hadn't combusted into flames.

She gripped him harder, a futile attempt at comfort. Closer and closer the cavalry raced. Not fast enough.

"We *will* find them, Atlas" she whispered into his back. He said nothing in reply, though his ragged breaths smoothed out ever so slightly.

The general arrived first, flanked by two soldiers of similar speed.

"How many?" Atlas asked

"Thirty-two," The general replied. "The rest; armed and alert, securing the camp in case of another attack."

Ayla bit back a reply that the only thing worth taking was already gone as Atlas nudged Ivelle into a canter.

For hours they followed the tracks west at a cruel pace to maintain sight of the trail. When daybreak came and the sky bled from black to blue, with more visibility they increased their speed once more.

Ivelle bucked and whined to a stop.

The trails forked.

"Four sets, on either side," the general puffed out.

They had more than enough men to split the party and investigate each route, but choosing the side to veer seemed to be tearing Atlas apart. Ayla could see the conflict in his eyes. *He* wanted to be the one to find them. It was a simple choice, yet so much at stake. It was not a puzzle he could solve. No amount of intellect could inform the decision. It was a gamble.

"We will go right," Ayla informed the general. A decision had to be made.

The general flicked his eyes to his prince who did not reject the decision and shouted back to his platoon. A gust of wind threatened to push Ayla off Ivelle as seventeen soldiers on horseback pelted past.

"Thank you," Atlas whispered back to her. Barely audible over the stampede of hooves beside them, but she squeezed him back in acknowledgement.

Atlas snapped out of his daze and pushed on to the right.

Less than half a mile later Ivelle's pinna twitch through her run.

"Stop!" Atlas shouted, and the soldiers complied.

Ayla listened. Through the morning chirp of starlings, they all listened.

Crying.

One nudge and Ivelle took off at full pace, leaving the rest of their party still comprehending her departure. It grew louder and clearer. A cry of pain. Cutting in and out with screams of protest. It was female. Luckily not that of a child, but it had every chance of being Niamh and they grew closer and closer.

Ayla felt sick.

The pair stopped at a ditch in the road. Ayla hesitated before they dismounted in utter shock of what she saw before her.

Hensella was slumped on a soggy bankside, throat slashed deep enough to see bone. Her blood pooled around her head. Her eyes screamed of fear, frozen forever in time. Ayla tried not to throw up at such a horrific sight.

She stumbled around the body, leaving a wide berth between herself and it, toward the origin of the noise.

Phena was leaning against the roots of a tree, paler than the dead, with a bloody dagger protruding out of her waist. She had lost so much blood, and was in so much pain, she didn't even notice their approach. It was only when Ayla was within a couple of feet that her vision lifted to see her.

"No!" Phena wailed, cut off by her pain "West," she breathed out, her voice barely clinging to the words. "They went west."

Ayla swallowed a lump in her throat, an unjust feeling of guilt building.

"Are there any more here?" Atlas asked sternly, looking all around to check for lingering attackers.

Phena shook her head lightly, "Not since daybreak."

It was pure coincidence that it was Hensella and Phena watching the princess at the time of her kidnapping, and not Ayla. By all means it should be her either lying dead in a ditch, or halfway there with a blade in her belly.

"Stay with her." Atlas said, swinging back up on Ivelle. "Take her back to camp, I will go after them"

"Atlas–"

"*Ayla*. Do you trust me?"

She worked through the tightness in her chest. "Always."

She blinked away her tears. He gave her a nod and took off like a bolt of lightning.

"Ayla…" her stare was brought back to the girl on the ground who clutched her hands. "I can't get it out…" she broke into a sob, but every cry shook her body and twisted the blade further into cut up flesh.

"Shhh, it's ok, help is coming," Ayla wanted pressure around the wound, but any movement would slice deeper. "A few minutes and they'll be here." She looked over her shoulder expectantly for the soldiers to catch up.

"Ayla please, I need it out. It–it's the one they…" she couldn't finish her sentence as her eyes fell to her dead friend laying in the mud. Ayla grimaced at what was being asked of her. She tried to rationalise it in her head. Cause the girl a moment of pain, so she may have a chance to live. Then she could apply pressure to the wound and relieve her of Hensella's murder weapon lodged in her gut.

"Alright," she whispered. Her hands drifted to the weapon, and she tried to cease their shaking. She slowly gripped the handle and even the slightest of movement had Phena screaming and cursing in her native tongue.

This was not a gentle task and could be done in no way that wouldn't cause suffering. The only thing she could offer the girl is get it over quickly.

Ayla pulled it free fast, screaming out with Phena as she did. The feel of cutting out flesh was disgusting, even if it was drawing the blade and not inserting it. The knife was thick, and so too was the gash.

Blood bubbled up and poured out at a horrifying rate, and Ayla was momentarily stunned before she grabbed the girl's skirts and pushed down on the wound. Phena screamed bloody murder, and All Ayla could do was hush her and assure her help was on the way. She checked again over her shoulder, craning her neck from an awkward position.

Still nothing.

When she swung back toward the patient, her eyes were half lidded and fading fast.

"No, no, no, Phena? Phena, I need you to stay awake with me. Can you talk to me?"

The girl opened her mouth, but it was dry and cracking on the skin, no words eluded. Instead, her heavy eyes widened for a moment and her grip on Ayla's arm spiked.

Ayla recognised the look on her face. Fear.

But what was she–
Everything went black.

Chapter 40

M ind your footing." Atlas shouted back to his men as they walked along a crumbling ridge of the mountain. They'd ridden at such a speed that they arrived at the convergence of the trails before the secondary group.

Tracks ran west until they met one of many mountain passes in Camelleah. The group were several thousand feet above sea level now, and while the threat of a slip was less consequential to a mare with wings, Atlas only had seventeen men. He'd hate to lose one to something as meek as falling off the face of a mountain.

He trained his eyes on the landscape around them. Heads popped out of the porous mouths of the face. The mountains had been carved out over the centuries into cavernous mazes, they ran right down to the root–where mines pulled precious metals and gems out of the ground.

In the harsh climate of Camelleah, over time entire villages had moved into the labyrinths of rock. Whenever they passed the hovel-like doors, any natives scurried inside.

The tracks stopped on a twenty-stride ledge covered in heather. The spongy flora masked precise footings of the abductors, but the area was trodden enough to suggest they had indeed stopped here. The soldiers dismounted and searched for an opening.

"General!" one of the soldiers called. The rest flooded to the crack of stone at which he stood. It was so narrow, every man turned adjacent to shuffle through the slit. It tapered, and the valley became smaller and smaller the deeper in they tread.

Atlas was suddenly glad for his lack of breastplate for he was sure it would catch. He heard several men curse behind him before shuffling back the way they came–too large to fit.

In the end only four fit through the sliver of stone.

Atlas, the general, and the two soldiers who had caught up with Ivelle the quickest. *The most competent among them,* Atlas concluded. It wasn't many, but he planned on tearing down this whole summit rock by rock if that was what it took, help or no.

"That's it?" the general echoed along the pass

"Yes sir," someone replied with shame underlying his voice. Every man at the camp had failed their primary task of ensuring the safety of the princesses. Their punishment for such a cock-up could range from expulsion of position to execution– depending on the outcome of this mission, that is.

It was more personal than that though, Atlas realised. These men would gladly lay their life down for the princesses they protected. Niamh and Twyla's sweet nature shone brightly, evident to every man who toured with them. Their innocence was pure and deserved to be safeguarded.

"On your command, Your Highness." The general drew his short sword and nodded toward the black chasm behind them. Atlas in turn drew his sapphire-hilted dagger from his coat and entered the abyss.

They walked in darkness for some time. Trailing his free hand along the walls, Atlas tried to feel a sense of direction. There was a slight slope as well as veer to the left as they walked on.

Eventually a faint light could be seen in the horizon. Small and sparkling, it guided them as would a star in the night's pitch sky.

It was eerily quiet in the belly of the mountain. Nothing but their breaths to be heard.

"What are your names?" Atlas asked, an effort to distract their minds from the chaos of darkness that could spin the imagination off its axis.

"Gunnar, your highness of house Lerinson." the general offered.

"Drury Orman." his second said after.

"Soren White." the farthest man added.

"An honour to meet you gentlemen." Atlas declared as they closed in on the burning flame. The torch was mounted on the wall next to a smooth stone door on iron hinges.

Atlas lifted his hand to the surface.

"Please, Your Highness, allow me." Gunnar offered.

"No need." Atlas replied calmly and pushed open the door. Its weight was immense, but the oiled hinges provided a smooth glide as it peeled away from the frame.

Gunnar and Drury lifted their swords with lethal concentration, while Soren guarded their backs, in case of attack from behind.

A frenzied gust of wind pushed against them as the door opened, as if they had just opened the mouth of the mountain and it inhaled for the first time in centuries.

They all froze, ears perked. No noise was detectable.

Beyond the unsealed door was another lit torch, this one illuminating a spiral staircase. Unlike those built in Balcarras castle that were laid brick by brick, these stairs were carved from the inside out.

Natural edges and earthy pores cascading all the way down.

Gunnar unhitched the torch at the top to carry it down with them.

Once again Atlas took the lead on their descent. He counted each step. Though they varied in size and depth, around one hundred and fifty down, his legs seemed to have forgotten the action. *Just one step in front of the other,* he told his mind. But his legs wobbled and hesitated with every move.

The stairway was narrow, the men could not outstretch both arms before hitting the walls, and the roof ghosted just above their heads.

The prince warmed the pommel in his hand. Rotated his wrist. Rolled his shoulder.

Atlas had seen death before. Had been at the hands of it as well as the butcher who bestowed it. Though for all his time in the army, he was so far removed from the risk of those he cared for. Anything that happened in those years of his training and service was a bubble in space and time. Any lives lived and lost in that bubble were without consequence once he returned home. Now two of the people he cared most for in this world been ripped from their slumber and stolen in the night.

By stair two hundred and seventy-four, Atlas paused.

He heard something. A roguish laugh echoed from below followed by muttering of others, amusement dripping off their tongues. It was loud enough to echo off the walls, suggesting that at the bottom of the stairs was an open, cavernous space. The spiral steps were tightly bound, and though they were close, he had no idea how many rotations they would make before they reached the end.

He signaled to Gunnar to put the torch down. There was still no light lining the spiral and if the mercenaries were to see it pouring out the exit, they would lose the element of surprise. Gunnar did as instructed, placing the steel on a step behind him. It kissed the ground softly and slowly, but the caves betrayed them, and the sound rung out.

Silence smothered the air from below. The quartered stilled.

A figure burst into view around the coil, roaring as he slashed his blade at Atlas, who met it with his own, driving it into the wall beside them. The blade clamoured to the ground before Atlas kicked the adversary in the chest. The bearded man let out a groan as he tumbled back into several other men down the opening of the stairs.

Atlas and his men used this moment to push forward into the open cavern. He sliced each of the worms flailing at the bottom of the steps with fatal precision across the throat, just as they had done to Hensella.

By the time he leaped over their squirming corpses, he was being charged at by half a dozen men and one woman. They came at him all at once, no plan of attack or strategy in nature. Atlas took on the first two that came close enough, the others were met with swords of their own from Gunnar, Soren and Drury.

Atlas tossed his favourite blade into his left hand while he drew his short sword with his right.

A man swung an axe sidelong which Atlas narrowly sidestepped. Before he had time to register, a woman with two hand blades was screaming bloody murder as she slashed them furiously. Her grip and footwork was of great skill, her blades were short and light which gave her speed. But Atlas' short sword met her gut from three paces away. Even then, she thrashed and waved her own at him like a wild animal. He pulled his blade out the side of her, leaving ropes of several important looking organs tumbling out of her.

He felt the air still before a swoosh of the axe came very close to clearing off his head. The weapon was large and fearsome, but heavy and tiring to its bearer. The man of golden hair was heaving breaths of rage, and his tired form slowed in the hoisting of the blade. He lifted it high over his head, and Atlas struck like a viper, stabbing him in the side, mere inches from where Phena was assaulted.

The blonde dropped the weight of the axe which landed behind him and gasped like a child at the steel in his side. Atlas bared his teeth as he withdrew it with force, and the man collapsed to his knees in a cry. The Prince of the Continent watched him for a beat, enjoying the sight of him in the same pain he bestowed upon others, before raising his short sword, and taking off his head, with cruel ease.

Atlas turned his attention to his comrades, who were finishing up their own messes. He stepped forward to aid but stopped short. These soldiers were in no need of assistance. Soren moved with feline speed, rounding up his assailants and skewering two of them at once. Gunnar took every swing of a man's sword and batted it away with his own like it was a toy. Drury disarmed a large man and proceeded to kill him with his own weapon.

When the brawl was reduced to heavy breathing of the four soldiers, they took in their surroundings. It was a large, cavernous hall, with dozens of small dark tunnels sprouting off it like veins, each one indistinguishable from the next.

Time was pressing against them and Atlas was running out of patience.

A gurgling splutter sounded from behind him, and the prince turned to find the woman inching away, her innards gathered in her arms.

Atlas walked over casually and lifted her by the collar, and her tired limbs dropped her spilling flesh to the ground with a splat.

"Where are they?" he asked with a menacing coldness.

The woman's eyes flared with fear. Her tongue worked to say something, but all that came out was a spit directed at Atlas followed by a crimson grin. She only had moments in this life left and Atlas planned on making them count. He slapped her harshly across the face.

"Where?" he screamed.

She looked shocked at his outburst, as if he hadn't just gutted her like a fish moments prior. He raised his hand again and something in her eyes broke, gave up on whatever hostility she held, whatever self-serving pride kept her from telling.

With a shaking finger she lifted her right arm to the side, without even looking, pointing in the direction of one of the tunnels. Atlas didn't look away as he redrew his sapphire dagger and pushed into her neck. Once the light in her eyes faded into the next world, he withdrew and dropped her without care.

He didn't bother cleaning the blood off the steel. Something told him it wasn't finished dirtying today. He made for the tunnel indicated.

"Your Highness, what if she lied?" Soren asked.

"She didn't." Atlas answered, still stalking toward the darkness.

"How do you know?" the boy persisted.

Atlas wrenched free a torch on the wall before entering the chasm, "Because she had nothing left to lose."

The cold of Camelleah did not seem to penetrate the mines of the mountains. Even though they were seemingly frozen solid. The life that bloomed within them, the torches and furnaces and warm bustling bodies were insulated in the husk of earth and stone.

Atlas hadn't bothered fetching his cloak when he and Ayla left the encampment, and while his limbs had frozen stiff in the cold ride to the mountains, it hardly seemed an important thing to register when so much was at stake. It was only now that he registered feeling in his toes as they wiggled in his boots that he realised he was thawing. The bustle in the hall had helped get the blood pumping, but as they descended deeper into the belly of the beast, they were met with a warming heat.

They passed several natives in the labyrinth, all unarmed and alarmed to see the prince and his men in their confines. None of them screamed for help, or to alarm the kidnappers. Neither did they attack. Most scuttled back into their holes, looking as if they just escaped a wild animal on the prowl. A couple held their ground, though looked submissive enough that Gunnar asked them where the princesses were.

Atlas did not suspect these residents had anything to do with the abductions. They were poor people, working to survive in the mines. Covered in soot and rubble, their skin as pale as the moon. He wondered if they ever saw sunlight at all. Most seemed malnourished and exhausted.

Atlas jolted to a stop. Caught off guard by what he saw before him. A man, weathered and worn from life in the mines, sat on a stump, sharpening a pickaxe.

Atlas recognised his eyes instantly. Ayla's eyes. Replicas of her own. The *sire* of her own. Big brown eyes with a molten centre. Dark lashes that looked dipped in coal.

At first, Atlas had to swallow a feeling of pity for Heath, wasting away here beneath the earth all these years. But then he reminded himself that this was a self-inflicted fall from grace. The realisation quickly soured into a simmering anger. *He left Ayla, for* this?

A sudden urge to beat his face until his skull caved overwhelmed rational thought. He could still remember the sounds of Ayla's crying flooding the castle halls after he abandoned her.

That terrible sound had chipped away at Atlas' heart. Nothing he could've said or done would've eased her pain. She deserved her father to be there for her during their shared time of grief.

No, she deserved better *than him.*

Atlas stifled his rage, and his eyes peeled off the man and back to their path–their purpose. *May he rot down here forever. Gods know he deserves much worse.*

The few mercenaries they came across stuck out like sore thumbs. Dressed in fine winter leathers lined with furs for the outside world unlike the rags of the villages inside. Their skin was burnished with the winter sun, unlike the ghostly residents. Their–*likely stolen*–weaponry clanked obnoxiously as they walked, giving them away before they even came into sight. One by one they were slain.

Atlas and his men passed the dungeons. The smell of rot and faeces permeated the space. There were at least two corpses in the farthest cell. Nothing but skin and bone left of them. They were likely forgotten and starved to death in this dark miserable place. Atlas wondered how far their screams for help must've travelled through these echoing tunnels. How many families were made to listen to them beg for mercy, forgiveness for whatever crimes they had committed.

To both Atlas' relief and surprise, neither of the princesses were being held in the cells. That relief was quickly drowned by fear for what could be worse than this.

They passed the dungeons and into the working heart of the mines. Carts on tracks were loaded with precious gems. The jewels sparkling even when covered in dirt

They were dazzling emeralds.

Distant crying snapped the four out of their shimmering trance and into a fit of panic. The crying was young and familiar–Twyla. A happy child who very rarely shed tears. When she did, it was gut wrenching.

There was a snapping male voice which quieted the child. Followed by a succession of laughter.

The pounding of Atlas' heart both blinded his senses and narrowed his focus. They could've been running the wrong way–the echoes made it hard to establish an epicentre of sound. But Atlas trusted his heart and his gut, and whichever gods were listening to guide him to them.

The walls began to change around them from less organic and more intentional carvings. First the walls, then the doors, then the floor–polished tile instead of raw rock.

They were in a residential quarter of the mountain. For the ruling family of the land and mines to reside in.

Refined gems of similar colour to those in the carts smothered the place. Encrusted into the walls, adorning the furniture, there were even lazy bowls spilling over with them. Like they had more wealth than most knew what to do with–yet their people were dirt soaked and living in hovels.

Atlas slowed his pace to a stealthy prowl. The others followed suit. Soren stayed on their tail while Gunnar and Drury checked doors on either side of the hall as they moved as a unit towards the noise.

They walked through the door to a large office with such casualty, one would think they owned the place.

Swallowing the urge to set the whole mountain ablaze, Atlas beheld Twyla sitting on the lap of a mammoth man behind a mahogany desk. A mosaic of emeralds coated its surface, and the beast ran his fat fingers over every bump and divot.

"Well, well. Looks as if we have more guests' boys."

Atlas trained his gaze on the princess who's eyes were red and face soaked with tears, a visible shudder every now and again as she tried to keep her sobs at bay.

"Has anyone given you the tour yet?" the stranger quipped and his men snorted various laughs to his poor attempt at humour. They wore carefree smiles, but their white knuckles over weapons spoke clearly.

It was only when Atlas took in the men at the back of the room that he noticed what was bunched at their feet.

Niamh.

Bound and gagged with a sizable egg swelling on her forehead. Her hair spilled around her, and she seemed unconscious. If it weren't for the little girl in the hands of the man responsible, Atlas would slaughter every living thing before him without hesitation.

Instead, he stared at the man behind the desk with such iciness he could've sworn the brute shuddered.

"Aren't you going to ask us what we want? In exchange for their safe release?" The man had self-inflicted a death sentence yet he seemed without care. He spoke as if this were a game of cards, and he was holding all the aces.

"You're not getting anything except a throat full of steel."

"Careful now," he tutted, lifting a carving knife and setting it delicately on the emerald slab before him.

Off to the right of the door, Soren kept his eye fixed on Twyla, hoping to catch her attention subtly. When she cast a sniffly glance his way he stared at her with wide eyes that settled into a smile, before slowly running a hand over his face and closing his eyes manually. When he looked back at the girl, she blinked, unaware of whatever he was trying to convey.

Atlas moved deeper into the room and brought the eyes of the men with him. Soren pointed his finger to Twyla and repeated the action. She stayed still and Atlas thought the effort futile, but then she closed her tear swollen eyes, and kept them shut. *Good girl,* Atlas thought.

"You haven't even asked *why*, which only confirms you brought this upon yourself." the leviathan professed.

Atlas pressed on into the room, closer still to Niamh. He bent to her side and checked her pulse, to no objection of the men. "Not at all, I just simply don't care."

Atlas slung his blade into the torso of the man leering over Niamh, then slid her limp body over the polished floor to Drury. Meanwhile Gunnar charged the men lining the back wall. Atlas dodged a short sword and struck the man's jugular. His attention whipped to the desk at the other end of the room.

As he had lured the attention of the eyes in the room, Soren had moved like a shadow behind the desk chair and now held the very knife laid down by the brute to his neck. The soldier did not hesitate to cut deeper into the flesh every inch the man moved. *He had plenty of it, so getting to the artery would require some depth.*

Atlas' eyes watched as Drury removed Niamh's bindings and Gunnar, the largest of the bunch, lifted the unconscious princess into his arms for safekeeping. Drury moved to the door to watch for any late members to the party.

The prince then proceeded to walk around the table with ease, sheathing his steel on the way, and picked the little girl up off the beast and into his arms. He kissed the top of her head and whispered, "You can open your eyes now, little princess."

She pried them open and looked up at him before placing her head on his shoulder and wrapping her arms around his neck, with a grip threatening to never let him go.

Now that her gaze was averted, he nodded to his man holding the knife, it sliced through flesh, but the abductor squirmed like a worm on a hook, beads of sweat trailing over his forehead.

"You don't want to do that, Your Highness" he said, an ever-ugly smile drawn on his mug. Atlas looked bored but wasn't given a window to respond as the man continued, "I'm the only one who can show you where she is"

Atlas refused to let the confusion be evident on his face.

"We already found what you left behind of the governesses."

He smiled and something ugly bloomed in Atlas' subconscious, warning him what was about to be said. His eyes raked over his peripheral, the lavish office in which they stood, the emerald desk he sat behind, bloody emeralds everyw–

He stilled. His blood drained from his face before returning with a thunderous vengeance.

Fucking Goldsworth.

Chapter 41

The world spun. Dark and cold, it started out as mere shadows swirling in the sky. Then came colour–or lack thereof. A miserable pallet of browns, blacks, and greys.

Slowly they defined themselves against one another. Deep brown wood on all four sides. A dusty black floor covered in heavens knows what. And worn grey steel links that formed a snaking chain on the floor.

A shift of her feet ignited her sense of hearing next. Those steel links dragged across the floor with every shift of her feet.

It took a long while to piece together these clues to understand where Ayla was. The rancid smell only confused her deductions. She sat up when a forceful gag rose up her throat. The foul smell was strongest on the floor, soaked into every fiber of the planks, so instinctively she moved as far from it as she could get.

Ayla ignored the shackles binding her ankles as she clambered onto her knees. She rose up a little too fast and her legs gave out, trembling with a fear her mind had not caught up to.

Bracing herself on the walls in front of her–with wrists bound in rough rope that burned with every squirm–she managed to her feet.

It wasn't just her weak knees that caused her to wobble, the space was moving. Rocking side to side. Little tremor like bumps that had rattled her head against the solid floor. *A carriage?* It was far from the comfort of the wagon she had moved north in with the tour, one of plush fabrics and cushioned benches, the finest curtains and scented with incense when they were stopped to feast. This was not fit for humans. *Livestock cart, then,* she concluded. That would explain the smells–that she refused to think about for the sake of her gag reflex.

The only light emanating the small space came from slitted windows at the top of the walls on either side of her. She could see out of them well enough, but didn't need an embarrassing attempt to tell her that she would not fit through the aperture. Ayla pressed her face as far as she could manage, eyes screwing at the sudden exposure to daylight, and tried to gauge her surroundings.

Hills. *No*, mountains. They were amid a large range. None were mapped nor visible from the woodland she was taken from, which meant she had travelled some distance while unconscious, either west, or north, if her memory of Camelleah geography served.

She became aware of the throbbing feeling at the back of her head and reached back with bound hands to soothe it. She winced when her dirty fingers met a wet, weeping wound. When she withdrew her hands, they were smothered in blood.

Tears threatened her waterline. Her lip wobbled as she battled the emotions stirring inside of her. Pain, confusion, fear. She dropped her head to her chest and tried to calm herself. She took long, steadying breaths, so sure she could smell the scent of Atlas clinging to her dress. After hours pressing against his back on Ivelle, it wouldn't be much of a stretch.

Less than a day prior they had practically promised themselves to one another, and now for all she knew, they were on opposite sides of the kingdom, and she was heading for certain doom. What said doom was… she didn't dare entertain the thought. But most friendly invitations didn't start with knocking someone out and shackling them to a livestock transport.

The enclosed cart rolled into a ditch, the jolt of which threw Ayla on the floor, landing on her side.

Hitting something solid, she hissed at the pain, but when she rolled away, there was nothing on the floor.

Hope bloomed in her chest. She drew up her muddy skirts, evidence of Phena's wounds soaking into its seams.

She suppressed a gasp when she beheld her dagger still strapped to her thigh.

Using her bound hands to withdraw the blade, she sat back down, lodging the handle between her knees. Her heart rate escalated with fear of the unknown window of time she had to execute the task. She began to cut, but the knife slipped out from between her knees a couple of times, shaking with anticipation. She cursed under her breath and squeezed them tighter, determined this would work. *It had to.*

Then she stopped. Considering her actions, and their outcome. If she did manage to cut through the ropes–which she was fairly sure she *could*–the blade would not break through the chains around her ankles. Her captors would find her, with cut ropes and simply retie her. Furthermore, they would know she was hiding a weapon.

Ayla swallowed, knowing what she had to do.

She sheathed the blade and dropped her skirts. If she hadn't been searched for weapons when taken, chances were she wasn't going to be. After she was cut from these chains and released from this box she could make her move. For now, she took to her feet again, determined not to fall back to sleep with what she was sure was a concussion.

Peering out the little window once more she tried to identify a route, familiarising herself with their surroundings. If she was going to escape, she would have no idea where she was or where she was going. The least she could do would be to retrace their path as far back as she could. Perhaps once she was far enough from wherever they were going she could seek out help, find someone loyal to house Marnoch. If ever her name meant something, she hoped it would be now.

Lost in overlapping streams of thought, she almost missed it.

A mare, white as snow, roamed on the parallel mountain. Her large, feathered wings, ruffling in the northern breeze.

Ivelle.

Tears of hope welled in Ayla and her throat constricted with joy. She knew it was Ivelle–and not one of the other nine pegasi–because of her socks, two grey on her forelegs, one just above the ankle, the other up to her knee.

Atlas was here. Or *near*, at least. Her eyes darted over the mountain face, but she caught no sight of him, nor his men and their horses. Worry crept into her chest. *If Ivelle was here, where in the hells was he?*

Ayla pushed her head against the window bars, checking to the right and left of her. She saw no kidnappers walking nor on horseback on either side. If there were any–other than the driver–they must've been so far in front or behind of the transport they fell in her blind spot.

She resisted the urge to call out to Ivelle. Instead, she awkwardly reached her arm out the window, her face barely fitting alongside her shoulder Her fingers stretched out with silent desperation, waving to catch her attention.

They were on the other side of a valley from one another. The chances of being noticed slim, but not impossible. There wasn't much movement on the heathered face save for Ayla and her captors. *Perhaps the sound of churning wheels alone would be enough to catch the ears of the ancient beast.*

The very thing that haunted her dreams, now her only hope at survival.

How could Ivelle help? She wasn't sure. Without a rider, pegasi were simply animals. Huge majestic, beautiful, powerful animals. But she prayed out to whatever gods were responsible for their creation, that had mercy on Atlas' family and sent their saviours in the form of wings, that they help her today.

Even from so far away she spied Ivelle's ears twitching with awareness. The mare lifted her stark white head and turned it in Ayla's direction. Her chest constricted and her heart thundered. A small whimper escaped her mouth as she waved her hands more frantically. The pegasus remained still, and Ayla's movements slowed. A mountain away, but she could've sworn she felt the eyes of the animal fixed on hers.

The moment was heavy. A thick space in time that could mean Ayla's life spared.

Until now she had remained silent, sure that any cries for help would result in her being gagged or hit over the head once more. But this chance was so potent she opened her mouth to scream out for help. She may not be Ivelle's rider, but perhaps she was familiar enough with her to be defensive. She'd seen first-hand how aggressive they could be in the past.

Ayla's mouth was dry despite the tears dripping into it, she inhaled as deeply as she could, sure her scream would carry over the rolling hills. The cart stopped with a jerk, and she was thrown into the front wall, subsequently tripping over her chains and tumbling to the floor.

There were a few beats of stillness, save for the tremor in her hands.

The sound of iron hinging was followed by the back door dropping open, falling from the top to create a ramp for cattle. Ayla was no expert on the matter but was pretty sure that cattle didn't need to be shackled down for portage.

"Morning sunshine," a woman cooed from outside. She was in her later years but bore the body of a tourney champion. Her greying hair was pulled into a single braid that fell over her shoulder. She gave a nod to the much younger, much larger man to her left who ascended the ramp, ducking to fit under its roof.

Ayla scurried away instinctively, though there was nowhere to go.

The man reached for the shackles and unlocked them one by one. By the looks of him, he could tear the steel apart if he so pleased. He grunted as he stood and knocked his head on the ceiling. Such a bump fueled his frustration, and he yanked Ayla by the arm and dragged her out.

The woman grabbed Ayla's jaw and inspected her face like fresh meat at market. Her eyes were particularly drawn to the scar slashing over her lips. She made an unimpressed scoff and stalked away. Her henchman silently dragged Ayla with them.

Ayla trained her eyes to the left scanning for any sign of her winged friend. Nothing. Ivelle had completely disappeared.

The trio weaved in and out of giant boulders before they reached a frame-shaped hole in the side of the mountain and stepped through. They walked along a narrow tunnel, lined with oil sconces, passed several downward leading staircases but never descended them.

"Take her to his room. I'll inform him of her arrival." the woman said without stopping, taking a left when they arrived in a round foyer, five doors on each side of the pentagonal space.

Her accomplice grunted in response and pushed Ayla forward through another.

There were no windows in the belly of a mountain, but there were so many oil lamps and candles adorning the room that everything was lit up.

She could see that the space was furnished for a bedroom. Surprisingly feminine, considering her abductor just alluded to the fact it belonged to a man. Soft colour palettes of blush and amethyst that independently may look agreeable, but alongside all the emeralds in the room, we're a nauseating mix. There were polished mirrors on every flat surface to bounce around the light. Velvet fabrics curtained the box-bed and draped over a chaise in the corner.

Captor and captive stopped in the centre of the room and he untied the bounds of her wrists. He wasn't gentle, and they burned as they pulled free. Ayla grimaced when she beheld how red and raw her skin was beneath. She took a baby step backwards, away from the leering man.

"Change," he snarled, nodding to something beyond her. She looked behind her warily and spotted a jewel-green dress laid out on the bed. She turned her gaze back to him but made no move toward his instruction. He crossed his arms and planted his feet, obviously not leaving any time soon.

She desperately wanted to change out of her dress. It was soaked with blood, sweat and fear.

"No." she said flatly. Her maidenly modesty aside, if he were to watch her change, he would see the weapon strapped to her leg and remove it at once, along with her only chance of escape.

"Change," he commanded again. Taking a predatory step forward. She steeled her spine and locked her knees straight, but her wide eyes betrayed her show of confidence.

"No." she said again, a hint more breathlessly and unsure. Something told her this man was not beyond changing her by force. But she wasn't going to willingly do so and reveal her only means of defence.

He began to march at her when the door reopened, and he turned in response.

What entered was arguably scarier than the man before her. Fergus Goldsworth. With a swollen, bruised and crusted face. *Of course.*

Ayla's eyes bounced around the emeralds littering the room and she cursed herself for not putting two and two together sooner.

"That will be all Preston," he said indifferently, not sparing a glance at Ayla as he sauntered inside. The man—Preston—gave a curt not as he exited on command.

The door clicked shut and even though it was a soft sound, she flinched.

Ayla couldn't peel her gaze from Fergus' wounded flesh. It had been smothered in blood the last time she saw it, the extent of his injuries undetectable. The continued swelling after so many days suggested to her that Atlas had broken several bones in his face, including his jaw, nose, and brow.

"You own this mountain?" She asked.

"I own the *Range.*"

"Then why reside in the smaller of the two peaks? Surely the larger is a bigger statement of power?" She asked, unable to hold her tongue through the outrage she was feeling. He looked offended by her observation. *Good.*

"What am I doing here?" She asked, feeling a tad more confident now that the monster behind such a plot had been unmasked.

"You're my guest," he replied plainly, "permanently."

Ayla suppressed the bile surging to her throat at such a thought.

"You're a fool if you think I will stay here willingly. Even more so if you think Atlas won't come for me–should you be stupid enough to hold me against my will."

"You think awfully high of yourself, considering you're damaged goods." He replied, drawing closer, eyes rested on her mouth. "He *was* rather taken by you," he went on, straining the muscles around his mouth to smile. "But he will soon forget. He has no idea where you are, and much bigger worries at hand. His *business* with my brother should keep him busy for a while."

"What business?"

He let out a long dramatic sigh, dripping in boredom. "Power, status, titles. He's always been hungry for more, my brother. Always scheming, never satisfied. I'm a far simpler man, myself. All I want is you."

Ayla scoffed in disbelief. "You just met me," she spat, "you don't know the first thing about me. You have only taken me because someone told you, *no.* And the little Goldsworth, born with an emerald spoon up his arse has never been told, no."

He ghosted a hand down her cheek, and she pulled away with a grimace. A reaction he didn't take kindly to and pulled her hair roughly back to him.

"Nevertheless, you are mine now. Forever." He seethed. "And you will learn to love it." he whispered into her ear, before licking up the side of her face.

She pushed his chest as hard as she could, and he stumbled back with a chuckle.

"I will *never* be yours!" she spat.

"I bet you said the same thing to Prince Atlas, once upon a time. Tell me, what would Prince Thian say if he found out his favourite whore was jumping from his bed into his brother's?"

Ayla went pale. "I'm no one's whore."

"Really? Didn't look that way before Morrigan's tourney. Or do you let all men touch you so intimately?"

Bitterness flooded her mouth.

"I heard Prince Thian doesn't like to share his toys. I wonder whose head he'll call for first. Yours, or his brothers, hm?"

Angry tears burned behind Ayla's eyes. "I am no one's whore." she repeated in lethal quiet.

Fergus wiped a disappointed look from his face. "Not to worry, a bit of resistance only makes the conquest more fun," He pointed lazily to the dress on the bed "dress." Sauntering over to a mirror behind him, the lord inspected his healing wounds. Something glinted in the reflection, and he turned with interest.

Ayla stood, chest heaving, and the promise of death awning her face.

Surprise lit his eyes. But then the bugger had the balls to bite back a smile, and opened his arms in clear invitation, daring her to try it.

"Come over here then," he drawled.

"Now why would I do that?" She asked. The blade flipped in her right hand, so her fingers and thumb pressed against steel. Drawing her arm back she hurled the weapon at her target. The weight of the handle flipped it mid-flight, pointy end taking its course. It struck true, right through his swollen eye.

She wasn't sure her strength in a throw could penetrate bone, but she had enough precision to target the soft flesh of the orbs. The blade was long enough it pierced through his brain, killing him instantly.

Fergus' corpse fell on its knees and wobbled slightly, its weight unsure whether to land forward or back. Ayla scurried over and pulled the dagger out of his skull before kicking him backwards.

Her hands shook violently.

She had never killed anything before. Throwing the blade was the only skill she had acquired with it, and even then, it had only found its mark in stumps or straw targets. Never a living thing.

She stumbled to the door, folding in half and vomited violently.

Chapter 42

A yla took several breaths, none of them successful in soothing her body or mind. She peeled the door open a fraction, as silently as physically possible. There was no one in the foyer. *Yet.*

She slipped out the door and didn't bother closing it behind her.

She kept her paces swift and steady as she walked through the foyer–

"Oi! You!"

Preston.

Her feet took over her mind as she sprinted down the long tunnel. She grasped her skirts higher, but someone grabbed her hair and swung her into the wall. She let out a strangled cry as the force of the impact had her repelling off it. Unable to find her footing, she fell down an opening of stairs behind her. Each bump was a sharp pain in her flesh. Her hands flew out to find purchase and stop the tumble, the pads of her fingers cut up by rough stone.

The staircase had no flame, so she limped in the dark, palms flat against the walls as she followed down the path. Every instinct in her begged she test the ground before stepping blindly. But such caution would slow her pace. And she had no time to lose.

Ayla heard Preston cursing a couple dozen steps above her, and a clatter of steel as he presumably kicked her dropped blade.

She continued to scrape her hands along the jagged rock wall, and eventually, she hit flat ground, illuminated by an oil lamp. With light on her side, she took off again, following the cramped tunnels until they seemed to be opening wider and taller. and eventually she stood in a cavern. It was a raw mining bubble.

Discarded pickaxes lined one wall, empty carts another.

She shuddered when she heard a maniacal female laugh somewhere in the distance. When she turned again, she realised why.

Beyond her was a huge gaping hole between her side of the cave and the other.

She was trapped.

"He's dead." Ayla confessed as soon as her pursuers were in sight.

"I saw," the woman replied.

"Then what use have you of me?"

"He died without *paying*. You're clearly of worth to someone," she grimaced as the spoke, looking at Ayla though she was spoiled meat. "We will put you up for auction ourselves."

Ayla blanched. There were about a dozen paces between herself and them. Another dozen to the drop behind her. It was as if the ground beneath had shattered in two, pulled itself apart. A bottomless pit with Stars knows what at the bottom.

She turned and looked at the gap. It was impossible to jump. About eighteen paces of abyss, if she had to guess.

"Really?" the woman asked dryly, anticipating Ayla's thoughts. "These are the Crankie mines, girl. They tremor with fury and split themselves open, swallowing any who dare stand on their cracks. There is nothing down there for you but death."

Ayla swallowed. She knew this. But she could not live with herself if she lay down now and let them take her to be sold. Her body was already bruised and broken. A swift fall wouldn't be the worst way to go.

Before her rationality could kick in, she listened to the heartbeat in her ears like battle drums preparing her to fight. She took off as fast as she could toward the pass, letting instinct tell her when to jump, swinging her arms with her ascent to propel her upwards. Time slowed and she realised she didn't like flying nearly as much when not mounted on something with wings.

Her torso thudded into the edge of the other side, knocking all the air out of her. Her legs thrashed and her nails clawed at the flat surface above. Willing every ounce of strength into action. When she scrawled up and stared back, the gap looked much larger than before, and her legs wobbled in horror.

The woman and Preston wore matching expressions of disbelief and regret that they had just lost their payday.

It was impossible. *Impossible.* She doubted even Olive could make such a jump. And yet she was here, alive. She had done it.

Before they had time to react, Ayla took off again. If anyone could make the jump it would be the giant on the other side.

Sure enough, when she weaved through the tunnel away from them, she heard the cry of Preston, which faded into silence as he made the jump, but not the landing.

Overwhelmed with emotion, Ayla's body shook. Tears streamed down her cheeks, cutting through the dirt on her face. Her run dwindled into a walk. Her aching limbs forced to limp. The urge to lay down and fall asleep was overwhelming. But she needed to get out of here.

Rounding a corner, she jumped out of her skin as she beheld a small child. He was carrying several large pickaxes–almost as tall as him–and seemed to have gotten just as much a fright as her. She realised she must've looked terrifying, like a phantom haunting the halls. Blood-soaked gown, dirt covered skin, matted unruly hair, tired eyes red-raw from tears. Though the boy did not look in much better shape.

Ayla ignored the ache in her legs as she sat on her haunches. She worked a smile, but the effort caused her eyes to well up again. "Hello there," she cooed, voice breaking as she tried to pacify his fear. "I need to get outside. Can you help me?" She tried her best to steady her wobbling lip and keep the desperation from her voice.

The boy looked over her shoulder–presumably where he was headed–before eyeing her up. He nodded and turned on his heels, taking her back where he came from. She let out a sob of relief, somewhere between a laugh and a cry as she followed suit.

"Do you want a hand with those?" she asked, pointing to his hold of tools. He did not spare her a glance as he shook his head firmly.

Ayla felt it first around her ankles. *An icy breeze.* Then the smell, not of musty dampness, but fresh air of heather and frost.

When she spotted a small bead of light in the distance her heart bloomed full, though she kept looking over her shoulder, expecting someone to come and rip her away from her freedom.

They arrived at the hole, which did not grow as large as she would have hoped. It was so small she had to crawl through the space, but it was the most grateful she'd been to see daylight in her entire life.

She wanted to hug the boy and cover him in grateful kisses, but simply said "Thank you. So very much." voice breaking on the latter words.

He looked unfazed by her emotions, gave her a polite nod, and made his way back into the heart of the mountain.

Chapter 43

I suggest you use your tongue before you lose it." Atlas snarled.

"My, my, we are hostile. This is a transaction. Do you subject all your business partners to such sharp words? I have given you back the girls, unharmed, and will lead you to the third when negotiations are done."

"*Unharmed*?" Atlas' face soured as she nodded to the bruised, unconscious princess to his left.

Lord Goldsworth shrugged his shoulders, his neck still as not to invite the blade at his skin further into flesh. "She was making a fuss," he waved casually, "best to let her sleep through the unpleasantries."

Atlas' jaw worked mercilessly but he honed his seething rage under control. Watching his target with predatory precision. "Where. Is. she?"

"Far away from here. You truly did upset my brother, Your Highness. He doesn't take kindly to embarrassment. You give me what I want, and I will take you to them."

"You would sell out your brother?"

"I would."

"Why?"

"Because Fergus is a sniveling halfwit! He was weak enough to let wounded pride drive his actions, backing himself into a treasonous corner. I agreed to… *hold* the princesses as a distraction while he took your real gem. Now they have brought you here and I have your attention, they are free to go. As for the Marnoch girl… I scratch your back, you scratch mine."

"What do you want?"

"Only what I deserve. To be Duke of Camelleah"

"Excuse me?"

"The Marnoch's are not the powerhouse they once were, Your Highness. My family's wealth has trumped theirs threefold in recent years. They have given away their lands, lost control of their tenants. They are soft, and weak. I can offer the continent, the *crown*, strength. I control over half of the mines here anyway. The wealth of Camelleah is *mine*. If the exportation of my jewels ceases, tell me Your

Highness, what will become of your continent's economy?"

"This doesn't sound like a transaction. It sounds like a threat."

"Not at all. If you let me finish, it is my understanding that even with the great tax increases these past few years, the crown is in great debt. Your father is a generous man. But the poor breed like bunnies, and it's hard to keep up with such charity when the population outweighs the food stocks of the continent. Make me Duke of Camelleah and let me relieve you of your dues."

"An interesting proposal." the prince replied.

A cat-like grin pulled over Goldsworth's face. "So," he outstretched his arms, welcoming, "We have a deal?"

Atlas returned his grin but there was no amusement behind his eyes. "Never."

He nodded to his soldier and the blade pushed up into his neck. Atlas was already walking away with Twyla still in arm. Protecting her ears from the gargled screams of the traitorous man.

He stalked back the way they had entered. Drury quick on his heels, Gunnar and Soren not far behind.

"Your Highness, what about Lady Marnoch? How will we find her without him?" Drury spoke.

"She's close."

"But… I… your–"

"He was a liar, Drury. He *lied*. He only looked down when he was lying. When he said he did not harm Niamh, when he denied he was threatening us, when he said Ayla was far away."

They marched back up the cavernous tunnels until they reached the hovels of the villagers. Instead of continuing their path Atlas stopped at the door of one, an old woman standing proudly in its open frame.

"You know who I am?" he asked.

She looked him over, lingering on his hair, the darkness of this place not enough to dull the enchanting bloodred. A curt nod was passed beneath bushy brows.

"Do you know where we can find the younger Goldsworth?"

Another small nod. She brushed past the group and walked through the open space, veering off the path they had entered on.

The men grew uneasy, steering off the tracks they were familiar with meant uncertainty of where they were going, what was to come. Eventually they arrived at a narrow, lit tunnel not dissimilar to the one they entered many hours ago. Daylight pierced through the end, a staggering contrast to the darkness they had been submerged in. Atlas thanked the woman and assured her aid would not be forgotten, as they all left the mountain.

They were now much deeper in the valley than they had entered. No sign nor sound of the men they left at the slivered entrance. Niamh stirred and

Gunnar's brow was beaded with sweat, but he refused to put her down. He may be the size of a tree, but it had been a considerable length of time since he first scooped her up, and his arms must be beginning to ache.

The sun had dipped behind the land, the skies were bruising as night set in. Without the warmth, frost crawled up the leaves of every blade of grass. They needed to regroup with the others soon and make haste back to camp or they would all freeze to death.

Atlas removed his leather doublet and draped it over the shoulders of Twyla who shivered in his grasp. His linen shirt did nothing against the icy chill in the air, but better him than the princess.

Without the sun, it was also hard to gauge their bearings. Which way was north, was as good a guess as any to Atlas. It was Gunnar who announced that they were facing east as he read the constellations above.

They made to move, getting higher ground would give a better view of the valley–and therefore chance of spotting both the royal guard and Ayla.

Only a mile along they were stopped by the rough descent of Ivelle. Glad to see his mare, Atlas smiled and patted her mane. She turned away from him though, adjacent to the mountain face, bowing her head and stomping her foot adamantly. Atlas followed her line of direction; he saw nothing but trusted her completely.

Torn once again, he had no desire to leave Niamh and Twyla in this state, but they were safe now, the conditions in which Ayla was being kept were unpredictable to say the least. His decision was made easier when a faint shouting was heard from the south. They followed the sound, and soon the smell of smoke.

Eventually they spotted the peaks of a blazing fire in the distance. The glinting silver armour of the royal guard reflected the light like a homing beacon.

"Take them." Atlas instructed, Handing a sleeping Twyla to Soren. "Don't wait for me, you'll freeze out here. Go back to the camp and see them–and yourselves–warmed and fed."

Atlas mounted Ivelle, who had trekked alongside them, discontentedly whining now and again in protest of their ignoring her.

The three men bit their tongues and nodded dutifully to their prince's request. He took off before they could think better of it.

Dropping off the steep cliff, Ivelle shot out her wings into a saving soar. Atlas forsook a leading clutch on the reigns, trusting her completely to take him where they needed to go.

She didn't need to take him far. Just over the valley to the mountain parallel.

From a bird's eye view it didn't take long to spot her dark dress against the pale landscape. Ayla was lying in the frozen heather. The top layers of her skirts were pulled up over her shoulders in attempt to stay warm. He could tell from how ghostly pale her face was that the attempt was not enough.

Ivelle circled the sleeping maiden and landed close, Atlas jumped off long before the steed was stationary, bounding over to the girl. His initial rush of relief was eclipsed by a pain in his heart. As he grew closer, he could see the true state of her.

"Ayla," he called, cradling her up in his arms. Her skirts fell from her shoulders and her hands that had been tucked beneath were almost as blue as her lips.

"Atlas?" she asked, eyes fluttering open, a delirious smile gracing her colourless cheeks.

Atlas lifted her into his arms and Ivelle kneeled on her front legs to accommodate his mounting with her in hand.

One nudge and they were off. He quickly overtook the group of soldiers, hesitating as he ultimately left the princesses behind. But they had torches of fire to ward off the chill, Ayla was frozen solid, and Atlas needed to get her to camp–and to a healer–immediately.

Ayla sat sidesaddle in front of him, leaning into his warmth. She cradled her hands that looked sore to move. Atlas lifted them softly and laid them flat against his chest, beneath his shirt. He was not immune to the bitter cold, with no more than a linen shirt he shivered with her. But his chest was a stark heat compared to her frozen limbs. She winced at the contrast of temperature.

Sleep chased Ayla the whole flight back and her head threatened to fall off his shoulder more than once, but he always guided it back home. He ghosted over her lips, sure if he kissed, they would forge together at the frozen contact. His hot breath fanning her face thawed some of the frost hugging her lashes.

"Niamh and Twyla will meet us at the camp," Atlas whispered to her. She was not conscious enough to ask after them, but he knew the concern would be burrowed in her mind.

"Hmm," she murmured incoherently in response.

They flew over a camp far closer than the one they had left behind. As soon as the search party had dispatched just a day ago, they had packed up and followed west. It took the company a day to cover the same ground the search party had in hours. Tents were still being erected as they landed.

Even slightly warm water would scold such frozen skin. So, Atlas ordered a shallow, tepid tub to be drawn, with boiling jugs on hand, ready to be added as Ayla's skin thawed out, and acclimated to the temperature.

Atlas carried her into his tent. She could stand, but her body shook so erratically he thought she might collapse. The space was warmed only by plentiful candlelight.

Her hands had gained some colour but were still incapable of functioning, so he took off her clothes as gently as possible. He couldn't believe how foul her dress smelled. Its colour was incomprehensible from the day before.

Atlas peeled off the clothing piece by piece, and his heart clogged in his throat at her wounds. She had several blooming bruises and swelling lumps on her limbs and torso. Her wrists were red and raw, the skin indented even hours after being tied up. Her hair was matted in her own blood.

He was so overwhelmed by the sight that he wanted to fall to his knees and cry. Someone had harmed her. Caused her pain and marred her body. He wanted to know how each and every mark had been laid upon her skin and flay every man that put them there.

But she would have to tell him in her own time. What was important now was getting her warmed up.

Working through the lump in his throat, he recognised now was not the time to be selfish. He had to be strong, for her.

Ayla clenched her jaw in an attempt to stop her teeth from chattering, but it only caused the motion to spread to her head, which bobbed uncontrollably. She gave no protest when Atlas scooped her up once more and lifted her over the lip of the bath. After hissing when she hit the water, she soon relaxed into it. She hugged her torso, claiming any heat that she could. Her eyes were half lidded and she could not yet muster words.

Atlas reached under the water and felt her frozen flesh. Once it had reached the temperature of the liquid, he added a jug of boiling water to the end, bending her aching knees for her, so it didn't burn her feet.

Jug after jug he poured in when she was ready.

Slowly her shivering faltered, and her breathing returned to normal. When the water level reached her neck, her cheeks began to flush. Atlas never thought he'd be so grateful to see the colour.

He picked up a soft cloth next to the bathrobe and began to tend to her head wound. Once he cleared the blood he could see no crack, just skin damage, which eased some of the worry in his heart. He'd have the healer check it thoroughly just in case, in the morning, but he was sure it wouldn't be fatal.

He tended to the rest of her dirty flesh, delicate over the sore spots. Ayla watched him intently as he worked.

"How did you find me?" she croaked finally.

"I didn't. Ivelle did. She led me to you." he replied honestly.

She told him of faint memories of Ivelle on the side of the mountain, but most was a blurry mess. She tried to piece together her memories of what had occurred, but the harder she thought, the more her head hurt.

Suddenly she shot straight upright, clutching the sides of the tub. "Phena!"

"Is alive," he finished, smoothing over her hands that white-knuckled the tub. "The unit arrived just after you were taken. They brought her back to the healer. She is still bedbound, but she will live." he assured.

Ayla released a breath. When she tried to draw another, it was broken and shaky. She tried again and a small sob escaped. She covered her mouth with her hand to suppress the sound. The attempt, however, was fruitless. Her cries slipped through the cracks of her fingers.

She was warming up, but she was far from a healthy temperature and Atlas did not wish to remove her yet. So, he pulled his linen shirt over his head, kicked off his boots and climbed in behind her—leathers and all. It was a tight squeeze, but he gently pulled her between his legs, their bodies melding into one.

Her back pressed into his torso and his arms wrapped over her own, holding her tight. He didn't ask her not to cry. She needed to cry—to release all her fear, pain, sadness and relief that she had accumulated in such a short time. All he wanted to do was be there for her through it.

Chapter 44

The familiar tumble of the carriage was welcomed by all. Even if each bump made Ayla wince at the reminder of her sore limbs. When she'd woken this morning, under about five too many furs, she still felt cold despite her sweat soaked skin. The chill was due to the absence of flesh that had held her through the night. The body that had seeped heat and comfort, protection and understanding even as her sobs slowed but her tears persisted to roll.

For the first time on their journey, Ayla was in Niamh's carriage with Twyla and Atlas. The four of them happy to sacrifice the comfort of space to stay amongst one another. Ayla and Niamh sat side by side, softly clasping each other's gloved hands, while Atlas sat across from them with Twyla perched on his knee.

The prince had only left Ayla that morning to check up on the princesses after their return to camp.

Ayla and Twyla's presence in this carriage also allowed Phena to be laid flat and watched over by the healer in Twyla's carriage.

It was still one person short though. Hensella was buried in Camelleah. Her body would not last the rest of the journey to the capital before the effects of decomposition took hold. So, it was decided to honour her where she was taken from this world and lay her to rest beneath Arianrhod and her stars.

Staring out the window, peaks of mountains grew few and far between as they progressed south. Since the entire camp had moved a day's ride west to meet them at the Goldsworth mines, it was decided that they would travel southbound over the Atholl border into a warmer climate, before turning east, back into Balcarras. This was pushed by the prince who declared he had business with the Duke of Atholl that had not been scheduled. There was little pushback on the matter by the soldiers, who would happily trade frozen mountains for lush forest lands, brimming with life.

As much as she tried to suppress it, Ayla couldn't help but feel guilt at her actions from the previous day. Not the act of killing Fergus per se, but the consequence of it. Now that both brothers of the emerald mountains were dead, she and Atlas had just subjected a whole community of desperate dwellers to fend for themselves.

"What will happen to the inhabitants in the mines?" She asked.

Atlas had already disclosed he had planned on sending resources and aid to the people suffering under the cruel hand of greedy Goldsworth. But now there was a question of inheritance and distribution of lands. Not just for the sake of wealth, but order and prosperity of the people.

Before he had time to answer, Niamh took the lead. "There is a third brother. I danced with him in Rydon Castle."

"Niamh, the boy is ten–" Atlas interrupted.

Seeing the hesitation in Atlas she raised a soft hand to cut him off, "Ten *and three quarters.* He is young, I understand, but he has a kind and fair heart his brothers were lacking. I'm sure he has no idea on the duties and responsibilities of being a lord of lands, but perhaps with guidance he can be molded into a leader worthy of the title. We could send a scholar from the capital to aid in this, couldn't we Atlas?"

Atlas' face shone of pride at the words of the gracious princess. Niamh, who seemed to pay not a wink of attention to lessons of politics in their youth, could be quite the diplomat when she wanted to be. Perhaps the continent would not suffer so, with Thian as King, should he have Niamh as his Queen.

"I think that is a wonderful idea. I shall send word to Rydon and the capital to correlate an agreement."

It lifted some of the weight off Ayla's conscience. *Perhaps something good would come out of this after all. A people liberated from brutality and inhumane ways of living. Supported and celebrated by a compassionate leader.*

When she noted Atlas' expression, it made her heart soften from the vice it was trapped in. He was so close, she could reach out and touch him for heaven's sake, but such distance still felt much too far.

In the moments of peaceful silence, it was hard to ignore the lack of babble from the little princess. She had no sign of physical injury, to everyone's relief, but her demeanour had not been the same since the mines.

She was so still and quiet, her eyes glazed and unfocused. It worried Ayla greatly when she recognised the look to be very similar to that of Niamh during her bad days, where she isolated herself from the world. There were no tears or anger, just a separation from everything around her. Twyla clutched her limp babydoll under one arm while holding Atlas' hand in the other but made no attempt to play.

"Twyla, would you like to go for a walk outside? We could visit the horses?" Ayla asked her, lowering her eyes to be level with the princess'. Twyla seemed to consider it for a moment but shook her head and leaned back into Atlas' chest.

"No? What about we try to find some cakes?" Ayla tried again in a sneaky, playful whisper. But not even the prospect of sugar was enticing enough for the girl. Ayla looked to Niamh as if for suggestions, but the princess had none to give.

"I have an idea," Atlas announced. He picked up the girl and turned her to face him. "What about... you take a ride with me? On Ivelle?" he asked.

Something sparkled in the girl's eyes at the possibility. Ayla's stomach dropped out at the thought of such a small and delicate child so high in the sky atop a pegasus. Images of her falling through the clouds invaded Ayla's thoughts and she paled at each and every one.

She looked to Niamh with desperation, hoping the girl's mother would protest such a wild idea, but alas the princess seemed almost as giddy at the proposal as her daughter.

"Atlas," Ayla started, racking her brain for any excuse to prevent such a scheme. "Isn't the first ride supposed to be with a child's father? Perhaps we should wait until we are back in Balcarras, and Thian can take her with Racjan." She looked to Niamh for support, who in turn looked at Atlas before returning her gaze to Ayla with saddened eyes.

"I didn't fly with my father the first time," she announced quietly.

Hells. Of course she hadn't. Her father was dead mere weeks after her birth.

"That's just a silly tradition of the past," Atlas declared. "Niamh perhaps you could take her?" He turned his attention back to Twyla, "What do you think little princess? Should your mother take you up in the sky with her?"

The little girl launched herself at her mother with the first smile they had seen all day.

They waited until they crossed the border into Atholl before Niamh took Twyla flying. The camp stopped and set up for lunch just south of the natural perimeter of mountains.

Every minute the rate of Ayla's heartbeat shot higher. Now that they were at the point of stopping, she shifted on her feet, unable to shake the anxious feeling.

Twyla was long past the age of needing a sling, but for the sake of strapping her to her mother, Atlas fashioned a makeshift tie to stop her slipping out of grasp. When he first took to the skies with Irlass, he had no such failsafe, but he was two years Twyla's senior. Not to mention the precaution would stop Ayla's heart from falling out her throat. *Hopefully.*

Ivelle was hovering around the group in a plain of grass before a forest. Ayla wanted to thank the mare for ultimately leading Atlas to her in time. But she wasn't feeling brave enough to walk over and pet her muzzle unaccompanied, especially in her state of anxiety. Instead, she rolled apples along the grass down the hill that stopped at the feet of the grateful pegasus. *Such a smart creature should understand the act as a presentation of gratitude. Right?*

"Ayla," a tiny voice squeaked from behind her. The governess turned to find her charge pulling on her skirts, beaming with anticipation. Ayla squatted on her haunches to meet the little girl. "Can you watch Maggie while I gone?" Twyla asked, holding out the doll in question. Ayla's heart warmed at the request. She took the doll and held it carefully.

"Of course, Bumblebee. We'll be here when you get back." she promised with a smile.

After mounting Twyla in front of her mother, Atlas tied the sling around the pair, tight enough it was secure, but not enough to cause discomfort.

Ayla watched them prepare with a knot in her stomach, rising up her throat and constricting her heart.

She clutched Maggie right to her chest. Pressing her nose in the doll's fabric from time to time, inhaling the calming lavender sewn into its stuffing.

This was dangerous. *A stupid fucking tradition.* But it was an important rite of passage for members of the Kinghorn and Solmund families. A tradition Ayla must respect and not speak against. She wasn't the girl's mother. It was not her place to have a say on such a matter.

Her opinion, however, was without question to shut down this whole idea. Even if it would disappoint the child. She had shown them that she could be cheered up–they could find alternatives that didn't include risking her life hundreds of feet in the air.

Too far from the trio, Ayla couldn't hear the words spoken between the prince and princess, but she could tell from each of their body language what was said. Atlas asking if Niamh was sure, and her assuring him with full confidence in herself and her pegasus.

Ayla searched Twyla's face from afar, picking it apart for any sign of fear or uncertainty. Ready to scream and shout and drag her off if she changed her mind about the flight. But there was nothing but a smile of anticipation radiating off the princess.

Atlas stepped back and Yvie took off, transitioning from a quick trot to a canter, before spreading her glorious wings and taking to the skies.

The pair circled the camp a couple times close to the ground, Niamh testing her daughter's reaction to the feeling of flight. It was enough to see the joy spread over every inch of Twyla's face in pure exhilaration. Niamh's face mirrored the emotions coursing through her daughter.

Ayla watched intently, her tight grip on the doll threatening the integrity of its seams.

A warm hand snaked around her waist from behind which eased her tension. It had been just over a day since they had been snatched out of the safety of their compound and dragged across the kingdom, but to Atlas and Niamh, there was no safer place for them than in the sky. There was freedom in the solitude of the world above the earth.

"They will be fine." Atlas murmured.

"I know," Ayla replied.

Atlas moved his head closer to hers, his hot breath next to her ear momentarily distracted her from tracking the pair in the sky.

"Let's go. You've never been to Atholl before, let me show you some of its gems." he said.

She spun under his hold, his arm now pressing into the small of her back as she looked up at him "Shouldn't we wait for them to come back?" she asked.

"They won't be back until sundown." he replied, smirking at the concern patterning her face.

"Sundown?! But that's hours away."

"Yes, it is. Niamh will take her over as much land as she can in that time." When Ayla's brows scrunched, and he could see her questions brewing he went on. "It is not just a rite of passage to fly. For us Kinghorns, it is a chance to see the land that we will one day come to serve as rulers, from the skies of the continent, just as our ancestors did as they descended from beyond the seas."

There was something precious and poetic in the sentiment, that Ayla felt a smidge better about the excursion.

She needed a distraction. If she were to stand here all day, all she would do is lose her mind staring into the blue beyond for hours on end, worrying herself to death.

"Where did you have in mind?"

Chapter 45

I velle plodded over the stony trail with grace, reveling in the odd scratch of her shoulder from a grateful rider.

The land over the border was a blend of two kingdoms. Hardy pines fought for space amongst oaks and sequoias. A trickle of mountains reached over the breach of the divided land, their mass covered in much more greenery and life than its northern neighbour.

Ayla reached down into the saddle pack again, trusting Atlas' hand on her hip to catch her should she slip.

She dug around and pulled out a handful of oatcakes and a chunk of hard cheese they had packed up before they left the touring camp. She tore pieces free of each and alternated feeding herself and Atlas.

Seeing his hint of a smile each time she turned to pass it to him, filled a part of her. More than oats and cheese ever could. Every moment with him added something to her soul she didn't know was missing.

"How many times have you been to Atholl?" she asked through a mouth full of oats.

"A couple. Only in passing. We move through it before crossing the Shallow Sea to Vorraine, to visit the Duke, my mother's father."

"So how did you find this *gem*?" she asked.

"Thian found it, actually. He shared it with me and Niamh when I was thirteen."

Ayla's heart skipped a beat at the sound of his name for reasons she couldn't quite decipher. Lost in the chaos of the past two days she hadn't even given thought to Thian.

Before she let her head spiral into itself, she shifted in the saddle, swinging one leg over, before pulling the other back up between herself and Atlas. The maneuver resulted in her facing Atlas, hooking her knees over his thighs. She instantly fiddled with the latches and ties of his jacket, avoiding eye contact.

"I don't want to go home," she whispered. He stilled. Sensing his jump to assumptions she corrected herself, "I *am* going home. I just… I don't want to go back to what we were. I don't know what to do–about Thian. What to say, how to act. I can't lie to him, but I know that this will hurt him. I *do* love him, Atlas," she said meeting his gaze "I just don't love him *that* way."

"What way?" he breathed.

She swallowed. "*This* way." She lay her hand over his thundering heart. Her eyes filling in the gaps that she didn't have the courage to articulate with words.

Atlas rested his brow upon hers. "I know it will break his heart, but I'm not sure there is a way to avoid that. He is unpredictable. I can protect you from him, Ayla. I'm just not sure I can protect him from himself."

Ayla moved her hands up to his face, stroking her thumbs over his strong jaw in the moments in between his words.

"Whatever we decide to do," Ayla started.

"We do it together," Atlas finished.

Unable to wait a second longer she pulled his head in for a fierce kiss. She drifted one hand from his face to the back of his head where she knotted his silken hair around her fingers.

His eagerness and hunger had him pushing her back into the saddle.

She suddenly giggled into his mouth at the taste of strong cheese on both of their tongues. The absurdity of the thought washed over her in a flash as he replied in a ravenous growl.

He abandoned the reins in favour of kneading her ass, trusting Ivelle to take the lead. She squealed as he dragged her hips closer in the saddle. The sound melted into a moan as she settled into him, feeling his swelling need for her. The sensation sent a shockwave of heat straight to her core. She moved her hips slightly, craving the friction it would provide.

Her dress had pulled up to her thighs when she had turned around, and when Atlas lifted her atop him, there were only her cotton underclothes and his leathers separating their desperate flesh.

Each slow roll of her hips drove her to the edge.

Both of them started a symphony of moans and pants, aching for each other yet hesitant to go further. So close, yet too far.

There was no one around for miles. He could take her here and now. Claim her and satiate the burning need inside them both. As her thoughts grew more sinful, his actions grew more erratic. His kisses were punishing, not letting her up for air, seizing every gasp she offered with his tongue. His hands roamed her body furiously, mapping every inch and curve as if he would never see it again.

Just as she readied herself to abandon all rationality, Ivelle stopped abruptly.

Atlas peeled his mouth from Ayla's to scope out their surroundings, in case they were being approached. Ayla–who couldn't be less interested if they had an audience right now–kissed her way along his jaw and down his neck as he swiveled his head like an owl. She licked his scars. Her teeth nipped over his pulsing artery, savouring the delicious taste of his flesh.

Atlas returned to her mouth for one more heady kiss, exploring her with the hunger of a man starved, before ripping himself away. He thumbed over her wet, kiss-swollen lips and the scar that crossed them.

"We're here." he announced, amusement sparkling in his eyes. Before she could claim him in another kiss, he dismounted Ivelle.

After stepping off a feathered wing, Ayla patted Ivelle on the neck in thanks. When she turned back to Atlas she was torn between slapping him for interrupting her pleasure and tackling him to the ground and taking it back. Instead, she braced her hands on her hips and huffed, looking around where they stopped on the trail, thoroughly unimpressed by their surroundings. No different than the pine littered landscape they had seen on their hour trek so far. She raised a questioning brow to which he suppressed a chuckle.

"We walk the rest of the way, " he said.

Consciously not taking his hand as they walked off the beaten path, Ayla didn't trust herself with the touch of his skin at this moment in time. Too much of it and she might lose control and beg him to take her against silver birch.

He had already proclaimed wherever they were going was a surprise, so she had given up asking miles ago. Instead, she looked around for clues as they strayed off the main trail. There was nothing special about this place as far as she could see.

"Can I at least have a clue?" she asked.

He chucked deeply and the sound sent vibrations over her skin, even though they weren't touching one another. "No. But if you spot any toadstools, don't step on them."

They trekked on for some time, toward the base of a small rock faced hill. When they broke through the tree line they emerged on a pebbled beach overlooking a shallow loch.

Now this *was a gem.*

Ayla dropped her mouth in awe of the pool before her. The freshwater shone an impossibly bright shade of bluish green. Its jewel colouring sparkled in the late sun. It was simple, really, just a loch. A body of water–one of dozens in the area. But it was stunning.

Atlas walked to the water's edge and laid out the rest of their crumbled oatcakes on a handkerchief atop a rock. He guided her to the mossy bank slope that bordered the tree line and the pebbled shore. They sat atop the incline and Ayla rolled her tired ankles.

She sat in the peaceful haven, drinking in the dipping sun, and all the sounds that nature had to offer. The rustling of leaves. Chatter of birds. Lapping of water when the wind pushed it farther up shore.

Ayla slid her gaze to Atlas, who was watching her with an expression she couldn't put into words. She suspected he had always looked at her lovingly, but the more time she spent with him, the more he stopped hiding it.

When his eyes slid past her shoulder, she apprehensively followed them to see what caught his intention.

"Oh wow!" She exclaimed, "Fireflies, how lovely!"

Little orbs of flying light began to emerge from the forest line opposite them, bouncing across the water surface, dancing amongst themselves.

"They *are* beautiful. But they're not fireflies, " Atlas replied.

Ayla looked at him with confusion, but he didn't say anything more. She turned her attention back to the beings of light. As they grew closer, they also grew larger. Much larger than any bug she had seen before. Almost the length of her hand she would've guessed. She squinted and leered forward but was too scared to approach the water's edge where they were collecting.

They had the wings of butterflies, almost transparent, but glowing like that of a firefly. Then they began to land around the little picnic Atlas had left on the rock by the water's edge. Landing on two tiny legs.

"Oh my Gods." Ayla whispered, "Fairies."

She looked to Atlas for confirmation, and his smile was answer enough. She covered her mouth with her hand. She wanted to get closer to see them better, but also felt like running away. Like she was stepping in on an ancient secret she shouldn't have seen.

Atlas leaned over to speak quietly into her ear, "They say the colour of the water is dyed from them washing their clothes in on the banks." Ayla let a half laugh slip through her line of defence as tears sprung into her eyes at something so silly and so lovely at the same time.

"Are we allowed to be here?" she whispered.

"They're enjoying our offering, aren't they?" He stood up and offered a hand to Ayla to join him. She hesitantly accepted and he pulled her up. Her cheeks instantly flushed, feeling though she was about to be caught doing something naughty.

He started walking towards the water's edge and she clutched his arm with her free hand. "Atlas." she warned. But he didn't stop. And the fairies didn't retreat as the pair approached.

They were so tiny, and the glow made their features hard to distinguish, but she could've sworn she saw a couple of them turn their heads to her and smile.

When they were a couple paces away, one of the creatures left their feast and took flight towards the pair. Unlike the swarming buzz of a bug, its fluttering wings were controlled and it moved slowly towards them. Ayla cowered behind Atlas and her shoulders swallowed her neck in anticipation of an attack.

The Atlas held out his upturned palm in front of him. The fairy hovered over it a few beats before landing on his skin and bowing towards him. An overwhelming rush of emotions flooded Ayla's system. *Did the creature know he was a prince? Or was this simply an expression of gratitude for an offering as simple as crumbs of crackers?*

"Can they speak?" Ayla asked. The fairy's attention darted to Ayla as she spoke, and she suddenly felt stupid asking such a question in front of them.

"Amongst themselves. But in no language, we can comprehend."

Now closer to the being, Ayla could make out its features through the haze of light. Its gangly limbs were covered in a sort of clothing. Not that of cloth or silk or leather. But what appeared to be petals. As delicate and lovely as its wearer, a strapless dress of bluebell, curling edges at the hem. She wore a hat of a smaller bud also.

Ayla wondered if all of these little fairies wore clothes of the same flower, but given the slight tint difference in their warm glow of light, she suspected this was not the case. Some emanated warmer pinkish light, others a green tinge. Though collectively, the light melted into a warm glow of pure light.

It was said that the magic that remained on the continent was densest in Atholl, but Ayla had brushed off most of the tales as nothing more than whimsical stories told to children at bedtime. But here she was, less than a day in the kingdom and witnessing the most beautiful show of light she had ever seen. But it brought the question: *If fairies were real, what other creatures truly walked these lands?*

The sun dipped farther behind the rock face, but the luminescent beings compensated delightfully. Once the offering of oatcakes was reduced to crumbs of crumbs, the fairies lifted off the ground. Some started to dance over the water, its glossy reflective surface multiplying the lustrous glow. There was no music being played. But the creatures danced in harmony with one another. Bouncing, leaping, soaring, spinning, all in a coordinated brilliance.

Despite the magnificence of the performance displayed before them, Atlas wouldn't take his eyes off Ayla.

Slowly the creatures of light dissipated over the water and back into the forest they came from. Without their illumination, the reality of dusk settled over the pair.

As their eyes adjusted to the inky sky, they made their way back to the trail. There was enough light to retrace their steps back to Ivelle, who waited patiently, chomping on a cluster of nettles.

They rode back to camp in a comfortable silence and Ayla found it hard to drop the smile gracing her cheeks.

Chapter 46

With a full belly and a fuller heart, Ayla was blissful as she pottered around Twyla's empty tent. The night's breeze had left her hair a tangled mess, so she grabbed a brush and began to rake through the tresses. Humming peacefully to herself, she picked out a weather-appropriate outfit for the princess tomorrow and folded the rest of the dresses into the trunk.

Her bed looked inviting. Soft, plump and warm, it would be so easy to slip under those covers and drift off.

But this wasn't the bed she wanted to sleep in tonight.

Twyla had slept in her mother's tent each night after the kidnapping. Atlas preferred it, as they could share double the guards.

Ayla hesitated as she approached his tent. Cheeks flushed hot with shame.

For months, posted guards of the castle had watched her sneak in and out of Thian's chambers. They might have stood dutifully silent, not even casting glances her way, but they were not blind. And she was not brainless enough to imagine for a second, they kept what they saw completely to themselves.

She swallowed her pride and approached the entrance. Clearing her throat and steeling her spine she prepared to declare herself, but before she made a sound, one of them opened the tent flap without a word. It was customary for a posted guard to both knock and announce the guest of arrival to their charge. These men ignored both.

Temporarily dumbfounded, Ayla flicked her eyes between them both, awaiting an explanation, but they still avoided her eye. Slipping through the flap into the dimly lit space, her eyes adjusted, taking in the matching furnishings to the little princess' tent.

The space was empty, Atlas presumably checking in on the princesses before bed, so Ayla felt free to nosy around. A tall trunk was open, and she spied a collection of books inside. An egregious amount for a tour, but it was so quintessentially *Atlas*, she had to smile.

Out of curiosity, she skimmed her fingers over the leather-bound tomes, screwing her eyes to read the faint embossed titles on their spines. She stopped on an account of his house's history, *'The Fracture of House Kinghorn'*.

There were very few fictitious titles, as far as she could see. But that was perfectly predictable for Atlas. He had no desire to spend time in the pages of fantasy when he had so much to learn about the world at hand.

She opened a page at random and began to skim over its telling's, but what caught her attention was the annotations covering the text centred in the page. She ran her fingers over Atlas' notes, thoughts and underlines.

Flipping through the book, she noted how every page was as covered as the last. She looked up from the pages in hand, to the dozens of volumes in the trunk, wondering if every book contained the same depth of analysis.

She stopped at a random page early in the book and began to read; *'With only ten to share between the two families, tension was brewing as the number of claimed beasts dwindled, and the eldest riders far from the age of passing.'* Ayla took a minute to catch onto the 'ten' in question being the pegasi, who were shared between houses Kinghorn and Solmund.

She read on; *'Queen Ayla,'*.

Her heart stopped dead in her chest.

Of all the books in the trunk, of all the pages in this book, she had stumbled upon her own name. An inspiration for her mother's choosing perhaps. She gave out a breathy laugh, but her hairs stood on end at the spooky coincidence.

'Queen Ayla, known to history as 'The Fruitful Queen' had given her husband three sons and four daughters in their twenty-three years of marriage. Six already mounted pegasi, as did the King. Leaving three in their native Articium, two of which were also saddled. The unbalanced scale of distribution left the Solmund's displeased. And strife was smoothed over by a betrothal of the throne's heir to a Solmund daughter.'

"Interesting read?"

She jumped out of her skin and slammed the book shut. "Mother above! Stop doing that!"

"Doing what?" Atlas asked with a cheeky grin.

"Sneaking up on me."

"Hmm. No, I think not."

"And why is that?" Ayla asked, tucking the book back between its neighbours in the case.

"Because I love the look of relief on your face when you realise it's me."

She was glad she was facing away from him so he couldn't see the stain on her face at the truth of his words.

"You should replace your posted guards, by the way."

"Is that so?" he asked, raising a brow.

"It is. They let me in–without asking whom I was *or* asking your permission for entry. I could have been an assassin."

"Are you here to assassinate me, Ayla?"

She rolled her eyes and made to move away from the books, but he strode forward, trapping her in front of the trunks.

"I'm considering it. We both know that I'm armed." she said, leading his eyes down to her thigh where the blade remained strapped.

"Still?" He asked.

"Always."

"Good." he said with the assurance she had a form of defending herself. "They know who you are, and they let you in because I told them to. You are welcome here whenever you wish. Whether I am here or not, they will let you in without question. The same goes when we are back home."

His body had drifted closer to hers, by intention or accident, it was hard to tell. The pull they felt to move towards one another was greater than gravity. It wasn't something she thought she'd ever be able to ignore again.

He looked down at her face as her smile faded and her chin dropped. He picked it up between his thumb and finger and tipped it back up to meet his eye. "What's wrong?"

"I wish that were the case–that I could come whenever I wished. Actually, I wish I could just stay with you indefinitely. But I can't–not yet." Glassy tears flooded her eyes. "I'm sorry," she croaked.

"For what?" he asked, brows drawn in confusion and worry.

Her hands shot to cover her face. To conceal the guilt and shame she felt pouring out of her. "I just– I'm scared. For so many reasons, I don't know how I'll tell him."

"Do you want *me* to tell him?"

"*No.* No, definitely not. I dread to think of his reaction either way, but Atlas if you were to tell him, he would see it as if you have *taken* me, when in truth I have *chosen* you. And he might even…" she swallowed. "Like you said, he's unpredictable."

"It's okay. I can be patient. I have gone many years without you, but now I know I will have you forever… I can wait a little longer." He tilted his head to the side and closed the gap between them, kissing her softly.

Her knees melted at the sensation she had been missing all day.

He pulled back an inch. "Twyla is with her mother."

"I know, that's why I'm here."

A devilish smirk widened his smile, and her heart drummed at the wicked possibilities that it could mean.

"So, that means I get you all to myself?"

"Tonight, and every night after." There was nothing playful in her eyes. It was an honest promise, and it wiped the smirk clean off Atlas' mouth.

He crushed his lips against hers desperately, once more. Needing not just to speak of his affection, but to show it.

Without warning, he spun her around. She let out a yelp of shock, but the surprise only increased her already soaring heart rate, sending a delicious pulse between her legs.

While Atlas kept his head close, panting with impatience as he worked down the laces of her dress, Ayla busied her hands, gripping the trunks at her waist.

"How does it end?" she asked a tad breathlessly, stroking the spine of the book she had flipped through. Atlas flicked the book a glance before answering.

"Not happily."

A chuckle. "Well, I gathered that from the title."

At the insolent tone in her voice, he was a bit rougher with the next pull of ribbon. The subsequent jerk bristled her already hard nipples. She let out a throaty laugh and waited for his answer.

"The youngest daughter of the crown, Thora, was outraged that as a daughter of the King, she would not ride the skies. The last mount would remain in Articium for one of the duke's children. What started as childish tantrums festered into unchecked malice. When the wedding between her eldest brother and the Articium daughter arrived. She killed the boy who would take the last saddle. Slit his throat where he slept."

Once he reached the last loop of the dress and it hung loose over her curves, he refrained from pulling it off as he continued the story. Turning to face him, Ayla clutched the buttery fabric against her chest.

"How old was she?"

"Twelve. History says she was found wandering around the castle, her crisp white nightdress smothered in blood. The guards thought her a wraith. When she arrived at her parents' chambers, it was not to confess her crimes, but to declare Racjan hers. Her father was so horrified by the sight and her actions that his heart seized where he sat."

"He died?"

"He did."

"What happened to her?"

"Duke and Duchess Solmund were rightfully distraught and demanded justice. The course of which was in the hands of a boy of twenty-two years who was declared King before his father's body was laid in soil. His mother begged him to spare his sister's life–she was only a child after all. But she was not innocent. And to spare her was to risk war. He was no longer granted the luxury of thinking like her brother. He was her King. And she had just committed treason."

Atlas pushed free strands of hair over her shoulder for a better view of her clavicle. "As far as the people were told, the execution was sequestered, to allow the family privacy to grieve. But in truth, Ayla stole her daughter in the night and fled across the Shallow Sea to Vorraine. They were never seen or heard from again. Simply a fracture in the bloodline."

"And now Thian rides Racjan."

"He does."

"How long ago was this?"

"Four generations."

The heavy weight of the story hung in the air.

"I told you it wasn't a happy ending."

"You don't seem so upset by it," Ayla replied with a smug grin. Running her soft pale hands over the front of his leathers, stroking what was concealed beneath.

Atlas groaned in response. "*That* is not for them. That is only for you,"

"All mine?" She lifted her brows and soaked in his heady eyes. "So, I get to do whatever I want with it?"

Atlas swallowed a growl. Instead, he dusted his lips over hers, echoing her words from earlier, "Tonight, and every night after."

She inhaled sharply but pulled her head back.

"Then go lay on your bed."

Atlas couldn't help but smile at her commanding tone. He did as he was told. Sauntering to the raised pallet.

She watched him kick off his boots but stopped him before he moved to climb atop the absurdly large bed.

"Shirt off." she ordered.

He looked back at her, though he said nothing, she swore she could feel the vibrations of his answer buzzing in the air as her body was assaulted with a wave of shivers.

He pulled the pitch-black shirt over his head and dropped it at his feet, next to his boots. He mounted the bed and lay on his back, throwing an arm behind his head so he could still see her, a grin beaming on his beautiful face.

She too kicked off her pumps. And as released the gown from her grip, her eyes never broke from his. She was slow and precise with her movements. Drawing out the moment with torturous intent. Her dress fell to her waist, and she caught it. Letting him drink in her pebbled breasts. She hooked her thumbs into the fabric and tipped over as she wiggled out of the garment. Not a shake, but a slow and sensual sway of her hips.

She could tell her audience was enjoying the show at the way his body twitched without permission, begging him to give his cock attention.

She was left wearing only the dagger strapped to her thigh, underwear and her sapphire earrings. She reached down to the buckle to remove the blade.

"Don't." Atlas instructed.

She sucked in a heavy breath.

Slinking over to the foot of the bed with feline grace, she shamelessly put in a little more sway than usual into hips. When she put a hand and an opposite knee on the bed Atlas shot up into a seated position, ready to grab her and throw her on the bed.

"Lay back down." Her voice was soft as velvet.

He ground his teeth as carnal desire swirled behind his icy eyes.

Little did he know, her show of confidence was just that. A *show*. She could barely hear her thoughts over the thundering of her heart in her ears.

Ayla crawled all the way up his legs until her face hovered over his. She stared at his lips but instead of bending down to take them for herself, she sat back on her heels, straddling him where he lay. There may be a sheet of fabric between them, but she moaned none the less when her heat sat down on the hardness beneath. She rolled her hips a couple of times, chasing the friction.

Atlas seized her hips in a bruising grip, just above where the blade remained bound by leather, and lifted her off him slightly.

Through gritted teeth, it was his turn to give orders. "Take. Them. Off. *Now*."

She did not argue as her flustered hands reached for his leathers and found the latches. Fumbling to unfasten them she bit her lip in desperation.

There was a thudding noise, Ayla's heart beating so hard he was sure Atlas must be able to hear it. It happened again, but sharper and louder. For it wasn't her heart at all, it was a spear striking a plaque outside.

"Prince Atlas, a moment?"

Atlas flipped Ayla over, so he was covering her body with his own.

Ayla on the other hand, gripped his flesh with wide eyes full of fear of being caught. With an exasperated huff he kissed her once and rolled off the bed. He reached the top fasten of his trousers though forewent replacing his shirt.

Storming out his tent, Ayla wrapped her naked form in a sheet before scrambling off the bed, grabbing her dress and pulling it on in a shadowy corner of the canvas room.

"I'm tired, make it quick." Atlas snapped outside.

Ayla clutched the loose, untied fabric to her chest. Listening to the muffled reply of whoever summoned the prince at such an ungodly hour.

Atlas re-entered the tent and did nothing to hide the disappointment from his face.

"What's wrong?" the question was out before the canvas flap settled.

"Some idiots don't know how to listen to orders, that's what. Cutting wild roots they have no business touching." Atlas grabbed his boots and pulled them on hastily, yanking the strings with frustration. "I'm sorry, I have to deal with it."

With regret in every movement, Atlas re-laced her dress to a decent state. She could tell he was slow with his movements, not because he was incapable of the fiddly work, but because he wanted to savour every brush of her skin.

"Stay here?" he asked lips brushing her neck.

She looked to the bed and nodded. "Hurry back."

Chapter 46

After two days travelling south, the tour was in the heart of the forestry kingdom, Atholl. Long gone were the sporadic pines and crumbling hills. In their place were dense woodlands rooted in fertile earth. The roots of some of the ancient chestnut trees broke in and out of the ground so tall and far that the entire company had to change course to evade them. The warmth of the sun trapped beneath the canopy was a blessed gift after weeks of frosty air.

Everywhere you looked, life was blooming. It was easy to keep Twyla entertained when every second spying out the window, a new animal could be spotted. Deer roaming through the bushes, frogs hopping through the roots of beech trees, every species of bird chattering in the branches above.

Atlas had ventured half a day west to the Duke of Atholl's estate for business unknown. He brought only Gunnar, Soren and Drury.

The tour had stopped by a market to await the return of their prince. Stocking up on previsions like meats, grain and firewood. It seemed ridiculous at first, to pay for wood when you couldn't take two paces without walking into lumber. But it was taken seriously by the prince of the continent not to cut unknown timber. He had made all his men swear to only source burning wood from local sellers, not collect themselves. The consequences of such an action in Atholl were unknown in detail, but the general consensus was grave.

Apparently not everyone headed the warning seriously, and Atlas had been left to clean up the mess two nights prior.

Among the timber stalls selling necessary goods, there were also local sellers offering trinkets and luxuries. Ayla, Twyla and Niamh were spending the afternoon grazing over the various tables. Ayla had brought no coin with her on the journey, but anything she showed the slightest interest in, Niamh insisted on buying her. Money was no object for the princess, and she would hear none of Ayla's protesting.

And so, Ayla's woven straw gathering basket–also a new purchase–was filled to the brim with goodies. A punnet of the sweetest blackcurrants she had ever tasted, a jar of local honeycomb, a beautiful, embroidered handkerchief with scalloped edges.

Ayla couldn't help herself from scanning the forest beyond the clearing. Didn't even realise she was doing it until Twyla would tug on her skirts. Her heart wished to find Atlas stepping out from behind a towering yew trunk.

After so many days spent together, his absence felt wrong. Like she'd left something as vital as a limb back at camp.

Most of the stalls in the outdoor market were trades of lumber–raw sellers, furniture, home trinkets, tools and weaponry amongst them.

Twyla pulled her mother and Ayla towards a table covered in small carved toys. Ayla lifted the princess to her hip for a better view of the spread. They were so small, but their designs were incredibly intricate. Wooden horses and knights, baby rattles, carved houses and trees.

"These are beautiful." Ayla praised the stall owner, a middle-aged woman with gorgeous hazel eyes.

"Thank you, my lady," she replied with a smile of pride, "Your Highnesses." She tacked on with a curtsy to Niamh and Twyla.

The former lifted a chiselled owl and ran her nails over the divots in the wood. "You are very talented," she commended.

"Thank you, Your Highness. But it was not I who made them," the pride in her eye remained, but was tinted with sadness "My son holds the talent with a chisel. I merely sell 'em on."

"Well, will you pass on our compliments?" Ayla asked with a smile, but she could see it was the wrong thing to say when the woman swallowed a lump in her throat and her eyes became very glassy.

"I... he has not been home in some time." she replied finally.

"That chair," Niamh said after a beat "it's so lovely, I simply must have it." She walked around the table to where the chair in question sat. It was coated in a blush pink colour, but every limb was carved with as much precision as the table trinkets. It reminded Ayla of the bed at the Rat and Mouse, in the borderlands of Camelleah that she had shared with Atlas.

"How much is it?"

"Eight gold feathers, your highness"

"Eight?! Nonsense. Something of this divine craftsmanship is worth a hundred, wouldn't you say, Ayla?"

"I couldn't agree more." Ayla said with a smirk, impressed by Niamh's masked charity. She looked at the woman whose eyes remained watery, but a happy smile lifted the apples of her cheeks.

She stammered and spluttered for words in response, instead Niamh walked over to her and outstretched her hand "Do we have a bargain?"

"I... we do indeed!" she shook it gratefully.

"Excellent!" Niamh exclaimed. She waved over a handmaiden to pay the woman and collect the chair.

Before they had a chance to leave, Twyla reached into Ayla's basket and pulled out a handful of blackcurrants, a couple slipping free beneath her chubby grasp. She toddled over to the merchant and handed them to her, with a shy smile. The act instantly stained her skin blue with the smushed ones, but the lady couldn't have been in the least bit bothered and just said her thanks to the princess who clutched at her mother's skirts.

"Niamh," Ayla said, as they drifted from table to table.

"Hm?"

"How are you feeling, about the coronation coming?" She kept her voice low; it was not public knowledge that the king would step down in a few moons time.

Niamh's eyes drifted over the pine needles they trod over. "Dread. Fear. A little bit of excitement I suppose?"

Ayla's heart dipped at the first two but relaxed at the third. Even though Niamh was never privy to their plans, Ayla had lived with the knowledge that she would take the throne with Thian, not Niamh, for near three years. Now that she was abandoning those plans, she felt an illogical guilt that she was leaving the princess with a role that was never hers in the first place.

"What are you excited for?" Ayla asked, genuinely curious. She barely made it past dread and fear when she used to consider the role before pushing it to a dark corner of her mind.

"The power."

Ayla's head whipped to the girl in surprise.

Niamh went on, "With resources and a title like that, a lot of good can be done in the world. King Irlass has done so much for the kingdoms; I hope to do the same."

Ayla smiled. "And what are you dreading?"

Niamh released a weighted sigh. "The people who will try and stop me."

Tables and benches lined each side of the creek for as far as the eye could see. Oil lamps suspended on rope were fastened tree to tree, illuminating the area below. The men and women of the tour were grateful for a hot meal that wasn't stew, bread or porridge for once, when Princess Niamh declared all were to celebrate Prince Atlas' name day with a feast.

Said feast was provided by three separate taverns and inns along the stretch of water that split the number of hungry bellies between them. The closer you drifted from one to another, a different merry tune could be heard on lute and fiddle.

Ayla, Twyla and Niamh sat at a decaying, moss sprawled bench, same as all the others. Every creek with movement had the girls mentally questioning the integrity of the furniture, but alas, it held.

Ayla was ripping apart a turkey leg basted in the most delicious spices when her eye snagged in the distance. Pale eyes locked with dark, flanked by Gunnar and Drury.

Atlas' expression was unreadable as he beheld her devouring the leg of meat, buttery juices dripping from her mouth all the way down her chin.

He ungloved his hands without breaking eye contact. After lifting one hand, he flicked one finger towards him, summoning her. The act sent a thrum though Ayla's veins, pooling low.

After nearly falling off the bench, Ayla sauntered over in her blue skirts, cleaning herself up with her newly purchased handkerchief. She had almost caught up to him before he took off in the direction of the inn next to them–The Wandering Maple. When she realised he wasn't stopping she snapped her head back to her table where Niamh was shooing her away with her hands.

Ayla bunched up her dress in her hands so she could quicken her pace after him. "Atlas!" she called.

"Ayla," he replied smoothly. Past the bustling bar he paced, through the dining hall and into the hallway of rented bedrooms.

"Where are you going? The festivities are in your name, you should join them,"

Once they reached a corridor dimly lit by candlelight, he stopped and grabbed her by the side of her neck, forcing her back against the pine wood wall. Her mouth dropped in surprise, but her eyes only darkened with interest.

"Yes, I should," he replied finally, "but I didn't want them all to see you like this."

"Like what?"

He leaned in and kissed her desperate lips. His tongue teased her mouth open, exploring feverishly, raking over every inch he could find. When he pulled back, with a smile in his eyes he replied, "Like *this*." And rubbed a thumb over her lips as she came down from the high of the kiss. "Seeing as it's my name day, can't I be a little selfish and spend it only with you?"

Ayla's heart did a strange little swoop as the sentiment poured out of his mouth. She lowered her eyes, but her mouth betrayed her attempt to mask a smile. "I suppose that is only fair."

Hooking her arms around his neck, she leaned back into the wall. "How was your business with the Duke of Atholl?"

"Concluded." he replied cryptically, with a secret smile in his eyes.

"Have you eaten?" She straightened suddenly at the thought. "Gods you must be starving. You should eat. I highly recommend the thyme turkey leg."

"I have eaten, I promise." he said, peppering her jaw in kisses. "And we all saw how much you were enjoying the turkey, Ayla."

She blushed at the reminder of how feral and disgusting she must've looked, lost in the delicious tender meat. But he didn't look at her with anything other than amusement. Then he leaned in close, pressed a kiss to the tender flesh under her ear and whispered, "But the only thing I want dripping out your pretty mouth tonight, is *me.*"

Her blush turned crimson, and the heated blood coursed through her veins in a heady rush. She tried to recover, but her mouth was suddenly too dry.

"Well… it is your name day." She said.

His breath fanned her face from above, but he remained an inch away from contact. They each stared at the lips opposite them with sinful desire.

"Take me to your room." Ayla whispered.

Atlas flicked his eyes up to meet Ayla's. He pulled away and took her hand in his, leading her through The Wandering Maple to where his trunks had been deposited by servants.

Just as they approached the locked threshold, Ayla pulled out of his grasp. "Wait! I almost forgot. I'll meet you inside," she promised. "I need to get something first."

She slipped another key out of her pocket and rounded the corner to her own room.

After fetching a velvet pouch, Ayla slipped into Atlas chamber and pressed her body against the door to close it softly. Keeping her hands behind her back only drew his attention to them. He stood up off the seat which he was perched on and stalked over to her with predatory focus. Each step he took matched the beat of Ayla's heart.

Her chest heaved as he reached past her waist to the key sticking out the door and turned its lock.

Pulling her hands to her chest she revealed the small velvet pouch. She clutched it tightly and said, "Happy name day, Atlas."

He took the pouch out her hands while trying to smother a giddy smile. When he undid the ties and tipped it, a small white gold ring fell into his palm. He picked it up and inspected the signet's design, a feathered wing–his family's sigil.

When he met Ayla's gaze, she was chewing her bottom lip nervously. "I bought it in Linton," she started "but I had the smith in Camelleah update the inside with an engraving." she said quietly.

Sure enough, when he turned it over, the flat head of the ring inside had a faint love heart with an 'A' etched in the middle. A warm smile spread over his mouth as he inspected the ring. "*A*, for Atlas?" he asked.

She breathed out a laugh and pushed his shoulder.

He slipped the ring onto his pinky finger. It fit perfectly.

"Now… you have my heart with you, wherever you are." she croaked out nervously.

He surged forward into another devastating kiss. This one much more aching and passionate, brimming with the words they didn't know how to say. Nor did she know how to process. All Ayla knew was that he was here, and she wanted to kiss him. Forever.

Shaking hands began tugging at fabric. Atlas forwent the laces of Ayla's dress and ripped apart the seams of the chest panel. She shrugged off the sleeves and the whole thing fell to her hips. Working in tandem she kicked off her pumps as Atlas drew his shirt over his head.

Her nipples hardened to stiff peaks in the sudden exposure and rubbed against Atlas' bare chest as they resumed their dance of tangled tongues. The sensation sent a shudder through her and a soft moan passed from her mouth to his.

Atlas' hands roamed her exposed flesh, fingers teasing the undercurve of her breasts before he wrapped both arms around her lower back and lifted her off the ground. A surprised yelp sounded from Ayla at the sudden change, but she just clung to his lustrous hair.

When he deposited her back down, the backs of her knees hit the bed frame. He peeled his face from hers, and though she mourned the contact, she seized the opportunity for air.

Her breaths were heavy as she beheld him drop to his knees, candlelight casting sharp shadows over his beautiful features.

He worked his way down slowly, kissing every piece of exposed flesh in the process. Slow and torturous he moved from the base of her throat, down to her collar bone, the flat plane of chest where she was sure her heart was visible with vigorous beats. If he couldn't see it, she was sure he could hear it as he rested his forehead on the very spot. Feeling how it beat just for him.

Next his kisses aimed for her breasts that ached to be touched. He teased with pecks and cruel licks around their full shape before sucking and nipping the rosy bud with a hunger that made her whimper. She fisted his hair, simultaneously pulling the strands and pushed him closer, a silent beg not to stop. When he was finished with one, he moved onto the next, showing it as much affection as he did the first.

Ayla clenched her thighs together as the needy ache spread lower and more desperate. Atlas smirked into her flesh and took the hint to hurry up in his descent.

He sat back on his heels and his hands worked down over the curve of her waist, to the swell of her hips on which the remainder of her dress rested. His thumbs tickled over the line between fabric and flesh.

Ayla shifted on her feet impatiently and when he looked up at her, his eyes were full of such sin it stole the breath right out her lungs.

He pulled the fabric down slowly, her underwear going with it, baring her wholly to him.

She looked to the sky and begged the Gods for strength against this man. For what he was about to do to her body. And inevitably, to her heart.

He drew a hand up her curly mons and drew his fingers back down like claws. The friction made her sway slightly where she stood. Ayla reached out to grasp the bedpost on her right, for some much-needed stability.

Atlas hooked one of her knees over his shoulder, parting her soaking sex. Groaning at the sight and smell of her arousal, his jaw worked.

He met her eyes as he lifted off his heels to his knees once more, stretching her leg up with him. Maintaining a fierce eye contact, he kissed her inner thigh and nipped along the trail to his prize. Each breath was sharp and audible on Ayla's part, while Atlas' fanned her aching entrance.

His strong nose made a whisper of contact, and the slightest touch had Ayla shuddering where she stood.

Bracing one hand on her hip and hooking the other around the thigh propped up on her shoulder, Atlas seized what was his.

No more teasing. No more waiting. He closed his mouth over her pulsing clit and sucked her to the edge of insanity.

Ayla cried out in pleasure, gasping hopelessly for air. His tongue flicked and swirled while his teeth grazed and pulled. He lapped up her nectar with the thirst that threatened stars in Ayla's vision.

Her legs began to shake under the pressure building, threatening to collapse even with the support of Atlas and the post.

"Atlas," Ayla pleaded, pushing his head away from her needy cunt. His displeasure of being torn away was worn on his face in a vicious scowl. "I need you." she panted out, "All of you."

His face softened and he rose to his feet, one arm snaked around her lower back, while the other gripped her face gravely. "I thought you wanted to wait. Until you were wed?"

"I did with him. But not with you. I want you, now and always. I could live out the rest of my days unwed and happy if it were by your side." She couldn't repress the tremor in her voice as she spoke.

"I *will* wed you, Ayla. Because I know, without a doubt, that I love you. Let me love you. Tonight, tomorrow, and every day until my last." He punctuated each word with a kiss to her jaw, "And even then, I don't think it will be enough. No number of days on this earth would be enough time to show you how much I fucking love you."

Ayla let out a sob but smothered it with his lips as quickly as it came out. Her tears smeared his cheeks, but he did not wipe them away, for they were not born of sadness, but of joy.

Atlas pushed her back onto the bed, and she crawled back into the centre as she watched him rid himself of his leathers. His desire sprang free, and she had to bite her lip to stop an expectant moan from slipping out.

He crawled over her and kissed her with a gentleness that was missing from before, while running his fingers through her wet folds to check she was ready for him. When he pulled back, nose to nose they lost themselves in each other's eyes.

"Do you trust me?"

"Always."

When he positioned himself at her entrance she sucked in a sharp breath. He kept a forearm braced by her head and she clung to his back with anticipation.

He pushed inside of her, and she let out a sound somewhere between and cry and a moan.

"Good girl," Atlas praised as he moved to her neck and kissed it languidly, distracting her pain with pleasure.

When she relaxed into the pressure he thrust in farther and she raked the whites of her nails down his muscled back. He shook with restraint, holding back a carnal desire.

When she rocked her hips beneath him, he pulled out almost to the head and pushed back in, giving her the friction her body screamed for.

"Gods, you're fucking perfect." he growled in her ear, loosing himself in her wet tightness that stretched to fit him inside. Ayla hooked her legs around his back, pulling him in deeper. He pushed almost to the hilt in a savage thrust. She cried out at that unnatural feeling of fullness, knowing he still had more to give.

The thought of him being inside of her, fusing their bodies in such closeness made her dizzy.

Ayla tested the feeling of movements, arching her back, circling her hips, stretching her arms above her head to grip the pillows above. His thrusts increased in strength and speed and the sensations were overtaking Ayla's control. Her breathy moans crescendo into cries of bliss.

Each call of his name only spurred him on.

She couldn't bring herself to open her eyes, lost in such euphoria, but then he bent over and whispered in her ear, "I love you, Ayla." and the crash of her heart pushed her over the edge.

She called out in a strangled scream as her back arched and her hips writhed on their own accord. Her legs shook as he rode her through each crashing wave of pleasure.

She was too numb to feel the ferocity of Atlas' final thrusts, which caused his own unravelling. After he collapsed on top of her sweaty form, Ayla wrapped her arms over his back pulling him into her. They lay there in the rapture of the moment for a long while.

He shifted to pull out of her, but she flinched and locked her legs around him "No, please don't go." she breathed.

He looked down at her with concern swirling through his eyes. "I'm not going anywhere." he promised and rolled off her. Grabbing her handkerchief off the floor that had been hidden in the sleeve of her dress, he also retrieved the jug of water and dipped it in before ringing it out. He stroked her legs softly and drew them slightly apart. She winced at the cold impact of the cloth as he cleaned her up.

Ayla flushed as she saw the blood staining the cotton but reassured herself it was normal for the first time. Maerine had prepared her more than most girls of the continent in what to expect of coupling. The blood didn't seem to faze Atlas as he gently wiped it all away. When he was done, he deposited himself on the bed once more, this time lounging on the pillows at the top. He threw one arm behind his head while the other wrapped Ayla up against his side. She drew a leg over his and her body melted into him.

Too hot and sweaty from recent activities, they forewent the bedsheets and simply warmed each other.

Ayla drew tired circles over Atlas' chest with her fingers, every time she looked up to meet his eyes, neither had anything to say. There was nothing that needed to be said. Their eyes communicated to each other in ways words couldn't.

When sleep was setting in and her eyes fought to stay open, Atlas finally asked "Are you happy?"

She didn't need to think about the answer. Nor answer mindlessly as she usually did. In this moment, she was sure, she had never been happier.

Chapter 47

The sun beamed down on the rolling grassy hills. Ayla turned over to see Atlas laying on his back, one arm hooked behind his head, the other atop the baby sleeping tummy-down on his chest. She reached out to take its hand and five little fingers curled round one of hers.

A flurry of giggles distracted her, and she sat up.

Running over the horizon was Twyla–or at least, Twyla but almost ten years older. And chasing behind her was a little boy with curly hair as dark as Ayla's. He was too far to make out his features, so she stood up to get closer. When she got to her feet, the earth beneath her spun, and she stumbled back away from Atlas and the baby.

She fell to the ground and her head hit the grass with a soft thud.

Chapter 48

Ayla opened her eyes as a soft tear rolled down her skin. In that moment, she wished more than anything that she had the gift of prophecy, for she wanted that dream to be a promised future.

She adjusted to the light shining in through the window, tinted green by the canopy of leaves outside. Rolling her head towards the bed, she noted the bicep she was using like a pillow. She couldn't help the smile that pulled at her sleepy cheeks.

She kissed the skin of his arm softly and breathed in his smell. Atlas' other hand was braced up her stomach, his thumb nestled just beneath her breasts. At the touch of her lips, Atlas stirred but did not wake. He pulled her impossibly closer and she burrowed into his protective hold.

As she came to, she noticed they were wrapped in bed sheets she didn't remember crawling under but was grateful for it in the brisk morning chill. She mindlessly stroked his arm as she basked in the sunlight with a giddy, delirious smile on her face.

As comfortable as she was in his hold like this, she missed his dreadfully gorgeous face, even after one night's sleep. Squirming in the little leeway Atlas allowed her, she rolled over. When she fully turned, she pushed one of her legs between his and lifted her hand to caress his face.

If he was awake, he was doing a damned good job at convincing her otherwise.

He looked so peaceful and a strange shade of innocent when he slept. She kissed the tip of his nose and he smiled in response. He didn't open his eyes, but pulled her tighter into him, resting his chin atop her head.

"Can we stay here forever?" she whispered.

He didn't answer.

Today was the start of the last leg in the tour back to Balcarras. And the reality was the foreseeable future was unknown. Entirely dependent on the actions and *reactions* of an emotional man with far too much power at his fingertips.

After changing into a fresh dress from her own room, Ayla and Atlas made their way outside to regroup with the others. The company was up and bustling for the day's ride ahead. Though the establishments along the river had provided plenty of food and ale, rooms were scarce and most of the tour remained in pitched tents that were already deconstructed and packed away for travel.

Atlas called over to Gunnar who was washing up by the stream with a few of his men, instructing him to ready the horses to depart. Meanwhile Ayla sauntered over to the same table she had sat at the previous evening, which was still occupied by Niamh and Twyla, and to her surprise Soren–one of the soldiers who had accompanied Atlas yesterday to visit the Duke of Atholl and on his mission to rescue the princesses.

She didn't realise she was this *sore*, in the throes of pleasure last night, but she was almost waddling. Instead of focusing on the pain, she homed in on the little princess spoon-feeding' bites of spiced apple porridge to Maggie who sat on Soren's lap. Ayla was surprised to see such trust put in him, by the princess who never let go of the babydoll.

"Good morning," Ayla said when she finally arrived, plotting herself down gently on the bench opposite.

"Good morning," Niamh echoed back to her. There was a foreign smirk on her face and a glint in her eyes that Ayla tried to decipher. She blushed profusely as she considered the princess knew of her exploits from last night, or gods forbid *heard* them.

Ayla dropped her head to hide the guilt spreading over her expression but raised it when she felt a hand clap over her own. Niamh very rarely initiated physical contact, but her face was one of complete comfort as she looked deep into Ayla's eyes.

"Can you eat on the way?" Atlas asked from behind her, holding an empire apple and paper parcel in his hands. "I'd like to make up the lost time and get everyone home."

"Of course." she replied, standing and resisting the urge to take his newly ringed hand in hers. She had no intention of keeping him a secret. But for now, there were too many eyes surrounding them, and if gossip were to reach Thian before she did...

"Are you finished with your breakfast, Bumblebee?" Ayla asked the little princess.

Twyla wiped the doll's porcelain lips clean of excess porridge and removed her from Soren's grasp. He smiled at her movements, far too mature for her fresh age of two and a half. She rounded the table and hugged her Governess' skirts until Ayla lifted her into her free arm.

"Your Highness'." Ayla said with a curtsy for sake of appearances. Her eyes skated over Niamh, who nodded politely but lingered on Atlas' until her breath hitched and she tore them away.

As the tour cut through the city and closer to the castle, a rumbling storm brewed overhead. Its furious grumbles a warning from the heavens if there ever was one.

As the stone houses became dense and streets narrow, Ayla's stomach tensed. It felt like a tide pulling her in against her will.

She considered the irony that the place she once dreamed to return to, was now the one place she dreaded to be. Not forever, though. Deep in her heart she wanted to return to this place and its people. And to Thian.

She missed him.

Five weeks that she had been without him, and she missed his smile, the most ridiculous antics, and the way he made her feel special when she felt so lost and alone.

Ayla was sure they would get back to that place, there was just going to be a transition period. An adjustment as he came to terms with the fact that their plans for the future were altered.

She knew he would see it as a betrayal, and that made her chest constrict with guilt. But that had never been her intention. And now he could be in her life forever and remain faithful to his wife. She wasn't sure how she was going to tell him, but when she did, she was going to make him see that it is for the best.

"Are you excited to see daddy?" Ayla asked Twyla.

"Can we see Esse?" she replied.

"You want to see Esse? That's a great idea, we can try to find her tomorrow, okay?" Esse and Twyla had spent very little time together, but the time they did, they had a ball, despite the age gap. With next to no other children in the castle, Twyla latched onto Esse whenever she could.

When the carriages ascended the cobbled road, past the castle gates and into the courtyard, everyone disembarked. Niamh went straight to her rooms and Atlas made for the King and Queen to debrief them on the success of the tour. Ayla and Twyla made their way to the gardens to stretch out their stiff legs and run off some of their built-up restlessness from sitting in a carriage all day.

Ayla picked stems of Lavender to dry out and replenish her stores, laying them in a pile on a stone bench. The winds picked up and kept blowing them off where they sat so she resolved to weigh them down with a couple of flat stones.

Despite tucking her hair into the collar of her dress to stop it blowing wildly in her face, it persisted pulling free. It was still mild, but the grass of the grounds was begging for a surge of rain

Twyla was crouched on her haunches inspecting a green caterpillar that was surrounded by raindrops as they fell from the sky.

"Will we pop him in with the hydrangeas so he can hide from the rain?" Ayla asked the princess when she came to see what caught her attention. In all honesty, Ayla hated creepy crawly bugs, so she was grateful that Twyla took the initiative to pick up the bug by herself. She didn't flinch or scream when it tickled her pale skin. She just carried it close to her chest before patiently waiting for it to crawl off onto a large green leaf near the stem of the bush as Ayla held open a gap in the flowers.

Just in the nick of time, too. For after a roar of distant thunder, the heavens opened, and the rain tumbled down in heavy pelts. The initial splashes shocked Ayla as they ran down her neck and soaked her skirts. She sucked in a gasp, ready to snatch up the princess and make a run for it. But then she looked to the little girl who was laughing wildly and reaching up to the sky, as if asking it for more.

Puddles began to pool in the grass and Ayla made the first jump. The water sprayed out beneath her feet, sending mud splattering over her dress as well as the princess'. Twyla let out another hysterical laugh and joined in. stomping her little booted feet in every wet patch she could find.

"My lady!" Ayla could hear through the downpour. She turned her head to find Soren stalking over, surely to escort them both inside. He had been appointed Twyla's personal guard after her previous was disbanded due to incompetence. It was an easy choice for Atlas after seeing how well she took to him at breakfast days ago and his demonstration of ability in her rescue mission.

Niamh had asked for Gunnar as hers, but he was a general who oversaw a platoon of more than forty men. Atlas had assured her that Drury was just as capable, and he trusted him with her protection.

"Just a few minutes," Ayla called back through the rain "I promise!"

He grumbled under his breath but not nearly loud enough to be heard. Instead of putting a stop to it, he walked over to the stone bench where Maggie and Ayla's lavender rested and picked up the former, tucking it under his cloak to preventing it from soaking any more.

Ayla lifted her skirts and started dancing round in circles and Twyla took to following. The little girl slipped a couple of times on the slimy grass, but every knock down only encouraged her laughter as she picked herself up and started again.

When Twyla's teeth began to chatter beneath her smile, Ayla knew it was time to call it a day and get her warmed up. She picked up the girl and held her close, offering what warmth she could offer as they made their way inside. Making their way through the castle, Ayla felt slightly guilty for the muddy trail they were leaving behind.

She made quick work of bathing the princess and tucking her into a warm bed for the night. Ayla apologised to Soren on the way out, seeing as he would have to stand there dripping while she was now released to dry herself off.

When she passed into the east wing where her own room was, she had a strange excitement about coming back to her own space. She didn't have many things of her own, but she loved what she had.

Opening the door, the smell of home hit her pleasantly as she breathed in the still air. Her eyes fluttered around; all was as she had left it.

Her trunks from the tour were deposited at the bottom of her bed. She would deal with them tomorrow after a good night's sleep in her own bed. For now, she–

She stopped. Her eyes reached the windowsill.

She walked over with a swelling dread in her throat. She dusted her fingers over the potted plants that lined it. Once vibrant green leaves were brown and shrivelled. Petals of flowers were brittle to the touch and dusted away with the wind. She pressed a finger to the pale soil. It was bone dry. It actually *cracked* as she applied pressure on it.

She had asked Thian to watch her plants when she was away. She didn't think it was too much to ask of him. She had placed a bucket of water on the floor under the ledge to make it easy for him, and a glass vial to dip and pour to feed the plants. Once a week.

That's all she had asked him to do. Water the plants *once a week*. Given how far gone they looked, she wondered if he even did it once.

They were just plants from the garden, propagated and repotted in her room. She could fetch more. But it still clogged her throat to see. She had nurtured these plants and loved them and asked him to do one godsdamned thing for her and he didn't even bother.

"You're here," A voice snapped her out of her teary trance. She jolted and turned to see Thian leaning against the doorframe. Her heart fluttered at the initial sight of him–at this point purely reflex. Gone was the limp and cane she had left him on.

"I am," she replied with a low smile. "What happened?" she asked, nodding her head to the crumbling petals in her grasp.

He looked at them and slammed his palm to his forehead like an idiot. "Gods, sorry Ayla. I forgot last week, I was busy training up my leg. Which is fine by the way." he said with a laugh that Ayla found entirely unfunny.

"Last week? This soil has not been tended to in weeks, Thian."

He stilled and a silent stretch felt like a noose tightening around her neck. A smile remained spread on his lips, but it did not reach his eyes.

"Are you calling me a liar?"

She blanched and stammered for a response as he sauntered farther into the room. "I will replace them. I don't know what's wrong with them. Must be too fragile to survive here." he said.

She bit back a response.

He stopped and sat on her trunk at the foot of her bed, knocking on it with his knuckles for good measure. "Want me to help you unpack?"

She shook her head dusting the remaining flakes of dirt off her hands out the window.

"I'm too tired, I'll do it tomorrow. For now, I just need to change out of these wet clothes and go to bed." she said, pulling bath sheets and a fresh nightgown out of her wardrobe.

"Yes, you looked like you were having fun outside."

"You were watching us?" Uncertainty flooded her. They weren't doing anything scandalous outside, but the thought of being watched unknowingly made her shiver.

"Of course. I can't help but watch you when you look so happy." he cocked his head and observed her. Drinking in every part of her.

She flushed under the scrutiny and fear took over.

What did he see in her? Did she look different? Now that she was no longer a maiden, could he see it written on her face? Could he smell the deceit on her skin?

"Anything exciting happen when we were gone?" she asked.

"Gods no," he let out a huff. "This place is intolerable without you."

She let out a snort of a laugh at his jest.

"I mean it, Ayla. I'm glad you're back."

She looked into his onyx eyes that glimmered with sadness. The more she looked, she noticed he had changed slightly. It wasn't just his leg that had strengthened with training. His shoulders seemed to stretch a little wider and his chest puffed a little farther. She sucked in a breath and turned around to pin up her mop of dripping hair.

He moved so quietly she did not hear his approach over the thumping of her own heart. His hot breath fanned the back of her neck, and a chill raked over her that had nothing to do with her damp clothes. He snaked his arms around her stomach from behind and rested his head on her shoulder.

"I missed you." he said, a slight break in his whisper.

A familiar prickle danced on the inside of her nose as Ayla looked to the ceiling, blinking back traitorous tears that threatened to fall. She tried to breathe steady, but there was a clog in her throat and her nose was suddenly sniffly.

She didn't know what to do. She used to long for these touches. And she *still* longed for them... just not from him.

When he lifted his head, he caught her chin in his thumb and finger instantly.

"What's wrong?" The look in his eyes screamed pain at seeing her in such distress.

"I... I just..." she sniffled and stammered but no coherent thoughts would form. "I'm just feeling a bit emotional. Tired and… *emotional,* I guess."

He took her meaning and took a micro step back.

"Okay… can I get you anything?" he asked innocently, and she leaned into the palm on her cheek.

"I just need to get some rest, I think. It was a long journey. I'll see you tomorrow?"

"Of course, love." He kissed the top of her head and his eyes scanned her face one more time to check she was okay before he moved to the door.

"You should go and see Niamh," she tacked on, wiping her nose with a soggy sleeve. "She will want to see you."

"Really?" he asked, surprise laced through his tone and in his wide eyes.

She nodded, "She went through a lot, Thian. It would be nice to have someone to talk to about it."

He gave an unsure nod of his head as he left the room.

Niamh hadn't asked to see Thian. And anything she wanted to share about her experience Ayla was sure she would've already told Atlas. But perhaps in strengthening the bond between man and wife, it would ease the pain of Ayla's admission when the time came.

Thian and Niamh didn't hate each other, and they were hardly estranged, seeing as they shared a child. But their relationship wasn't filled with love. Not the way Ayla wished for both of them.

Chapter 49

Grey days were few and far between in Balcarras. Being the kingdom in the centre of the continent made it so. After a few strong days of sun, however, soaking up all the moisture on the ground, the sky was ready to repay the earth.

Without the streaming sun to wake her from her slumber, Ayla arose groggy and confused. She wandered over to her sill where her saplings were taking to their new home. After pouring a vile of water in each terracotta pot she stroked their leaves lovingly, inspecting for any signs of disease, malnourishment or pests. During her ministrations, she noticed how quiet the gardens were this morning. *Perhaps everyone was sheltering from the skies above that promised a downpour,* she thought.

After combing her hair, washing her face and changing into a fresh dress, Ayla slipped on her ankle boots that would have suited last week's puddle party better than her velvet flats.

Wandering out of her chambers, she headed for the kitchens to fetch something to eat before she picked up Twyla.

There was a prickle swarming down her skin.

The halls were mostly empty. And quiet. *Too* quiet.

She tried to catch one of the chambermaids carrying bed sheets into the servant's passage but she scurried away with her head down. Ayla's heart started to drum with unease.

Forgoing her breakfast, she turned on her heel and darted to the nursery. Hall after hall she fluttered through clutching her heavy skirts. She rounded a corner and thumped into a solid chest.

"I'm so sorry–" she started pulling herself away and straightening her skirts, until she recognized the face sitting atop said chest. Atlas.

He didn't have a face of amusement at their collision. Something was troubling him as much as her.

"What's going on?" she asked tentatively. He did not give her a verbal answer. Instead, he surveyed the empty halls around them. He clutched her hand and tugged her along with him, his other hand resting on the pommel of his blade.

"Your Highness," a guard called from an adjacent corridor, catching the prince in his sights. "His Majesty requests your presence in the throne room."

"There are a dozen post guards missing from their station on this floor, Ser. Where are your men?" Atlas snapped back.

"His Majesty requests your presence in the throne room." the guard parroted.

Ayla could feel Atlas tensing beneath her grip at the soldier's lack of cooperation. Before he snapped, she interjected, tugging on her arm with her free hand. "Come on, let's just see what he has to say."

Level after level they descended to the ground floor where the throne room was located. Every floor as deserted as the last. Atlas bristled at the soldier who shadowed them the whole way down.

Two guards *did* maintain their post at the entrance to the throne room. The tall slabs of wood groaned in protest as they were parted from one another into the great space. Ayla dropped Atlas' hands as they did so, not wishing to show such a public display of affection before the King. But as soon as his skin left hers, she wished to clutch it once more.

The pair looked at one another before stepping into the room.

Warily, they crossed some distance over the threshold before the sounds of the doors slammed shut.

The room, in the belly of the castle, had no windows except one large semi-circular glass panel on the wall above the door they just entered. Sunlight normally gleamed through the wheel of glass and bathed the throned in golden hews. Today however, the sun did not bless these halls. It was a cold, bereft shade of gloom. Several bowls of flame were lit up to try and compensate, but they were puny and swallowed by the darkness.

Because of this darkness, it took their eyes a moment to adjust. Ayla had never been in the hall without the populace of a great many people, always for a celebration of some kind. Today, however, it just felt… solemn.

"Thian?" Ayla called out. Her voice echoing off the sharp stone of the castle walls. She continued to step forward for a better look at him while Atlas had stilled.

The prince sat not only atop the dais, but on his father's throne. His form slumped over, one elbow resting on his knee, the hand of which braced his forehead.

"Today is a special day." he murmured downward from his seat, barely loud enough to reach the ears of his two listeners. But he went on, "I'm free." he stated. A chuckle started to shake his shoulders, and he threw his head back against the chair.

That prickle of unease started to sweep over Ayla's skin anew. "What do you mean you're free, Thian?" she asked. She had learned to deal with Thian in a multitude of moods and found that soothing him like a child worked best most of the time.

"I suppose you're free now, too." he said, ignoring her question. "We will be free together. Well, together with my other one." he waved his arms in front of him dismissively. His words were slurred, but Ayla did not think he was inebriated. No, she'd seen enough of *that* too, to know the signs. It was more like he was in a deep state of exhaustion, muddying his mind.

"It was time... so I got rid of him."

Despite her fear of the answer, she whispered out the question, "Who?"

"My father."

Immediately Ayla's heart dropped out of her stomach, and she began to shake her head in disbelief.

"I gave the bastard a cleaner end than he was heading for, a mercy really." He gave a snort of a laugh at his own cruel words.

When Thian finally focused his eyes on his audience, Atlas was stepping forward with a grip set on his sword. He stepped just beyond Ayla, and put a hand out to shield her. She, in turn, clutched his outstretched arm, tears falling from her lashes.

Their body language spoke more than words could say.

Thain blinked. He stared. And something in his breathing changed.

It was visible on his face; wave after wave of emotion rolling over him. Each one cresting and breaking over each other.

Confusion.

Suspicion.

Betrayal.

Rage.

He surged to his feet and took a step to the edge of the dais, overlooking them.

His breath was seething through his teeth as he asked, "What have you done?"

Acknowledgements

Dear reader, thank you for taking the first step into the *Scarred by Feathers* series. This is my first book-baby, a labor of love and much needed escapism from my own head.

Camille, I could fill a book this size with the amount of gratitude I have for you. Every painful draft I put you through, and the countless hours of talking about this big magic world mean everything to me. May our two-person book club be forevermore, love Uta x

I can't go any further without thanking my beautiful mum. I can't describe how grateful I am that I'm yours. Your infinite support, love, and wisdom are things I take for granted, and don't tell you enough how much they mean to me.

Thank you to Alessia for your editing wizardry. I'm so glad you pushed me to make this book what it is now!

About the Author

Elle Rhaeser is a Scottish author and lover of all things fantasy. When she's not writing, you can find her snuggled up with a romantasy book, binge watching a new series or hyper fixating on another creative project! *Where North Meets South* is her first book.

You can find her on Instagram and TikTok @ellerhaeseroffical

Sign up to Elle's mailing list via the link in her Insta Bio for the latest news on all future books and exclusive content.

Printed in Dunstable, United Kingdom

66308476R00272